RACHEL L. SCHADE

FORTRESS OF BLOOD AND POWER

A FAE OF BRYTWILDE NOVEL

Cover by GetCovers

Map and interior designed with Canva

ISBN 979-8-9876059-4-3

www.rachelschadeauthor.com

RACHEL L. SCHADE

FORTRESS OF BLOOD AND POWER

A FAE OF BRYTWILDE NOVEL

DRAGON SHADOW
PUBLISHING

For anyone who's ever longed to feel seen.

ALSO BY RACHEL L. SCHADE

Silent Kingdom Series

Silent Kingdom
Forsaken Kingdom
Broken Kingdom

Cursed Empire Series

Empire of Dragons
Empire of Traitors
Empire of Monsters
Empire of Ruins

Fae of Brytwilde Series

Castle of Dusk and Shadows

MAP OF
WILLOWBARK
ASHWOOD

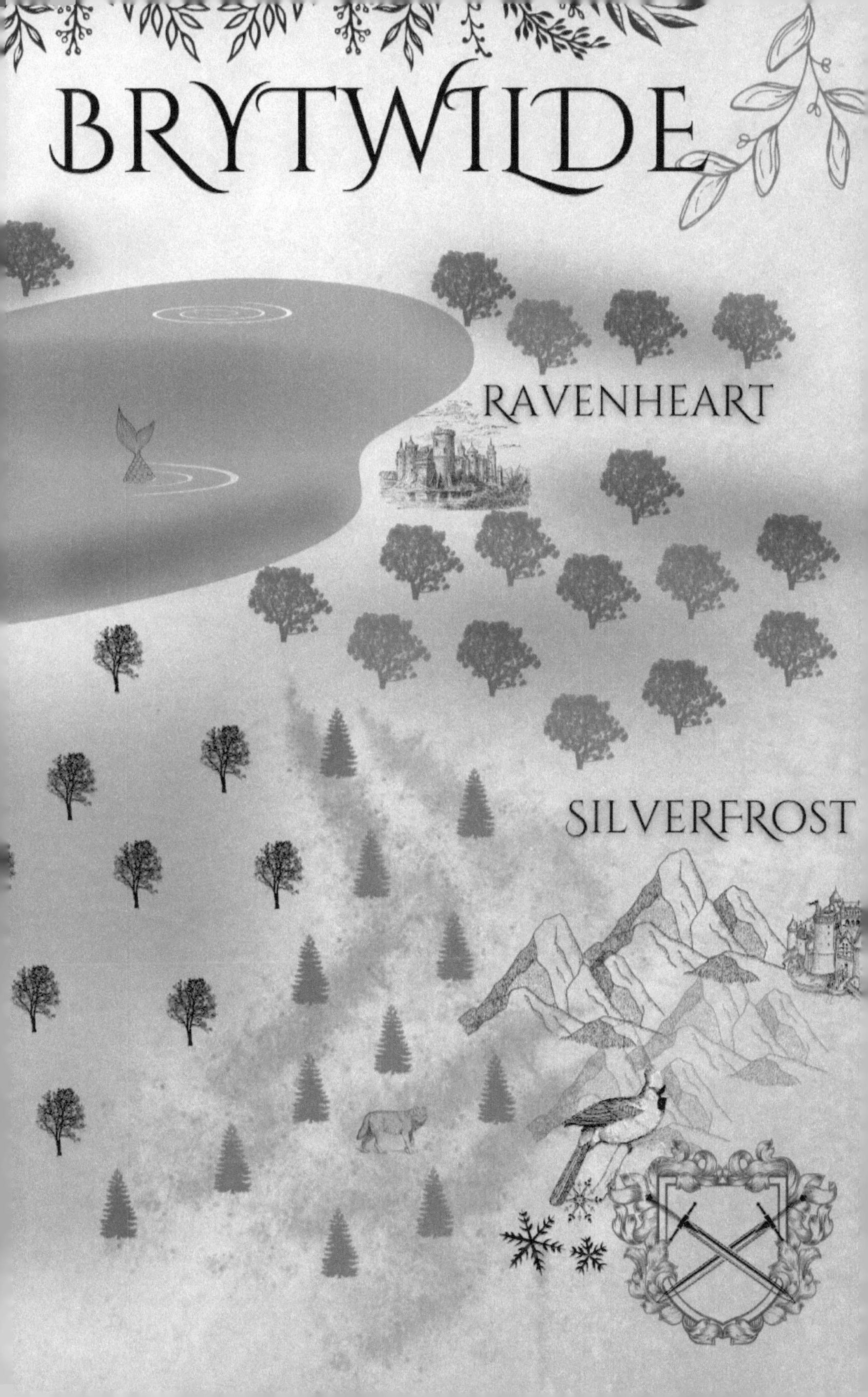

BRYTWILDE
RAVENHEART
SILVERFROST

CHAPTER ONE

A single drop of scarlet blood welled against my pale skin, threatening to stain the pristine fabric. With a hiss, I withdrew my finger before I could ruin my dress and set my needle aside. Besides, there was no more time to fuss over the gown, and it was finished. Even if I wished I could spend the rest of the night adding delicate details like lace or tiny bits of embroidery—anything that could keep me confined to the relative safety of my room and away from the oppressive atmosphere of tonight's town ball.

Kate was already there, her face an expressionless mask as she offered me a handkerchief. Though my maid had learned to school herself, I could sense the judgment emanating from her, as heavy as the dark clouds painting the evening sky outside my bedroom window. I was used to her coldness, but tonight, my nerves were frayed, and it grated on me.

Cringing, I pressed the kerchief to my finger, waiting for the bleeding to stop, and succumbed to letting Kate begin preparing me.

"Your brother has enough for you to pay a seamstress to make your gowns," Kate muttered at last, tugging harder than necessary on the laces of my stays.

In my heart, I knew I should rebuke her. There was nothing unladylike about making one's own dresses, and it wasn't a servant's place to give her opinion on my brother's wealth or my hobbies. But my tongue remained frozen, stuck to the roof of my mouth as she tugged me into my petticoats and finally my dress.

As I studied my reflection in the mirror, taking in the soft lavender fabric I'd spent so many hours carefully stitching together, pride warmed my heart. It offered the barest relief from Kate's icy looks and the unwelcome howling of the early December winds outside.

When I settled into the chair before my vanity so Kate could start on my hair, she paused, her permanent scowl deepening. Her eyes flicked disdainfully toward the long locks cascading down my shoulders, gleaming bright silver in the flickering candlelight. "Perhaps you should cover it for once."

Instead of answering, I looked down, silently fidgeting with the folds of my skirt until Kate sighed and got to work, barely trying to repress her grimace as her fingers brushed through my hair. As if touching it would harm her in some way.

Shame and hopelessness smothered my earlier pride. My brother Charles and his friends had been gossiping about me more than ever. I suspected it had much to do with the fact that Charles was hoping to make a match with Louisa Eggerton, a woman whose beauty was fine, no doubt, but whose father's fortune and influence in our town had a far greater pull on every eligible young man's heart. The more he distanced himself and made cutting remarks about me, the more the townspeople warmed toward him.

While the wind continued to howl and the clouds smothered the dying sun, threatening either icy rain or snow, I concentrated on ignoring Kate and her disapproving looks and erecting an imaginary world to escape into. One where Charles remained my affectionate younger brother, where my stepfather was still alive, and where I could dream of a peaceful existence. A gentleman falling in love with me and taking me to a comfortable house, somewhere in the countryside away from town gossip and superstition, somewhere I could stitch dresses to my heart's content and know peace and love and security. Somewhere I was wanted, not tolerated or scorned.

The illusion shattered as Kate finished, and not a moment too soon. Persistent knocking sounded on my door, jolting me from my chair. While Kate crossed my bedroom to open the door, I shoved my feet into my slippers and seized my jacket from where I'd laid it across my bed.

"The carriage is ready," Charles said impatiently from where he hovered in the doorway. His eyes were the same rich brown as mine, but when they locked on me, there was nothing but hostility in them. "Don't make us late."

My heart ached, remembering all the times we used to laugh together. Back then, he'd let me mend tears in his clothes and had appreciated my skill the same way Father had. He'd enjoyed games of chess with me and evenings reading together by the fire.

Now, the only remaining member of my family was a stranger. He cared only for the approval of the town, for gaining their favor now that he ran Father's house, and for marrying well.

"I'm ready," I said softly, stepping toward the door.

My half-brother's eyes landed on my hands, taking in the callouses adorning them. "Put on some gloves."

I seized a pair from my vanity. As I trailed him along the hall, down the steps, and toward our front entryway, I dared to ask the question that had pestered me all evening and every other event Charles had forced me to attend with him. "Why not spare yourself embarrassment and permit me to stay home? It's not as if anyone will want to dance with me. I can sit alone at home just as well as at the ball."

When we approached the door, I buttoned my jacket and braced for the night's chill wind. As soon as we stepped outside, its fingers raked along my cheeks and toyed with my hair, pulling unruly strands free to frame my face.

Silence hovered between my half-brother and me as the coachman handed me in and Charles followed after. But as soon as the door shut, I turned to him expectantly.

A muscle ticked in Charles's jaw, and for a moment, I imagined I saw a shadow of regret in his eyes. But it was gone too fast. Perhaps my memories with him were a dream, some strange farce, and this was the true Charles. Not the laughing, teasing one I remembered, who'd looked up to me fondly. "As your guardian and provider," he said stiffly, staring out the window rather than meeting my gaze, "it is my responsibility to assure you want for nothing."

"And I don't," I said. Though my allowance was pitiful, Charles had never withheld anything from me. He'd let me keep my old room, clothes, and maid. I had everything I could ever need or dream of—except what I desperately longed for most. Love. Peace. Family. "A ball is not a need, Charlie."

At the sound of his name, Charles cast me a sidelong glance. The carriage rolled forward, horse hooves clopping along dirt and wheels creaking over holes and pebbles as we wound toward the town hall. "You're out in society, and a proper lady. Not a recluse. Perhaps if you made an effort to cover your hair and *try* to be normal—"

"I am as human as you," I interrupted, my voice trembling around the lump in my throat. My vision swam, and I glanced away, staring out the window at the passing houses, the scattered leaves tearing across the road, the looming clouds blotting out the last of the evening light. "And Father loved my hair. He said it was beautiful and unique and nothing to be ashamed of. Certainly nothing to *fear*."

"It's a sign of fae blood," Charles snapped. "And you can't tell the citizens of Altidvale not to be afraid of the fae, not when we've all heard the stories and the warnings. You've lived through the winter solstices with the rest of us. You've seen them—with all manner of strange colors of skin and hair and eyes—dancing and cavorting. The violence. The bloodshed. The horrors."

I ground my teeth. *And that's why you, of all people, should know I'm not like them.* But I let the argument die. Charles's distance was hard enough to bear. I wasn't sure I could withstand a full-fledged fight if I dug in my heels and tried to counter all his wild theories. According to him, my fae blood meant that eventually, I would crumple to their allure. Maybe I'd leave the safety of our home one winter solstice night—the only night the creatures of Silverfrost, the nearest fae kingdom—were allowed to freely roam our town. Maybe I'd conjure magic, wild and unpredictable and violent.

In his mind, fae were untamable, and that meant I was destined to follow in their ways no matter what I thought or how human I behaved now.

All of Charles's suspicions had begun a year ago, once Father had confessed on his deathbed that he'd married my mother *after* I was born, after my true father, a man whose identity my mother had kept a secret, had died. It had turned my world upside down, realizing the man I'd called Father wasn't related to me at all, and that Charles was only my half-brother. The town gossip had started not long afterward, everyone talking about how they'd known my silver hair wasn't natural. How my late mother must have had a romantic dalliance with a fae. How I was not to be trusted.

Perhaps I'd been naïve to trust that Charles would come to my defense, to assume he'd care for me more than his own reputation.

Instead, he'd made me an outcast in my own home.

As we neared the town hall and the carriage slowed, Charles sighed. "Try to behave yourself," he said, as if I'd ever caused a scandal. "Maybe someone will want you for your dowry at last and take you off my hands before I marry. Father should have known better than to let someone unnatural like you under our roof."

The young men were whispering about me again—just as I'd expected. Sitting in the corner with the matrons and other ineligible women, I plastered a demure smile on my face and pretended I wasn't listening.

It was a game I'd played often over the past year. Smile. Sit up straight. Act as if I couldn't hear the words, as if nothing could upset me, and try to lose myself in a daydream of the happy past or some unattainable future.

In my mind, my heart was as impenetrable as stone, as cold as ice. The scathing words, the suspicious looks, and the frequent rejection didn't cut me.

Of course, that was all a lie.

"Her hair has turned even greyer—or perhaps it's silver," Frederick Rains muttered. "Did you see how it glistened when she came in? Like moonlight. Unnatural."

"Perhaps this winter solstice will be when her magic manifests," Jacob Wick insisted, crossing his arms. "I can't believe Charles hasn't cast her out."

My stomach tightened. For most of my twenty-one years, I'd loved my unusual features because Father had, and because he'd told me that, before Mother had passed of a fever when I was too young to remember her well, she had loved them too. Back then, the townspeople had been led to believe I was Father's child by blood, not marriage, and though they'd sometimes muttered or looked at me strangely, they'd been pleasant enough. But nowadays, with my true heritage constant speculation, I was forever shunned and whispered about.

And now I had the growing fear that Charles—who'd promised Father before he died that he'd care for me—would decide his loyalty to his dead father wasn't as strong as his desire to be rid of me and the taint I spread on his precious reputation.

"Sweet Miss Florentia Cantwell," came a wheedling tone as the young men ended their talk in favor of seeking out partners for the next dance. "Too shy to mingle with the other young ladies?"

I stiffened and turned, my muscles already tensing with my urge to flee. Mrs. Eggerton studied me with false sympathy.

"I think we are well enough acquainted that you can call me Ren," I insisted. Florentia was too formal, too extravagant, and I'd always disliked it.

Mrs. Eggerton tsked. "Would you disregard the name your own mother bestowed on you?" Her eyes roved over me. "My dear, I think you should try to put yourself out there. How do you expect to catch the eye of one of these handsome gentlemen if you're always hiding in the corner? False modesty doesn't become a young lady, especially someone of your age who should be thinking of finding a suitable match."

Heat flared in my veins, but Mrs. Eggerton wasn't finished. "You know that it hasn't been easy on your devoted brother to care for you, and I have reason to expect he'll be married soon. I'm sure his generosity—and my daughter's—will know no bounds, but is that something you want to take advantage of, lingering in their home after the wedding?"

My fists scrunched in the fabric of my dress, but I swallowed back my growing hurt. Unfortunately, I wasn't sure I fully concealed it. Her daughter Louisa wasn't the worst of the young ladies who scorned me, but she hadn't gone out of her way to befriend me either. We exchanged passing pleasantries, especially now that she'd captured Charles's attention, but it all seemed superficial.

And I'd already heard more than one of Charles's berating remarks about how I would be even less welcome once he was a married man. He'd reminded me of this fact at breakfast this morning.

"Tonight, I'll see Miss Eggerton again, and I expect to make my intentions toward her known. If I end the evening an attached man that much closer to marriage…well, it is that much closer to the day this house will have a woman running it. My new bride won't want to share this space with you. At twenty-one, you should be trying to be useful and strike a match yourself, not continue to live off my charity."

My throat burned. "If you want me to marry, perhaps you should stop encouraging the rumors about me."

Charles leaned forward, his dark eyes alight with a livid glow. "But saying you have fae blood is the truth, is it not? Look at your grey hair, like a crone before your time. You are not *one of us." Sneering in disgust, he turned away, as if I weren't worth wasting another moment on.*

Inhaling deeply, I forced my pain and fear about the future down. I wasn't an old maid, but the constant reminders from everyone around me about how generous my brother was in continuing to care for me were growing repetitive and worrisome. I clung to the hope that Charles would be too afraid to break his word to our deceased father to turn me out. But what if that lingering loyalty eventually faded?

Standing without bothering to do more than dip my head in the barest of curtseys toward Mrs. Eggerton, I shifted past everyone on the sidelines. They had no trouble enjoying themselves, all conversing politely, laughing easily. They hadn't a care in the world—at least not here, at a ball. This was where the rest of society set aside their grief and worry.

It was the opposite for me, a constant string of rejection and loneliness. At every ball, if I dared to gather my courage enough to even attempt to socialize, I was faced with the same treatment. Gentlemen whose gazes wouldn't linger, who muttered excuses before I could converse with them even though we'd grown up together. Or those who dared to speak or even dance with me, but never deigned to treat me as more than an acquaintance.

Superstition ran too deeply in the veins of these people, despite the fact that I'd never once shown a propensity toward anything fae. My ears were curved and delicate and utterly human. Only the flash of gold in my brown eyes and the silver stream of my hair marked me as unusual, but those meant nothing when I didn't have magic. My mother had been human.

If there was fae blood in my heritage, it was so diluted as to be nearly nonexistent. I wasn't like the half-fae we occasionally saw wander into town or dance in the streets on winter solstices, the ones who possessed pointed ears and wielded magic proudly.

The song drifted to an end and the dancing couples parted, many spinning away from the dance floor in favor of finding food and drink. My eyes skimmed the crowd, searching for one of the men who'd humor me with a conversation. I'd smile and laugh and pretend so Mrs. Eggerton and Charles would have no grounds to accuse me of not trying.

I swallowed back the regret threatening to clog my throat. Once, I'd dreamt of marrying for love. Now I knew that was a fool's dream. The best I could hope for was a marriage of comfort, one that would offer me a place in this world where perhaps I'd be respected as the lady of a household, a wife, and not a strange outcast girl with no future.

A flash of blond so pale it appeared white burned in my vision, and my gaze sharpened. Across the dance floor stood a stranger, clothed all in black leathers vastly different from the coats and trousers the town gentlemen wore. His short hair was the shock of white-blond I'd noticed, a bright gleam against the darkness of his attire and his gold-toned skin. His piercing eyes met mine, burrowing into my soul.

The heat of the room vanished, and my blood turned to ice. *Fae.*

I knew before my eyes raked over his pointed ears. He was too handsome, his aura too...*other*. Even from across the room, I felt an unnatural pull toward him, the sort I'd been warned about all my life. Fae were beautiful and charming and magical on the outside so they could attract their unsuspecting victims, but their hearts were ruthless and bloodthirsty.

It wasn't unusual for fae or half-fae to wander across the border of their world, called Brytwilde, and into ours. Fae from the winter kingdom of Silverfrost climbed down from the mountains to explore the mortal towns that lived in their shadows more often than we humans liked to contemplate. What startled me most was that this fae man hadn't glamoured himself to appear human, and that no one else seemed to find his presence unusual.

Rarely did the fae come for peaceful reasons. Sometimes they came to strike dangerous bargains, to glamour mortals into obeying their every whim, or to steal someone outright. My town of Altidvale was relatively safe due to old deals struck between its founders and the fae, ones that kept the fae from meddling with us as long as we allowed them certain liberties. One was that anyone who ventured past our borders too close to the mountains was as good as theirs, and we humans promised not to search for our lost loved ones. Another was that anyone who left their homes on the night of the winter solstice also belonged to the fae, who were allowed to wander our streets freely then.

And occasionally, our mayor agreed to let a fae servant or messenger enter our town and share news from Silverfrost and offer to take the boldest and most foolhardy among us to their royalty to bargain for their greatest wishes.

But if a fae stranger had been invited to our town ball, the gossip would have spread like wildfire.

As far as I knew, this man was an intruder. A dangerous one.

The music resumed and couples started to dance. The stranger circled the ballroom, making his way toward me on sure, lengthy strides. No one else gave him more than a passing glance as he moved along the edges of the dance, his eyes never leaving mine. Perhaps he hadn't glamoured his appearance, but had instead glamoured every guest in the ballroom to leave him alone—and had glamoured *me* to remain still. For, as much as my terrified mind screamed at me to run, I couldn't move. Could hardly breathe.

As he drew nearer, candlelight flashed in his eyes, revealing them to be an unnatural shade of gold—and sparkling with a predatory gleam. Ice skittered down my back, but I was still rooted in place.

He paused a mere yard away, and rather than offer an elegant bow, he smirked and dipped his head in greeting. "Miss Florentia Cantwell?"

I frowned. "I'm afraid we have not been introduced." My eyes scanned the ballroom for a familiar face, anyone who might know this man and give us a proper introduction. It seemed foolish to cling to etiquette in this moment, yet I was desperate for any excuse to get away, to find someone else so I wasn't alone with this fae man.

"Your mortal customs are charming, but unnecessary." The stranger held out a hand, and I noticed callouses and faded scars tracing his palm and fingers. "Dance with me."

"Who are you?" I asked, my composure slipping. I wondered if he could read the fear on my face, if he could already scent it on me. It was rumored the fae had far superior senses, everything from stronger smell to better hearing.

He didn't pull his hand back. Dark amusement traced his full lips. "Garrick Darkgrove. And now that you know my name, and I've already learned yours thanks to your numerous town gossips, we have been introduced. Come dance, and I'll answer your questions."

One more time, I glanced about the ballroom, but no one seemed to sense anything out of the ordinary. There was no fear on anyone's faces, no suspicion. "Do they even see you?"

Mr. Darkgrove listed his head. "They see what they expect to see. One of the young men you grew up with, being polite and offering you a dance. Later, they won't remember who you danced with, but it won't be of any importance to them."

The comment burned. Had he already noticed how little anyone in this town cared for me? Perhaps it was the bite of rejection that granted me the courage to set my hand in his and dare to dance with the only man here who seemed to find me interesting.

A lump lodged in my throat as a new song began and Mr. Darkgrove steered me toward the dance floor. I cast another furtive glance around, but no one noticed us. The music swelled, and the fae released my hand to stand across from me.

I met his eyes despite my fear, determined to exercise the propriety that had been instilled in me since I was a girl. The fae danced to our human music like he'd spent his life in the mortal world, his every step exuding as much grace as any gentleman present. Perhaps that was due to the predatory litheness all fae possessed, an elegance that was as entrancing as their otherworldly beauty.

"Mr. Darkgrove," I said, swallowing, hoping my voice didn't tremble. I pretended instead that he was like any of the other men present tonight, and that it was my responsibility as a lady of good upbringing to make pleasant conversation. "You said you would answer my questions. What brings you to Altidvale?"

The man huffed a laugh, his smile surprisingly genuine. A flash of white teeth proved that he did not, thankfully, possess any fangs or wickedly curved canines like some of the fae I'd seen on solstice nights. "Call me Garrick, please. And I wandered near your town on business."

I frowned. "What sort of business?"

"I'm a hunter. Though tonight, I confess, I was drawn to your town ball in the hope of some warmth and entertainment. The mountains' solitude can grow lonely."

I stepped away, circling the room as part of the dance, but continuously casting sideways looks Garrick's way, trying to see how the other dancers responded to him. Garrick grinned and dipped his head, all pleasantness, and ladies and gentlemen merely smiled in return.

As I wound my way back toward Garrick, I repressed a shudder. Though all children in Altidvale were taught that fae couldn't lie, we were warned that they could twist their words and bend the truth. I couldn't help but suspect that Garrick was doing that now, for would a fae truly sneak into a human ball only for entertainment and companionship? Their revels were far rowdier than our mortal parties.

And why was I the only one who could see what he truly was?

Maybe Garrick wanted me to see he was fae, and he hadn't glamoured me. Though I wasn't sure why that would be the case. Why had he chosen to speak with *me*?

Charles was right, I thought wildly. *Impossibly, I have fae blood after all, blood that lets me see through glamour, and now they've come to claim me.*

I tried to shove my fear down as Garrick and I twirled around one another and then apart. When we stepped together again, his eyes flicked to my hair. "Have you always seen through glamour?" he asked.

"What?" I stumbled and righted myself, a flush creeping across my cheeks. But no one else had seen my embarrassing misstep. I was as invisible as ever, and never had I been more grateful for that.

"You knew immediately what I was."

I inhaled sharply, the dance all but forgotten. I was vaguely aware of music twining through the air, subtle and lovely, but turning discordant as it mixed with the thundering beat of my pulse in my ears. "I—I don't know what games you're playing at, sir," I stammered. "But you aren't supposed to enter our town without permission."

Garrick leaned in, dropping his voice lower. "Why would I need permission for doing something no one will ever know about? I'm only dancing. I don't plan on harming anyone."

I wanted to flee to the other side of the ballroom, but, as if reading my thoughts, Garrick grasped my wrist. His hold was gentle, yet it made me feel trapped, and my heart stuttered. "There are rules we honor, and that you must honor as well."

Garrick's eyes darted to my hair again. "Why are you different from them, Florentia?"

I grimaced. Father had called me Ren. My full name sounded pretentious and wrong.

"You have eyes that pierce through glamour and hair of starlight. Is that why you sit all alone while they gossip about you?"

Ducking my head and refusing to meet his gaze, I resumed the steps of the dance, managing to tug out of his hold on me. I had the impression that now he'd found me, he wouldn't let me go. That if I walked away, I'd only be more interesting, like a fleeing mouse capturing a cat's fascination. Perhaps if I danced quietly, I'd seem dull, and Garrick would leave me alone. I was overcome with the fear that my earlier courage might prove fatal, and I inwardly cursed myself as a fool for giving into it and allowing this stranger to lead me to the dance floor.

Whether he'd come for entertainment or to fool humans into terrible bargains, I no longer cared. I wanted to leave this floor, leave this ball, and return home. Away from the stares, the noise, the gossip. Away from the danger and cruelty of humans and fae. Away from all my forced smiles.

I was awfully, bone-deeply weary of pretending.

But I'd have to do it a little longer. Lifting a hand to feign fanning myself when inwardly I was clenching my teeth to keep my teeth from chattering with cold, I sighed in relief as the song ended.

"Thank you for the dance," I murmured, staring at my feet as I dipped my head to Garrick, "but I feel faint and need to sit down."

It was a reasonable excuse, one I hoped he'd accept without following me. Plenty of young ladies grew overheated during the exertion of dancing for hours, especially when they forgot to take a rest and drink. The crush of bodies was warm enough—or it had been, before this strange chill had started overcoming me.

I walked on wobbly legs toward the nearest table, eager for a glass of water, anything to distract myself. My slippers skidded along the polished floor. The sound of footsteps trailing me made me turn, skirt swishing about my ankles.

Garrick.

"Please, sir," I said, but as soon as I unclenched my teeth, they began to chatter.

Garrick's eyes widened. "Are you unwell?"

Surprise momentarily eased my fear. He sounded concerned, as if he were a compassionate fae. Not heartless. "I—I don't..."

He stepped forward, cutting me off as he brushed his fingers along my forehead. They were calloused but gentle. Heart in my throat, I was too shocked at his forwardness to step away. "I have heard of fevers afflicting mortals, but not deadly cold." Something flashed in his eyes, and I didn't like it. It seemed too calculating. "Do you need to sit down?"

I shook my head, wanting him to leave but not quite able to brave saying the words aloud. Instead, I decided that if etiquette didn't matter to a fae, I wouldn't let it matter to me, and I turned my back on him to approach the table. As soon as my fingers closed around a glass of water, cold flared through my body. The water frosted over, black as the darkest night.

But the ice didn't stop. It coated my arm, tracing lacy patterns up my bare skin. It crackled beneath my feet.

And now, everyone was watching me.

CHAPTER TWO

Charles's grip was unyielding, digging into my arm so painfully that it distracted me from my smarting, bleeding palm.

"Charlie, please!" I cried, but he ignored me, his expression stiff, his eyes locked straight ahead.

The night air nipped at the exposed skin of my arms and face. Heavy cloud cover blocked the stars, and a frosty hint on the wind threatened snow. It was not a night to be out in nothing but my short-sleeved gown. There hadn't been time to search for my jacket after chaos had ensued.

Everything was a hazy blur in my mind, even though mere minutes had passed since the incident at the ball. Black ice. Biting cold. Shattering glass splintering in my hand and warm blood, shockingly bright and red against the frosty darkness surrounding me.

Screams had filled my ringing ears, and I'd stumbled, slipping on the ice. When I'd whirled to search the room for Garrick, sure he'd been the cause of the strange winter magic, Charles had been there instead, seizing my arm and whispering furiously into my ear. "Walk. Now."

The people of Altidvale had panicked, fleeing the ballroom as if they were under attack. And no one was searching for the gold-eyed fae I'd danced with, the one they hadn't even noticed. No, their horrified, accusatory gazes had all pinned on *me*.

Now, teeth chattering and breath steaming before me, I stared down at my bleeding hand. The cuts were shallow, but they still stung. *I didn't conjure that ice,* I thought, even as another shiver rippled down my spine. I'd been afraid and consumed by cold, but I was sure that was due to Garrick's presence. For the past year I'd been accused of being part-fae and dangerous, but I'd never manifested any magic before, never had any reason to suspect I could do anything unusual.

It wasn't mine, I insisted to myself again, trying to nudge aside all lingering doubts.

The rattling of carriage wheels and the clop of horse hooves echoed through the street, but they were all heading the opposite direction that Charles and I walked. While the rest of the townspeople hurried toward the warmth and safety of home, my brother was dragging me to the foot of the mountains, toward the barrier that marked the gap between our mortal world and that of the fae. If Charles threw me beyond the border, he'd be leaving me for the fae. Altidvale's agreements would bar anyone from coming for me—not that anyone would want to. And I could try to return—if a fae didn't find and claim me first—but what would I be returning to if Charles refused to let me go home?

"Please, Charles—" I began again, my throat already raw from pleas and sobs that had fallen on deaf ears.

His jaw was rigid, and his eyes remained straight ahead, dark and fuming with the blackest emotion I'd ever seen from him. The final threads of his vow to Father—the last of his restraint that kept him from tossing me out—had frayed.

"I knew you were a monster," he growled, but he seemed to be speaking more to himself than to me. "Perhaps you spent all this time glamouring everyone to love you." He sneered. "You're a danger, and you betrayed us all. Did you always plot to take us lowly humans unaware with your deadly magic? Have you always hated us?"

"Charles, I would never—"

"I'm marrying Miss Eggerton, and you will not live under the same roof as her, terrorizing and threatening her with your dark magic." His fingers dug in deeper, and I yelped in pain, thrashing in vain against the strength of his grip.

"I'm your *sister*!"

"You are *not* my blood!" Charles screamed, the words louder than the pounding of my own pulse in my ears. "We might have shared a mother, but that's not enough, not when you're clearly more fae than human. You're not one of us—you're one of *them*."

Tears burned my eyes. I knew better than to cry. I'd grieved the loss of my brother months ago, as he'd grown more suspicious of me and all the ways he claimed I was different. Somewhere along the way, his fear had transformed into loathing. But once, he'd been my younger sibling. The one I'd tucked into bed at night and read stories to. The one I'd looked after.

Now, it was his turn to look after me, and he found the task to be a burden.

Charles dragged me toward the outskirts of our town, winding past shadowed buildings and up the incline that marked the edge of our world and the beginning of Brytwilde. The scent of evergreens enshrouded us, coming on a gust that rolled off the snow-capped mountains.

"Think of this as my last duty, my last act to protect you," Charles bit out as he finally stopped, his own breath clouding the air. He loosened his hold on me, only a little, as he cast a glance over his shoulder. The warmth of candlelight gleaming through windows danced like distant fireflies, and my heart ached. "Altidvale will never accept you after your dangerous display back there. You belong in *their* world, in Silverfrost. That's your home. They'll accept you."

My eyes burned. "That's not true. That ice wasn't from me. There was a—"

"Goodbye, Florentia," Charles said, and he shoved me, hard.

I choked back a scream as something in the air flickered and a pulse of warmth, of power, flowed through me. When I struck the ground on the other side of the invisible barrier, I landed on a worn dirt path that wound upward, into the mountains.

With the air knocked from my lungs, it took me a moment to move, to even breathe. Struggling to inhale, I gaped up at Charles, whose expression changed for the briefest of seconds. Something wide-eyed, almost like regret, filled his eyes, and then his face became stony once more. "Never threaten us with your magic again," he said, his voice low. "Go home. Leave us in peace."

Charles lifted his gaze to the mountains. "Here is your gift!" he shouted. He knew the Silverfrost royalty would hear, whether through magic or spies, as he launched into the terrible words we'd been taught to recite if ever we sacrificed one of our own to the fae. "Rulers of winter, accept my offering freely and generously given, and in return, I plead your graciousness and goodwill upon my household and my town." I knew what he would expect—to return the next morning to find a pile of gold awaiting near the barrier, or even a fae servant waiting to grant a single wish or blessing upon him as a sign of gratitude. "Come yourself or send one of your humble servants to fetch her, and may you welcome her warmly into your kingdom, where she belongs."

Silently, he turned, stalking back toward home without glancing back.

"Charles!" I screamed, launching to my feet, determined to race back into Altidvale with him. If a fae didn't murder me out here first, I'd freeze to death. Surely I could find someone in my mortal town who would take pity on me.

But when I charged forward, my hands struck something solid and hard, despite the fact that there was no visible wall. Staggering backward, hands smarting, I choked on a sob. *The border.* The fae must have enchanted it, ensuring that mortals who crossed into their world truly belonged to them. It wasn't simply that our people were forbidden to retrieve their lost loved ones—they couldn't do it without belonging to the fae as well. I *couldn't* return to the human world.

A new chill swept through me, having nothing to do with the temperature.

Whether he knew it or not, Charles had left me to die.

I lost track of time as my brother's form faded down the street. My mind whirled with panic and desperation. I pounded my fists against the barrier to no avail.

There was nothing to do but accept that I was trapped in Silverfrost, a fae kingdom known for its cruelty toward humans. I could lie down and wait to freeze, or I could turn and face my fate.

For a wild moment, I wondered if dying of exposure would be more peaceful than venturing deeper into Silverfrost and braving the fae. But I shook my head, refusing to entertain the notion. I couldn't give up that easily. I had to search for shelter, and then I'd try to formulate a plan.

Wrapping my arms around myself, I trudged up the path, my slippers dislodging rocks and roots. Soon, evergreen boughs swayed overhead, blocking out the grey sky. In the thickening shadows, the cold grew icier, and my tears froze to my lashes. I swallowed back my mounting terror. Somehow, I had to find a place to wait out the frigid night.

I scanned the path, my eyes searching the trees edging it. They thickened into a forest, creaking in the wind. The shadows between them were too dark to discern anything but the occasional moving form or pair of gleaming eyes. I prayed those belonged to animals and not bloodthirsty fae or other monsters. *If there is a path, surely it leads to one of their towns or dwellings.* The fae would be eager to collect any humans who wandered beyond the barrier, whether to torment, enslave, or murder them.

A bitter laugh escaped me. Hoping for shelter among a people who would enjoy my misery seemed like madness, but at least that gave me a slim chance of survival. Maybe.

Footsteps on the path made me pause. They didn't come from ahead, but from behind, making me hope—foolishly—that Charles had seen reason and returned for me. That he'd chosen to brave the dangers of Brytwilde rather than leave his elder sister to die here.

But those thoughts faded when I turned and found none other than Garrick approaching, his gold eyes bright in the dimness. This time, he wore a fur coat and was fully armed, like a hunter venturing through the woods in search of prey.

"There you are," he said, as if he'd been scouring the town for me since Charles dragged me from the ballroom. He rushed forward, shucking off his coat and offering it to me.

"You!" The single word came out in a rush, full of accusation.

Garrick blinked, as if stunned.

"*You're* the reason I'm here." My teeth chattered, but I was too upset and distrustful to take the coat he still held out to me. Tears stung my eyes. "You unleashed that magic in the ballroom, framing me, and then you disappeared."

His brow furrowed. "I can't wield winter magic." Without waiting for my response, he stepped forward and wrapped his coat around me tightly. I was shivering too violently to resist. It smelled of pine and earth and fresh mountain air, and it enveloped me in a warmth that sank into my bones.

Garrick scanned the path ahead. "We need to find shelter," he said, taking my arm gently and guiding me forward.

My face was numb, making it difficult to speak through my cold lips. "Can I trust you?"

Garrick cast me a disparaging look. "Firstly, your people were already against you. Secondly, that magic was your own. And thirdly," he added, his teeth flashing in the night as he grinned, "why would I give you a coat if I wanted you to die?" Before I could try to argue further, he added, "I left because I worried my presence was the reason you lost control of your magic. I didn't think your people would be so rash as to cast you out after one incident, without a single question asked."

My mind whirled, refusing to latch onto the idea that I had magic. Cold as I was, my resistance to walking with a stranger was swiftly breaking down in the face of my need for help to survive. I allowed Garrick to lead me forward. "Perhaps you want me to survive long enough to run and provide entertainment," I suggested. "You told me you're a hunter, after all."

Still smiling, Garrick shook his head. "I wouldn't do that to a magical creature like you, Starlight."

I frowned but chose to ignore his nickname—reminding me of the way he'd said I had *hair like starlight*—and his insistence that I possessed magic. I was too overwhelmed. "He *sold* me to the Silverfrost family," I muttered as Garrick drew me off the path and into the forest, shoving branches out of our way.

"Who?"

"Charles, my half-brother." I sniffled, feeling pathetic, but Garrick didn't offer me a pitying glance. Instead, he stared into the darkness, seeming to be mulling something over.

"There'll be a penalty to pay if you don't arrive on their doorstep soon," he explained. "They'll send some of their servants from the castle to find you. They may have already."

A shiver darted down my spine despite the warmth of Garrick's coat. "What will they want with me?" I breathed.

In the darkness, I couldn't read Garrick's expression. "It depends. With most humans? Slaves or entertainment. With you and your magic? I cannot say. They might accept you as one of their own."

Might. I couldn't risk my entire future on a chance.

"Is that where you're taking me?" I asked, my voice tremulous.

Garrick hesitated, a long moment passing between us, and I was reminded that fae could not lie. "I am taking you to shelter, or you won't survive the night. There's a cabin not far from here that I often stay in. After that, we will decide what to do in the morning."

I paused, contemplating his words. "What do *you* want to do?"

Garrick didn't miss a beat as he pressed further into the woods. "Ensure your survival."

"Why?"

This time, Garrick's rich laughter echoed off the trees. "Because no one deserves to freeze to death simply for being different."

I couldn't argue with that. "Why were you in Altidvale?" I went on as the trees began to thin and starlight flooded through the forest canopy. We entered a glade covered in pine needles. Nearby, a stream burbled over stones, winding deeper into the wood.

"I told you. I wanted to join your ball."

"Doesn't Silverfrost offer entertainment?"

Garrick gestured to the cabin ahead of us, nestled on the edge of the glade. "This is where I've spent my nights for the past month. Wouldn't you also be drawn to company?"

"*Human* company?" I asked pointedly.

Something flashed across his face—loneliness or pain, I wasn't sure. "Any company."

An icy breeze swept through the clearing, and I noticed the way Garrick flinched. I'd assumed up to this point that maybe his magic somehow kept him warm, and he didn't need his coat. Apparently I'd been wrong. I picked up my pace, eager for the promise of shelter.

The cabin door creaked as Garrick swung it open, but the interior was cozy, if cramped. Other than a small washroom in the far corner, there was only one room, containing a fireplace and a bed layered in heavy blankets, a chest resting at its foot.

My eyes snagged on that bed, and my heart thundered in my chest. Until now, I'd been anxious for safety and a chance to survive. I hadn't considered what it would mean to spend the night in such close quarters with a stranger.

Garrick might have saved my life, but that didn't mean he wouldn't harm me later. I'd been taught all my life that the fae were cruel and deceitful. Their generosity generally came with a steep price. If Garrick was right and I did possess magic—outlandish as that was—then maybe he'd saved me in hopes of using me. Or maybe he was the one the royals had sent to fetch me after Charles had offered me to them. If he retrieved me for the crown, perhaps he'd receive a lavish reward.

I hovered near the door, rubbing my temples and willing my sluggish mind to work faster as Garrick clicked the door shut behind us and strode toward the fireplace. Silently, he built a fire from a stack of logs waiting on the hearth, leaving me alone to my thoughts.

We will decide what to do in the morning. As if Garrick would give me a say in my fate. I shivered.

"You'll feel a draft by the doorway," Garrick said, never taking his eyes off the flames he was coaxing to life. "I promise I won't bite." He smirked. "Not after we've only known each other for one day, anyway. Perhaps after two."

Embarrassment stained my cheeks as I tried to decide if his jesting tone meant he was flirting with me. "What sort of promise is that?" I managed to choke out.

Garrick studied me, amusement still dancing in his expression. "Fae cannot lie, so I would say it's worth far more than a mortal one. You can trust me when I say I won't bite...unless you ask me to."

I gaped at him, but rather than dignify his words with a response, I wrapped his coat more tightly around myself, longing for the comfort of my own home. What I'd give to be in my bedroom sewing, away from this brazen fae and the ways in which he made me feel both terrified and scandalized.

Garrick's humor melted as anger darkened his face. "Come sit before you freeze. You can trust me, and my word, far more than you could trust your brother or the promise he made to your dying father."

My heart dropped into my stomach. "How do you know about that?"

"Like I said before, I heard the townspeople whispering about you," the fae said, his tone as disgusted as I felt. "Their constant gossip. Their judgment. They bemoaned poor Charles Cantwell's vast generosity and sweet temperament, the way he sacrificed in order to uphold his vow to your father." Garrick placed a hand over his heart in mockery. "Tonight, we saw the true worth of his words."

"Indeed," I whispered, tears burning my eyes.

Garrick leaned back on his heels, scanning me slowly. "I'm sorry. It was insensitive of me to speak that way. Please, warm yourself. I promise you that no harm will come to you in this cabin."

I arched an eyebrow. "*Outside* of it?"

"I can make no promises about that, Florentia."

"I...prefer Ren," I said hesitantly, before relenting and approaching cautiously, sitting as gracefully as I could on the floor. I held my hands out toward the growing fire. Though there was an acceptable distance between us, I couldn't help but feel uncomfortable. I'd never been unchaperoned like this with a man who wasn't family. "It's not proper for a lady to be alone so long with a strange man," I ventured. Not that I wanted Garrick to leave...I simply hoped he would take note and behave like a gentleman, though that was probably too much to hope from a fae.

"It's also not proper to throw your sister out into the night and leave her to freeze," Garrick growled.

Startling, I glanced at him, surprised at the hostility in his tone. And maybe a little bit afraid. His guttural voice was a sharp reminder that he wasn't human.

Garrick cleared his throat. "I'll stop speaking of your brother." He turned away, shaking his head. "It's just...my kind value loyalty above all else, especially to loved ones. It's hard not to think of him as the vilest of men to break his word and threaten your life so callously."

I had no response to that.

For a long while, we sat in silence, letting the fire crackle and pop, its warmth slowly enveloping the cabin. My tense muscles began to relax as Garrick rose, moving about the room to gather a kettle, filling it with water from a supply he must have kept on hand, and setting it over the fire to boil.

"Do you truly live here?" I asked after a long while, studying the way the firelight cast flickering shadows over the sharp planes of Garrick's face. His piercing gold eyes remained focused on the dancing flames, not turning to look at me. He was handsome, in the breathtaking way that fae tended to be, but there was a ruggedness about him. It wasn't only the leathers and fur clothes he favored or the fact that he had bows and quivers of arrows hanging on the wall. It wasn't the mud-encrusted boots he'd shucked off at the door. It was something in his very appearance, one that told me he was as dangerous as he was beautiful. He was predatory, lethal—with or without magic.

"I'm a hunter," Garrick repeated, shrugging. As if that alone answered my question. But then he went on: "I travel throughout the mountains, and there are cabins scattered everywhere. I keep necessities stocked in each so I can take shelter while I await my prey." He collected two mugs from a cabinet, added tea leaves, and poured hot water from the kettle into each.

When he offered a mug to me, I cradled it in my hands, letting the rising steam caress my face. "Do you set out traps and bait them to come closer to your cabin?"

Garrick turned to me, his mouth twitching in another smirk. "Why? Are you hungry for venison? Hare?"

I shook my head. "But I don't understand you," I ventured. Perhaps it was the fact that Garrick didn't scorn me, or maybe it was my hope to become better acquainted with this fae until I believed I could trust him, but I felt bold enough to ask personal questions. "If you grow so tired of living and hunting alone in the mountains that you chose to seek mortal company, why not live among your kind?"

Taking a long gulp of his tea—to give himself time, I imagined, since it hadn't steeped nearly long enough—Garrick leaned back on his hands. "And what *is* my kind, Starlight?"

This time, I scowled at him. "We are not familiar enough for nicknames."

"I've already asked you to call me Garrick, and Miss Cantwell is entirely too formal for my world. Here, we don't think it too formal to call someone by their given name. And a nickname?" His lips curled into another dimpled smile, and unbidden warmth spread through my chest at the sight. He reached out, tugging gently on a lock of my hair. "It doesn't mean the same thing here. In my world, flirting doesn't mean I'm proposing marriage."

I swallowed thickly at his closeness. Among humans, it would surely mean he was courting me, trying to win my affections, or that he was a rake, carelessly breaking women's hearts. But Garrick seemed to speak the truth. He seemed the type of man to be friendly and open with everyone, maybe even to flirt without it meaning anything. He possessed a natural charm. His nickname only meant he saw me as a possible friend. I could accept that.

"So tell me," Garrick continued, "what is my kind?"

I frowned in confusion. "What do you mean?" I scanned his face, searching his gold eyes, focusing on his pointed ears. Misgiving clutched my heart, turning my growing warmth into something chilly. I'd heard stories of the monsters and other creatures that lived in Brytwilde, but they'd never had faces that looked like the high fae. "You're fae...right?"

Garrick tilted his head. "I'm a shifter, considered one of the weakest types of fae. All I can conjure is the weakest sort of glamour, enough to occasionally trick humans with a few illusions, but not enough to control them. And I couldn't trick anyone with magic in their blood, like you. Most shifters are ridiculed and looked down upon. Our magic is never strong, save for our ability to transform into another creature and occasional related abilities."

I stiffened. "What sort of creature?"

Garrick didn't flinch, didn't look away. A slow grin crept up his face, wicked and wild. "A wolf."

I jerked backward, sloshing my tea and cringing when the hot liquid soaked my dress.

"Are you all right?" the fae asked hurriedly, reaching for my mug.

More embarrassed than hurt, I nodded.

"No need to worry," Garrick reassured me. "I was only teasing. I promised not to hurt you, remember?" He swept toward the cabinets, setting down my mug, withdrawing a cloth, and returning to dab at my wet dress.

"But...what do you hunt?" I asked, voice strangled, torn between flinching away from Garrick and trusting the promises he'd made me.

Another grin twisted his lips, this one less mischievous and more friendly, framed by dimples. "As a shifter, I don't eat humans or fae, not even in my wolf form. That would be too close to cannibalism." He sneered with disgust. "I *am* still fae. Not a monster."

I shuddered despite his words, but his expression remained earnest. "And the law I'm sure you learned about us fae applies to *all* types of fae, Starlight," he went on. "I cannot lie. But perhaps now you see why I'm looked down upon. I'm little more than a dog to most fae, unable to even wield strong glamour, unable to use any sort of magic but to transform into a furry beast." He chuckled, but there was bitterness in it.

"Does that mean you choose to be alone? Do you...have family?" I asked, hoping my question wasn't too invasive.

"I, like you, have never fit into my world," Garrick explained. "The rest of my family died during a vicious battle at the Silverfrost castle over two decades ago." His expression was distant, as if haunted by snatches of awful memories as he spoke. "I'm accustomed to being alone. No matter the adventures I experience in these mountains, there is never anyone to share them with while I'm out here. However, I do go into towns and cities—sometimes even the castle—to trade the meat and pelts I gather for other items. Sometimes I'll stay a bit for the company, but I think you know as well as I that often, you can be even lonelier in a crowd than when you're secluded." There was a lightness in his tone that made me think maybe he was trying to make his life seem less sad. It was difficult to know how sad he truly was, when he continued to smile and jest as if it all were nothing.

Eventually, he sat back, laying the wet cloth aside and glancing at my still-damp dress. "I can offer you a change of clothes," he suggested.

My eyes scanned the single room cabin and the one bed again, tension coiling in my stomach. I needed the safety of this shelter, and whether it was foolish or not, Garrick's promises reassured me I would be better protected with him than on my own. I couldn't face the cold or the creatures outside as I was. But I hadn't really considered what an entire night alone with this man would entail.

In Altidvale, it would have provided endless scandal and gossip, and Charles would have been forced to bribe Garrick into marrying me. Here in the kingdom of Silverfrost? There was no one to care about scandal, and this was only survival for me. But what was it to a fae?

As if reading my thoughts, Garrick lifted his hands, palms facing me. "I'm not trying to take advantage of you. I couldn't leave you to die out there. That is all. And now that I've saved you, I'm duty-bound to protect you. It's in my blood, being part-wolf." He winked before gesturing toward the washroom. "You can change in there, and then you can sleep in the bed. I'll sleep on the floor."

Before I could open my mouth to question his generosity, feeling the polite thing to do would be to refuse to take his bed, he grinned. "I can manage sleeping on the floor just fine, Starlight. I *am* considered a dog, after all."

CHAPTER THREE

For a long while, I gazed through the window above the bed, studying the glow from the stars streaming through the bare branches of a tree outside the cabin. They rose toward the sky like skeletal fingers grasping for a shred of distant light. Meanwhile, the wind continued to whisper through the forest, causing the trees to creak and the cabin itself to tremble. The low-burning fire helped chase away the frigid air that seeped through each crack in the walls, but I was still grateful for the fur blankets I'd burrowed into.

Garrick had offered me a loose shirt that hung overlarge on my frame but covered me enough to avoid feeling too scandalous. Still, my legs had been bare, so I'd demanded that he turn away as I settled into the bed, piling the furs over me until I was comfortable and completely covered.

Now, I rolled over restlessly and studied the darkened cabin and then Garrick. Stretched out on a heap of blankets before the fire, he'd gone so still and quiet that I imagined he was already asleep. That was, until he stirred, as if sensing the weight of my gaze. His gold eyes met mine in the dimness.

Embarrassed to be caught staring, I tried to draw attention away from the fact by asking the question that had been haunting me. "You said we'd decide about my future tomorrow. But what does that mean? You're a Silverfrost, and you told me you sometimes hunt for the king and queen. Would you turn me over to them?"

Garrick's eyes flicked to the fire. "I don't want to. Though they're my sovereigns, I don't like the way they treat humans. You don't deserve that life. As I said, I'll protect you. But I'm not sure how long you can run from them, Starlight. They'll send their soldiers after you, and I doubt they'll care much for the condition you're in so long as you arrive at the castle."

I inhaled sharply. "As a hunter, don't you know places to hide in these mountains?"

Garrick picked at a thread on his blanket. "I can't guarantee you could hide forever. Or that the royals would ever stop looking for you. We could try to cross the border and enter another fae kingdom. Ashwood is far friendlier toward mortals. Though I'm not sure they'd welcome me. The relationship between Ashwood and Silverfrost is...strained."

The way he spoke the words made me think he was greatly understating the tension between the two lands. I swallowed. "And the other fae kingdoms?"

"I'm not sure they'll be any kinder to a human than Silverfrost would be."

I leaned back against the pillows, closing my eyes. Imagining spending the rest of my life on the run and in hiding, praying to distant gods to defend me. "I can't ask you to leave your life behind for me," I muttered into the shadows.

Garrick's head was turned away once more, studying the fire, but I could have sworn he whispered, "What kind of a life?"

Running my hands down my face, I tried to calm my pulse, tried to believe I'd be able to escape the Silverfrost royals. They were the center of every nightmarish story told in Altidvale, the villains all children feared when they drifted off to sleep. I didn't want to believe Charles had truly cast me off to them, that I had no hope of freedom or happiness. That my miserable life might end at their hands, or worse—that I might be enslaved or glamoured into their service.

I wiped at a tear before it could slide down my cheek. *That will not be my fate,* I promised myself, even though I had no reason to believe I could fight it.

"This cabin is close to your town, and therefore where Silverfrost's servants will begin their search," Garrick said. "In the morning, we'll travel deeper into the mountains, to another of my posts. It will take us nearer to the Ashwood border."

"Are you sure you wouldn't rather send me on my way alone?"

Garrick huffed out a laugh. "Starlight, I'm a wolf with protective instincts and no pack to defend. Let me at least see you to a safer location before you cast me away."

"I'm hardly more than a stranger. Why risk your king and queen's wrath for me?" When I sat up, I met Garrick's gaze.

"Perhaps I'd like a friend, someone worth risking my life for." He tossed me a careless, dimpled grin before turning over. "Get some sleep, Starlight. We'll have a long walk tomorrow."

A scraping sound against the window jolted me awake. The cabin was even darker, immersed in night's shadows, the fire burnt down to nothing but embers. I sat up in bed, blinking bleary eyes and turning. My heart froze in my chest, a scream rising and dying in my throat.

The scraping sound came from a claw running down the glass as a headless creature—its flesh grey and sagging, like an undead thing—stood at the window. In its other arm, it cradled a head, its fierce red eyes glaring straight at me. There was a hungry gleam in the severed head's gaze as the monster scratched its claws down the windowpane, the noise grating against my ears.

Stifling another scream, I staggered up and out of the bed, slamming against the wall.

Garrick bolted from his blankets, his gaze fastening on the monster outside the cabin. "Dullahan." He snarled the word like a curse. "The king and queen sent it to find you." He drew a dagger from a sheath at his thigh and seized a bow and quiver from the wall. "Stay in the cabin. It cannot enter with the protective wards placed upon it." As he approached the door, he cast a fierce look over his shoulder. "Bolt the door behind me, and do not let me in unless I call you Starlight. It can mimic voices."

With that, he strode outside, slamming the door behind him. I darted forward and bolted the lock, shivering more with fear than with the blast of cold air. It was in that moment, as I slid down the wall and hugged my knees to my chest, that I wondered what I'd do if Garrick never returned. Gritting my teeth, I rose, scanning the wall across from me for any blade or bow that looked small enough I might manage to wield it. What a preposterous idea—me, a sheltered lady of Altidvale who had never even touched a weapon before in her life, fending off that nightmarish monster outside. Hysterical laughter threatened to bubble up, but I choked it down.

Another shudder racked my body, tickling my spine and cooling my palms.

Low growls shattered the quiet of the night, and I lurched to my feet, scarcely daring to peer out the window to catch a glimpse of what was happening. There was the scrape of a blade being drawn, and an animalistic hiss I assumed belonged to the monster. I caught a glimpse of shadows colliding before the forms vanished out of view.

Long moments passed, my heart pulsing in my ears and my breath fogging in the air. I wrapped my arms tightly around myself, determined not to lose control to the chill that was building within me. What if Garrick was right, and I unleashed more magic?

I was almost as terrified of the thought of wild magic as I was of the dullahan hunting me.

A spray of scarlet arced through the darkness outside the window, splattering along the ground. Blood. My mouth turned sour.

"Garrick." What would I do if he was killed? It struck me fully then how vulnerable I was, how dependent I was on having a guide and protector in this strange and dangerous kingdom. I couldn't cower behind wards in this cabin forever, but I knew without any experience in defending myself, without any clue how the magic I supposedly possessed might work to help me, without any hunting or survival skills, I would perish if left on my own.

Or the king and queen would find me.

I squeezed my fingers into fists to stop their trembling. If I thought living with Charles and his resentment and malice had been stifling, I couldn't fathom what life would be like as a slave or captive to the cruel, bloodthirsty fae. If they even let me live, they would ensure I suffered and served them all my days. I'd already felt trapped for the past year. I would not be trapped again.

I will die before I am their prisoner.

The doorknob rattled, and my heart leapt into my throat. Another chill snaked down my spine. *"Florentia, open the door."*

The voice sounded like Garrick's, but I knew better. My skin prickled and I squeezed my eyes shut, praying that this didn't mean the blood had belonged to the fae shifter. If he was dead, it was my fault. He'd chosen to protect me.

And it meant I was doomed, that his efforts had been in vain.

A thump shook the door, and I scrambled back. Ice crackled beneath my feet, frost tracing delicate patterns along the woodwork. What if this creature knew of ways to break the wards placed upon the cabin? What if the wards couldn't hold forever?

Clenching my teeth, I strode toward the wall and wrenched the smallest blade from its hooks, drawing it slowly from its sheath. Its hilt was marked with the silhouette of a wolf against a full moon, and the knife was perfectly polished, gleaming in the dim room. If the dullahan broke down the door, maybe I could plunge this blade into its chest—or into one of those glowing eyes in its severed head—and run.

The blade shook in my hand. I was a seamstress, a creator. I was quiet Florentia, the young woman who strove for peace and evaded conflict and masked her grief over the cruel rumors about her. I wasn't a fighter.

Another slam made the door quake and groan. I swallowed and squeezed the blade until my fingers ached. In the stillness, I prayed to the gods for protection. I glanced toward the bed, wishing I could hide beneath it but knowing that would be foolish. The dullahan would find me easily. There was no hiding in this little cabin.

There was a muffled groan and more thumps, but the knob stopped rattling. Garrick's gruff voice came again.

"Starlight!" He was panting, like he was hurt.

Starlight.

I charged for the door, unbolting the lock and flinging it open. A gust of icy wind billowed within the cabin, raising gooseflesh on my bare legs and brushing silver strands of hair across my face. Garrick stood hunched in the entryway, a shapeless heap in the glade behind him. Blood gleamed on the blade he clutched.

Staggering back, I scanned Garrick's pale, taut face.

"Are you hurt?"

He swayed on his feet, and I caught sight of scarlet dotting his shirt front. "Bolt the door," he said, pushing into the cabin and striding toward a cabinet. Rifling through it, he withdrew a bag with bandages and vials protruding from the top. He dropped it on the table.

Securing the door, I turned to find his back to me. His shirt was shredded, revealing bloody gashes in his skin. With a stifled groan, he plucked his shirt over his head and leaned against the table. My foolish eyes, unused to seeing so much bare skin, traced the muscled planes of his back until my throat went dry. The cold that had enveloped me earlier disappeared, melting with the warmth spreading through my chest and across my cheeks.

Shaking my head to clear it, I approached the table. Unfortunately, that vantage didn't help, as his toned chest and golden skin were just as distracting.

"Ren." Garrick's serious tone and use of my name jolted me to attention. My eyes darted up to his. "Are you squeamish?" he asked.

"I hardly know."

"Well," he muttered with a crooked smile, "you haven't fainted at the sight of my blood yet, so that's a start." He nodded to his bag of medical supplies, pulling out a roll of gauze and what appeared to be a sewing kit. "I need your help. I heard your townspeople talking about how you sew your own dresses."

I frowned in confusion.

"I need you to stitch my wounds."

I lifted the kit, pulling out the needle and thread and gaping at them. "Your skin is hardly like fabric..."

"Please," Garrick ground out, leaning heavily against the table. "I need you to help me clean the wounds and stitch them closed to prevent future infection. I can't very well stitch my own back."

"All right," I said, my voice firmer and more confident than I felt.

Under Garrick's instructions, I gathered water from the pump in the washroom and clean cloths. Garrick tossed another log on the fire, making the flames rise and flooding the room with better light for my work. He stretched out upon the table, instructing me on how to pour an antiseptic over his wounds and start to stitch them closed. I willed my hands to stop shaking. To distract myself, I began to talk.

"Why didn't you transform into a wolf to stop the dullahan?" I asked, threading the needle and starting to work on his back. His breaths remained steady, a soothing rhythm I tried to concentrate on, rather than let myself shudder at the way his skin resisted each tug. As much as I tried to pretend I was working with fabric, every pull of the thread reminded me I was working on flesh, and my stomach turned. The only benefit to my discomfort was that it banished any feelings of awkwardness. I couldn't be scandalized by the amount of male skin I was touching when I was focused on my work, and I was too desperate for the distraction of conversation to feel shy about prodding Garrick with more questions.

"A dullahan is a difficult creature to kill with mere animal instincts," Garrick explained softly. "Claws and teeth might have injured it, but it will not die unless you're a bit more precise, something I'm not always adept at in wolf form. That's because the only way to truly defeat a dullahan is by destroying the head it carries. Once that happens, the headless body quickly loses power."

I was quiet for a long moment. "There will be more creatures coming for me," I said. Not a question.

Garrick hummed his affirmation.

"Are you sure you want to—"

"Yes," Garrick said, cutting me off. "Besides, I already made a statement by killing the dullahan. More of their servants will search for you here, and they'll find the body outside one of my cabins. The Silverfrost family knows who I am, and they'll know what I've done."

"I'm so—"

"Don't apologize. I made my choice."

I frowned as I finished with his first gash, moving on to the next. My greatest virtue in Altidvale had been in being kind and quiet and unobtrusive. Apologizing for my existence and striving not to cause trouble or disturbances was second nature.

As if sensing my surprise and discomfort, Garrick reached around, seizing my hand in his before I could make the next stitch. Warm and calloused, his fingers enveloped mine. My pulse jumped, but not unpleasantly. I couldn't recall the last time I'd felt a friendly touch.

I was also painfully aware of his state of undress and the fact that a gentleman clasping my hand like this back home would mean something far more intimate. It would have been a declaration of affection. A gesture indicating that he wanted to court or marry me.

Heat singed my cheeks.

"Thank you," Garrick murmured, before dropping my hand and allowing me to stitch the second gash in his back.

"For what?"

"For tending to me," he responded, as if it were obvious.

"If it weren't for me, you wouldn't be wounded."

There was a smile in Garrick's voice. "Nevertheless." He paused. "Besides, there is a thrill to fighting for one's survival. It makes you feel alive."

"Hmm. Must be the wolf in you."

He chuckled softly. "None of my other prey is such a challenge."

I finished stitching up his back in comfortable silence, then soaked one of the cloths in the bowl of water, cleaning off the blood.

Standing, Garrick stretched and grinned. When he turned to face me, his gold eyes were bright. "You're a talented seamstress indeed."

My eyes skimmed over the scratches lining his chest, trying to focus on the injuries and not the skin. "Shall I stitch the others closed?"

"They're not that deep. I can clean them myself, but if you don't mind, I'd appreciate your help with bandaging them."

I nodded, too embarrassed to speak. Garrick sat on the table and cleaned his wounds, giving me a chance to collect myself before he handed me a roll of gauze.

"If you wrap it around my body, you can cover the scratches in front and protect your stitches on my back," Garrick suggested.

"This would be a compromising position back home," I said, my voice sounding almost like a squeak.

"No one in Altidvale will find out about your forward advances."

"Advances?" Cheeks aflame, I glanced up to find Garrick's teasing grin.

"I'm jesting, Starlight. I know you're not trying to seduce me." He winked. "You're doing good by helping an injured man. There's nothing scandalous or compromising about tending to the hurt."

Finding comfort in that reassurance—which was true, I knew I couldn't leave him to suffer, especially after he'd earned these wounds defending my life—I stepped up to the table. My heart pounded. I was close enough to him that his knees pressed into my legs and I could feel the heat of his body consuming me. Refusing to meet his eyes, I placed the gauze over one of his scratches and then unwound the roll, reaching around his back. I realized my error a moment too late, when I was forced to stretch my other arm around to grasp the gauze, practically embracing Garrick.

I was too rigid, my footing too unsure, and I slipped, falling against him. Seizing my waist, Garrick chuckled, the sound vibrating through his chest as he held me. Without meaning to, I glanced up and met his eyes, which appeared molten gold in the firelight. Its flickering glow cast shadows along the planes of his face, highlighting his inhuman beauty.

His lip quirked in the start of a grin, and I worried he could read my every thought written in my expression.

I leapt back. "Forgive me," I gasped. Fumbling, I returned to fastening the bandages around his chest, trying my best to put more distance between us.

"I didn't mean to make you uncomfortable," Garrick said.

When I leaned forward to tie the bandage, I could feel his breath caressing my cheek. I swallowed. "It wouldn't have been proper for me to be in this cabin at all, with bare ankles and knees." I laughed, but it came out sounding too high-pitched. "But if not for you, I would be dead somewhere on that mountain path. Helping you after you've rescued me—and risked your life for me—is the least I can do."

Garrick pressed a hand to his chest. "Well, I give my word that I'll try to be a perfect gentleman, Starlight."

That time, I couldn't help the way my chest warmed at the nickname. I'd spent the past year longing to be cared for and understood, and here in the space of a few hours, a stranger had chosen not only to learn about me and accept me as I was, but also to risk his life to defend me. "Try?" I asked, handing him the roll of gauze and stepping back.

He shrugged. "Well, I am part dog."

I bit my lip to avoid smiling at his jape. Outside, the wind howled, and my eyes tracked toward the window.

Garrick noticed my look. "Nothing can get in," he reassured me. "Try to get some sleep. We'll need to cover some miles tomorrow."

When I climbed into bed, bundling into the furs, it took a long time to stop glancing at the window and relax against the pillows. Finally, I drifted into sleep, dreaming of monsters clawing against the glass…but also of muscled skin and a pair of golden eyes.

CHAPTER FOUR

My breath steamed in the air when I woke up the next morning, repressing a groan at the thought of leaving the toasty sanctuary of the fur blankets I was wrapped in.

"Good morning," Garrick greeted me from where he crouched at the hearth, feeding logs to the tendrils of flame he'd started. His eyes, twinkling with mirth, flicked to mine. "I was starting to worry I'd have to lift you out of bed and carry you for the next leg of our journey."

Squinting against the morning light that struck my face as soon as I sat up, I blinked and glanced out the window, noting the sun was already high in the eastern sky. It was much later than I usually slept, but then again, I didn't usually wake in the middle of the night to dullahan attacks and a need to stitch a man's naked skin back together.

"I only have dried meat and tea for breakfast, but I think I might have a bit more stored at our next stop, if we can make good time today." Garrick stood and went to rummage through his cabinets, returning with strips of jerky.

I accepted two and bit into one gratefully.

"I have more clothes you can borrow. We'll be increasing altitude and trudging through snow soon, and you can't do that in a ballgown—or only my shirt, as lovely as your legs are."

My cheeks flamed, scandalized that he'd noticed.

Garrick nodded to the chest at the foot of the bed, where he'd laid out a pair of trousers, shirt, belt, and stockings, as well as a heavy fur coat, gloves, and leather boots. My cheeks threatened to redden when I thought of borrowing a man's clothes. It seemed intimate. And yet, I shook off the sensation. It was practical, a way to avoid suffering from frostbite. All my societal niceties didn't apply here, where my goal was to survive the wilderness and the creatures that would be hunting me.

Silently, Garrick went about preparing tea, bringing me a steaming mug before offering me an uncharacteristically sheepish smile. Already clothed in layers of leather and fur, he appeared ready to leave at any moment. "I'll give you some privacy while I...dispose of the body," he said quietly. "I'll knock before I return so you can warn me if you're not dressed yet."

His thoughtfulness warmed me. I hadn't expected such manners from a fae, much less one who could shift into a wolf. As he exited the cabin, leaving me to finish my tea and jerky and then reluctantly climb out of bed, I thanked whichever god had been looking after my interests when they'd sent Garrick to help me. Flirtations aside, he was friendly, and though his charm made me feel awkward, it also banished any uncomfortable need for me to fill silences between us.

I scurried to the washroom, where Garrick had left a pitcher of water I could scrub my face with. It was cold, probably gathered from the stream outside, but it was fresh. Then I scrambled into the clothes he'd given me, blushing furiously when I was immersed in the same smells that clung to him—the scents of evergreen and cedar, fresh air and leather. Everything was overlarge on my frame, but I did the best I could before stuffing my feet into the boots and wrapping the coat about myself.

By the time Garrick knocked, I was cozily stationed before the fire.

"Come in," I called.

Garrick stepped through the doorway, pausing when he saw me. A strange look flickered over his face, gone too soon for me to read it. "We shouldn't delay any longer," he said, and I nodded, watching regretfully as he put out the fire with a bucket of water. When he offered me a hand, I didn't hesitate to accept his help. "Another servant or soldier could already be nearby."

Before we left the cabin, Garrick strapped a sword and a series of hunting knives in leather sheaths to his belt, shoved another knife into his boot, and hefted a bow and quiver full of arrows to his back. "Best to be prepared," he said, flashing me a smirk and leading me outside.

I inhaled the fresh mountain air, studying the thin, sparkling layer of snow that had fallen sometime in the early morning hours. The sun shone brightly, but fluffy clouds were gathering, promising more snow. A chipmunk scurried up a nearby tree, scolding me for being so near its home. Nearby, the stream burbled along merrily, clear and glistening in the daylight. Everything seemed normal and cheerful, the terrors of last night dashed away as if they'd never occurred. It was a little disconcerting.

"You need to be prepared too," Garrick said, drawing me from my appreciation of nature. He handed me another knife I hadn't seen him clutching in his palm.

I blinked at it, studying the marking of a wolf silhouetted against the moon etched into its hilt, and thinking of how hopeless I'd felt with a blade last night, not having a clue how to wield one. Or even if I'd have the courage to defend myself. "Ladies aren't exactly taught how to fight," I said at last.

Garrick's piercing eyes never left mine. "I'll teach you. For now, take it, and if an enemy gets too close, do your best to shove the blade into anything tender. Eyes, face, torso, hand...whatever it takes to stop or slow them."

I took it, shoving it into my coat pocket and praying I wouldn't have need of it.

Studying the clouds overhead, I kept my head down as I trudged through the growing piles of snow, my breathing turning shallower the higher the trail climbed. We'd only been traveling a few hours, but I was already exhausted and sore. My toes ached and blistered in my borrowed boots, each step arduous when my stockinged feet slipped around inside them. I'd tripped and nearly fallen so often I'd lost count. Garrick had stayed by my side, faithfully offering a hand each time to keep me from injuring myself.

"I wish I could offer you better-fitting gear," he'd said with a frown, but we were in the wild, with no towns nearby. We had to make do with what Garrick had.

Now, I paused to catch my breath and wipe the sweat beading on my brow with my mittened hand.

"We're not far," Garrick said, but that encouragement only made me want to groan. He'd said that a few times already, and I was starting to think his definition of far and mine were very different things.

"I can scarcely breathe."

The hunter reached into his pack and withdrew a canteen, passing it to me. I sucked down the water greedily. "You're unused to this elevation." When I finished and handed him the canteen, he took a gulp. I tried not to watch as his lips pressed against the same place mine had just been, tried to ignore how intimate sharing a canteen was. I knew it meant nothing and was silly to be scandalized when my life was in danger, and yet, I couldn't ignore the uncomfortable squirm in my belly each time one of the careful boundaries polite society had erected was challenged.

"Is it...too soon to stop?"

A teasing glint entered Garrick's eyes as he replaced the canteen in his pack. "I could carry you."

My face burned. "I'll walk," I gritted out, trudging onward before he could embarrass me with further flirtations.

"Forgive me," Garrick said, holding out his arm. I hesitated before taking it. "I'm making you uncomfortable. Your human formalities are unusual to me."

I didn't respond.

"To distract you as we walk, I could tell you about the time I outwitted a cantankerous troll."

"A troll?" I scanned the trees surrounding us, imagining a bulky troll lumbering out and threatening us. So far, the only creatures we'd encountered had been harmless—squirrels, rabbits, birds—but I couldn't banish my fear of every story I'd heard about fearsome creatures living in the fae world.

"They're too thick-headed to be much of a danger," Garrick said, brushing aside my concerns as if trolls were simple pests. "This particular one was no exception. I'd tracked a deer to a pond with a nearby cave. A foul-tempered troll stalked out, swinging a club and threatening to crush in my skull for waking him." While my eyes widened, Garrick merely laughed. "Trolls aren't known for their cheery dispositions, Starlight. Most seek the solitude of the mountains and threaten death when anyone is unfortunate enough to stumble upon one of their lairs."

I missed another step, sliding through snow, but Garrick's hold on me tightened, propping me up. "Thank you," I murmured.

"Rather than take on the lumbering giant, I proposed something else: a challenge. If he won, he would have the pleasure of killing me. Well...he specified eating me."

I couldn't help but cringe, making Garrick's smile broaden at my reaction.

"If he lost, he'd be forced to tolerate my presence near his cave until I was finished tracking my own quarry."

This wasn't the first story Garrick had told to keep me entertained. His liveliness and zest for adventure seemed to know no bounds. I also knew he preferred it when I humored him by asking questions, because each time, his eyes lit up. It had been so long since someone truly enjoyed my company, so long since anything I did brought joy to anyone, that I couldn't help myself. "What was the challenge?" I asked, glancing sideways so I could see his dimples flash and his gold eyes sparkle.

"Tracking."

"What?"

"I don't know how many stories you've heard about trolls, but they're excellent trackers. Many consider them to be the best, with their keen sense of smell and animal instincts. Naturally, when I told the troll whoever was the first to track down and kill the buck I'd been hunting would be the winner, he laughed and agreed."

"Why do I sense you tricked him?" I asked, amusement lacing my tone.

"Well, he didn't know I was a wolf shifter," Garrick said. "He set off in the direction of the buck, and I shifted—easily outrunning him and finding the deer first. Not even a troll can best a wolf's hunting instincts. I darted in front of the troll before he could creep up behind the buck and raise his club. Slaying a deer in wolf form is a little messier than I prefer, but..." He shrugged. "When I shifted back into my fae form, the troll was furious, claiming I'd cheated. But I reminded him that I hadn't specified *how* we would track the deer. Precise language matters among the fae."

I laughed, shaking my head. "What if you hadn't won? Wolf form or no, there was still chance involved. Wouldn't you have been committed to your word to...let him eat you?" I frowned at the thought.

"Me? Lose?" Garrick scoffed. We both laughed, the sound echoing off the surrounding pines.

A sound greeted us from ahead, like distant humming. I froze, forcing Garrick to a stop to avoid dragging me by the arm. My heart hammered against my ribs, screaming at me to run.

Garrick's fingers tightened on my arm. "Don't be afraid. It's the mountain witch, Shavonne. She's only trouble if you don't grant her request when you pass."

"What sort of request?" I hissed as the hunter calmly led me forward up the incline and around a bend in the trail.

"It's never too steep a price, or I would have taken us another way. But this is the most direct route."

Ahead, a rickety wooden bridge spanned a small chasm that dropped into a clear mountain stream. Just at its start, a stooped figure draped in a heavy cloak awaited us, humming and twisting something in her gnarled fingers.

"I thought trolls guarded bridges—that's what my childhood stories said."

"The stories mixed it up, then. Trolls prefer caves and hunting. Witches like bargains and trickery like most other fae. They're generally long-lived hags and other beings who dabble in potion-making as well as our usual elemental magic, but they're unable to use glamour."

Garrick led the way confidently, flashing a charming smile as the witch turned her head, revealing the wrinkled face tucked beneath her hood. When she returned his grin, it was all gums, without a single tooth in sight. "Garrick Darkgrove, renowned hunter," she crooned, setting aside the stone she'd been fumbling with. "I was attempting to see the future, but apparently my gifts don't lie that way." She chuckled to herself. "Otherwise, I would have known you were bringing this curious mortal with you." Her watery eyes latched onto me, scanning my silver hair and my human ears.

"Yes, it's not often I have such a lovely traveling companion. But I'm afraid we're in a hurry, Shavonne. We need to pass."

"Then you know you must humor an old woman."

Garrick dipped his head. "Of course. What price must I pay?"

The witch's toothless grin widened. "Oh, not you this time, my pretty dear. Her." She pointed her crooked finger toward me. "I make my request of you...?" She paused, clearly awaiting a name.

"Ren," I supplied, though my voice wavered.

"This will be entertaining." Shavonne clapped her hands together. "We cannot lie, but you humans can. So grant me this, young Ren: two lies and one truth about yourself."

"Why would you want lies?"

"So you're more likely to tell me a deep truth."

"But how will you know which is the truth?"

She cackled. "Oh, I'll puzzle it out. That's the fun." Shavonne waved her hands at me. "Bare your heart, and you can pass."

I swallowed. "Very well." My mind felt hazy as I sifted it for truths and lies that would be personal enough to satisfy this woman. "I hate my brother for betraying me." In my head, where my anger and hurt churned like a restless storm, I'd been sure this was true, but the words tasted wrong as soon as I spoke them. A lie.

Shavonne nodded along, her watery eyes gleaming. I wondered if she could sense the untruth in my words, or if she was waiting to hear everything.

Hesitating, I tried again. "I've never felt like I belonged anywhere, not even when my stepfather was still alive and my brother didn't shun me." Tears burned my eyes, and I blinked to avoid crying. This was true.

"Very interesting," Shavonne muttered.

"What do you do with lies and truths?" I asked. "You don't even know me."

"And it seems you don't always even know yourself." She gave me another toothless smile. "Share something else."

I frowned. "Are you using magic?"

The witch shrugged. "I think there's magic in sharing the contents of your heart. But perhaps I help it along, help you see what you're truly feeling." She winked.

Disconcerted, I closed my eyes. One more lie. My heart focused on last night, when black ice had shattered my glass and frosted my skin. When Garrick's glamour had had no effect on me. "I don't believe I have magic. I've always known I was a perfectly ordinary human."

Shavonne cackled. "Well earned." She gestured with a hand. "You may both pass. Thank you, Mortal Ren, for amusing an ancient woman."

I stared at her, wondering if there was more to it all. Surely the bargain wasn't that simple. I expected a fae trick—some hidden sacrifice I needed to make, some way she'd twist my words and use them against me. But she merely grinned as Garrick took my arm and led me across the creaking bridge.

Chill wind blew strands of hair across my face as we crossed to the other side and up another incline, deeper into the forest marching up the mountainside. "You believe me about your magic?" Garrick asked after a longer silence than usual. I'd been mulling over the revelations the witch had forced me to face about myself and hadn't even noticed he'd gone several minutes without speaking, as lost in thought as I was.

"I think, deep down, along with feeling different—and not just for my hair—I knew I wasn't quite like anyone else. I didn't *realize* that meant magic, or fae blood, or anything like that. For a while it simply meant I didn't fit in. I wondered if maybe there was something inherently wrong with me, that made me invisible or unworthy to everyone else." I bit my lip, embarrassed for sharing so much. Maybe the witch had used some magic that was making me speak more truths than I'd normally be comfortable admitting to a man I'd just met. Or maybe, though it had only been a short while, Garrick's charm and openness and protective nature were making me feel safe enough to tear down some of the walls around my lonely heart.

"Invisible?" Garrick's lips quirked. "The whole town was talking about you."

"I meant...unseen in the ways that truly matter. They looked at my strange hair and imagined what they wanted about me. They didn't see *me*. They didn't care to know who I really was."

Garrick squeezed my arm. "And what a shame for them. I've only known you for one day, and already I can tell you're kind and thoughtful and a lot braver and more interesting than anyone in your sad little town would ever give you credit for. *And* you have magic, which makes you more powerful than the lot of them. More powerful even than me."

He laughed, and I couldn't help but smile, just a little. Even if my mind was overwhelmed, trying to comprehend how I carried more power in my veins than the immortal I walked beside.

CHAPTER FIVE

"Can you tell me more about my magic?" I asked as Garrick and I settled before the fire he'd started.

Evening had fallen and snowflakes were beginning to descend by the time we'd reached the next cabin, which was much like the last, except it had an entire kitchen and several bedrooms attached. Garrick had explained that this one had once been his family home, though now, when he wasn't staying here during hunts, messengers for the royal family used it—along with the other smaller outposts—while traveling throughout the kingdom. For a short while, he'd left me before the fire to warm myself while he'd hunted, saying we needed a proper meal. He'd returned with several hares, which he was now roasting over the fire. The aroma permeated the cabin, making my stomach growl after subsiding only on a few pieces of jerky for the entire day.

While he turned the meat on a spit, Garrick considered my question. Outside, the sky was dark and heavy with clouds, and thickly falling snowflakes blocked out any views we might have had of the surrounding forest. But within, the firelight bathed the room in a cozy golden glow that now reflected in Garrick's eyes as he watched the flames dance. "Considering I don't have magic like yours, I'm not sure I can be of much help. But I can tell you this: your magic is tied to the land. It's true for all fae. Our kingdoms are as much a part of us as anything. And now that you're on Silverfrost ground, you'll be more connected to your power than ever before. It'll grow even stronger once we reach the winter solstice, because every fae's magic is tied to the primary season of their kingdom. That means right now, the autumn kingdom fae are at the height of their power, and once winter ends, Willowbark will be at its strongest."

I considered his words. "So I draw magic...from the land?"

Garrick dipped his head in affirmation. "Based on the ice you conjured, you likely could also wield a snowstorm. But who can even guess at the full extent of your abilities until you learn to tap into them?"

Withdrawing my hands from beneath the blanket I'd wrapped around myself, I studied my palms. "Is it dangerous?"

"All power is dangerous, Starlight. And magic is in your blood, which means it's tied to your emotions and thoughts. It'll take practice for you to gain control and know how to wield it confidently." His gaze flicked to the scabbed cuts on my palm from the glass that had shattered just last night when I'd unintentionally frozen it. "Once you know how to use it well, it'll only be dangerous if you mean for it to be."

"If I don't practice, will I...have more incidents like the one at the ball?"

"In moments of unbridled emotions." He gave me a crooked smile. "I suppose I brought those out in you last night."

As he turned the meat again, grease sizzling into the fire until it popped, I considered his words. "I'll have to practice or risk unleashing something more dangerous."

"Don't practice in an enclosed space," Garrick warned. "On a night when we stop outdoors, you can work at it."

"Won't we freeze if we stay outside?"

The wolf shifter flashed me a smile. "I'll keep you warm, Starlight."

I hoped he meant by fire, but I didn't press the matter.

Once dinner was finished, Garrick removed some jars of fruit and a wrapper of hard cheese from the kitchen to add to our fare, along with plates and silverware. He set the table as I approached. "This fruit is still fresh—as is the cheese. I was here not too long ago." He smiled softly at the plates. "And Mother always insisted on stocking each cabin with fine porcelain," he said as he cut into the first hare and dished out servings for each of us. "She said just because we could shift into animals didn't mean we needed to eat like them."

Settling myself in the seat across from him, I studied Garrick's expression curiously. I hardly remembered my mother, so hearing him speak so fondly of his own made a strange, unexpected ache spread through my chest. "Were you close with your family?"

Garrick's expression turned solemn. I was already so accustomed to his easy, dimpled smiles and mirthful, bright eyes that it was a little jolting to see darkness pass over his face. "As close as one can be, I suppose. I was only a boy when they were killed. At seven, I was spoiled—my parents hadn't expected to have another child, and my two older brothers were young adults themselves. I looked up to them, admired them and their strength and courage so dearly. I was too young to fight as the rest of my family did, but I'd trained every day. When..." He hesitated, gaze distant as he chose his next words. "When the battle happened and they were all slain, I felt as if I should have been able to save them...as if, somehow, I should have been able to stop it."

"You were only a boy."

With a bittersweet smile, Garrick met my gaze. "I wish that helped the guilt." As suddenly as the grief had consumed him, he shook his head and forced a grin. "Enough about me. I'm sure you're hungry."

I followed his example, cutting into my meat and taking a bite. I'd never imagined wild hare would taste so delicious, but as the flavor filled my mouth, smoky from the fire and perfectly cooked, I decided either it wasn't bad or I was simply that hungry.

"What about your parents?" Garrick asked softly after we'd eaten in a comfortable silence for several minutes. "I hope they were better toward you than your brother."

"My stepfather loved me," I murmured. "He used to sit with my brother and me by the fire and tell us stories. He loved to stargaze on clear nights, sharing the tales of the constellations and then making up his own. I..." My throat tightened. It was odd to open up to a fae, to a man I hadn't even known a day ago. And yet, after the adventures we'd already faced, after his openness with me, it felt right. "It's only been a year," I continued, "and I miss him dreadfully. He was the only parent I really knew, for my mother died of fever when I was very young, and I apparently never knew my true father."

Garrick's brow pinched, perhaps in sympathy. "I think I might have known your father."

My eyes widened as Garrick nodded to me. "The hair and the winter magic." He smiled. "I know you probably think unusual hair colors are common among the fae, but silver isn't one we see as often among high fae. And though magic isn't always inherited—the land gifts various types of abilities as it chooses—it sometimes is, especially when the bloodline and magic are powerful enough. I was only a boy, but I did encounter him a few times. He worked at the castle. I wish I could tell you more, but...it wasn't as if I knew him well." He shrugged. "But he was always kind to me. Quiet, but in a strong sort of way. Like you."

I shook my head, grinning. "I'm not like that at all."

But when I lifted my head, Garrick's expression was earnest, without a hint of teasing. "You're stronger than you realize, and not only because of your powerful magic. Trust me, Starlight. We wolves have a way of picking out the strong and brave from the weak and cowardly. Your town—your brother—didn't appreciate you, but you're so much more than what they led you to believe."

A gentle nudge woke me the next morning. I was tangled in the bed-clothes as if I'd tossed and turned, though my dreams were hazy. Had it been a nightmare of the dullahan? Fear about my uncertain future? Grief over my stepfather and the father and mother I hadn't known?

I glanced up at Garrick, who hovered over me, and a blush suffused my cheeks when I realized how exposed my legs were in the shirt I wore. Hurriedly, I sat up and tucked the blankets around myself.

Amusement danced on his face, but Garrick fought to conceal it. "You were embarrassed when I saw your legs before, so I tried my best not to look," he said, and though it seemed like he meant it to be comforting, my cheeks only heated further. Eager to change the subject, and a little ashamed I hadn't thought of it before now, I asked, "Do you need me to check your back?"

But the wolf shifter shook his head. "I was able to glance at it using the mirror in the washroom. No signs of infection, and your stitches are holding well. Thank you."

This time, we ate some of the leftover hare, which Garrick had salted and wrapped last night so we could carry it with us as we journeyed onward. Then he left my room, giving me privacy as I once again clothed myself in layers that were too large and smelled of him. He'd already apologized last night for not having any clothes of his mother's, but I'd told him not to worry. Even if he'd held onto them all these years, there was no guarantee they'd have fit either.

"Do the messengers who stay in these cabins ever leave their belongings?" I asked Garrick as I left the cabin to meet him outside. It was such a different life than what I was accustomed to, the frequent travel, the multiple shared outposts, and the lack of servants to tend to every need.

"Not often. They know to pack lightly. We aren't likely to encounter any up here right now either," he added, as if predicting the next question already on the tip of my tongue. "Tensions always run high among the fae kingdoms of Brytwilde. The royals are always coveting one another's power and land. There are constant wars and threats of wars. And right now, there is a war between Silverfrost and the autumn kingdom of Ashwood. I've heard there are soldiers stationed on the border currently. Messages between the two sides are only occurring through swordfights and blood. And messages to the kingdoms of Ravenheart or Willowbark would be carried across our northern border to avoid the battles."

As we crunched through the freshly fallen snow from last night, I stuffed my hands into my coat pockets and wondered if this was reassuring or not. "So we're traveling toward army encampments—or even a battlefield?"

"I didn't want to speak of the war before and worry you needlessly. But I know these mountains well. Trust me, we'll find a way around," Garrick reassured me. "But in the meantime, I'll train you in how to use that knife when we stop."

I didn't tell him it wasn't the lack of knowledge with a blade that terrified me so much as the fact that I didn't *want* to ever have to use it.

But true to his word, he began teaching me that afternoon. We paused by a stream to drink and eat more of our salted meat. Garrick set some fish traps he stored nearby, ones he said he kept near the stream and tended to whenever he traveled this way. "Draw your knife," he said once he'd finished.

"What?" I was seated on a boulder I'd dusted clean of snow, resting my weary legs and aching feet. Some of the blisters that had formed yesterday were bleeding, and every step was painful. I glanced at the burbling stream longingly. With today's sunshine and milder temperature, chilly but without any brutal winds, I could almost imagine the water would be inviting. But ice glistened along its sides, reminding me it was frigid and soaking my feet wouldn't be soothing.

I flicked my gaze back to Garrick, who stood a few feet away along the stream's bank. "Draw your knife and use it on me," he challenged.

Stifling my urge to sigh, I stood and plucked out the knife, sliding it free before pocketing the sheath. When I held the blade up, I squeezed the wolf-marked hilt with a death grip and swung it half-heartedly through the air.

Garrick arched a brow. "Fearsome."

"I can't stab you," I protested.

He smirked, flashing brilliant white teeth as he set his legs shoulder width apart and bent his knees. "You won't. Try again."

Frowning, I stepped nearer and swung, aiming for his chest. In a single smooth motion, Garrick stepped aside, using one hand to seize my wrist and the other to steal the knife from my grasp. Spinning it, he held it toward my neck.

I pursed my lips. "You're flaunting your training."

Garrick burst into a good-natured laugh. "I wanted to see what we needed to work on."

"Everything?" I asked sheepishly.

Reaching up to brush some snow from my hair, Garrick shook his head, still smiling. "Not everything. You know where to aim it, at least."

By the time the sun was staining the western sky orange, my stomach ached from laughing at Garrick's constant jests. He'd made even the exhausting work of learning how to stand, how to duck and dodge blows, how to parry a strike, and even how to swing a blade at an opponent surprisingly enjoyable. Though I hated to think of actually needing to fight to kill, he'd kept me smiling and laughing the entire time.

Sometimes, when he teased me, his gold eyes studying my face without fear or disgust, my heart would skip a beat and I'd almost forget he was fae. He was only a young man, friendly and good-hearted and quick-witted, and he seemed to enjoy my company.

"We can rest now, and I'll teach you to build a fire," Garrick announced.

"What, shall I burn my enemies to death?"

Dimples framed the wolf shifter's mouth. "She jests. I knew you'd warm up to me."

I turned away to conceal my reddened cheeks, though I wasn't sure why I was embarrassed and couldn't quite meet those brilliant eyes.

"No," Garrick went on, "I just think it would be useful for you to know how to fend for yourself in the mountains. In case..." He trailed off, shrugging. "Well, you're ever robbed of my delightful company."

Spinning on my heel, I tossed him an alarmed look. "When you leave me?"

I felt like a fool. Garrick had a life here, and though he'd promised to see me to safety, he'd also said the royals might never stop hunting me. What if he planned to equip me to survive the wilderness and then return to his life? It seemed only fair. I couldn't expect him to uproot his life for me. And yet, my heart sank at the notion. Which was utterly ridiculous. He couldn't stay with me for the rest of our lives. He wasn't family, or a man courting me for my hand and pledging marriage. He was only...a protector. An unexpected friend.

Eventually, I would enter Ashwood and find new friends there. I hoped.

"Leave you?" Garrick appeared as taken aback as I felt. "I only meant we never know what could happen, Starlight. Come, let me show you how to choose the driest firewood, even in the snow."

Sheathing my knife and stuffing it back into my pocket, I followed him into the forest, trying to ignore the tangle of emotions that had taken up residence in my heart.

CHAPTER SIX

After Garrick showed me how to start a fire and we ate a dinner of fresh fish drawn from his traps, the wolf shifter pulled aside some tree branches to reveal a hidden cave resting near the stream's embankment. "Troll-free," he said with a wink. "I stay here often."

He removed a bedroll from his pack and laid it out near the edge of the cave, close enough to our fire to receive its warmth. It worried me that he only had one, but shyness overtook me when I considered asking him about it. Hopefully, as with the single beds, he had a plan.

Instead, I settled on the floor close to the cavern's mouth to soak up the fire's heat. When I peered out and up, through the pine branches swaying overheard, I could pick out the first stars sprinkling across the evening sky.

"Which was your stepfather's favorite constellation?" Garrick asked, noticing my look. It startled me, filling me with a pleasant jolt of warmth to realize he'd been watching me so closely and remembering my words about my stepfather.

"The hunter," I said, laughing a little. "He loved to share the story about his feats against the..." I shrugged apologetically. "Well, about the dark fae who tried to kidnap his daughter. I always liked to imagine he would fight that hard for me, if ever a fae crossed the border and wanted to take me away." For a moment, I frowned at the sky, thinking painfully of the times Charles had sat beside me listening to that very same story. How easily he'd offered me to the fae.

When I glanced back at Garrick, I found his eyes already on me, soft with understanding. As if sensing I didn't want to discuss it, he let his somber expression melt into an easy grin. "I was always told the hunter was defending a lover. He was fae, but he'd fallen for a mortal woman that was betrothed to a greedy and cold king from another land. Forced to escort the woman he loved to her wedding, he protected her from every sort of dangerous creature and curse along the journey."

"And then what happened?"

"He asked her to run away with him, but when they tried, the king's soldiers tracked them down. They killed the hunter, and the human woman married the king."

I frowned. "Stories are supposed to end happily."

Garrick leaned back against the cavern wall to study the sky. "Fae ones aren't meant to have any sort of endings. They're either pieces of history, passed along over generations until one can't tell truth from myth, or they're told as warnings and lessons. I think our version of the hunter's story might be a piece of one of our kingdoms' histories, though the details are so vague now, it's hard to tell."

"Father's stories were to let us escape into a happy world for a time," I said wistfully. "And perhaps to teach lessons too, but they were about good deeds overcoming the bad."

"Let me tell you a happier story then," Garrick said, pointing to a bright star, one of the first that had appeared in the gathering darkness. "In Brytwilde, we call that star *aeveld*, which in the old language means hope. It's the brightest star in the winter sky, the one that banishes the most darkness. Some like to say it's a gift from one of the goddesses, her parting reminder that even in the blackest of nights, starlight will make a way for you and give you hope." He tossed me a grin. "What do you think of that, Starlight?"

My face flushed. "I thought you called me that because of my hair."

"True," he said, his expression sincere, "but also because you shine brighter than any of those sad mortals in your town. Why do you think I chose to speak to you?"

I smirked. "Because I saw through your glamour and you wanted to know why?"

Garrick laughed. "Even before I realized that, I knew there was something special about you."

Covering my face to conceal my awkwardness, I shook my head and laughed along with him. "You're a horrible flirt. I don't believe anything you say."

"I can't lie, can I?"

Pretending to be furious, I lifted a pinecone from the cavern's floor and tossed it in his direction.

Garrick schooled his expression, tucking away his laughter and teasing. "In all seriousness, I'll try not to flirt and make you uncomfortable, but I think you should know your worth after all the rot your townspeople spoke about you. Magic or not, you deserve a better life, far away from that town. I'm sorry for the way things happened, but I can't say I'm sorry you have a chance to experience Silverfrost. Tomorrow, I'll try to help you practice your magic, unfit as I am for that." He stood, stretching his arms. "You should get some sleep. I'm going to keep watch. I warn you: I have to put out the fire now that it's growing dark or it'll attract others for miles around, but I have a makeshift door I can use to shut you in, so you'll be all right."

"Won't you need sleep?"

He shook his head. "I'll stay outside in wolf form. When I shift back, it'll be as if my fae form slept all that time, dormant while I prowled about as a wolf." He grinned. "I have to enjoy the benefits of the little magic I'm granted while I can, and this seems like a good time. I'll wake you if there's any trouble." He lifted one of the pine branches to step outside, but before he left, he glanced over his shoulder. "Sleep well, Starlight."

Garrick's makeshift door was made up of bark and sealed the cave entrance well enough to keep the lingering warmth of the fire inside. Curled up in my coat and bundled within the bedroll, I was able to stay comfortable, with my own body heat soon filling the small space until I drifted off to sleep.

The scrape of the door pushing inward woke me just as Garrick filled the entrance, silhouetted by the pale grey light of pre-dawn. He tossed a pair of boots, a tin, and some thick woolen socks beside me. "Sorry to wake you," he said, voice hoarse. "I know my boots were hurting you, so I traded with Shavonne for a new pair. You'll need to apply that salve to help heal your feet and prevent infection. And you'll need to hurry." He leaned against the wall, shoving the door closed and immersing us in darkness.

But not before I caught a glimpse of an arrow shaft protruding from his leg and blood drenching his trousers.

"You're hurt!" I gasped.

The sound of a striking match filled the space as Garrick reached for a lantern on a natural shelf in the cavern, lighting the candle within and setting it on the ground. In its flickering glow, I noticed how pale his face was as he grasped the arrow and, with a muted grunt, tore it free. "I'll be fine. Please hurry."

Gritting my teeth, I hastened to obey Garrick, yanking off my bloodied socks and applying a generous amount of salve to my feet. I wrapped them using a roll of gauze from Garrick's pack and shoved them into the thick socks. Instantly, the pain eased, making me wonder what magic the salve contained. The relief made it bearable to tie on the new boots, which fit perfectly, and stand. "Let me see your wound," I insisted, crouching before Garrick and studying the blood staining his trouser leg.

"It'll heal," Garrick said, but when his eyes met mine, they were glassy. "I was struck while in wolf form. Give it a little time, and the wound will improve. That's one benefit of being a shifter—the injuries you sustain in your animal form don't affect you nearly as much when you're in your high fae form." He flashed me a smile, a little less brilliant than his usual grins. "There's a party of soldiers hunting us, and it won't take them long to draw near. We need to leave. Can you walk?"

"You're asking *me* if I can walk?"

Garrick just shot me a pointed look, refusing to let me worry over him.

I stood, setting my jaw. "Yes."

As we packed, Garrick's limp grew less pronounced, and the color began to return to his face. "Already much better," he insisted as we stood in the dark. We paused long enough for him to listen for any approaching footsteps, and then he slid the door free.

The growing daylight burned my eyes.

"I'm afraid we'll have to travel hard to stay ahead of them," Garrick said grimly. "There won't be time to stop for resting or training. Can you manage?"

My legs were already sore from days of walking further than I'd ever gone before, and my stomach ached with a demand for breakfast after all the exertion, but I nodded. I didn't have a choice.

Even with our fast pace, Garrick retained his cheerful attitude, joking with me whenever he could as if he knew I needed the distraction so my thoughts wouldn't stray toward danger. I didn't want to imagine what was after us—one dullahan had been terrifying enough and left its marks on Garrick, though he'd never complained about his back again. Four pursuers—ones that had shot the wolf shifter already and incited this level of urgency in him—made me nervous.

As daylight faded, I was stumbling, hardly able to keep myself upright, and Garrick seemed unable to conceal his distress. "I'm afraid we weren't able to travel as far as I'd hoped," he confessed as he scanned the thick forest around us. Shadows were growing long and the air was turning more frigid, nipping at my cheeks and making my fingers ache even in my gloves. "We're too far from the next outpost to stop soon."

Heavy-lidded, I didn't even try to waste energy acknowledging him. It took everything in me to put one foot in front of the other. My legs throbbed and my lungs burned with each uphill step. I clung to his arm with a death grip to prevent myself from sliding in the snow.

"Starlight," he said, gently. He stopped so suddenly I almost collapsed.

I turned to him in confusion. "Yes?"

"I'm sorry if this makes you uncomfortable." Without further warning, he scooped me effortlessly into his arms.

My gasp died in my throat. I was too exhausted to care about propriety, too desperate for warmth and rest. Leaning my head against his chest, I relished the heat that emanated from his body and the scents of leather and fur and snow. A sense of safety banished all my fear, and without meaning to, I drifted.

It was full dark when I jolted awake, still cocooned in Garrick's arms. My breath misted in front of me, and when I glanced into the wolf shifter's face, I saw tension in his furrowed brow and clenched jaw.

That was when I realized a sound had awoken me. More noises followed. Crunching twigs that seemed to split the air in two, and then muffled voices. Our pursuers were closing in on us.

My heart slammed into my throat, and ice shot through my veins, a rush so sudden and violent that black frost crackled around us, spreading across the ground beneath Garrick's boots.

Garrick dipped his head low, his mouth so close his breath brushed my ear. He spoke in such a quiet whisper I had to strain to make it out. "Your magic is wild and unpredictable, connected to your emotions. Calm your thoughts and will the magic to stay within you. I'm going to set you down so you can hide while I draw them out and distract them. Be as quiet as possible. If anything goes wrong—run."

But when he set me down, I couldn't force my legs to move. Garrick was no longer a stranger—he'd become a friend, someone I was learning to trust, to admire. How could I even consider leaving him? What if he was injured again and needed my help? But I couldn't object to his plan aloud and risk the approaching fae with their keener hearing catching my voice.

As if reading my rebellious thoughts, Garrick shook his head at me and gave me a gentle shove.

My steps crunched over the ice forming at my feet, each one far too loud. Garrick waited patiently behind me, his bow still fastened to his back and his blades sheathed.

I found a nearby pine and crouched behind it, struggling to control my breathing and the shivers racking my body. Ice splintered around me. When I grasped a branch for support, frost laced its bark. I staggered back, pleading silently with the distant, apathetic gods.

Garrick straightened, sliding his hands casually into his coat pockets, and began to whistle. Loudly.

Not a second too soon.

Four figures emerged from the shadows deeper within the woods. As they drew nearer, the starlight filtering through the forest canopy dappled them in a silver glow, making it easy for me to discern their features. The man in the lead had skin like tree bark and mossy green eyes. When his gaze met Garrick's, he lifted his chin in greeting. Three other men—one appearing more human, another with feathery wings the color of dust, and the final looking like a gnome with his grey features and short, stocky frame—all brought up the rear, their hands on their sword hilts.

I inhaled a frosty breath, listening to the tree branch groan from the ice weighing it down. Squeezing my eyes shut, I clenched my fists and willed my magic to return to wherever it had come from, to sink back down deep inside me.

"Why, Garrick Darkgrove," called a self-satisfied sounding voice. My eyes flew open. The bark-skinned man was the speaker, a smirk I didn't trust spreading across his face. His eyes scanned the area, roving about as if he already knew I was nearby. My heart hammered against my sternum. "I apologize if our arrow put you a little on edge," the man went on. "When I saw you running about in your animal form, you appeared like nothing more than a common wolf." His cruel grin broadened, and I took note of the way he'd crafted his sentence. He'd made it sound as if the shot had been an accident, but he hadn't said outright that he'd thought Garrick had merely been a wolf. I was certain he'd shot him intentionally. "Are you on another hunt?"

Garrick responded with a smirk of his own, not even bothering to remove his hands from his pockets as he offered a lazy shrug. "That little pinprick? It was nothing but a nuisance. And why else would I be trekking through the mountains, Ian?"

I hugged my arms to my chest, trying to stave off my chills. Blessedly, the ice had stopped spreading, but I didn't trust that I wouldn't accidentally unleash more.

Ian's eyes turned sharp, and the winged man at his side crossed his arms. "Why else? Perhaps for the same reason we are. I'd imagine word spread to you about the girl that was given to the Silverfrosts. They've offered a handsome bounty to whoever claims her first." His grin turned devious, revealing sharp canines. "And they didn't specify what condition she must be brought in, other than alive." He stepped closer. "Tell me, does a lone wolf like you grow greedy, hoping to keep a new plaything all to himself?"

Garrick stiffened, the smirk freezing on his face. His gold eyes turned blank and eerily cold, suddenly looking more wolflike. "You have me all wrong," he said, a warning snarl edging his tone. "Does it look like I have a girl in my possession?" He spread his arms wide, as if inviting the royal servants to search the forest. "I don't want trouble. Be on your way. Find this girl you seek. Leave me out of your search."

"Hold still," Ian commanded.

And, without question or hesitation, Garrick obeyed, his eyes turning glassy.

Without warning, Ian seized Garrick by the neck. Garrick choked, his complexion turning red, but he didn't resist, didn't even try to fling off his attacker. Even his expression remained strange and distant, his eyes seeming to stare at something no one else could see.

The other fae laughed, the sound bouncing harshly off the trees.

I sucked in a furious breath, resisting the urge to launch myself forward. What would I do? One afternoon of training with a knife hadn't equipped me to fight off four fae. And my magic was unpredictable.

All my life, I'd been taught to be proper, to be agreeable, to not take up too much space. *Kind Florentia. Quiet Florentia. Strange Florentia.*

My emotions sent another rush of cold through me, and my magic spread, making more branches quake. This time, I did not fear being heard. The fae were too distracted by their cruel antics. And in that moment, I was too terrified for Garrick to know terror for myself.

"How does it feel," Ian purred, "to be helpless? To be a pathetic little *dog*?" Still Garrick didn't strike out against his attacker.

Helpless. I remembered what Garrick had told me about his weak glamour. Did that mean he was also helpless to resist the compulsions of other fae? Had Ian forced Garrick to remain still while he choked him? Was he going to murder him right here in front of me?

Perhaps this was the moment in which Garrick expected me to run. Maybe he knew he couldn't fend off these men, and he'd only hoped to be a distraction.

Another wave of cold made me shiver. Garrick had been prepared to risk his life for me. He'd been nothing but kind and good, perhaps the truest friend I'd ever known. I could trust him more than I could trust the people

I'd lived among my whole life. I couldn't watch him die. I couldn't lose him.

The icy knot building in my chest seemed to bloom outward, like a spreading snowstorm, overtaking everything in its path. My body was full of cold fury and purpose. The magic felt instinctual, natural.

And it burst out of me.

This time it wasn't merely ice. It was the full strength of a raging snowstorm, frigid winds lashing at my coat and hair and huge flakes tumbling from bloated clouds that wrapped about me like a cloak. They misted and whirled in a beautiful, hazy dance, throwing snow until all I could see was blinding white. There was a rumble, and the earth shook. A roar like the mountain was descending upon us shredded the air, but the storm within and without me didn't relent, not even with my mounting fear.

Perhaps it was fueled by my continued rage, or perhaps it was something beyond me now, too powerful in this magical land for a mere mortal like myself to control. Shrieks and screams joined the whistling wind, mingling into a clamor that made me utterly disoriented. I staggered, terrified I'd fall or be buried alive in the blizzard I'd conjured.

"Avalanche," a voice growled, startling me with its closeness. Garrick. His warm hand seized my wrist, and I wondered if his fae or wolfish senses had been what allowed him to navigate through the snow and wind to find me. "I think even if you manage to stop your magic, it'll be too late to stop the snow coming from the mountain peak. We need to find safety. Now."

My teeth chattered as I searched for Garrick's golden eyes. Whether from his warmth or the distraction of his presence, the reassurance that he was safe, the fury of the storm was already dying. The snowflakes had thinned, and the wind didn't roar quite so loudly. "Is there time?" I asked.

"Climb on my back. It'll be faster."

Before I could fully register the change, Garrick had vanished—or rather, he had transformed. A beautiful white wolf with Garrick's piercing gold eyes, standing as tall as my waist, stood before me. Without hesitating another moment, I seized some of his fur in my hands and slung myself onto his back.

My heart lurched into my throat as Garrick launched us down the mountain, snow tumbling beneath his paws as he charged around trees and leapt fallen logs with astounding grace and speed. Icy wind bit my cheeks, and, even through my gloves, my fingers grew numb, threatening to lose their grip on his fur. Behind us, the rumbling of the oncoming avalanche and the cries of our enemies grew more distant.

But I knew for as fast as Garrick ran, the avalanche would be easily twice as swift.

Tears filled my eyes and froze on my lashes from the cold, but I couldn't fully release my magic either. Snowflakes turned into hail, chunks of black ice large enough to pelt painfully against my face and hands. I shivered so violently now that I thought I'd knock myself off Garrick's back even before my fingers could lose their grip.

I swayed, nearly slipping off. Gritting my teeth against their chattering, I dug my knees into Garrick's sides, hoping I didn't hurt him as I struggled to keep my seat. He released a low growl, but it didn't sound threatening. I imagined he was trying to encourage me to hold on a bit longer.

Behind us, the roar of the avalanche was growing in its rage. I dared a glance over my shoulder to see a wall of white churning past trees and rocks, devouring everything in its path. Swallowing down my terror, I leaned forward as far as I could, ducking close to Garrick's warm body to keep my balance.

How much longer could he outrun this? I knew from growing up in the shadows of the mountains that avalanches could tumble for miles, killing animals and people in their merciless paths. I wondered if a death like that would be more like being crushed or suffocating as one drowned in a sea of snow. Squeezing my eyes shut against the stinging cold, I willed Garrick to run faster, willed my fingers—now completely numb—to somehow continue to cling to fur I could scarcely feel. No matter the heat of Garrick's body, my own was freezing, like my very core was made of ice.

I wondered if my magic could kill me, turning me into a woman of solid black ice like the hailstones raining around us.

The world tilted abruptly, and I stifled a yelp as my eyes opened and I struggled to right myself, nearly tumbling off Garrick's back. The roaring was so loud in my ears I couldn't hear anything else, not even my own pulse. Ahead, a cavern loomed, and I realized Garrick's intent. He knew we couldn't outrun the wall of snow plowing toward us, so he meant to seek shelter.

My mind counted out the seconds as the snow rushed down the slope, trees groaning or splitting and crashing, only to be swallowed up in its relentless course. One tree slammed into another trunk, making the bare branches of the standing tree waver and shudder.

Suddenly, I feared being crushed by a tree before the snow even reached us.

But I didn't have time to contemplate that further, as Garrick took a running leap, forcing me to cling with every last ounce of my strength to his fur. In the din surrounding us, my scream was silent, nothing but a vibration tearing at my throat. We landed, my forehead slamming against Garrick's back. He leapt again, climbing a short ascent toward the cave in a rocky outcropping. Its elevation would be our salvation, the cave mouth hopefully high enough that the oncoming snow wouldn't cover it and trap us inside.

Two more heartbeats and we were in the cave's dark interior, the damp walls providing enough of an obstacle to slightly dull the avalanche's thunder.

Exhaustion clung to me, as if the absence of an imminent threat to our lives had sucked all the energy from me. I sensed my magic stutter and stop, and I knew without having to turn that the low-hanging storm clouds had vanished and the hail had ceased. The cold building within me, however, had not.

I tumbled off Garrick's back, shivering so much that my muscles ached.

Garrick was back in his fae form in an instant, fully clothed in his fur coat with his bow and quiver strapped to his back and blades at his sides, as if he'd never even been a wolf. He stooped beside me, laying a hand against my forehead and cursing. "I have no way to build you a fire, Starlight."

"This isn't proper in your world, I suppose, but I promise, I'm not trying to be forward." Garrick flashed me a dimpled grin. It was beautiful, lighting up his whole face, but the humor didn't reach his eyes. That was enough for me to worry that he was right—I could kill myself with my lack of control on my magic. "I'm going to hold you so we can share body heat beneath this coat. It'll warm you faster." He hesitated. "I'm going to remove your coat too, because fewer layers between us will be more effective." The cave was too dark for me to see his expression.

Even if I could have protested, I wouldn't have. There was no one left to impress; I had no reputation to uphold. In this world, the only thing that mattered was survival.

Garrick unbuttoned my coat with nimble fingers, his face inches from mine. I tried to speak, to thank him, but my teeth chattered too violently. The cold air was almost unbearable as he slid the coat off my arms. Thankfully, he worked quickly, shucking off his own coat before drawing me down to the chilly cave floor, positioning us on our sides and draping our coats over us like blankets. For a moment, my face was so close to his I almost lost myself to embarrassment, but I was too frigid to let the feeling consume me. As he enfolded me in an embrace, pulling me flush against him, I tucked my head beneath his chin to avoid looking in his eyes. Instead, I let myself relish in the comfort of feeling myself gradually thaw.

Garrick's body was warm and solidly muscled; his grasp was firm yet gentle. With my ear resting against his chest, I listened to the steady rhythm of his heart while his breath brushed through my hair. It felt peaceful. Safe.

My stomach lurched in a way that wasn't unpleasant. I'd never been this close to a man, and so I couldn't deny the feeling caught me by surprise. Being in Garrick's arms should have felt foreign, but it was comfortable, giving me a sense of belonging.

Slowly, warmth crept through my body, stilling my quaking muscles and filling me with a more soothing version of my earlier exhaustion. Eventually, I realized that it had gone quiet outside, leaving nothing but a haunting silence over the mountainside. But in our cave, our little refuge, I had the music of his heartbeat and his breathing to lull me into sleep.

CHAPTER SEVEN

I woke cradled in warmth, something solid and steady beneath my head and a soft breeze ruffling my hair. With a contented sigh, I stirred, relishing the comfort of the fur blankets cocooning me. That was when I noticed the heartbeat drumming beneath my ear. One of Garrick's hands was tangled in the loose strands of my hair, while his other rested at my waist, fingers digging gently into the fabric of my shirt.

My eyes flew open, heat flooding my cheeks. Even when I carefully lifted my head from his chest, Garrick was close, his expression peaceful in sleep, his breath tickling my face. His arm was wrapped around my body, holding me near. The heat that emanated from him was a gentle contrast to the frosty air.

Back home, my reputation would have been ruined by such proximity with a man. I would have been the subject of constant gossip and scorn, shunned even more than I had been before. Charles would have demanded a wedding, though that still wouldn't have stopped my neighbors' tongues.

It seemed silly to consider now, when I was in the wilderness. Even without worry for my reputation, I still felt shy. I didn't want Garrick to wake when we were this close, to see me studying him. To know I'd been starting to experience new emotions—ones that a woman didn't feel toward a mere friend and that had no right to be growing in my heart.

Sitting up, I stifled a groan as the coats covering us fell and the unforgiving cold ran its fingers over me. Whether from my movement, the chill, or my noise, Garrick's eyes flew open, his face instantly alert. He sat up, catching me about the waist and scanning the cavern.

"Are you all right?" he demanded, his fingers rigid where he held me.

"Yes," I said hastily, feeling like a fool.

Garrick's eyes flicked over my face, taking in my discomfort. His eyes widened and he wrenched his hands away from me as if he'd been burned. He stood and seized his coat. I staggered to my feet as he began buttoning the fur and gathering the bow and quiver he'd shucked off before curling up beside me last night.

I busied myself with shoving my arms into my own coat and buttoning it. I couldn't shake the embarrassment consuming me, and I couldn't meet Garrick's eyes, not without feeling my cheeks burn.

Why did I want Garrick's attentions to mean more than they did? I was grateful for his kindness and companionship. I knew I couldn't expect him to give up his life in Silverfrost to stay with me in Ashwood, which meant eventually, we would have to part ways. Was it only because I was lonely? Or was it him? His charm, his humor, his wit. His dimpled smiles and protective nature and good heart. The way he listened when I spoke, the way he saw who I was and wanted to know me.

I'd never experienced anything like it, and, as short as our time together had been, I didn't want to lose whatever we were building. Thinking about saying goodbye made my heart feel hollow.

Garrick's voice pierced my reverie. "Stay here while I scout outside. I won't be long."

A sobering thought struck me as memories of last night's avalanche returned. "Do you think any soldiers survived?" I asked quietly. It was surreal to think I might be responsible for killing four fae.

Garrick shrugged. "Perhaps, or someone or something new could be nearby. Or there could be snow and shifting rocks." He studied me, con-sidering. "Your magic is dangerous right now when it's difficult to control. But do you think if anyone threatens you, you could try to use the knife I've given you?"

It was unsettling enough that I might have taken lives unintentionally with my magic. Imagining using a blade to deliberately take a life was vastly more so. "I-I think so."

"Good." Garrick's eyes were hard, his voice gruff. "If *anyone* tries to harm you, don't hesitate to stop them." He strode out the cavern mouth, leaving my mind whirling. I crept as close to the edge of the cave as I dared, glimpsing the morning light shimmering peacefully on the mountainside.

Gilded trunks stretched toward a cloudless, pure blue sky. Snow draped the trees' bare branches. The scent of pine was rich in the air, sweet and fresh, almost calming the whirlwind of emotions within me.

Almost.

I'd killed men. I'd wielded power my wildest imaginings could never have fathomed possessing. I'd survived more hunters seeking me, an avalanche, and the chill that had wracked my body afterward.

And somehow, along the way, I was finding myself captivated by a man who seemed to flirt as easily as he breathed—without meaning anything by it. Though Garrick had confessed to loneliness, though he'd shown me kindness and friendship, he'd never offered anything more. He'd shared that his loyalty and protective nature stemmed from his wolfish side.

Sighing, I ran a hand through my hair, dislodging strands from the knot I'd pulled it into yesterday. Silver locks fell into my eyes. Perhaps I was fooling myself, hoping to survive this harsh world, forever evading the Silverfrost family's reach. Perhaps I should try leaving Brytwilde behind and trying to venture back into the human world.

Though I had no money, no other living family apart from Charles, and not a single friend I could depend upon to care for me, I supposed I could find a way to make a living. In a town away from Altidvale, distant enough that no rumors of my magic had reached them, I could try to find a position as a seamstress. I could make a life for myself, secure and apart from public scrutiny. Everyone gossiped about a strange young lady out in society, expected to gain suitors, but no one would pay a lowly seamstress much mind. Especially if I forever tucked my hair beneath a bonnet and kept my head down.

Resolve hardening, I lifted my chin when I heard Garrick's approach. His form filled the cave entrance, freezing as if he sensed my intent before I opened my mouth.

"It's safe," Garrick said, at the same moment that I announced: "I'm returning to the human world."

For a moment, he merely stared, his gold gaze sweeping over me. "Is it your magic?" he asked at last, brow wrinkling.

"What?"

"Do you fear it? Now that you've seen what it can do?"

I shook my head. "No." Then hesitated. "Perhaps. I...it's not as if I've killed a man before. Let alone *four*." My voice trembled.

Garrick closed the distance between us, his expression softening. "You had no choice. And think of it this way: you saved my life."

"That's just it," I whispered. He was near enough now that I had to lift my head to meet his eyes. "You shouldn't have to risk your life for me, not again."

"Oh, Starlight," Garrick said, the corner of his mouth twitching. "I've so rarely had the chance in my life to do anything noble. Don't take this from me."

"I'm serious!"

Amusement flashed in his eyes.

"I can't bear to be responsible if something bad happens to you," I said, "and it's become clear I can't run from the king and queen forever. My best chance of survival—and freedom—is to return to the human world."

The laughter died from Garrick's eyes, replaced with such gravity that it frightened me. "That's not possible, even if you had a home to return to. At least, not until you leave Silverfrost behind. The barrier between this kingdom and yours will forever prevent you from leaving. The land itself will recognize your blood and the fact that you belong to the royal family. Once a mortal crosses that barrier and is offered to the Silverfrosts, the magic forever restricts your passage."

"What?" Despair flared, cold and devastating. I recalled the barrier I'd struck the night Charles had offered me to the fae. I'd thought it only extended around Altidvale, not around the whole of Silverfrost.

Garrick grasped my hand, his touch tender. "We'll flee to Ashwood as planned. From there, you can choose to stay or to take your chances in the mortal world. Whatever you desire. But your only option for now is to run."

I blinked at the tears threatening my vision. "Why didn't you tell me before?"

A muscle twitched in his jaw. "I'd thought we already agreed that attempting to turn back to the human world was hopeless, so I never believed you'd consider it as an option." His eyes scanned my face. "Are you sure this doesn't have to do with your magic? Those soldiers threatened *you* first.

They would have shown you no mercy, had they captured you. And as I said before, in stopping them, you also saved my life. What you did wasn't wrong."

My smile was frail. "It doesn't feel right, either."

As if realizing he was still grasping my hand, Garrick dropped it abruptly. Before, I'd been shy, and he'd learned to be considerate. But now, the distance between us frustrated me more than I wanted to admit. *Don't mistake all his kindness for deeper feelings,* I admonished myself.

"It will never feel right, not for someone with a good heart like yours," Garrick explained gently. He flashed me a self-deprecating grin. "But take it from a wolf: Killing for one's own survival is part of the natural order of things."

After Garrick cautioned me to beware of shifting rocks, I left the cave to take care of my needs. I returned, cursing the bitter cold, to find my companion digging through his pack for the few rations we had left.

"I have bad news," he began as he offered me a piece of jerky and our canteen of water.

I stifled a groan as I sat on the floor across from him, biting into the dried meat. "Haven't you already shared enough bad news for the day?"

"I wish." He sighed. "As helpful as your avalanche was, it also forced us deeper into Silverfrost, further from Ashwood's border and closer to the royal family."

My stomach churned, and suddenly my hunger vanished. "How much closer?"

Garrick cleared his throat, not quite meeting my eyes. "Their castle is within a day's hike from here."

Fear scraped a ragged claw down my spine.

"And unfortunately, we can't dig a path through all the snow you brought down, so our only path toward Ashwood will force us deeper into Silverfrost first. We'll have to travel around the foot of the mountain until we can find a clear path to climb."

I picked at the jerky with shaking fingers, still unable to take another bite. "Are you saying we have to continue *toward* the Silverfrost royals?"

Regret shone in Garrick's eyes. "I'm afraid so. We'll have to be especially cautious. I'm sure there will be more soldiers and bounty hunters eager to find you and procure the royal family's favor." He hesitated. "And I can't be sure you killed all four of the others who were already after us."

Swallowing, I scanned the dim cave, my eyes lingering on the thicker shadows near the back, making it unclear whether it continued deeper into the earth or ended in a stone wall. It was cold and harsh, without food or water to help us survive. And yet for that brief instant, it felt like a haven.

"It wouldn't do to linger here," Garrick added, as if reading my thoughts. "Though I haven't met another wolf shifter in far too long, there are plenty of other ways to track us. Other shifters could scent us, or a more powerful fae than me could cast a spell that would help guide them straight to us."

I frowned, unsure I wanted to understand the depths of magic such as that.

Lifting my chin, I searched his face. "Is there a way to continue onward and *not* walk straight into my enemies' arms?"

Garrick's lips twitched. I'd never been so direct with anyone back home save for Charles when he threatened to turn me out, but then again, other than with my sorry half-brother, I'd never had a reason to speak my mind so openly. With Garrick, it was easy. His mission was mine. Sitting back, he raked a hand through his white-blond hair, standing it on end as he mused. "We can do the best we can, but we will have to venture close to them. I know how to avoid being seen, and I know of another cabin not far from here, also enchanted by wards. But the closer we draw to the capital, the more soldiers and bounty hunters we are likely to encounter."

I cringed, but I didn't relent. "Are you sure you want to risk their wrath? This is your kingdom, after all."

Garrick's mouth was a grim line. "Don't worry about me."

As we emerged from the cave, Garrick offered a hand. His skin was pleasantly warm against mine, contrasting with the frigid morning air and sending a jolt of reassurance down my spine despite the knowledge that we were heading *toward* danger. "You needn't be afraid or ashamed of your magic," the fae hunter said, almost too casually.

I cast him a sidelong look. "Like you're ashamed of using yours?" It was a guess, but considering he'd only let me see him in his wolf form once, under the direst of circumstances, and he sometimes called himself a dog, I was confident I was right.

Garrick flinched. "When you're taught all your life that your power is meaningless, that your value is akin to nothing in the eyes of other fae, it isn't easy to appreciate it."

My brow furrowed, but Garrick nudged me gently, his grin seeming forced. "As flattering as it is to see you care about me, we have bigger troubles to worry about, Starlight," he said. "Don't fret. My feelings about my shifting abilities won't stop me from using them if the need arises. You're safe with me."

CHAPTER EIGHT

"At last," I breathed, rubbing my gloved hands together as Garrick bolted the door behind us. It had been a long, grueling trek through deep snow—made longer because of frequent stops to rest because I wasn't accustomed to such arduous tasks, and because of our need to take a circuitous route to avoid a company of soldiers Garrick spied leaving the castle to enter the mountains and head toward Ashwood. After our long day, I was overjoyed to be in this next cabin. To be safe, behind the wards that wouldn't allow anyone else to enter once the door was bolted.

Unfortunately, we were also much closer to the enemy. As we'd approached this cabin, I'd caught glimpses of great stone walls rising in the distance, resting on the swell of the next mountainside.

"The castle," Garrick had muttered. "It's built like a fortress, for the royal Silverfrosts were known for their warlike tendencies. It's said the first of their kind created it to withstand any siege, so they could go out and conquer the other three fae kingdoms but never fear anyone taking theirs."

Thinking of those warlike fae, notoriously cruel to humans, had made icy fear clutch my heart. I'd turned away hurriedly.

Now, I settled on a pile of blankets Garrick laid before the hearth as he set to work building a fire. I sighed with relief as the flames began to crackle, then wondered at the irony of my possessing winter magic yet hating the cold. Would I ever build up a tolerance for it, the way Garrick seemed to have done? Was it because of his fae or shifter blood, or merely the fact he'd lived his life in these rugged mountains?

"There hasn't been anyone here in some time," Garrick said as he rifled through the cabinets for supplies. He sighed, shoulders slumping. "I'll have to leave you."

My heart dropped. "What do you mean?" I asked, pausing mid-removal of my boot, my fingers still tangled in its damp laces.

"Well, I assume you're hungry," Garrick said, a half-smile on his face. "I don't think the little salted meat we have left will sustain us much longer." He shrugged, seizing his bow and quiver from where he'd hung them on a hook on the wall near the door. "Besides, you're secure here."

"The wards will hold even when you're gone?"

"Did you think I had anything to do with them?" The wolf shifter's laughter came out forced, his gold eyes dim with sadness he couldn't quite conceal. "I don't have such magical abilities. They hold with or without my influence, Starlight. They were placed generations ago, to secure all who would stay here. As long as you bolt the door, only those you welcome will be permitted to enter."

I nodded, concealing the way uneasiness slithered along my skin in spite of Garrick's reassurances. I couldn't forget the dullahan and the way it had imitated his voice.

As if reading my thoughts, Garrick added, "Don't let anyone in—no matter *what* you hear—unless I can tell you exactly where we met and the first thing you said to me."

"I'm afraid we have not been introduced," I recited with a grin.

Garrick dipped his head. "I'll return as soon as I can. Bolt the door behind me."

As soon as I'd slid the lock into place, I returned to the fireside, pulling off my boots. No part of me wanted to climb into the bed to warm myself, not when it was set against the wall, near a window. Instead I found a tunic and a pair of leggings in a chest and changed into the fresh, dry clothes, folding the men's pants and rolling the hems to fit my body.

Curling up in a fur blanket before the fire, I clung to my hunting knife. My mind ran wildly through the moments leading up to the avalanche I'd unleashed, wracking me with guilt and tension despite the knowledge that the men who'd hunted us wouldn't have hesitated to kill Garrick. I didn't regret what my magic had done, not when it had saved him, but that didn't ease my guilt, the sobering knowledge that I'd taken lives. And that I had the power to take more.

If my magic was strongest during winter in the Silverfrost kingdom and was connected to my emotions and thoughts, I feared I'd never gain control of it. My quiet actions and calm demeanor back home had always been a front to mask my churning pain and intense feelings. From grief to fear of the future to the pain of never being wanted, never fitting in, and the constant ache of loneliness, I had always been a storm on the inside.

The avalanche had felt like a natural extension of the wildness within, as deadly to myself as it had been to others. Somehow, I wasn't surprised by that either. Endangering my own life with my magic seemed fitting, like the old, silent gods' way of amusing themselves with my pain. How ironic that the power others had always feared had not only truly been a part of me, but also threatened me as well.

Unfortunately, I wasn't sure how to strengthen my grasp on my abilities short of practicing with them, and I wasn't about to risk summoning another storm or avalanche.

Sighing, I huddled deeper within my pile of blankets, trying to remain alert. But the arduous walk through the snow and the pleasantly toasty air from the fire made my eyelids grow heavy, and I slipped into a dreamless sleep.

"No desire for company to keep you warm? A shame."

The words jolted me awake, sitting up and staring toward the door. Something scratched along its surface outside, slowly and deliberately. That deep, taunting male voice spoke through the keyhole again.

"All alone, I see. Your dog left you to fend for yourself."

Seizing the knife, I stared at the door, willing myself to be unafraid. *The wards won't let him in.*

The fire burned low, casting an umber glow around me but leaving the cabin's edges in flickering shadow. Through the window beside the door, I caught a flash of movement in the night.

How long had I slept? And where was Garrick?

The scratching started again. "A quiet little human," the stranger crooned. "You can't hide in there forever. Why don't we strike a bargain?"

I gathered my courage. "I'm no fool," I said, tightening my grasp on the knife. "You want whatever price the Silverfrost family placed on my head, and the only thing I want is my freedom. There is no agreement we can come to, and nothing you say will convince me to let you in. You cannot pass the wards."

There was a long, drawn-out sigh, almost as if the fae were using it only for dramatic effect. "Very well. Be difficult."

My heart hammered in my ears as I heard the scrape of a blade being drawn.

"They want you alive, but considering you killed my friends, made hunting you challenging, and forced me to draw my own blood, I think they'll understand if I take my time with you first."

I stood, letting the blankets fall to the floor and holding the knife point toward the cabin entrance, as if the creature could see me. "What are you talking about?"

"Playing with my prey. Little worm that you are, I've heard your blood tastes intoxicating to my kind. Perhaps I'll take a sip or two."

The earlier warmth of the cabin had vanished in an all-consuming chill. I shuddered as my breath fogged. Nearby, the fire sputtered and dimmed, fighting against a frigid breeze gusting around me and tangling in my hair. "You'll never make it inside."

Laughter, deep and threatening, made me feel like claws were being scraped down my spine. "Unfortunately, Garrick Darkgrove failed to realize that it was *my* ancestors who created the wards for these cabins. The same blood that marks them for protection runs in my veins. All I need is a few drops of my blood for the magic to recognize me and let me pass."

There was a click as if to emphasize his point, and then the deadbolt slid open of its own accord. The knob turned and the door swung inward, wind and snow swirling inside. In the entrance, the hulking form of the winged fae man loomed before me, his mouth open wide to reveal black fangs.

My heart throbbed in my throat, but my scream died before it could fully form.

The fae swallowed the distance between us in two huge strides, his grey, feathered wings unfurling to their full length. He was like a bird of prey, dark and feral and entirely too swift. I staggered back, unsuccessfully trying to stumble out of his reach.

Ice popped beneath my stockinged feet, spreading outward over the hardwood floor in a frosty layer. I slipped and crashed in a heap, my elbow slamming painfully on the ice's hard surface. My entire arm went numb, and the knife fell uselessly from my limp fingers.

Seizing me by the throat, the fae laughed, his eyes a red so deep they were nearly black. My teeth chattered as he lifted me, opening his mouth still wider. Ready to consume.

I reached for the magic rippling through my veins. Chill wind whistled as it tugged at the man's feathered wings. Thrashing, I tried and failed to wrench his hand off my neck, to punch his leering face and knock him away. Snowflakes fell in a flurry into the cabin, churning around us in a furious white blanket.

Again, the man merely laughed, digging his fingers in harder, until his nails bit into my skin and warm drops trickled down the back of my neck. His nostrils flared and a terrifying gleam shone in his eyes as he inhaled the tang of my blood. "Snow won't stop me, worm."

I screamed as his head dipped lower, his fangs brushing my flesh. Their points stung as they began to pierce the place between my neck and shoulder.

Black ice climbed up the man's arms and devoured his booted feet, rooting him in place. Snarling, he lifted his head to glare at me, his fangs dripping with my blood. His hands could no longer hold me in place, and his trapped legs couldn't chase me.

"Starlight!" My heart leapt with hope at the sound of Garrick's voice.

Not even pausing to seek my coat or knife, I stepped into my unlaced boots and launched myself across the slick cabin floor, skating along the ice and charging into the night. Warmth and pain pulsed in my neck, and I lifted a hand to where my attacker's fangs had pierced me, grimacing.

Outside was a whirlwind of snow, frigid and painful. The sensation of a thousand needles pricking my bare skin consumed me, cutting through the fabric of my clothes. I shivered and charged toward the sound of Garrick's voice, still calling out to me. No matter the risks of the storm outside, I couldn't linger in the cabin, couldn't trust that my unpredictable magic would keep the winged fae bound for long.

Pines rose ahead of me, but otherwise, it was difficult for me to make out clear shapes in the snow. Flakes coated my hair and dusted my eyelashes.

"Ren!"

Garrick couldn't be far.

A stronger gust tore my hair free, letting silver strands whip against my numbing face. "Garrick?" I shouted. "I'm here!"

"Starlight." His voice was warm and relieved, and when I spun around, he was there.

Heedless of how he might react or what the world I'd left behind might once have thought of me, I threw myself into his arms. His warmth enveloped me instantly, thawing the cold in my veins. I buried my face in his coat, snow melting against my face and mingling with the tears stinging my eyes.

Before I could speak, the storm ended as soon as it had begun. Quiet descended as Garrick hesitantly threaded his arms around me. My heart ached. He wasn't returning my embrace, not really. "You're bleeding," he murmured, but his voice sounded strangely distant.

I lifted my head, and he dropped his arms and stepped back, leaving me to the cold. The cool light of stars bathed the trees in silver, and I could just make out the cabin and its fading glow a short distance away. Footsteps approached from the forest behind me.

"There you are, Snowflake," called an unfamiliar voice, grating on my ears.

When I met Garrick's gaze, the usual warmth of his golden eyes had vanished into something cold. Foreboding lurched through me.

"Thought you could run and hide from us forever, did you, Miss Florentia Cantwell?" came an amused feminine voice.

I spun to face two approaching figures, the silver light tracing their sharp features and taunting grins. Both stood tall and slender with rich brown hair and deeper, darker eyes. Their high cheekbones and pointed chins appeared chiseled from marble, and their pale skin seemed almost luminescent. Crowns of white and yellow gold engraved with snowflake detailing and sparkling diamonds gave them away.

The Silverfrosts.

Garrick dipped his head deferentially and addressed the royal siblings by name. Or perhaps he spoke their names for my benefit, in an awful, unwanted introduction.

"King Preston. Queen Nerissa." His voice was low and deep, betraying none of his feelings.

A shudder rippled through my body.

"Well done, Garrick," Queen Nerissa said as she sauntered forward, a self-satisfied smirk twisting her full, red lips. "See, Preston? I knew your hunters could never compete with my Garrick. Their tracking abilities could never compare to what a loyal dog can do."

My breath caught and I staggered backward, as if I could outrun the immortal fae stalking toward me. I slammed into a solid chest, and muscled arms coiled around my waist. Garrick held me against him—but, though his warmth continued to envelop me, it was no longer comforting. He was confining me, preventing me from escaping.

"Let me go," I hissed, the tears on my eyelashes freezing. I tried to glance over my shoulder, but my head was pressed too closely against him, his chin tucked against my hair.

The sting of betrayal slammed into me so forcefully I ached. How could I have been so foolish as to trust a fae? How could I have believed, because he'd talked of running away, because he couldn't outright lie, that he wasn't deceiving me? Had I truly been that starved for kindness? For companionship? I'd attached myself so quickly to the very first person to offer me an ounce of decency for the first time in a year. Shame consumed me.

As the siblings paused mere feet before us, their eyes raking over me, I struggled vainly against Garrick's grasp. Something dark churned in Preston's eyes. He took another step closer, his boots crunching in the snow. Extending his arm, he seized my chin with one gloved hand, tipping my head to inspect me like I was an animal at a livestock exhibit.

"Just a delicate little snowflake," he muttered, as if to himself. "A shame that our magic was wasted on the likes of a sad little mortal like you."

Both his and Nerissa's eyes snapped to my bleeding neck in the same instant. Preston inhaled sharply. "Smells about as appealing as an animal."

But Nerissa's pale face had turned vicious, her taunting manner melting into something far more terrifying. "Where is he, Garrick? A failed hunter must be punished. Find and dispatch of him." She snapped her fingers as if she really were commanding a dog, and Garrick's arms released me. Nerissa's gaze flicked to her brother, who still gripped me painfully. "He's your servant. Would you like the pleasure of punishing him?"

Preston snorted. "No, you and your dog can have your fun."

As Garrick and Nerissa trudged back toward the cabin, where I assumed the winged fae was still encased in ice, Preston lifted his hand in a silent signal. His other remained firmly on my chin. I had the urge to struggle and try to flee, but I knew better than to give into the impulse. Years of being taunted and mocked and feared had taught me to become quiet and unobtrusive. I suspected such behavior would serve me equally well among the fae. Fighting back would make myself a more interesting challenge, a plaything they wouldn't soon tire of.

At Preston's gesture, several guards slunk from among the trees, naked blades shimmering at their sides. Two carried shackles that gleamed a strange bluish color when the light caught them.

"Restrain her," Preston said, grinning wickedly and releasing my chin. He stepped back to allow the guards to flank me, seizing my arms.

This time, my magic responded to my terror, and I didn't try to resist it. Maybe I had no choice but to try to run, even if it encouraged them to give chase. A chill rippled through me, and the breeze picked up, whipping stinging snowflakes against my cheeks.

"Tsk, none of that now," Preston taunted. "Resisting and running will only give us reason to let our dog chase you again. And he does so love to hunt."

As if to punctuate his statement, a ragged scream rent the air, echoing through the cabin behind me. My heart dropped as the scream cut off.

The guards tugged my arms behind my back and snapped the shackles around my wrists with a clank. Instant pain burned through me as the cold metal brushed against my skin. I hissed through my teeth and my eyes watered as the agony intensified, like countless hot coals searing along my skin, their heat burrowing into flesh and tendon and bone.

"Forget-me-nots melded in with our metal," Preston explained, meeting my gaze with a hungry look. Now that he was nearer, his eyes looked red. The color of dried blood. He leaned forward, his breath caressing my face. It smelled of decay, and I choked back a gag. "The flowers have an interesting effect on fae magic. You essentially forget how to use your power—and in that forgetting comes enormous pain. To be cut off from something that lives in your blood is to lose a piece of yourself. Awful, is it not?"

My very bones ached, every muscle in my body going taut with the agony churning through me. Now the burning seemed to go even deeper than my bones and my blood, consuming organs. Devouring me. I struggled for breath, my lungs heaving with effort. My vision started to tunnel, and I wondered if I'd pass out right there, collapsing in the snow.

From the corner of my eye, I was aware of Garrick and Nerissa returning. Blood splattered Garrick's clothes, and when I tried to meet his gaze, he turned away, his expression shuttered. Nerissa strode closer, holding...a severed finger. My stomach cramped as she lifted it high, showing off the gruesome, bloody thing like it was something to be treasured.

"Care to go collect a trophy, brother?" she asked Preston.

The world swayed and lurched around me. I keeled over, heaving the pitiful contents of my stomach—which was mostly bile—into the snow.

"Don't be so dramatic," Preston muttered, grabbing me by my injured shoulder. Fresh pain lanced through me. His gloved finger traced the blood trickling down my neck before he lifted it to his nose, sniffing. Grimacing, he wiped his glove on his trousers. "The stench of mortal blood. As disgusting as I thought."

I tried to *move,* but I was frozen in place. Horror and an aching, unending sense of betrayal and loss slammed into me. The agony from my shackles reached a peak, until I thought maybe I was being shredded apart or burned alive, and this time, I screamed.

I screamed and screamed until I was breathless, until my throat was raw, until Preston scowled, drawing his blade and lifting the pommel over me. There was a flash of pain as it struck the back of my head, and then darkness.

CHAPTER NINE

Piercing sunlight jolted me awake to find my head throbbing and my entire body aching with the memory of my agony. Worse still was the pain punching my heart. *Garrick.*

I scanned the stone-walled room I occupied, with no visible entrances and exits but a high window letting in light from an overcast day, and a single wood door. On my right was a chair resting before an unlit fireplace, lending to the room's chilly atmosphere. To my left was an open entryway leading to a windowless washroom with a copper tub. Glancing down at the bed I was reclined on, I found fur blankets draped over me. My boots rested on the floor at my bedside, but there was no sign of the knife I'd possessed. Either it remained in the cabin where I'd left it, or the royals had confiscated it.

My shackles were gone, but I could still feel phantom pain. Perhaps the forget-me-nots' effects lingered even after they'd been removed from someone's skin. I didn't want to test this theory, as, enclosed in this room as I was, the only person who would hurt from my ice and snow would be me.

I sat up, blinking as the world lurched, and scanned my surroundings more intently. Was the door locked? If they'd left me unrestrained, it seemed too much to hope that the Silverfrosts hadn't left me guarded.

Footsteps echoed outside as if in answer to my questions. A bolt slid free, and the door swung inward. I gaped at the figure in the doorway, his white-blond hair contrasting sharply with the brightness of his gold eyes. His jaw was taut, all warmth leached from his features. Perhaps the charming, loyal, gentle man I'd known, the one who'd confessed to loneliness, the one who'd made self-deprecating jests about his weaknesses, didn't exist. Maybe this cold hunter was the true man.

Renewed pain flared in my chest. "*You.*"

Ignoring me, Garrick kicked the door shut behind him and strode silently across the floor, settling himself on the edge of the bed. It wasn't until he sat that I noticed the bag he carried. Resting it on the bed between us, he withdrew a jar of ointment.

I gritted my teeth, my eyes darting over his shoulder toward the door. *Foolish,* I thought. There were likely guards waiting for me out there, not to mention miles of frigid mountains and no guarantee I could find the Ashwood kingdom by myself, let alone that its people would welcome me.

Not to mention Garrick's icy presence.

King Preston's words echoed in my head. *Resisting and running will only give us reason to let our dog chase you again. And he does so love to hunt.*

I'd always survived by being unobtrusive, but if I refused this fight, I'd be resigning myself to a lifetime of slavery and cruelty. Or torture. The image of Queen Nerissa and that bloody finger haunted me.

Without letting myself overthink it, I launched from the bed. The world spun and my steps fumbled as I slid on stockinged feet across a cool stone floor, charging for the door I prayed was still unlocked. I didn't feel any cold chills or other indications of my magic brewing, and I was unarmed and in an unfamiliar place. But I couldn't just lie down and give in to this nightmarish existence. Not without trying to find something better...

Warm hands seized my wrists just as I reached the door. My breath caught in my throat as Garrick whirled me around to face him, pressing my back against the wood. His face was inches from mine, his gold eyes bright with emotion for the first time. I thought it might be fury.

"Not a good idea," he growled, locking my arms on either side of me, his fingers firm on my wrists. He had me hemmed in, his chest rising and falling unevenly, so close it pressed into mine. I knew chasing me hadn't winded him at all.

He was breathless with his anger.

I wished for magic that didn't come, longed for the cool touch of my ice to temper the heat from Garrick's body encasing me. Wished I could entrap him the way I'd stopped the winged fae the night before.

But I couldn't fight back, couldn't resist. Instead, dizziness struck again, and my vision blurred. I swayed unsteadily on my feet, trying and failing to speak. All that came out was a groan of protest as Garrick lifted me effortlessly in his arms and carried me back toward the bed. My heart plunged into my stomach as the familiar scents of mountain air, leather, and fur filled my nose, reminding me of when Garrick had carried me to help me. Not to trap me, as he was now.

And yet his touch was as gentle as ever, a sharp contrast to the unfeeling look on his face.

"You're injured and weak from the shackles," Garrick said, his tone still guttural. It reminded me that he was a wolf shifter. Animalistic. A heartless hunter loyal to his wicked king and queen. "Running would encourage them to play with you more, to hurt you. And if you did somehow escape the castle? It would be suicide."

He lowered me onto the bed, hovering over me as he searched my face.

"Says the man who turned me into those...revolting creatures," I managed, still breathless from my exertion when my muscles remained weak and achy. "It seems...you want me to die. I thought you were better than the fae who use and abuse humans...but you're just an animal with...a predator's instincts. All along, you were tricking me so you could be the bounty hunter that brought me to them." My voice cracked.

A muscle jumped in Garrick's jaw. Something flashed in those gold eyes—and then vanished, replaced with a blank look concealing all emotion. "You don't know what I am." Without pulling back, he brushed strands of silver hair out of my face and off my neck, revealing the place the winged fae had bitten me. It still stung, though the blood had long crusted over my wound. "Hold still so I can tend to you."

"I don't want you touching me."

Garrick leaned forward even closer, his nose brushing mine. My heart jumped into my throat, my throbbing pulse so violent I was sure he could hear it. I glared at him, but he didn't let my expression affect the stony look on his face. "Would you prefer I fetch the king and ask him to treat your wounds?"

I shuddered, and Garrick pulled back to retrieve the ointment. "As I thought," he muttered.

"Isn't there a servant to do this?" I demanded as I sat up, turning my head away so as to avoid his eyes as he brushed the ointment over my neck with a calloused finger. Every brush of his skin against mine stirred a jolt of energy and heat. Though I wanted to forget my foolish earlier feelings for this man and lose myself in the bitter sense of betrayal, I couldn't ignore my attraction quite so easily, not when his touches were tender and attentive. They reminded me of the good-hearted, conscientious man I'd thought he was. The one I'd trusted and felt safe with, the one I ached to have by my side now.

"The king and queen sent me," Garrick said simply.

He settled closer to inspect the back of my head, brushing aside strands of hair to find the lump Preston had left when knocking me unconscious. I hissed when his fingers touched it, then immediately clamped my lips closed, not wanting him to know how much I hurt. Any sign of weakness, any symptom of the broken pieces I'd shattered into, would be something a fae would happily exploit.

If only I'd been this cautious of my heart before, when I'd been alone and eager to listen to Garrick's own story of solitude and loneliness.

"You would probably do better cleaning this on your own," Garrick said stiffly. "I can draw a bath for you, let you wash your hair. I'll apply the ointment afterward and add more to your neck. What I already used should dull the pain somewhat."

I shot him a look before my eyes flicked to the open washroom. "I'm not bathing with you here."

Garrick sat back, lifting his hands in surrender. "I won't look."

Scoffing, I turned away. "And I'm to trust your word now? You aren't a gentleman. You're a fae. A deceitful, lying scoundrel—"

"I cannot lie, Ren." It was jolting to hear him call me Ren and not by his nickname for me.

I scowled. "You lied by withholding the truth." Daring to meet his eyes, I sought any sign of remorse, any hint of feeling at all behind that cold mask he wore. Nothing. "What is the purpose of tending to my injuries? I've been told they torment and wound humans for sport. Or am I being trussed up before I'm executed?"

Garrick looked away, and I wondered at his unwillingness to look into my face. He couldn't lie, but he could omit things. What did he have to hide this time? "As far as I know, the king and queen have no wish to kill you currently. They ordered me to tend to you, to ensure you're cleaned up for a feast. They will present you to their court."

I threaded my fingers together in my lap, trying to still their trembling. "As their new plaything?"

"I don't know their plans, as I am not in their confidence."

Inhaling deeply, I forced myself to ask the question that haunted me, the one I feared would only have painful answers. "Why did you do it?" Tears swam in my eyes, blurring my vision. "You told me you don't agree with how the king and queen treat humans. Why did you betray me?"

Garrick remained stoic, not reacting when a tear slipped freely down my cheek. Like he'd never cared. "I am their obedient hunter and servant." It sounded rehearsed, as if he'd told countless others he'd tracked down for the royals this very same thing.

"You serve a woman who murdered her subject and cut his finger off like it was a trophy," I whispered, my voice shaking with disgust. I studied him again, taking in his broad, muscled frame, the stubble on his square jaw, the absence of emotion in his gold eyes. "Or is that what you are too? A careless murderer of your own kind?" I swallowed back my rising bile. "Did she have you kill him for her?"

His expression was stony. "The Silverfrosts aren't like the rest of us. They are powerful. Our rulers. The highest of fae-kind. It's our responsibility as their citizens to obey them, and it's their right as our king and queen to punish us if we do not."

"They're *monsters*."

Darkness seeped into Garrick's gaze, the first hint of emotion. His tone pitched low. "And have you forgotten what *I* am?"

I swallowed thickly, remembering how at first, the idea of him shifting into a wolf had terrified me. How quickly—and foolishly—I'd grown comfortable with him, trusting him. Thinking he would only protect me and never hurt me. But he'd only ever defended me from the other fae so he could have the honor of taking me to his king and queen himself. All along, he'd been hunting me. Fooling me. Using me.

"Why did you come to the ball in Altidvale?" I asked hoarsely. Garrick couldn't lie, but had he twisted the truth in some way when he'd spoken of coming for entertainment? Hadn't he first told me he'd been in the area on business? Had the Silverfrosts somehow known I had magic and wanted me even before Charles had offered me to them?

But Garrick shook his head, as if reading my thoughts. "If you think King Preston and Queen Nerissa sent me to find you that night, you're wrong. They didn't know you existed until Charles offered you to them. It wasn't until then...when you told me what he'd done...that I knew they'd send fae to find you. That's when I knew they'd expect me to bring you to them."

Pain pierced my chest to hear him speak of the transaction so plainly.

Before I could collect my thoughts, Garrick stood abruptly, turning so his back was to me. "I'll prepare your bath. It's nearly noon, and we don't have long. Their feasts begin early and continue long into the night. It wouldn't do for you to be late and...upset them. Don't try to run again. There are guards in the hall who will stop you nearly as easily as I did."

He strode into the washroom without another word, leaving me to seethe on the bed. When I heard water running, somehow trickling from some faucet in the washroom that made me wonder if the fae had wells inside their castle, I stood cautiously and tested my balance. The world swayed, my head pounded, and nausea swept over me in waves, but it was manageable. True to Garrick's word, the pain in my neck had already dulled too, leaving only my headache and strained muscles to plague me. I crept toward the window, peering out onto a frosty, unforgiving world.

Beyond the foreboding stone wall encircling the castle, the mountainside descended in a pure white sheet toward clusters of pines and mist. More mountains rose on the horizon, breathtakingly beautiful and gilded by the sunlight. Far below, tucked between the mountain I was on and the next, there was a city, idyllic and peaceful where it settled beside a glistening lake. From this height, I could just make out puffs of chimney smoke rising from the buildings, all painted in cheerful shades of pale yellow and blue and green, as if the city's inhabitants were determined to bring color in their world of white.

It was startling how peaceful it appeared, a city of fae I'd been taught were vicious. A city in the shadow of a fortress-like castle belonging to terrible fae. Ones who were worse even than the stories portrayed them.

And I was trapped, their newest plaything with an unknown destiny. Cursed to a life of torment.

I couldn't climb out of the window, even if I thought Garrick wouldn't stop me before I made my way over the sill. The sheer drop from my room to the courtyard below told me I was several stories up.

Doomed. Tears pricked my eyes, but I swallowed back the urge to cry once more. I didn't want Garrick to see me break again, not when he'd only watch me coldly.

My mind ran through my options. If I had fae blood that granted me magic, I wondered if it meant I also possessed glamour. If I could command Garrick, I'd have the might of a wolf on my side. Maybe I could order him to tear out my attackers' throats and lead me to safety.

I both hated and loved the thought.

"Your bath is ready," came Garrick's voice, pulling me from my thoughts.

I whirled, finding him leaning against the washroom entryway. His face remained chiseled from stone, though there was a more casual air about him that reminded me of the more carefree man I'd met. Now I realized it had all been an act. He'd made himself charming, made himself into the type of man I'd begin to fall for. He'd seen my loneliness and preyed upon it. Preston's words again echoed in my head. *He does so love to hunt.*

"I don't see why they won't lock me in their dungeons and be done with it." I lifted my bare wrists. "Why remove my shackles? Why give me a room and send you to help me heal? Why invite me to a feast?"

Garrick's eyes were hard. "I already told you, I don't know their plans."

"Why did they send *you*?"

He shrugged.

"When you call yourself their obedient dog, does that mean you never ask questions or wonder about their intentions?"

Garrick flinched, avoiding my gaze. I'd hit my mark. "Bathe, before you're late and there are consequences," he said instead, storming away from the washroom. Toward me.

I laughed bitterly. "What more can they do to me?"

"You have *no* idea what they can do," Garrick snarled, leaning closer. "No inkling of the hell they can inflict on their living subjects."

For a long moment, we stared at one another. My pulse beat in my ears, and the world continued to sway. My aching head was dizzy and light. I *had* to escape.

Praying my glamour would come naturally to me, I made an attempt to use it. "I command you to help me escape," I said, dropping my voice into something I hoped sounded alluring and irresistible.

Garrick stared, a furrow forming between his brows. "What?"

My heart dropped. "I command you—"

He cut me off. "Your powers won't work here. The king and queen used blood from your wounds to place an enchantment on this room that prevents you from accessing any of your magic. Or your glamour."

"But I can use my powers in other parts of the castle?"

The shifter glanced away, but his silence was confirmation enough. He couldn't lie and didn't want to admit the truth. That knowledge gave me hope, even if it was brittle.

With that possibility in mind, I relented, pushing past Garrick to enter the washroom. I would bathe and attend the Silverfrosts' feast. I'd feign obedience and weakness. I'd play the role of quiet, good, unobtrusive Florentia once more. And when they least suspected it, I'd find a way to fight back. "Turn around," I called to Garrick as soon as I stood before the tub.

Garrick shook his head, though I watched as he turned his back to me, staring out the window. "I'm not here to seduce you."

"You wouldn't succeed if you tried." I peeled off my tunic and leggings and submerged myself into the tub.

A hiss escaped me. It was hot, a layer of steam rising from its surface. Some lavender soap rested nearby, its soothing aroma fresh and lovely. I inhaled deeply, willing the scent and the sensation of blissful warmth enveloping me to melt away my pain, defeat, and fear. If only for a moment.

As if Garrick had heard my surprise when I climbed into the tub, he explained how the water and heat worked. "There are a few fae from Ravenheart who made their home here, and they're gifted with fire. They're able to keep the water warm, while those Silverfrosts who control water help direct water into our pipes. I'm told every kingdom in Brytwilde has such luxuries, but you mortals do not."

"We mortals are forced to go without many things," I muttered under my breath.

As comforting as the bath was, tempting me to linger and pretend I wasn't a prisoner to two monstrous immortals, I heeded Garrick's earlier warning not to waste time. I hurriedly scrubbed my skin and washed my hair, cleaning the crusted blood off my neck and the back of my head.

The door swung open, and footsteps pattered about my room. I glanced over the edge of the tub to find two human women dressed like maids—though I'd always been told the Silverfrosts kept slaves—darting around. One laid a dress on the bed, while the other built up the fire and exchanged quiet words with Garrick, too low for me to hear. They showed no signs of wounds or even malnutrition, but their eyes were eerily glassy with glamour. I could hardly stand to look them in their faces. They were prisoners as much as I was.

As swiftly as they'd arrived, they swept back out of the room.

"You need to hurry," Garrick said to the window.

I frowned. *Quiet. Obedient. Don't let them know you're dreaming of a way to escape,* I reminded myself. I'd play their game for my own survival. And I'd win. I had to.

Determined, I stood, setting one leg out of the tub. But I'd risen too swiftly, and my shaking limbs and pounding head rewarded me with a wave of dizziness. I cried out, barely managing to catch the edge of the tub with one hand as I slid toward the slick tile floor.

Warm hands caught my waist, callouses scratching against my bare skin. I choked on a gasp.

"Don't look at me!" I cried out as Garrick lifted me.

"I'm not looking below your eyes," he grunted, heaving me up until we were face to face.

Despite the steam still curling through the air and the heat of his hands burning through me, gooseflesh rose on my skin. I wanted to be embarrassed or ashamed, but Garrick couldn't lie, and his eyes remained fixed on mine.

This time, there were emotions churning in his gaze—an entire storm that I couldn't begin to sift through.

"Are you hurt?" His breath caressed my face as he leaned forward, brushing his thumb over my cheek. His touch was gentle, his gaze warm, and I ached for the man I'd thought I'd known to be genuine. For this to not be only a trick, a mere mask.

I so wanted the look of concern, of *wanting*, in those searing gold eyes to be real.

But if he'd fooled me before with behaving as if he cared, he could do so again.

"I'm fine," I said, shoving back and teetering dangerously again. He caught my wrist, his eyes still fixed on my face. "Leave—please!"

Garrick blinked, a muscle working in his jaw. He drew back slowly, as if coming out of a trance. Or letting his pretenses fall away to reveal his true feelings. Cold and distant again, he looked at the ceiling. "You're not going to fall and break your neck before the feast, are you?"

"I'm fine," I repeated, hurriedly seizing the towel from a shelf near the tub and wrapping it around my body. Though Garrick had kept his word and I never once saw his eyes stray, I felt a semblance of relief with the cloth over me, even if it left far too much of my legs bare.

"The maids will return to help you dress, and they'll bring a medicinal tea for the dizziness. And some food—you must be starving, which doesn't help with those feelings of weakness. They'll tend to your head injury while they fix your hair, but I'll apply another layer of ointment to your neck again. How does it feel?"

The pain had dulled even further, leaving it almost numb. "Why not wait until they've dressed me?" I demanded, feeling scandalized. "Or better yet, let the maids do it?"

Garrick's gaze was piercing. "I was ordered to personally ensure you're all right. Though the blow to your head is causing your unsteadiness, I'm more concerned about possible venom in the bite on your neck. I can leave the maids to deal with the rest."

"Venom?"

"No reason to fret. We've cleaned and tended to it swiftly, and you're not showing any worrisome symptoms. But best to be sure. Come," he said impatiently.

I strode out of the washroom, trailing droplets of water. Sitting rigidly in a chair before the fireplace, where a fire now roared pleasantly, I held my breath as Garrick brought over his bag.

Carefully, he tugged my soaked hair off my neck, trailing his fingers over my bite wound. My lack of pain made me hyperaware of his skin on mine as he rubbed another layer of ointment into the punctures. His fingers lingered over my racing pulse, and I prayed he didn't sense it. Didn't know he still had an effect on me. Didn't realize my foolish heart couldn't forget the growing feelings I'd been harboring.

Traitor. Liar. Hunter. Killer. Captor. I listed all the reasons I had to not trust his tenderness, to banish all memories of the man I'd thought he was.

And when he strode out of the room, leaving the maids to flock in and dress me in fae clothes for a feast hosted by my captives, it was easier to remember why I needed to distrust and hate him.

CHAPTER TEN

Clothed in layers of delicate silver silk overlaid with lace that was far too thin for the chilly halls of the castle, I trailed my maids down some flights of stairs and into a small stone antechamber. Torches set in sconces on the walls cast eerie orange light flickering over the space. I scanned the room, my eyes snagging on the two guards at the far end by a carved set of double doors. Both were heavily armed, and each had inhuman features that reminded me how far I was from Altidvale. One had horns, while the other had a pair of tusks jutting from his mouth in a terrifying sneer.

Garrick stepped out of a shadowy corner just as my maid curtsied and slipped away without a word. I glanced over my shoulder, wistfully watching the maid retreat. Though neither she nor any of the other human girls who had tended to me had spoken or offered me more than a chilling, empty sort of presence—the glazed look in their eyes had told me they were all glamoured—I'd felt a sense of solidarity with them. They weren't starving or visibly injured, but they weren't free either. Just like me, they were prisoners in this palace, serving monstrous masters they didn't want to. The only difference was they were less aware of it than I was.

I didn't know if that made me—or them—more fortunate.

At least I could try to fight back. I couldn't be controlled or tricked with glamour.

But they? They were in some blissful state of otherness, blinded to the harsh world around them.

If I couldn't escape, would I grow to envy them? Was it better for one to be a prisoner without knowing it, or to know it yet be incapable of freeing oneself?

My chest tightened as Garrick approached, his expressionless eyes raking over me. There wasn't a trace of glamour in his gaze though—they were clear and piercing as ever, if stony and unyielding. His eyes flicked to the healing wounds on my neck, left exposed by the way the maids had styled my hair in a complicated arrangement of braids atop my head.

"You look cold."

I pressed my lips together, refraining from glaring even though my churning emotions made me want to scream at him.

Garrick shrugged out of his fur vest, and before I could protest, offered it to me.

I swallowed back the rejection burning the back of my throat and slipped it on. Though it still left my arms bare, it radiated warmth. Garrick's warmth. It smelled of fresh mountain air, of freer times when I still believed he was my friend.

I gritted my teeth as my heart sank all over again with a fresh sense of betrayal. This stone-faced man was not my friend. Certainly nothing more. Everything he'd done before was to gain my trust and lure me to his king and queen, and everything he did now was in service to them.

"Come," Garrick said, holding out his arm.

For a moment, I blinked at it. "Are you their servant to usher me in and announce me, or my escort?"

Garrick only shrugged.

I forced myself to take his arm, to ignore how warm he was, how even now I felt secure near him when, logically, I knew I should feel most frightened of all at *his* side. At least the Silverfrost siblings hadn't pretended to be anything other than monsters toward me.

The pair of guards swung the double doors inward at Garrick's and my approach, and we were immersed in a flood of flickering gold light and heat. We passed through the entryway and into a huge curved room full of several tables laden with food, permeating the air with a tantalizing aroma that reminded my aching stomach I hadn't eaten since yesterday. Multiple fireplaces roared at intervals along the walls, and countless fae chatted and dined at tables interspersed throughout the room.

But it was the left side that drew my attention, open to the floor below us, which offered nothing but a plain stone floor and windowless walls.

Cold. Uninviting. And adorned with rusty stains, almost as if it were covered with old blood.

No one was down there, but I had the uncanny thought that the room below us was an arena, and the space above it was for the fae court to dine and watch as those less fortunate fought to the death.

I couldn't stop myself from shivering.

"Welcome," came a familiar voice. Yet it wasn't the cold touch of my magic creeping through my veins—no matter how I reached for it, even outside my rooms, I felt no sign of it—it was the icy sensation of fear.

Queen Nerissa leaned back in an elaborate gold and silver chair, its size and design making it look much like a throne. At her side, King Preston was seated in a similar one, their presence at the end of one of the tables seeming to overtake the entire room.

Everyone quieted as their queen went on, gracefully gesturing toward me with false warmth. Countless fae stares bored into me like dozens of needles pricking at my skin. "Miss Florentia Cantwell, our honored human guest."

The word *guest* was a lie I was surprised her fae lips could even utter, but I knew even with their limitations, they were masters of deceit. Swallowing my despair, I plastered a smile onto my face as I broke free of Garrick's arm and dropped into a curtsey.

I lifted my head, studying Nerissa where she continued to lounge on her chair, clutching a wineglass full of golden liquid I knew to be fae wine. Her white gown glistened with countless pearls, its neckline rising on one side in a stunning mimicry of icicles. The dress's train spilled along the stone floor and nearly reached the foot of Preston's chair, where he reclined in a simple black jacket and trousers. The color of his eyes matched the wine in his own glass as he swirled it, staring at me expressionlessly.

My heart pulsed in my throat.

"Rise," Queen Nerissa said after a long moment, lazily flicking her hand. Her eyes narrowed as my skirts rustled around my feet while I straightened, as if she were taking in my attire for the first time. "Little Snowflake, you look lovely, but what are you wearing?"

I followed the direction of her gaze, my fingers brushing over Garrick's fur vest. My words stuck in my mouth.

But Queen Nerissa didn't wait for my answer, pinning Garrick with her eyes. For the first time, a sense of foreboding for Garrick swept through me. *But he's their faithful servant,* I reminded myself bitterly.

"I thought our honored guest appeared cold," Garrick said, his tone blank, "and that you would want her to be comfortable."

Queen Nerissa rolled her eyes. "Snowflakes don't grow cold. But very well. Bring her to her seat."

Garrick took my arm again, leading me stiffly toward the royal siblings' table, where there were two open chairs on Queen Nerissa's left. To my surprise, Garrick pulled out the furthest chair for me before settling beside the queen himself.

Glazed-eyed human servants scurried forth from other doors set at even intervals opposite the open end of the room, bearing trays full of countless delicacies I couldn't have even imagined back in my humble town of Altidvale. I supposed while the kingdom of Silverfrost was immersed in winter, either fae magic or trade with surrounding lands permitted such variety in foods. Everything from roast duck to glazed ham to steaming potatoes to the finest and freshest of fruits was laid upon the table. *Including* unfamiliar fruits in richer shades of plum and navy and gold and silver, ones that I knew better than to touch. Magic and glamour or not, I was still human, and I'd heard plenty of stories about the effects fae food could have on mortals, ranging from embarrassing to lethal.

"I've heard so much about you," a woman beside me crooned, her lips stained blue from the fruit she was eating. Juice dribbled down her chin and she wiped at it carelessly. Her dark eyes had no pupils and her skin was so pale it was translucent, making the purple veins tracing her temples and neck visible. Her wispy black hair hung about her in a wild curtain. "King Preston and Queen Nerissa were just talking about how…unfortunate it was that your avalanche slew some of their best men."

My heart lodged in my throat. If the royals were talking about the strength of my magic, that meant Garrick had told them just how much I was capable of wielding. I shouldn't have been surprised, and yet this knowledge cut me deeply.

"It's been such a heated topic of conversation," the woman went on, her blue-lipped grin cruel. Her eyes flicked to my hair. "A mortal with such powerful magic?" She sneered. "What a waste."

I tucked my hands into my lap, wishing she'd look away and focus her attention on someone else.

"Tell me," she went on, leaning closer until I could smell the strangely sweet scent of the fruit on her breath, "did you know all this time you had fae blood? Did you offer yourself to the royals on purpose in order to challenge them?"

I stared at her in confusion, but before I could scramble for words, a blank-eyed human stepped between us and poured golden liquid into the wineglass in front of me. I stiffened, darting a glance toward the king and queen. While Nerissa was ignoring me, laughing and talking to a grey-skinned fae who'd approached her, Preston's gaze pierced me. Disgust and foreboding crawled over my skin.

Play along. Quiet Florentia. I reached a trembling hand toward the stem of my glass, not breaking my gaze from Preston's. Did I dare pretend to drink? To take a small sip?

Did I dare to defy them and pour it out?

The servant stepped away and the pale-skinned woman at my side opened her mouth as if she were about to press me with her questions again when all chatter at the table died and a figure came bolting through the doors.

"Your Majesties!" the horned man cried, and for all his fae grace, he nearly tripped in his haste as he rounded the guards who'd stepped forward upon his abrupt arrival. He paused before our table, gasping for breath and dipping into a quick bow. "I bring an urgent message from the border—our forces are in dire need of—"

"You burst in unannounced and uninvited on this most important night?" Queen Nerissa's tone was sharp as a knife as she interrupted him, standing from her seat.

The man blinked and stammered something unintelligible.

Queen Nerissa waved her hand impatiently. "Guards, escort this messenger to a waiting room. We will speak to him later, when he's not interrupting this important night with our guest." Her gaze shot to me, something eerily hungry in her expression.

After all she'd all but ignored me at the start of this feast, I found it strange she was speaking as if my presence and this feast were so important. Especially when there was an ongoing war with lives at stake. But guards ushered the messenger out swiftly, and as Nerissa settled back into her chair, everyone around me returned to chatting and eating, some shrugging carelessly as if they were interrupted with urgent messages daily.

I braced myself for my pale companion to return to prying me with questions, but this time, a woman across from me stood on her chair, clapping her hands and startling the room into silence. The king and queen both beamed, clearly not upset with this interruption. I concealed my frown at the informality of someone standing on their chair at a feast. What would have been shocking and humiliating back home, however, was met with applause and cheers from the rest of the fae.

With white hair cascading down her back and a wizened old face, she wasn't like the high fae around her. She was a hag, with crooked fingers, yellowed teeth, and a bent back. She didn't possess the startling, endless beauty of immortals like Nerissa and Preston. And yet, she moved energetically, and her eyes seemed *young*. Despite the crow's feet surrounding them, they were clear and lovely and deep, full of ageless wisdom matched with a strange sense of youthfulness. She was ancient, but she retained the energy and grace of an immortal. "I have been called upon to share a story," the hag announced in a raspy voice that still managed to carry and echo throughout the space, to every single table.

It hardly seemed possible, but the room seemed to become even stiller and quieter at her announcement. Everyone leaned forward, entranced, and for an instant, I was caught up in the magic of the moment as well.

The hag lifted her age-spotted hands, spreading them wide as...*sounds* rushed into the room. Winter wind howled around us, followed by the crunch of footsteps in snow. The cries of babies and the laughter and chatter and music of dances and celebrations. As the noises died down, the hag raised her voice once more. "I am a Memory Keeper, older than Silverfrost itself. I have witnessed and stored the history of this kingdom, from its founding to the tragic moment that nearly became its downfall.

Listen as I share. Those who were there, remember with me. Those who were not, learn and do not forget these lessons."

Once more, sounds whirled around us, like drifts of the memories the hag stored were all being carried to us on an unseen breeze. She moved her hands as if she were a musician, directing the memories like a song. "For centuries, the Silverfrost family ruled our kingdom with strength and power. Their fierce spirits were only matched by their skill with magic, granted by our land. Many of the Silverfrost line possessed abilities to control the winter wind and snow and ice, just like numerous other fae outside of the royal family can do in our frozen kingdom." A roaring filled my ears, matching the fury of a blizzard. "Others could manipulate animals around them, like our snow foxes and birds, commanding them to do their will." The blizzard was replaced by the gentle sounds of a fae woman speaking, intermingled with the chatter of birds. "Some, long ago at the beginning when fae strength was greatest, could even read minds."

I swallowed back a rush of fear, thanking the silent gods that those powers had died out among the fae long before my time.

"Their might was befitting, for they, like all the fae kingdoms in Brytwilde, had been given an important task by the gods. One that affects both immortals and mortals alike." This was something I hadn't learned in Altidvale. Aside from stories about their cruelty and power, or cautionary tales against trusting the fae or wandering into their dangerous lands, the human children of my town weren't taught much else about the fae.

A sound like stones scraping together filled the air, making the hairs on the back of my neck stand. I grimaced, resisting the urge to cover my ears. "For in Silverfrost," the hag went on as the scraping sound blessedly diminished, giving way to the sound of a creaking door, "we guard the entrance to the underworld."

My heart froze. Screams rent the room, heart-wrenching and terrifying. Groans of pain. Thuds of bodies. I sat so rigidly that Garrick, even from his position beside the queen, shot a glance my way. His gold eyes burned into me, but I refused to meet his gaze or acknowledge his attention. I wouldn't trust him or his false comfort.

"Every winter solstice, the door separating our realm of the living with that of the dead becomes the weakest. It can be manipulated to be fully opened or fully closed only then. The Silverfrosts were granted great power, enough to seal the entrance on that crucial day, keeping those undead monstrosities out of our world." The inhuman noises sweeping through the room after this proclamation were so chilling, so awful, that I clenched my teeth until my jaw ached. Everything in my mind screamed at me to run, even though the more rational part of my thoughts knew the sounds were merely that. Not the approach of demons or undead things.

"While the kingdom of Ashwood sends the spirits of the dead along to their rest in the afterlife, Silverfrost has the even heavier duty of keeping the restless dead—those who have been condemned to eternal punishment—from returning. Our heavy responsibility is why our kingdom has always valued strength in battle and in the mind. Power to hold back the dark forces beyond death that would drag us all, mortal and immortal together, into ruin and chaos. Into an underworld brought here to our living world, tainting our life, our magic. Everything."

A shudder coursed through me, but I tensed my muscles, refusing to let anyone see my mounting terror. Imagining creatures worse than the Silverfrost siblings was horrifying. I didn't want to see what Preston and Nerissa feared.

The hag leaned forward. "Unfortunately, even the greatest power in our land—those with the most potent magic, the best strategic minds, and bodies and training honed for battle...even it wasn't enough when the creatures of the underworld escaped and ravaged this castle. A mere two decades ago, everything changed for our mighty rulers. Something went wrong. Even I was not here to witness it—not until it was too late. Few survived, and I scarcely made it out with my life."

More screams erupted, shredding the air with such intense notes of agony that my eyes glimmered with unshed tears. The hag swirled her hands, letting the sounds envelop us with crushing clarity.

"Death came through the door that night," she announced, "and slaughtered our entire beloved Silverfrost family."

Silence descended over the room. Heads bowed all around me, the faces of the fae who'd been celebrating earlier turning solemn. One of the logs in a fireplace popped. A jolt of compassion Garrick didn't deserve pierced my heart as I realized this was the fight that had killed his entire family.

The hag gestured toward King Preston and Queen Nerissa, who smiled contentedly, as if they hadn't just been listening to a gruesome tale of an entire family being murdered.

"We were blessed that night by our mighty king and queen, siblings from a noble estate across the kingdom, who arrived for a scheduled visit in the middle of the attack. Using their magic, they gave me the chance to flee with these memories I've caught for you of that most tragic day. And they cast those creatures back into the abyss. It is under their rule that we have managed to live in relative safety for nearly twenty-two years."

Applause rang out, wild and fierce.

"But without true Silverfrost blood, our new king and queen could only take that family name and the throne...they could not inherit their most important power. The ability to close the entrance to the underworld and seal its inhabitants inside it." The hag's eyes grew even more somber as another awful sound—an ominous breathing with the scrape of claws—permeated the room. "Our only hope is to be stronger and smarter than anything that escapes at night. To subdue those creatures until, someday, the gods send us someone with the power to send them back into the abyss they crept from. This is why we fight to the death. This is why we train. And this is why, when anyone comes forth claiming long-lost Silverfrost blood, we honor yet test them. No liars will be tolerated."

"And," Preston cut in, his voice echoing through the room, "this is what makes today so special, and our guest so honored. For it has come to our attention that Miss Florentia Cantwell wants to be tested, to see if she somehow possesses an ounce of this precious Silverfrost blood." His grin was wide, but it was all teeth.

What? I never claimed to be a Silverfrost. I sat up hurriedly, my gaze snapping toward Nerissa and Preston. Nerissa ignored me, leaning back in her seat with her wineglass carelessly dangling from her fingers, while Garrick perched on the arm of her chair. She trailed lazy fingers up his bicep in a lustful way that had my stomach lurching. As if I had any right to feel possessive or jealous or hurt regarding anything that traitor did or didn't do.

But Preston's eyes were locked on mine, those red irises twinkling in the flickering light. He was silently laughing at me. Mocking me.

I curled my fingers into fists, my words trapped in my throat. When Garrick had shared the story about the avalanche I'd unleashed, what else had he told Nerissa and Preston? When he'd said he'd known my father, had he been speaking of one of the dead Silverfrosts? Or was this all some awful trick contrived as an excuse to torment me?

I couldn't scream, couldn't protest. What good would it do? It was clear the king and queen had prepared some awful test for me, and resistance would only make it worse.

Wouldn't it?

"Florentia Cantwell," King Preston drawled, standing from the table and circling toward me.

"Ren," I whispered. As if he heard. As if he cared.

He paused, towering over me and smirking, delighting in my frozen expression. "I'll do you the honor of escorting you to the arena myself."

CHAPTER ELEVEN

Preston grasped my upper arm so tightly that it throbbed as we swept from the invitingly warm room, away from the piercing stares of countless fae. A winged woman bared her fangs at me as I walked past, reminding me of the man who'd tried to kill me not too long ago. I wondered if she was his family, and if she blamed me for his death.

She would just be one more enemy on my increasingly large list of those who wanted to use or murder me.

As King Preston led me through a door I hadn't noticed, hidden in a shadowy alcove, and dragged me down a winding set of stone steps, I finally found my words. "I never claimed to be a Silverfrost," I protested, my words echoing off the windowless walls. Torches flickered around us, their orange light dancing in Preston's bloody eyes.

Pausing on the steps, the king turned to face me. His grin was slow, malicious. "And yet, the people believe you did. We must honor our tradition and test your strength to see if the claim is true. We couldn't let someone with royal blood go unrecognized."

"But fae cannot lie."

"All it takes is a bit of clever phrasing to avoid an outright lie." Preston turned, yanking me further down the staircase. "When one is immortal, one has infinite time to expand one's wisdom and excel at deceit."

Desperation clawed through me, cold and hard like the ice I'd wielded. As intense as the avalanche I'd unleashed. But now, when I hoped for my magic to respond to my despair and terror, there was nothing. It was lost to me, even though I was outside of my room. Had the royal siblings used spells elsewhere within the castle, created with my blood? "What do you plan to do with me?"

"You'll fight in the arena to show off your strength of body, mind, and magic. Surely a Silverfrost on her own land in the height of winter would be most connected to her power now." He arched an eyebrow at me, his sidelong glance wicked. He *knew* I couldn't access my magic. He and his sister had planned this moment, all to send me to my execution in a very public display.

My stomach churned as we paused before a dark corridor where even the torchlight lining its walls seemed to barely touch the blackness writhing through the air. I caught a whiff of earth and blood and filth, like the passage dove deep into the bowels of the earth where unspeakable things took place. As if to punctuate my thought, a distant shriek split the air, echoing deep below us.

Gooseflesh rose on my arms.

"The dungeons," Preston said. "But that is not your fate, not today." He steered me away, toward a barred metal door flanked by two bored-looking guards.

"Your Majesty," one said, while each dipped low in respect.

The female guard on my left, with skin so pale it was nearly translucent and eyes and hair the shade of snow, stepped forward, eyeing me with disinterest.

Preston shoved me at her. "No weapons," he proclaimed.

The woman nodded, and Preston spun on his heel, disappearing the way he'd come.

"This isn't right," I pled. "I made no claim—"

Preston paused before the staircase, his eyes locking on mine. An unspoken threat lurked in his gaze. "Humans can be such liars, I'm afraid. She's learned the error of her bold claims too late, and now she is terrified. Don't listen to the way she begs."

Dipping her head in acknowledgement, the woman smiled slowly. "I wouldn't dream of doing so, Your Majesty," she said, her tone low and predatory. "She will make this fight entertaining for us, I hope."

As Preston's footsteps retreated, the male guard lumbered toward me. Based on his grey skin, bulky build, and overlarge features, I guessed he was an ogre or troll of some kind. "Little weakling, will you walk on your own with what dignity you have left?" he demanded, his voice rumbling so deeply I could feel it reverberate in my chest. "Or will you give us the thrill of the chase and force us to catch and drag you in?"

My knees trembled and my head spun, turning so light I wondered if the effects of the medicine Garrick had given me had worn off...or if I was that terrified. Numbly, I met the ogre's eyes, taking in his leering expression, and set my jaw. "I will walk."

Both guards launched forward, shoving the creaking metal door inward and then pinning me with twin glares. Somehow, I staggered toward the entryway, blinking at the way the firelight from the balconied floor above painted the stone arena floor in bloody hues.

This is what you do? Stumble meekly to your death without protest? Rage flared in my heart, a swirling storm that wouldn't be unleashed. It was trapped inside me, just like all my frustrated words of protest had always been back in Altidvale. Each unkind word. Each piece of gossip. I'd sat by and swallowed my pain and anger down, burying it beneath my calm exterior, pretending all was fine. If I'd made a scene, if I'd lost my temper, I would have only proven their fears right. They'd seen me as dangerous and unlike them.

How true they'd ended up being.

But now? Now I was among monsters who'd rendered me powerless.

I walked and pretended I had a shred of dignity to care about, praying all the while to the distant gods that there was a way out of this.

Or maybe this was my path to freedom. Maybe my only chance in the cruel world of Brytwilde was to give in to death. At least this way, I wouldn't be enslaved or tormented. I would be able to see my mother and stepfather again in the afterlife.

Tears blurred my vision, but I blinked them away. If death was to be my fate, I could accept it.

But I wouldn't face it without trying to fight, even if I didn't have the faintest idea how to defend myself in an arena.

I curled my fingers into fists at my sides as I stepped out into the empty arena. Curved walls, smooth and plain, encircled every side...except for the one opposite me, which bore a heavy metal door matching the one I'd walked through. When I peered upward, I found the countless fae above gawking at me from their comfortable chairs, which they'd pulled away from the tables to move closer to the railing. Some jeered or taunted, clearly eager to see me die. Others were quieter, more contemplative. Maybe they thought there was some truth to my alleged claim of being a Silverfrost.

My eyes skimmed over King Preston and Queen Nerissa, with their soulless eyes boring into me, and snagged on Garrick. I didn't want to seek him out in the crowd, didn't want my heart to skip when I saw him. But I found him anyway, and my heart jolted in spite of myself. His gaze was steady on mine, that expressionless mask concealing whatever he was thinking or feeling.

Please, I thought, begging him to understand me, to read my desperate expression. *You defended me before. Show me I'm more than prey you were ordered to fetch. Show me you truly do care. That the man I thought I knew wasn't a lie...*

He remained silent, motionless. Nothing more than another observer to the entertainment the royal siblings had prepared. The storm within roared ever louder, full of aching pain that provided a sharper edge to my anger and fear. I tried again to draw on the magic in my veins, but it felt trapped—contained inside my body. Something was wrong, and I was going to die because of it.

Behind me, the door slammed shut, making me jump.

"Good citizens of Silverfrost," Queen Nerissa began, standing and strolling toward the edge. She leaned over, her dark hair cascading over one shoulder as she peered at me, her lips curling in a chilling smile. "I do hope you enjoy the test we have prepared for our honored guest. As you know, anyone who claims Silverfrost blood must prove their worthiness. You have heard the rumors about this mere mortal's powerful magic."

As Queen Nerissa droned on about their revered traits of strength and ability and power, how I'd have to face my opponents as I was—weaponless, with only the magic I bore—I tried to steady my breathing and focus. Garrick couldn't be trusted, but as a fae, he also couldn't outright lie. And he'd told me my magic would be easier to access on this land. That it would be a natural extension of my thoughts and emotions. Maybe the royals had interfered with my magic, but it still lived in me, did it not? Surely, with enough effort, I could access it.

When I'd caused the avalanche, I'd feared for my life and Garrick's. I hadn't been able to control and hold back the power. When the winged fae man had attacked me, the ice I'd locked him within had come almost effortlessly.

Yet nothing was coming to me now, when I was awaiting death to pour forth from the opposite door and murder me in a spectacle before all these onlookers.

A tremble started in my fingers, rippling through my body. Did the siblings actually think I *was* a Silverfrost, and that was why they'd used forget-me-nots on me? Had my father been a *royal fae?* Were they trying to protect their power, their places on the throne, by murdering me this way?

Did they truly see *me* as a threat to their throne?

My mind whirled with the questions, but I didn't have time to consider them. The door across from me swung inward, and not one but several opponents launched into the arena. I tensed, a fierce desire to live spiking in my chest. Even if I wasn't sure what I was holding onto.

If I survived, what new torments would these siblings invent for me?

Swallowing my fear, I held my ground, refusing to allow the jeering crowd to see me retreat. There was nowhere to flee, anyway.

"A human thinking she's a Silverfrost? The gall!" someone spat, so loudly I could hear past the screams and shouts piercing the air.

I tried to block it all out, tried to ignore the chant growing as more and more fae cried: *Kill the mortal!*

But my stomach dropped when I paused, allowing myself to study my opponents, who'd scattered and spread out throughout the arena, apparently hoping to hem me in.

They were all human. Every single one of them stared ahead with glazed eyes, not really seeing this arena or me. Not truly aware of what they were even doing.

My mouth dried. I couldn't kill glamoured humans, not even if they were being forced to attack and murder me. Even if I found a way to fight back without magic, how could I spill their blood to save myself? I'd be a murderer. They were innocent.

They were...

They were armed with weapons, each one of them bearing a glinting sword or pair of daggers. One man lifted a heavy axe with both arms.

"Come here, little girl," the man with the axe taunted, and I had the chilling impression that his lips were moving, but someone else was speaking.

I gritted my teeth, studying the four humans who were stalking closer, each staring through me with empty expressions. Though they were slaves to the royal siblings and probably ill-treated, they weren't malnourished or weak. Perhaps they were trained and used as regular entertainment in fights like these, for both men and even the two women were toned and muscled, moving with graceful steps.

My head felt light. Women didn't fight in Altidvale. It was unheard of. And in proper society, men didn't hurl punches at one another or engage in bloodthirsty fights with onlookers. Only when one gentleman challenged another to a duel. I didn't even know how to incapacitate these armed men and women, let alone kill them.

And this was a fight to the death. If they didn't die, I would.

Footsteps pounded closer as I pled for my magic to manifest. *Come on*, I thought. *You run through my blood. You are a part of me. Defend me now.*

I drew on my fear, imagining ice crackling from my fingertips and coating the arena floor.

Sweat dripped down my spine as the axe-wielding man stepped forward, grinning. The other three fell back, allowing him his moment to attack. He leered closer, and I stumbled away, head spinning.

Overhead, the fae were laughing, the roar of their cheers and mocking cries so loud I couldn't hear my own breath anymore. Couldn't hear my own pulse. I could only sense it throbbing in my throat and in my head.

The man swung, a flash of blood-red steel in the torchlight.

I swallowed my scream and threw myself to the floor, my knees and palms stinging when they slammed against stone.

Snarling, the man stepped nearer, giving me just enough time to realize the foolishness of my action. Now I was on my hands and knees, an easy target without a simple route of escape. Towering over me, the man surprised me when he didn't swing his weapon again.

Instead, he aimed a kick at my side. My cry of pain was lost as all the air left my body. I choked and collapsed, my torso throbbing and my chest terrifyingly empty. Spots flickered in my vision while the man laughed, dropping the axe with a clang. I couldn't move swiftly enough—he seized me in both hands, continuing to laugh. I gaped at his face, which remained expressionless even as that awful, mocking chuckle rumbled through his chest. His eyes were empty as they met mine. This wasn't him killing me, but the fae controlling his movements, his choices, even his words.

Air rushed into my lungs, providing a moment of blessed relief, and I thrashed in the man's iron grip, but it was too late. He hurled me across the arena with unnatural strength. I heard the crack of bone as I landed hard, pain ripping through me. Nausea danced along my tongue as I skidded along the smooth floor.

Ice. Snow. Rip this world apart, I begged. Nothing but a moan escaped my lips. Spikes of hot agony flared everywhere, and darkness swam before my eyes. Blood trickled from my nose and into my mouth, filling it with the taste of copper and my rising bile. I couldn't hear anything but the screams of the crowd now.

I was barely aware when the humans encircled me, weapons raised.

My terror peaked, shredding through me with a helpless certainty. This was the end, and I'd meet it because my brother hated and feared me and left me to die at the hands of these monsters. I'd taste death while these heartless fae looked on, laughing and applauding like this was nothing more than a play at the theater. I'd be murdered in front of Garrick, the man who'd once protected me, but now couldn't even bother to move from his position beside Queen Nerissa.

Pain flooded me, and somehow, even amidst the blackness flooding my vision, even with my opponents towering over me, my eyes found Garrick in the crowd and locked on him. He leaned forward, his white-blond hair bright in the darkness enveloping my world. His jaw feathered, and for an instant, I thought maybe his gold eyes flashed with emotion. It had to be a trick of the flickering light, because his face remained chiseled as if from stone.

The man with the axe stepped nearer and swung.

I screamed.

In fear.

In agony.

In defeat.

In *fury*.

The air crackled and something cold and solid filled my hand. The man cried out, his gaping mouth revealing blood coating his teeth and dribbling down his chin. I blinked at the shard of ice clutched in my hand, honed perfectly into a sharp blade. He'd launched himself onto its tip as he'd lunged to deal a killing blow. The ice pierced him clean through—a fatal strike to his chest.

Blinking, his glazed blue eyes cleared, finding mine. There was shock and sorrow there as his arms fell and his fingers went limp. He dropped the axe with a clatter. For one awful, endless moment, we stared at one another. The pain and betrayal and confusion in his bright eyes nearly undid me.

Then he slumped forward, dead at my hands.

A wave of dizziness and darkness swept over me as more agony flashed through me, reminding me of my injuries. I was going to lose consciousness. I'd murdered an innocent man, and it still wouldn't be enough.

The trio of remaining humans stepped closer amidst screams and boos from the fae crowd. I struggled to sit up, to move at all, but my body refused to obey me. Weakness and pain flooded me in equal measures, and my grip on my ice blade slackened. It and the man pierced upon it both fell to the floor, useless.

My ears rang as the world slipped away from me. I was proving my mortal weakness to my hateful onlookers, and the glamoured humans were going to murder me while I was helpless. *Mother? Father? Are you waiting for me?* I wondered.

As I faded, I thought I heard a shout, louder and deeper than any of the others echoing through the arena. *"Enough!"* Snarling and screams filled my ears. Something white tore across my vision, something that made the floor shudder with its pounding footsteps and rumbling growls. But I couldn't tell what was happening as everything went dark and still.

CHAPTER TWELVE

I opened my eyes to a familiar bedroom of stone, the high window to my right admitting a watery light that told me it couldn't be past mid-morning. Every inch of my body ached, but it was a relief compared to the sharp agony of earlier. At least an entire night had passed, and somehow, I was still alive. I tried to brush the blanket back and sit up to survey the damage to my body, but a voice interrupted me.

"I wouldn't do that if I were you," a woman said in a smooth tone. "Though," she added with a chuckle, "I don't know the first thing that goes through you mortals' heads."

Turning, I found a tall, slender fae woman seated in the chair at my bedside. Lovely golden hair framed her pale, angular face, while her full lips twisted in a bemused smile. It didn't seem entirely kind, but there wasn't any open hostility about her either. Her eyes were an unusual shade of turquoise, bright and cunning as her gaze slid over me.

On her shoulder sat a pixie, lounging as if she regularly reclined on others. Her curls hung loose, framing a face with a dark complexion and rich brown eyes. They glittered with mischief, reminding me of all the stories I'd been told about pixies and their fun, carefree ways. She made me feel a little more at ease, while her golden-haired friend made me nervous.

"What—what happened?" I whispered, my words sounding raspy as I pushed them out of my raw throat. My mouth was dry, and the ache as I spoke reminded me of my screams in the arena. "Who are you?"

The golden-haired fae crossed her legs primly, drawing my attention to the fact that she was clothed in some form of tight trousers and a tunic rather than a dress. I frowned at the strange sight. "You can call me Isolde, and this is Aspen," she said, gesturing toward the pixie on her shoulder.

"I'm a healer, so I was sent to tend to you. The magic was especially taxing on your frail human body."

I didn't protest, for she was right.

"Why am I not dead?" I asked. Had they sent Isolde to heal me only so they could put me through some new trial that would finish me off?

Isolde pursed her lips, looking as if she'd tasted something sour. "You displayed powerful winter magic, hinting at the possibility that you could indeed possess Silverfrost blood...despite your mortality." Her forehead scrunched.

Aspen hopped off Isolde's shoulder, walking across her lap and settling on the edge of my bed. "It was quite a sight." She sat, crossing her legs and resting her chin in one hand. Like Isolde, she wore fitted trousers and a tunic in bright, cheerful colors at odds with the dull winter light filtering through my window. "Slaying that human with a spear of ice? Impressive. We haven't seen magic like that in...well, decades."

Bile filled my mouth at the memory. The man's final look pierced my thoughts, filling my head with the painful image. His confusion. His hurt. His sorrow. He'd been nothing more than a tool in fae hands, and I had ended his life.

Did he hate me in those last moments? Or had he found relief in being freed of the control?

I swallowed back a building sob, knowing these fae wouldn't sympathize with my guilt.

"The way Garrick Darkgrove came to your rescue was also something I haven't seen the likes of in years," Aspen added, a mischievous glint in her eyes.

"What?"

"Once you displayed your magic and killed the first human, he became a bit...unhinged." Isolde shrugged. "Usually the hunter is calm and in control, and it's so rare for us to see him in his wolf form. But he is loyal to the crown, so I suppose his reaction last night was to be expected. He was the first to intervene, no doubt when he realized the extent of the magic you'd wielded. He transformed and killed the other mortals before they could harm you further."

Despite Isolde's earlier warning, I sat up, too overcome with this news. Garrick *had* intervened for me? But according to the fae, it was only because I was valuable. My *power* was valuable. Not because he cared.

"Of course," Isolde continued, "King Preston and Queen Nerissa realized Garrick was right to stop the humans, and they called on me to tend to you, to piece you back together." She studied me thoughtfully. "Two broken ribs and some fractured bones in your wrist. How easily that man shattered you. It's strange to imagine that such power could reside in such a pathetic frame."

I swallowed my indignation, but my throat was so dry, I proved Isolde's comment accurate by choking on my own saliva and falling into a coughing fit.

"She probably needs water," Aspen piped up, tossing Isolde a look.

Isolde stood, sweeping toward a side table that had been set up beside my bed, full of a pitcher, glasses, and a tray of food. She poured me a glass of water and handed it over.

As I swallowed, Isolde settled back in her chair, waving a careless hand toward me. "You slept two full nights and a day healing those bones, and you'll probably remain a bit tender for a few more days."

I stared, processing her words. No wonder my stomach ached with a hunger that nearly matched the pain in my muscles and bones. Each breath I drew sent an ache through my torso, reminding me of my still-healing ribs.

But I was alive. I sat up further, trying to turn to inspect the tray of food, but a wave of pain jolted through me, and I cringed.

"Not everyone is convinced you have Silverfrost blood," Aspen observed.

"What does this mean?" I asked, head pounding. "Did I pass the test? Are there more?"

Isolde arched a brow. "You passed the test...barely. Most of the court is convinced you must have some drop of Silverfrost blood in your veins to be able to wield winter magic in such a way. Creating a blade from ice *is* impressive," she added, almost begrudgingly. "However, this doesn't change the fact that you are a mere mortal. And nothing will be certain until the winter solstice, when we will find out if your blood can truly close the entrance to the underworld and keep the undead and demons at bay."

"In the meantime, we are here to prepare you, now that you're awake," Aspen announced, standing and setting her hands on her hips. "And we haven't any time to lose, as you're in rough shape. It's going to take a while."

"Prepare me?"

Isolde rolled her eyes. "We don't have time for ridiculous questions. The king and queen called for you, of course." She pointed to the tray, which I was finally able to turn and study. There was a bowl of fresh sugared berries alongside some pastries, eggs, and thick slices of bacon. "This food was delivered recently, once we noticed you were stirring more in your sleep. Eat quickly."

Isolde and Aspen chattered about various court gossip as I shoveled food into my mouth, delighted by how delicious and fresh everything tasted. As soon as my ravenous hunger was abated, the women scurried me into the washroom and into a steaming bath. I could have relaxed and soaked in it for a long time, relishing the way the hot water soothed my aching body, but Isolde remained impatient. She dressed me in a simple silver gown, overlaid with a corset that she laced so tightly I cringed as it tugged against my ribs.

"Drink this," Isolde said, plucking a vial from her pocket.

I frowned at it as she steered me toward a chair by the fire. "What is this?"

"It'll help with the pain." She raised her eyebrows at me. "Healer, remember? Don't tell me mortals are *that* forgetful."

Ignoring the jab, I settled into the armchair, gulped down the bitter tonic, and sat still as Isolde coiled my hair into a complicated braid atop my head. Meanwhile, Aspen gracefully climbed the chair to perch on the arm, setting a small bag before her. "Now close your eyes and don't move," she said.

Obeying, I felt her climb up and down my dress sleeve, perching on one shoulder and then the other as she swept various brushes and other cosmetic tools across my features.

"Lovely!" Isolde proclaimed at last, allowing me to stand and ushering me toward the door. She pointed at a pair of boots, and I stepped into them. When I hesitated, my pain flaring when I tried and failed to crouch down to reach the laces, Isolde sighed and kneeled to tie them herself. As she straightened, she scanned my face. "Good work, Aspen."

"My work is always perfect," Aspen retorted.

"You must hurry," Isolde went on when I hesitated at the door in confusion. "Darkgrove will be your escort. There's no time for you to go gawk at yourself in the mirror, though I suppose for a plain human you'd be amazed what we were able to do for you." She rolled her eyes.

Without another word or any further explanation, she turned the knob and gently but firmly shoved me out the door.

I blinked up at the flickering chandelier overhead, filling a stone hallway that would otherwise be austere with buttery light. Before I could move, Garrick stepped forward from a shadowy alcove beside a tapestry depicting a brutal war, extending a heavy fur coat toward me.

"What is this for?" I asked.

Garrick himself was clothed in a fur coat that hung to his thighs and trousers tucked into heavy leather boots. Contrary to the cold expression he'd worn the last time I'd seen him, the night I'd been forced into the arena, a bit of warmth flared in his eyes. Was he relieved to see me well? His gaze skated over my form. "To stay warm, Starlight. Unless you've learned how to wield fire magic as well."

I swallowed, trying to reconcile the man before me—the one who reminded me of the friend who'd protected and flirted with me—with the one who'd watched me stone-faced while I'd walked into the arena. Silently, I slipped my arms into the coat and buttoned it up as Garrick started strolling down the hall, clearly expecting me to follow.

Thankfully, the vial Isolde had given me had finally taken effect, dulling the pain in my ribs so that my movements and breaths were no longer accompanied with a throbbing, stabbing sensation. I picked up my pace, my silver skirt swishing around me as I trailed Garrick down a long flight, our steps muted on the heavy carpet. The castle itself was quiet, full of the dull grey light of winter. Each window we passed afforded a view of a land freshly laden in snow, the clouds that shrouded the sun promising even more snow.

"We're leaving the castle?" I ventured, trying to ignore how weak I still felt as we reached the end of the stairs only to enter another hall that seemed to stretch on forever. Hope, brittle as it was, swelled in my chest, and my mind sifted through possibilities. Leaving the castle could provide more opportunities to escape, and though I wasn't as adept at using my magic as I'd like, maybe there were fae out there who would be kind to me when they saw the power I possessed. If the citizens of Silverfrost thought I might have royal blood, maybe they'd be willing to help me.

Or maybe they'd do anything in their ability to force me to stay, desperate for my blood to hold back the creatures of the underworld from flooding into their land.

Garrick slowed his steps enough that I was able to match his strides, coming alongside him. He shot me a furtive glance, his expression neutral, yet not cold. My absurd heart twinged in response. "Yes, we are venturing outside, to the capital city. The people are eager to meet you, and the king and queen have agreed you should."

Nerves danced in my stomach. Somehow I didn't believe that they were truly happy about my surviving their arena and tricks. Maybe they planned to murder me in some other public way beyond the castle walls.

I shoved it aside and searched Garrick's face. "You saved me."

Something like fear darted across his expression. "It was the least I could do."

I swallowed. "Did you do it for them?"

He stepped closer, his eyes desperate, and opened his mouth.

But whatever he'd meant to say wasn't meant to be. At the end of the hall, a pair of guards opened a set of carved double doors leading into a great hall. Garrick jerked away from me. "Come," he said, striding toward the hall's entrance.

Heart throbbing with a confusing mixture of hope and hurt, I obeyed. The hall was full of warm hearths burning brightly and countless tables and chairs where fae were deep in conversation. Servants—both fae and glamoured humans—strolled back and forth, carrying trays or relaying messages. Heavily armed guards lined the walls.

At the far end was a dais with two exquisitely carved thrones of white birchwood, but both sat empty.

"Miss Cantwell." King Preston's voice caused a feeling to skitter down my spine akin to the sensation of ice melting along skin. "Or perhaps I should say...Miss Silverfrost?"

I turned to find him and his sister behind us, clothed in lavish fur robes, their crowns sparkling in their dark hair. A longsword was strapped to Preston's back, while Nerissa bore no weapons that I could see. She was in another sweeping gown, though this one was pinned up on one side, revealing heavy boots that indicated she, too, was ready for travel.

Meeting King Preston's bloody gaze, I dipped my head in silent respect. "I have always been Miss Cantwell, and that is the name I am comfortable answering to," I said diplomatically.

Queen Nerissa laughed, the sound rich yet haunting. She studied me like one would eye a bug pinned beneath them. "It's true we aren't entirely convinced of your bloodline just yet, though your magical display in the arena was impressive."

King Preston shrugged and extended his arm toward me.

I bit back the urge to grimace as I took it and let him sweep me close to his side. Dipping his head, he whispered in my ear, the unwelcome sensation of his tickling breath making me flinch. "Try anything, and we'll set our wolf on you. It's your blood that makes you important, mortal, and that is all. Don't grow too comfortable."

Revulsion swept through me as Preston tugged me down the hall toward another set of doors, which a pair of guards pulled inward with a heavy groan. Icy wind bit my cheeks and deposited snowflakes in my hair as we descended a set of stone stairs leading into a courtyard. Already, servants stood beside a cluster of horses that were stomping their hooves and snorting in the cold air. While Queen Nerissa and an assortment of servants and attendants mounted their own steeds—including, I noted, Isolde, who must have hurriedly dressed after preparing me—King Preston released my arm and gestured toward a horse.

"Am I to have my own mount then?" I asked, trying to keep my tone even and disinterested as Preston approached a fine black stallion.

He laughed as he swung effortlessly into the saddle, his gaze cutting into me like a knife. "Not at all." He nodded to Garrick.

"My faithful dog will be watching you," Queen Nerissa supplied, tossing her long hair over one shoulder. In the soft winter light, her pale skin and sharp cheekbones were even more harshly beautiful. "That way if you have any unfortunate ideas of abandoning your people, *Your Majesty*, you'll have a hunter on your trail."

Garrick's expression was stony as he approached the dappled gelding. It bore no saddle, only a thick blanket draped over its back. When he glanced down at me, offering his hand, my heart lodged in my throat.

"I've never ridden without a saddle," I protested weakly, but the human servant had already reached for my dress, lifting it to the side and expertly pinning it up. Unfortunately, that left far more of my leg bare than I was comfortable with, leaving my skin exposed to the frigid air.

"A little cold, but that's what your furs are for," Queen Nerissa said when she saw me cringe.

Swallowing, I turned to Garrick, who set his hands on my waist. A gasp lodged in my throat at the sudden touch, and I was thankful for the gloves he wore that provided an extra layer between us. Still, the warmth of his body seeped into me immediately, and I couldn't ignore the jolt of awareness that spread over me. As he set me on the horse's back, he leapt easily behind me and accepted the reins from the servant. I tried to move forward, fighting to put distance between Garrick and me.

But that was impossible. There was only enough room for me to sit flush against him, my back pressed to his chest. His warmth enveloped me, chasing away the chill as his arms wrapped around me to secure the reins and lead the gelding. I was effectively in his embrace, all too aware of his every heartbeat and every breath as his chest rose and fell behind me.

As the gates creaked open, our horses cantered out of the courtyard, their hooves clattering against the cobblestones.

Embarrassed, I leaned away, trying to let the winter breeze cool the flush in my cheeks. Hoping to distract myself, I tried to focus on my surroundings rather than the man seated far too close to me.

Beyond the iron gates was a twisting stone road made precarious with its slick layers of ice and snow, especially when it dipped downward, toward the foot of the mountain. But as we slowed to a leisurely pace, I found the view was stunning, affording glimpses of nearby snow-capped peaks.

Pine trees added jolts of bright green color to the landscape and filled the air with their fresh scent. Far below, our destination crouched beside the lake I'd spotted my first day here, just a smooth sheet of ice dusted with snow. Chimney smoke curled up from the rows of snow-powdered homes, looking inviting in a way I hoped wasn't deceptive.

As we rounded our first bend, I tried to shuffle away from Garrick even more.

"Trying to fall off the horse?" Garrick teased, his voice rumbling in his chest until I could feel it against my back. He tightened his arms, pulling me against him.

I squirmed, failing to get away and only sliding backward. I hadn't thought I could fall any closer to Garrick, and yet I did, until I was nearly in his lap.

My face burned with embarrassment and frustration. I was supposed to be furious with this man. My mind screamed that I couldn't trust him. But I couldn't forget that he was the one who'd come to my rescue repeatedly, who'd tenderly carried me from danger. The one who'd joined me in studying the stars. The one who'd looked at me like I mattered.

"This is...unbecoming for a lady," I whispered fiercely. Glancing over my shoulder, I found myself startlingly close to Garrick's face, his breath warm against my cheeks as his mouth twisted in a smirk.

"No one cares here. They only want to know you won't leave Silver-frost, and that means they want you as close to me as you can be."

"To ensure I don't escape?"

Was that regret in Garrick's eyes, melting the lighthearted grin that had concealed his cares? I wasn't sure, didn't know what I could trust about him anymore. He looked as if he wanted to say something, but like earlier, he didn't.

"If I promise not to run," I pressed, "could I have my own horse?"

As if the pained look had never existed, Garrick's eyes shone once again with mischief. He bent his head until his chin rested on my shoulder, his lips brushing against the shell of my ear. The scents of leather and fur wrapped around me. "Then I wouldn't have the pleasure of your company."

Against my will, my stomach flipped, and my whole body tingled pleasantly from his close proximity. "You betrayed my trust, Mr. Darkgrove," I said. My gaze darted about, ensuring that no one riding before or beside us could hear our quiet conversation, though I wasn't sure if their fae hearing would pick up what a human's could not. "*And* you told me before you weren't flirting with me. It certainly sounds as if you are now."

"I may have said I was *trying* not to flirt, Starlight, but you're awfully fun to tease."

I didn't know what to make of this man, or the conflicting emotions he stirred within me. "I'm not speaking to you anymore."

We rode on in silence to the foot of the mountain, our pace picking up once we reached the flat path leading into the city. The scents of woodsmoke, roasted meat, and sweet pastries wafted on the breeze, making my stomach grumble even though I'd had my fill at breakfast. Sleeping and healing for so long had left me ravenous.

King Preston pulled his stallion up beside Garrick's and mine as we neared the first cluster of homes nestled on the outskirts of the city, a collection of wood cabins alongside grand estates of fine stonework. "Your people are eager to see you, Florentia," Preston murmured, his gaze cutting to mine.

I swallowed. "I prefer Ren." My voice was quiet, meek. I wished I had the courage to make it stronger, more commanding.

Preston arched a brow in silent question, while behind me, Garrick stiffened. The king leaned over, lowering his tone so that only Garrick and I could hear. "Your preferences don't matter, mortal. We'll test you again...and even if you do prove to have Silverfrost heritage, you are still a lowly human. Unworthy of the crown. As I said before, the only thing important about you is your blood. The people may celebrate you, but most of us see you for what you are: pathetic, with a short life with little meaning."

As he sat back in his saddle, plastering on a fake smile, I turned away, feeling that angry storm building within me again. Unfortunately, my magic was once again distant, leaving nothing but an ache in my bones.

I scanned the area, but unless forget-me-nots could influence magic without one directly touching them—in which case, the other fae would be affected too—I saw no sign of any nearby. So why was my magic so difficult to wield, when before it had come so naturally? I might not have known how to control it well, but I'd been able to manifest it easily enough.

My thoughts scattered as we entered the city proper, where, despite the frigid air, countless people were gathered around fire pits along the road, cheering and waving silver ribbons. I blinked, shocked when I realized the name they were shouting was mine.

Or close to mine.

"Florentia Silverfrost!" they cried, fae of every color and size beaming at me as if my blood truly could hold back the creatures of the underworld.

Everywhere, cozy shops and cottages were adorned in sheets of ice, some appearing magical and impossible, as if they'd been carved from blocks of ice themselves. Others reminded me of miniature snow-capped mountains, their floors topped with rocky peaks and their cavernous entrances adorned by engraved doors or sparkling sheets of ice. A few others seemed to be only made of snow, pure white and almost blinding to look at, crafted in beautiful layers.

Despite their cozy homes, it appeared every citizen was gathered outside, strumming instruments, dancing, or roasting spits of meat or fruits.

"It's a celebration, all in your honor," King Preston muttered, just loudly enough that I could hear over the music and the shouts. "Smile and relish it, *Your Majesty.* Our court knows how powerless you truly are."

I pursed my lips as Garrick tensed again, but he didn't say anything. *If you despise me, why keep me alive?* I wanted to demand of Preston, but the crowd was growing louder the deeper we wound into the city, and I wasn't sure he'd hear me if I tried to speak. Besides, the answer was in front of me. I was a symbol of hope for the people of Silverfrost, and if Preston and Nerissa killed me without covering it up in some way, their citizens would likely revolt.

My skin prickled as I scanned the countless people—a woman with butterfly wings, a man with antlers, pixies like Aspen dancing on top of a box outside of a shop, and green-skinned children laughing and tossing snowballs at one another. These people were my power. Maybe they wouldn't help me escape, but would they help me gain my freedom in some other way? As long as the citizens of Silverfrost loved me, I had a modicum of strength against the cruel fae who owned me.

Once we reached the town square, Preston and Nerissa paused our procession and lifted their hands, calling for silence. Everywhere, people hushed to listen, wings fluttering, tails flickering, and faun hooves stomping. A sprite alighted on a nearby fountain, its water drained for the frozen months.

"Citizens of Northelm, words cannot express our joy at seeing your festivity and happiness today," Queen Nerissa began, her words echoing off the walls around us. "It gives us great hope to know that there is a possibility a member of our dear Silverfrost royal line survived, and that we may have found that survivor at last."

Cheers arose, their thunder reverberating in my chest. I swallowed and shifted in the saddle, uncomfortable with the attention from the countless eyes boring into me. Most seemed reverent, but a few looked greedy, as if they, like Preston, only saw me for the blood I carried. The tool I could be.

Garrick's arms tightened around me, though I wasn't sure if he meant the motion to be comforting or restraining, keeping me from running.

Like I had anywhere to go.

"Though Miss Florentia Cantwell's magical display in our castle arena showed great promise, we know we would be remiss if we didn't ensure she was who she claims to be before we celebrate fully. We unfortunately have days of waiting left until the winter solstice, when she could use her blood to seal the entrance to the underworld and erase all our doubts with her enduring protection. I expect you to remain here in Silverfrost for this grand occasion to celebrate, rather than partaking of your usual revels in the human city of Altidvale."

This time there was scattered applause. Men and women glanced at one another in confusion and doubt. I could practically read their thoughts: *If our queen isn't certain she is a Silverfrost, have we begun to hope too soon?*

"Thankfully, we need not wait that long. She can prove herself before then. As you know, we already have creatures of the underworld in our midst, the ones who slip through our unsealed door each night." Quiet and fear, so heavy it felt like a tangible thing weighing the air, settled over the crowd. "Florentia Cantwell can prove her mettle in another trial."

Queen Nerissa turned toward me, her smile wide. Though some might have seen the look as admiring and respectful, a proud queen eager to welcome a long-lost royal, I saw right through the façade. She was only eager to see me fail. Her dark red eyes sparkled with glee. "Just as her ancestors managed to do before her, fulfilling their duty to protect our people, Florentia will incapacitate an underworld creature."

CHAPTER THIRTEEN

My heart pulsed in my throat, making it difficult for me to swallow or even breathe. The numbing effects of the tonic Isolde had given me seemed to already be wearing off, making my ribs ache with every step, every gasping breath.

The inn's hallway was cozy and inviting, its floor cushioned in thick carpet and its walls adorned with countless burning lanterns to brighten the dim light of winter spilling through the windows. Crackling fires burned in each room we passed, where various fae cleaning the vacant spaces paused to bow or curtsey in our direction.

And all the while, the city's celebrations continued outside, the music and singing and laughter following us even into the inn.

King Preston sidled up behind me, placing a hand on my lower back. I struggled not to gag. "You can prepare here," he said, gesturing toward a closed door before us, "and rest if you choose. Or you can join the celebration." He grinned, as if at some private joke. I wondered if he was inwardly laughing at the thought of me participating in a party that precluded my death.

"Prepare?" I demanded.

After Queen Nerissa's proclamation, she'd bid the citizens continue their partying and feasting for the rest of the day until it came time for my next test, which would take place tonight. Then she'd led our entire group toward this inn, where apparently I was to...prepare.

"Well, you can celebrate in that," he said, his bloody eyes skimming the silver dress and too-tight corset Isolde had bound me in, "but I imagine you don't want to fight a demon in it." He shrugged. "Though the choice is yours. You're the one with royal blood, after all. Your wish is our command."

Fury lanced through my chest at his lazy smile. My eyes flicked around the hall. Queen Nerissa and the others had remained downstairs, sitting by the fire, likely prepared to enjoy the festivities, but Garrick had trailed after Preston and me. He leaned against the wall, arms crossed over his broad chest, watching us blankly as if our discussion meant nothing to him. Courage gathered in my heart, fueled by my anger and desperation. Quiet obedience would do nothing for me now. "Hardly. You *own* me, and you're clearly trying to kill me. What happens if I truly am a Silverfrost, but the fact that you're somehow stifling my magic means I die tonight? What about my blood then?"

"So, the quiet human has found her voice. Charming." Preston stepped closer, his hand seizing my neck, wrenching my gaze up toward his.

My ears rang. His cold fingers didn't squeeze enough to stop my airflow—only enough to remind me that I was his prisoner.

"If you die tonight, then I suppose that means you'll spill all your blood for your kingdom, and we'll collect it," he snapped. He released me, and I stumbled back. "Garrick, keep an eye on her," Preston demanded, storming back down the hall.

My mind whirled. What Preston had said had to be an idle threat, or he and his sister wouldn't have bothered to keep me alive this long. Or so I assumed. But that line of reasoning didn't assuage my fear.

I didn't wait to see if Garrick moved from his position against the wall before I lunged for the door, turning the knob and hurrying into the solitude of my room. A tunic and a pair of the same type of tight-fitting trousers Aspen and Isolde had worn rested on the bed, while a fire crackled merrily in the hearth.

Eyes burning, I clicked the door shut and strode past the fireplace, the fur-covered bed, and the side table laden with a pitcher of water and a tray of refreshments. I stopped before the window, staring out at my view of the outskirts of town, where the landscape stretched toward an imposing mountain. My gaze scanned upward, snagging on a fortress perched on a cliffside. Its stone walls appeared high and impenetrable. Its iron gates were securely shut.

The sound of the door opening and closing behind me made me stiffen. I sucked in another breath, trying to still my racing heart, and another wave of aching pain roared through me. Had my corset grown tighter?

"I don't need help getting ready—not from you," I murmured, crossing my arms and staring resolutely out the window. It was a childish thought: that if I refused to turn and look at him, he'd leave me alone. He wouldn't have the power to hurt me anymore. Deep down, I knew that was impossible. He'd been ordered to hunt me down, and now he had been ordered to ensure I didn't run. Ever the loyal dog, he wouldn't be going anywhere.

"Thinking about running?" Garrick's tone was cool and even, completely at odds with the man who'd teased me on horseback earlier.

The storm building inside me broke free, just a little. I turned, lifting my chin defiantly. "Maybe I am."

"You wouldn't get far." There was no threat in his voice, no animosity in his gold eyes. He was only stating a fact.

"I'd inconvenience you."

"Oh," Garrick said, prowling closer. I swallowed, noting that, backed against the window, there was nowhere else for me to go. "You're not hoping to escape then? Only *inconvenience* me?"

I ignored his question, answering with one of my own. "Would you have stood by and watched Preston strangle me?"

Garrick's expression was a mask, his eyes empty. "He didn't."

"Do you even think for yourself, or are you such a faithful servant you're merely his puppet?"

He surged forward, setting his hands on my shoulders, startling me into staring up at his face. Warmth lurked in the depths of his gaze, sparking a foolish, lingering ember of hope in my heart. "I didn't like that he put his hands on you," Garrick confessed, his words a growl. It reminded me of his wolf side, and it made my skin prickle. "I—" He struggled to speak. "I hate what he does to you. I wanted to break his fingers one by one."

Don't believe him, I urged myself, even as my heart thundered at his touch, at the look in his eyes. The coldness was melting away, exposing something raw and vulnerable. Something that looked like...concern. Maybe even more.

I shook my head, both to clear it and to deny his words. "Then why didn't you? Why serve them at all? Why not help me escape to Ashwood as we'd planned?"

Sorrow pooled in Garrick's eyes. "There is no escaping."

"Because you're keeping me here on their orders."

He grasped my shoulders more tightly, and I froze, staring into his eyes. "There is no escaping for *either* of us. They have many hunters. You met some of them—were injured by one."

My mind tried to comprehend his words. *No escaping for* either *of us.* Wasn't he a willing servant?

Garrick's fingers curled into the fabric of my sleeves, holding me firmly. I couldn't tell if he was trying to hold me close or restrain me. "I'm not saying to never run. I'm only saying that tonight—tonight I don't know if even you could make it. Not when the entire city is waiting to see you. And now that word is spreading about your Silverfrost blood...the other kingdoms might not be so friendly."

My breath hitched. "What do you mean?"

"Every kingdom in Brytwilde has a tenuous relationship with one another. Many fae crave power—a taste of magic makes them want more, and any royal who overtook another kingdom's throne would gain some of the magic of that land. It means, though we trade peacefully to share resources and send diplomats and play at polite politics often, we are often at war with various kingdoms, just like we're at war with Ashwood now. It means that no kingdom would ever trust the ruler of another if they set foot unannounced on their land."

"So Ashwood might not welcome me?"

Garrick's brow pinched. "It's hard to be certain, but they would have as many reasons to suspect you as to believe you. It was uncertain enough when you were a human crossing the border while they're at war. But now that you're the rightful queen of the kingdom they're fighting? You could be running toward new enemies."

The world spun, and I couldn't tell if it was from the way my corset pinched my painful ribs, turning my breaths shallow, or from my own fear. I felt more trapped than ever before. If I escaped, I could very well be running from one deadly situation to another. *If* I survived the harsh climate with only the barely-formed skills Garrick had taught me.

Garrick released my shoulders and stepped back, ducking to peer into my face, but I avoided him, stumbling back and leaning against the windowsill. My ribs throbbed. I couldn't breathe, couldn't think clearly. "Are you truly their prisoner, or are you trying to confuse me?"

There was a pause. "I'm limited in what I can say—and when," Garrick confessed. "I..." His voice trailed off.

"It doesn't matter," I said at last, not meeting his gaze. "I'd rather take a chance than stay. Staying here will be certain death."

"You're a Silverfrost. I saw your magic. You'll be able to fend off any underworld creature."

"Preston and Nerissa are suppressing my magic!" The force of my raised voice made my corset strain against my skin even more, and I winced.

"That's impossible. They told me they wouldn't, as that would prevent our ability to perform a true test, and fae cannot lie."

I finally met Garrick's gaze, finding his mask firmly back in place, the warmth leached from his eyes. I wanted to scream. Who was he? What was true and what was false? What was trickery and what was real? "If you don't help me escape, my blood will be on your hands. If our friendship ever meant *anything* to you—"

"I am bound to serve them, Ren," Garrick ground out. "They're my sovereigns."

"If you think I'm a true Silverfrost, would that not make you duty-bound to *me*?"

Garrick studied me helplessly. "When a fae vow is made, it is an unbreakable thing."

"You made a vow?" I demanded. Was that why he'd chosen to betray me? Why he served his cruel master and mistress so faithfully, even though their ways seemed unlike what the man who'd trained and protected me would support? Why he turned into another person when in their vicinity—this cold, emotionless version of himself?

Garrick didn't speak, only continued to stare, a muscle working in his jaw.

I narrowed my eyes. "Do they have some hold over you? A spell? Something stronger than glamour?"

Again, Garrick was silent. But his silence and the pleading look that had entered his eyes was answer enough. Maybe part of the hold the siblings had over him forbade him to speak of it, but he still couldn't lie. And if he couldn't lie and claim they weren't using him...they *were.*

But that didn't change my circumstances. It only solidified the fact that I couldn't trust Garrick.

I spun, undoing the window latch to slide it open. Biting wind swirled into the room and cooled my heated skin as I leaned out, finding the drop to the ground below wasn't too far. Though I knew I couldn't escape with Garrick here, I could test his allegiance, once and for all.

"What are you doing?" Garrick's footsteps thundered behind me as I did my best to swing my leg over the sill. The corset tightened even further, until it was more like a vise around me, half-strangling my breath. I swayed, spots dancing across my vision.

Just as I expected, Garrick's arms wound around me, yanking me into the room. Holding me upright with one arm securely around my waist, he used his free hand to close the window and secure the latch. He was gentle about it, but in this moment, willing or not, he was still my captor.

"You have to...fight it," I choked out, my breathing too rapid. "Let me...go. Fight whatever hold they have on you. You can't leave me to die."

"It's an honor to serve them, the same as it is an honor to undergo a trial and prove you're a Silverfrost." Garrick's voice was low again, dangerous. And I had the strange sense his words weren't even his own. He pulled away, scanning me and frowning. "Why can't you breathe?"

Frustration flared inside me. *Quiet, kind Florentia.* That side of my personality that had served me in the human world would do no good here, in this moment. Though a part of me hated the very idea of controlling Garrick without his permission, just as others were doing, I was desperate. And I was no longer in my spelled rooms, which meant I should be able to use glamour—glamour that would work on him. "You need to let me go," I said calmly. "Lead me safely to Ashwood. Let no one see us escape."

For a moment, Garrick stared at me, brow pinched. No glazed look entered his eyes. No sign that he felt stirred to listen. Then he scrubbed a hand along his jaw. "Your glamour can't work against..." He hesitated, as if searching for words he was permitted to speak. "Their rules."

My hope withered. But it made sense. Of course the siblings wouldn't have dared to make Garrick my bodyguard unless they were certain I could never glamour him. Whatever power they held over him was somehow more powerful, more unbreakable, rendering mine ineffective.

Instead, I took advantage of Garrick's distraction and bolted toward the door. But spots continued to flash in my sight, and I stumbled, barely catching myself by seizing the bed post. My chest heaved, every breath sending agony through my bones.

Behind me, Garrick swore as his footsteps stalked closer. "Hold still." There was the hiss of a blade being drawn from its sheath, and my heart staggered in fear. I tried to whirl and face him, but he coiled one arm around my waist, holding me in an iron grip. I thrashed, and he sighed. "Hold still," he repeated. "Unless you want me to cut you." His voice was tender, more like the man I remembered, like maybe in this moment he was himself and not whatever Preston and Nerissa made him to be.

I obeyed, relaxing my body against his. Something slid beneath my corset, the sound of fabric and ties snapping and coming undone accompanied by a sudden release. The constraining pressure against my ribs vanished as my ruined corset fell to the floor. I took a deep breath, my head clearing as air flooded my aching lungs.

"Who bound you so tightly?" Garrick demanded.

His arm loosened, letting me face him. His free hand sheathed his hunting knife at his hip while his other continued to grasp my waist, as if expecting me to collapse again.

"Isolde, the healer."

Garrick's scowl deepened. "Seems she did a shoddy healing job. May I..." He hesitated. "Could I check your ribs?"

My cheeks flamed. "I'm not undressing for you."

His eyes widened. "I wasn't asking you to. I was going to do the undressing."

"What?"

Garrick shook his head. "Not like *that*. I'll only unbutton the back of your dress enough to check the bruising around your ribs. Unless Isolde added a hundred more layers under that outfit?"

I shook my head, still speechless, my face too hot.

"Starlight," Garrick said, his voice softening. Compassion shone in his eyes. "I'm not trying to take advantage of you. I'm trying to help you."

Slowly, I nodded and turned around.

Garrick sighed, his breath warm on the back of my neck as he began unbuttoning. Every muscle in my body tensed, but I was in enough pain that I couldn't protest anymore. If he could help me, I would accept that. It wasn't as if I could escape very far in my condition.

When he'd unbuttoned me all the way to my lower back, he paused, kneeling to inspect my skin and hissing. His calloused fingertips skimmed along my side, softly enough not to hurt. I swallowed my gasp, not wanting him to hear me. That would have been embarrassing.

"It looks awful," he muttered. "Fae magic should have healed you more than this by now. You can't fight like this." He stood, circling me to look me in the eyes. "I'm fetching a healer." He hesitated. "Just because I'm not in the room, doesn't mean I can't stop you. I have orders."

Garrick's fingers caressed my neck, so lightly the touch seemed like an accident.

I nodded sadly. Waves of exhaustion swept over me, and I teetered on my feet.

Noting my unsteady legs, Garrick wrapped one arm beneath my knees and another under my lower back, his warm fingers splayed against my bare skin. I tried to ignore the way my heart and body reacted all at once. "You're so soft," he whispered, but my thoughts were hazy, and I was sure I was imagining it. He held me close to his chest as he carried me to the bed, gently laying me down.

Bleary, I blinked my eyes at him, startled when he took my hand in his tenderly. I was sinking into exhaustion, and I wanted to welcome blissful unconsciousness rather than continue to feel the pain shooting through my ribs. Even my earlier fear seemed distant.

"The healer will help," Garrick murmured. "I'm sorry, Starlight."

I'm sorry, Starlight. I jolted awake as agony tore through my body.

A fae woman with large, owlish eyes and snowy feathers for hair hovered over me. Crying out, I thrashed in the bed, instinctively trying to slap her away. "If you want to heal, Your Majesty," she said through gritted teeth, "you'll hold still. Otherwise, I'll have him put you to sleep again."

Again? Betrayal slammed through me as my thoughts fully cleared. My eyes found Garrick on the other side of the bed, his face once again expressionless. How had he drugged me?

The pain in my ribs was swiftly melting into a soothing warmth, helping me to breathe easily. The owl-like woman glanced at Garrick. "Why didn't their healer do her job correctly?"

"I'll talk to the king and queen about it," Garrick said.

The woman scowled. "You'd better. This woman might be trapped in a frail human body, but that means we need to protect her all the more. She's our only hope, hunter."

"I know this." This time, Garrick's tone was a growl. "Why do you think I'm tasked with guarding her?"

Something flashed in the woman's eyes, like suspicion and dislike. Maybe she had the same thought that I did: that Isolde hadn't fully healed me because the king and queen had commanded her not to. That they wanted me to look weak, so they could remain powerful.

I wanted to seize the healer's hand, to beg her to stay and help me. She was on my side.

But then she continued speaking. "I have a potion to help inspire wakefulness. It's a drug one should only use sparingly, but a small dose of it should be enough to keep her awake to perform her trial." Her eyes shot to me. "You'll be healed enough for tonight. Prove you are truly worthy of the throne, mortal. I lost my closest friends and two children to those bloody underworld creatures. We need you to seal that door once and for all."

My hope dulled. Of course, even the citizens who were eager to welcome and help me still wanted something from me. They'd never let me escape.

Everyone in this accursed city would do everything they could to throw me into the next arena, the next deadly trial.

Worse still, exhaustion from being healed was making my limbs turn leaden and my eyelids grow heavy already. I would be in no condition to flee. They'd only drug me to wake me just in time to drag me to the next test. To my death.

I was doomed.

CHAPTER FOURTEEN

B itter liquid spilled into my mouth, waking me up. Instinctively, I tried to spit it out, but a gentle hand covered my lips. "Swallow," the owlish woman bid me. I blinked up at her face as I forced myself to swallow and accept more of the concoction when she pressed a vial to my mouth.

The world was hazy on the edges, and it was only as I drank the last drop of liquid that I became conscious of voices muttering nearby. My eyes flicked toward the corner across the room, where Garrick and Isolde were engaged in a heated conversation, apparently unaware that the healer had woken me. The room was dark, and the pair was shrouded in shadows from where the light of the candle at my bedside scarcely reached.

Night had fallen. My next trial was soon. Fear dug talons into my chest.

"You're supposed to be the best healer in the kingdom," Garrick was saying, his tone as harsh as a blade scraped against stone.

"I am," Isolde responded, crossing her arms.

"Then if you won't tell me what happened, answer me plainly. Did you fail to heal Ren completely?"

"Apparently so," she said sharply. "The human is pathetic. It took much magic and was quite taxing on her frail body."

Garrick cursed. "That's no excuse. You've healed humans before—"

"Maybe she's weaker than the rest," Isolde interrupted. "Besides, what do you care? She's nothing more than a worm that *possibly* has valuable blood. The idea that a Silverfrost ever considered bedding a human and creating that thing is..." She winced. "Disgusting."

This time, the growl that rumbled out of Garrick's throat was all animal. The hairs rose on the back of my neck as I imagined him transforming into a wolf right there and leaping at Isolde. "Was your failure to heal her completely *deliberate*?"

Isolde spun away, her long blonde hair whipping around her shoulders. "You insult me."

"And you're avoiding my question."

Turning back to him, she stalked closer, her words venomous. "Everything I've done, I've done on *their* orders, Garrick. Just like you. Except I find it to be an honor to obey them, and I don't try to fight it. Remember your place, dog. That girl doesn't deserve our allegiance. Even if she's a Silverfrost, she isn't fae. She's mortal. Nothing like us. She can't rule. All she can do is faithfully obey our sovereigns, same as us, and be the shield we need."

Turning on her heel, the fae stormed from the room, slamming the door behind her. At my side, the healer shook her head, eyes full of anger as she glanced at Garrick. "Human or not, if Florentia Cantwell is a Silverfrost, tampering with her healing and her ability to pass a test is treasonous."

Garrick strode across the room, towering over the small woman sitting in her chair. His gold eyes were fiery, but I couldn't decide if his rage was all directed toward the healer, or also toward Isolde. "You will say nothing," he said. "If you speak a word about this to anyone, I will hear of the rumors, and I will hunt you down and tear out your throat."

From my prone position, I stared at him breathlessly, frozen in fear even though his threat had nothing to do with me. This was confirmation enough. Preston and Nerissa were sabotaging my trials, and Garrick was choosing their side once more. He was their faithful hunter and killer, through and through. From slipping me into unconsciousness so I couldn't escape to covering up the king and queen's deceitful ways, he was betraying me again and again. No matter what vows he'd made or what control they held over him, no matter how much of his actions went against his own will...it didn't matter. I could never trust him.

As much as I longed to be able to believe the man underneath their control was my friend, he was theirs.

Not my ally, not my friend.

Never mine.

After Garrick had threatened the healer and made her vow to never tell a soul what she'd overheard, she'd brought me an outfit sent from the king and queen themselves and then promptly disappeared. I didn't even know her name. Though her kindness toward me had been self-serving, I still wished I knew it, still wished I'd had a chance to thank her properly for preparing me for this fight. Even if I knew, healed or not, I still couldn't win. Not as long as my magic remained unreachable to me.

Now, outfitted in leather boots, a pair of leggings—as she'd called the fitted trousers—a type of half-corset that rested comfortably over my chest without restraining my thankfully less sore ribs, and a loose tunic that allowed for free movement, I trailed Garrick out of my room and into the hall. I shoved my arms into my coat as I walked.

But then Garrick paused, turning to offer me a sheathed hunting knife, and I frowned. Like his others, the hilt was marked with the silhouette of a wolf before the full moon.

"I thought this fight was a test of my magical power," I murmured, glancing down the hall to find no one else about.

"Just take it, Starlight," he said, his expression unreadable. "Find a place to hide it. And finish buttoning your coat. We must hurry."

"Turn around," I ordered, and Garrick didn't waste time questioning me. As soon as his back was to me, I hastily shoved the knife down the front of my tunic, letting the small corset hold and conceal it, and then buttoned my coat over it all.

I knew there was no hope in running, so as soon as I'd finished, I fell into step beside Garrick, going downstairs to exit the inn and meet the rest of our group outside the nearby stables. Everyone was already mounted.

"Don't keep us waiting. The citizens are in such suspense," King Preston said, a hint of mockery in his bored tone.

A cold sliver of light from the waxing moon pierced through the hazy clouds, reminding me that a full moon was gradually approaching. A moon I would likely never see. Would Preston and Nerissa keep my blood and use it that night anyway? My stomach hollowed at the thought.

My breaths streamed out in a frosty mist as I burrowed deeper into my fur coat and hurried over the cobblestones toward Garrick's and my waiting horse. Garrick set his hands on my waist to help me onto the gelding first. I held still as Garrick swung up behind me and wrapped his arms around my torso as easily as if he held me all the time.

"Showtime," Queen Nerissa murmured, and she and her brother took the lead, guiding our group in a trot through the city streets and toward one of the towering mountains hemming it in.

"You drugged me?" I asked Garrick under my breath as our horse lurched forward. When Queen Nerissa's head turned, the starlight catching on her pointed ear, I froze. Of course her keener hearing had caught my words.

But Garrick didn't seem concerned. "It was no drug. There is one other ability granted to us wolf shifters."

Of course there was something else you didn't tell me. I kept the thought to myself, bitter as it was. If Garrick couldn't even speak about whatever magic kept him under the siblings' control, then it stood to reason there'd been plenty of information he'd either been forced to withhold or hadn't been eager to share with the woman he'd been ordered to hunt.

"We have the ability to subdue others—to calm them or put them to sleep," Garrick continued. "I suppose because we are meant to be predators, it is another way our magic manifests and allows us to secure our targets."

Glancing down at where Garrick's hands rested at my waist, I reminded myself to be wary of his nearness in the future. *If* I found a way to survive past tonight.

And yet, he'd given me his knife. He'd admitted he was a prisoner as much as I was. I was starting to believe the man I'd met was the true Garrick. The trouble was knowing when it was him, and when he was under Preston or Nerissa's control...and always being wary. His mercurial moods lately indicated their control was sporadic, but frequent. Unpredictable. And even when he wasn't fully under their control—whatever strange sort of glamour or spell it was they used on him—he seemed to be bound by specific orders or promises all the time, like the one that compelled him to hunt me down, to guard me from escaping.

I gazed up at the craggy mass looming over us, blotting out a portion of the dark sky. Its snowy peak was ringed in mist that made the distant stars seem even colder and harsher. My eyes sought something familiar out of habit, scanning the patches of velvet sky visible through the clouds until I found *aeveld*. Though my heart ached at the sight, I also found a crumb of comfort in studying those stars and remembering the closeness Garrick and I had shared while stargazing. That easy camaraderie, his bright smiles...

As if sensing the turn of my thoughts, Garrick leaned forward. King Preston and Queen Nerissa rode a fair distance ahead, winding out of the city and into the shadow of the mountain. "Do you know what the Silverfrosts said about *aeveld,* the star of hope?" he murmured, his lips tickling my ear.

Afraid to turn back and meet his gold eyes when I was all-too conscious of the other fae trailing behind us, I forced myself to stare rigidly ahead. "What do they say?" I whispered.

"According to *their* stories, it represents their powerful line of fae, always able to banish the demons and creatures of the underworld to the darkness where they belong. It is a symbol of the light they carry, their crucial responsibility." His arms pulled me against his chest so I could feel the beating of his heart. "*You* carry that light and power, Starlight. It's in your blood. In your soul. No demon can defeat you."

"I wish I had your confidence." I paused, breathing deeply enough I could feel the edges of the hunting knife's leather sheath digging into my skin beneath my bodice. A steadying reminder. "Will you stand by and watch if...if the worst happens?" I couldn't help the note of accusation creeping into my voice.

Garrick's fingers tightened, digging into my fur coat. "When I am under..." He hesitated, his voice strained. "Not even my words are my own. My body is not my own." I sensed the way he trembled, either from fury or grief. Horror seeped into me at the idea of being a prisoner not only in their fortress, but also in my own body. Subject to the royals' every whim and cruel order.

"*How?*" I demanded. I'd never heard of such powerful glamour.

"I cannot speak of it. They won't... I cannot," Garrick finished. His body tensed, his grasp on me loosening. Our horse trotted up closer to the royal siblings, and it seemed that the nearer we drew to them, the less Garrick was himself.

I wondered if it was out of a desire to not draw their attention, or if his proximity increased their level of control over him.

My heart throbbed in my ears at this information. In a way, it bolstered my hope and eased my pain to have this proof that Garrick cared, that he didn't betray or entrap me willingly. But in another, it was far worse to know Garrick was as much a captive as I was. If I died facing this demon tonight, he would be forced to watch.

I would be forced to see his expressionless face in the crowd and know he could do nothing to spare either of us.

Time lost all meaning as we rode on in silence, the cold breeze unable to permeate my heavy fur coat or the warmth Garrick's body heat surrounded me in, but the chill growing in my blood making me shiver anyway. Garrick spared no more comforting words as we ascended a rocky path leading up the mountainside. He didn't tighten his grasp on me in quiet reassurance as our horses wound the final bend to face an imposing fortress set upon a cliffside partway up the mountain.

Clearly under the siblings' control again, he was lost to me once more.

As King Preston and Queen Nerissa led us through the gates, already open and awaiting our arrival, my skin prickled, and I swore I could sense something unearthly. Attendants scurried forward to take the reins as we dismounted in the courtyard. My boots slipped on the icy cobblestones, but King Preston stepped forward in that moment, catching my elbow.

"Mortals are clumsy creatures," he said, shaking his head and drawing me forward, away from Garrick and the rest of our company.

Queen Nerissa fell into step beside us, tossing me a smirk. "Citizens have already gathered in the arena, awaiting your test."

My head was light with fear, the world turning hazy. I wasn't sure if I would have been able to keep my feet but for Preston's iron grip on my arm, tugging me relentlessly toward the fortress.

Two guards swung open the double doors, allowing us to step over the threshold into inky darkness punctuated only by pinpricks of light from flickering torches. The orange light cast by the flames painted the chiseled stonework of the floor and walls in eerie shades. Overhead, the ceiling was swallowed in shadows, giving the impression that there was nothing but emptiness above us. Despite the airy feel, it was somehow stifling and oppressive, like the darkness itself held weight and invisible eyes boring down upon me. The scent of smoke and earth and iron permeated my every breath.

Again, a sense of foreboding swept over me as our footsteps echoed in the empty space. Evil resided here.

And I had nothing to defend against it but the knife digging into my ribcage, a feeble weapon against undead creatures that could not be killed.

As Preston turned and half-dragged me down another hall, Nerissa and Garrick on our heels, I practically begged my magic to come back to me, like it was a living thing that could hear me. There was nothing but a hollow ache where that sense of power had once resided.

The air grew thicker, its scent turning stale as the hall ended in two sets of staircases. On the left, stone steps spiraled upward, lined with flickering candles. To the right, a few steps descended toward a heavy iron door, padlocked and guarded by two well-muscled ogres, each dripping with every manner of weapon I'd ever seen. An uneasy feeling settled in my gut as I stared at that door, until the hairs on the back of my neck stood on end.

Preston paused, noticing the way the door drew my attention. His smile was sharp, his blood-red eyes piercing in the flickering light. "That is the door to the dungeons where we secure all the pesky creatures that escape at night."

Somehow, I found my voice despite the way my throat seemed to be slowly closing up. "You don't secure them in the castle?"

Preston scoffed. "Is that what you mortals would do? Invite an enemy to one of your civilized tea parties? Keep a monster in your bedchamber? Why would you hold that which could destroy you near at hand?" He shook his head. "No, we secure them here, in this mountain, away from the citizens of Northelm and the inhabitants of our castle. We will not have another massacre."

I swallowed. "How many...of those creatures do you have here?"

"At first, we only saw one or two creatures slip through each month," Queen Nerissa said, striding forward to dip her head in acknowledgement toward the guards. I thought I heard a sound like claws scraping against stone, but that was impossible. The door was too thick. "But as the years passed, and what Silverfrost blood was left to mark the entrance to the underworld faded away, the veil thinned. More and more skulked into our world at night, forcing us to erect this fortress to secure them all. Only a Silverfrost can banish a creature—and even then, only on a winter solstice, when the veil is the weakest of all. Now we see demons creep out nearly every night, haunting our castle halls or sneaking down to the city to feed."

I ground my teeth at the thought.

"We have hundreds secured here now."

My head whirled. *Hundreds.* An army from the underworld, contained by steel and might but never banished. Ever a threat to the people of this kingdom, and constantly increasing.

"Most nights are still manageable," King Preston said, shifting his focus toward the ascending stairs. "Some, no creatures emerge at all. But others, we must prepare for an intense battle. So we are forced to always be on our guard once the sun goes down, never knowing what sort of night we will endure. This is why our people will not accept you, a mere mortal, unless you prove yourself. They have had to demonstrate their might and courage for two decades in order to survive. All we ask is that you subdue *one* creature. If you cannot even do that, then you're no Silverfrost. They have no reason to put their hope in you."

"If you want me to prove myself, then don't sacrifice me. Allow me to *use* my magic."

Preston and Nerissa burst into laughter.

"If you can't access your magic," Nerissa said, "then that is because your pathetic human nature won't let you." She shook her head. "You don't wear forget-me-nots any longer, Snowflake. Whatever fae blood is in your veins must be something less powerful."

Preston shrugged elegantly. "I'm not surprised. Can you imagine a royal fae choosing to breed with a mortal?" He grimaced. "Disgusting."

Garrick's voice was quiet. "Other royal families in Brytwilde marry humans."

Nerissa startled, as if she'd forgotten the hunter was there. Then she turned, running a hand along his cheek. "Beautiful, I don't keep you around for your thoughts. Silence."

Obediently, Garrick clapped his mouth shut, his expression settling into one of cool indifference.

Footsteps echoed down the stairs to the left, and a man with ram's horns and flowing blond hair emerged. He dipped into a hasty bow. "Your Majesties, the people began gathering hours ago. They grow impatient."

"Good." Preston shoved me forward. I stumbled, catching myself before I fell into the man. "Take her to the arena. My sister and I need to find our seats so we can enjoy the view."

CHAPTER FIFTEEN

There was no remorse in the horned man's eyes as he escorted me up the seemingly endless flight of steps, until sweat beaded on my brow and slithered down my back and I had to pause to catch my breath in the stairwell. Above, the murmuring of an unseen crowd thundered toward us, muffled but overwhelming all the same. How many citizens had walked from the city and waited here for hours? How many truly thought I was headed toward victory, and not my slaughter?

"Nearly there, Your Majesty," the man said, startling me from my thoughts.

"If you truly think I am a Silverfrost," I panted, "why lead me to my death? This is a spectacle! A horrifying show."

Though his silver eyes were kind, his brow furrowed with confusion. "It is an honor to show your courage and power to your people, Your Majesty. A time-honored tradition among your ancestors."

I had a wild desire to tear back down the staircase and rush from the fortress, to take my chances in the cold among the monsters that lurked within Brytwilde. As if sensing my thoughts, the man went on, "Come, there's no reason to resist. If you run, the guards will kill you. At least in the arena, you'll have an opportunity to defend and prove yourself."

Swallowing back the urge to cry or scream, I gritted my teeth and forced my legs to move. One step. Another. The pulsing of applause and shouts and pounding footsteps rattled my chest the higher the horned fae and I rose, until I could hardly hear my own breaths.

"Here," the man announced as we stopped at a landing. The steps stretched onward above us, but to our left, a narrow hall led into shadows.

Like the entrance to the arena in the castle, this hall stopped at another heavy door, guarded by two fae who watched me impassively. But unlike at the castle, I could sense wrongness clinging to the air. It was the sickly-sweet stench of rot mingled with a sensation that made me feel as if the air was slithering across my skin. Like the shadows were alive and moving—and toying with me. An icy chill snaked through my veins, but no power accompanied it. This wasn't the cold of my winter magic. It was the cold of sheer terror in the presence of something evil and awful.

"I hope, for all our sakes, that you pass this test," my escort muttered, and then without formality, shoved me toward the guards. A tall, curly-haired woman seized my wrist.

"Quick!" her companion shouted, unbolting the door.

The woman practically threw me inside, and the door slammed behind me.

Darkness.

Eerie silence.

Flickering torchlight filtered through barred openings at least two levels above, where fae were seated in rows of rising stone benches encircling the arena. The acrid tang of smoke mingled with the odors of death and earth and iron. It gave me the feeling of being trapped in a dungeon cell, with the bars overhead casting eerie shadows and the distant flames casting red light that didn't fill the dark corners of this new arena.

I swallowed, trying to summon magic or some scrap of courage. My audience had gone so silent and still that my ears began to ring from the sudden lack of roaring sound. And no matter how I scoured the shadowy room, I couldn't find my opponent.

Welcome. The voice seemed old and deep, and I couldn't tell if it rumbled from everywhere or nowhere at all. If it spoke aloud or only echoed in my head. It gave me the prickling feeling of steel scraping over stone. Of a discordant note. *I've waited years for this.*

Stomach clenching, I stepped forward, my boots scraping along the floor. There was no movement—no sign of any other living thing in this enormous cage. Above, the countless eyes boring into me only exacerbated the feeling of being trapped.

Though I knew the citizens hoped I would be their salvation, I was, in this moment, little more than entertainment to them. I was putting on a show that would either grant them hope and joy, or would satisfy them by bringing a supposedly lying human to justice.

Movement flashed in the corner of my eye, but when I turned, I saw nothing. The sound of sniffing filled the air, making gooseflesh rise on my arms. Instinctively, I reached for the knife tucked inside my bodice.

A human. *How interesting. I haven't yet had the pleasure of encountering prey so...fragile.*

I ground my teeth as something finally emerged from the shadowy corner of the arena. It was a tall, willowy figure shrouded in darkness, slipping forward on silent feet. In place of a head was a skull bearing two curving antlers, and where its eyes should have been, there was nothing but gaping holes.

Every muscle in my body went rigid. As the creature stalked forward, its fanged maw never moved, but the voice in my head grew louder.

As a human, you are so aware of your mortal state. Death trails you everywhere.

Sweat slithered down the back of my neck. My mind screamed at me to run, to fight back, to do anything. This being was unnatural, its very presence sending off every sort of instinctual alarm in my body. It was wrong. Terrible. Something created by the gods at the dawn of time to punish the evil souls not worthy of a peaceful rest in the afterlife—not something meant to creep through the veil and attack the living.

The air turned stale and the orange and red shades cast by the torchlight seemed to dull, turning to greys and blacks. Everything faded and altered, like the world could scarcely stand this creature's presence.

And I still couldn't move, couldn't speak. Could barely even breathe.

My lungs burned with the effort to suck in air that tasted of ash and despair, and my body, though still locked in place, turned heavy.

But my art is not in death, poor little mortal, the creature went on, pausing before me. Those empty eye sockets gave me the impression of something staring into my soul, searching out my every fear and doubt and weakness and flaw. Weighing my worth and finding me wanting. *It is in pain.*

At his words, crushing agony, like my heart was being carved from my chest, slammed into me. It was the bone-deep ache of every heartbreak I'd ever experienced. It was the searing hopelessness of knowing I would never feel peace or joy again. It was the soul-shredding torment of loneliness.

Every loss I'd ever borne weighed me down until I could scarcely breathe. My stepfather was dying all over again. Charles was shoving me across the border, condemning me. Garrick was betraying me and watching me with a stony expression. My freedom was being ripped away forever.

I couldn't think, couldn't move. My knees buckled beneath me, slamming into the stone floor, but the ache of impact was lost to me. All the pain swiftly transformed into numbness, emptiness, so all-consuming I wasn't sure I'd ever find strength again.

You have endured much loss and rejection, the demon taunted, cutting through my haze.

Alarm crashed into my heart, throbbing through my veins. But it was terror as I'd never experienced it before, raw and full of despair.

Vaguely, I was aware of shouting above me. The fae, cheering for my death, relishing the way I was being brought low.

Strange they sent a human to me. Are you a sacrifice to appease me at long last?

When I managed to lift my head, I found the creature towering over me, its empty sockets boring into my soul. The chains of its shackles clinking together, it lifted a skeletal hand ending in fiercely sharp claws that glinted red in the torchlight, as if they were already stained with blood. An animal moan filled my ears, and it took me a moment to realize it was mine. The sound of utter hopelessness, of resignation as I faced not just my death, but my annihilation. This demon was going to destroy me, piece by piece, and I was helpless to stop it.

Starlight!

Physical anguish replaced my emotional suffering as the creature's claws sliced into my arm—no, *through* my arm. I screamed as blood and pain became my entire world. I would lose the limb. I would bleed out, left here forever reliving every terrible feeling I'd ever endured. The tang of copper permeated the air while the taste of blood filled my mouth. As the demon yanked its claws free, fierce heat burned through my veins. Something was horribly, irredeemably wrong with my left arm.

Aeveld. You *carry that light and power, Starlight.*

I couldn't tell if I was remembering what Garrick had told me earlier, or if he was saying those words again, screaming down at me. My ears rang, and everything was foggy.

Fight, I thought, recalling the knife in my corset. If I'd lived these crushing emotions before and survived, I could do it again. Even if this time, they were all consuming me simultaneously. Gritting my teeth, I used my good arm to drag myself out of the demon's shadow. My body slid across the floor painfully slowly, but the creature didn't pursue. It seemed to relish my pathetic attempt to move away, to struggle back onto my shaking legs.

My mind struggled to grasp at my magic. Surely if my emotions channeled it, all the feelings this creature was forcing upon me would draw it out. And yet, not a shred of power flowed through my veins. Instead of that familiar cold that accompanied my magic, I was overwhelmed with heat. It was like I was burning, endlessly consumed by relentless flame. Blood dripped from my arm, a crimson stream trailing across the floor. As if I could stop the flow, I pressed my good hand to my shredded flesh, hissing when fresh agony surged through my arm from the force.

The demon approached again, raising its claws, aiming for my heart.

Desperate, I shoved my now-bloodied fingers into my corset and withdrew Garrick's knife. As the creature swiped, I ducked, slamming the blade into its torso with the remaining strength I could muster. I scrambled backward before the demon could strike again, slipping in my own blood and collapsing. My pulse pounded in my temples as I blinked up at the advancing creature, staring at the place where the blade was lodged in its body. There was no blood, no sign of injury or weakness or pain from the monster at all. Only a knife trapped harmlessly in its flesh—if the creature was even made of real flesh.

Foolish human. You can't kill me, and you can't injure me with a mere piece of metal either. I am eternal, crafted of darkness to defy death and wreak havoc.

The demon hovered over me, and this time, I could almost imagine a grin stretching across its face—if its skull had anything but an empty maw. A scream clawed up my throat as it attacked. I was going to die. Despite Garrick's confidence, despite my magic.

I lifted my hand and shoved at its arm as hard as I could, my final feeble attempt to deflect its attack.

And then—the demon jerked away, a strange, agonized cry piercing my thoughts, like it was crying out wordlessly in a way only I could hear. I stared as it squirmed and crumpled to the floor like it was being burned. I glanced from the bloody hand I'd lifted to try to stop it, to the blood on its skeletal arm. My blood.

It's in your blood, Garrick had said. Of course. My power lived in my veins.

Staggering to my feet, I charged for the flailing demon, slapping my bloody palm onto its chest. It unleashed another horrifying cry in my head, and then went still.

Blackness swooped in from the edges of my vision, and the shaking in my limbs increased, combining with overwhelming exhaustion. I collapsed, and the darkness devoured me.

CHAPTER SIXTEEN

Shouts. The door slamming and countless footsteps. Jangling chains and muffled curses.

My body ached, but my arm wasn't as ruined as I'd thought, like the demon had tricked me into experiencing more pain than it had truly inflicted. The scratches along my skin stung and bled, but I wasn't bleeding out on the floor as I'd imagined, with an arm shredded down to the bone.

As a heavily armed group of fae approached the shackled creature, rough hands seized my arms and heaved me to my feet. I blinked at Preston as he glowered. His gaze flicked to the knife in the paralyzed demon's body. He snapped his fingers, a silent order that one of the guards obeyed by rushing forward to yank the blade from the demon.

His voice was deadly quiet, indiscernible beneath the roar of our audience. But it was easy enough to read what he said by the way he enunciated the words. "After you, Your Majesty."

I led the way toward the exit, my steps wooden. I hadn't thought I could taste fear and misery as intense as what the underworld creature had forced upon me ever again...until this moment. Now I knew I'd been sadly, foolishly wrong.

What it had filled me with hadn't been real, disintegrating as soon as its power over me slipped. But the emotions choking me now were rooted in a problem that wouldn't vanish so easily.

Surely Preston had recognized the mark on Garrick's hunting knife. They knew he'd broken the rule against weapons to aid me.

Outside the door, Nerissa and Isolde already waited with Garrick between them. His expression was blank, but I couldn't tell if it was from fae control or an effort to appear unperturbed. The guards were nowhere in sight.

My gut twisted.

"How disappointing, my pet," Nerissa said, her eyes latching onto the incriminating knife the guard held up for her to study. She turned to Garrick, reaching up to run her fingertips over the stubble on his jaw. "You knew better."

A muscle jumped in Garrick's cheek, but he didn't look at Nerissa. He didn't look at anyone. Even when I tried to meet his gaze, he stared resolutely at the stone floor.

Nerissa pulled back, frowning. "Do you have no excuse for yourself?"

Garrick said nothing. He barely even blinked.

"It was my faul-" I began, but Preston shot me a fierce look.

"No human lies," he bit out.

"Very well," Nerissa said, waving her arm. "Get it over with. A dog must be trained. I can't have an unpredictable hunter. Garrick, hold still. You won't move again until I command you."

Nodding at his sister, Preston snapped his fingers. "Isolde."

Isolde stepped forward, placing her hands on either side of Garrick's head.

"What are you doing?" I demanded, trying to press forward, only to be held in place by Preston's painful, unrelenting grasp on my arm. "Stop!"

My shouts turned to screaming as I thrashed against Preston.

"We are teaching our dog to obey," Preston explained. "And since it's clear you care for one another, we are, by extension, teaching you to as well. You may have proven you bear royal blood, but you are still a frail mortal. You will learn to defer to us in all things, as our healer, Isolde, does. Just as she can speed a body's natural healing process with her magic, she can also cause the body great pain by attacking itself."

I cried out in fury, in horror, as Garrick's chiseled expression melted into agony. Blood trickled from his nose, but he was locked in place, compelled to hold still as Isolde did something that clearly wasn't healing to him.

Tears burned my eyes. The raging storm inside reached a crescendo, its roar seeming to come alive through my own screams. My skin went cold, then hot, and something snapped within.

Black ice crackled along the floor, distracting Isolde enough that she loosened her grip and Garrick's eyes flashed open, still glassy from pain.

"Stop," Preston snapped, his fingernails digging into my skin, but there was a tremulous hint to his tone. He was afraid.

And I couldn't stop. "Let. Him. Go!" I cried. "You'll kill him!"

Isolde met my eyes, her own wide with fear and defiance. "I obey my fae king and queen." She clapped her hands on Garrick again, and the hunter groaned, trembling from the pain she was inflicting. Though I knew the siblings wouldn't want Garrick to die, Isolde's eyes darkened with reckless malice, and I remembered their heated conversation over my unhealed ribs.

She was going to kill him.

And I wasn't going to let that happen.

An unnatural calm settled over me as the strength of my magic returned to me fully. The connection was restored, and every one of my veins tingled with life and power. Quiet, kind Florentia was gone. I couldn't abide this cruelty, this evil, one second more. She wouldn't torment Garrick ever again.

I'd killed before with my magic to save Garrick. And now that I could feel its cold consuming me, its power surging through my body, I knew I wouldn't hold back now.

"Then you've chosen the wrong sovereign," I said.

Preston clutched my arm so I couldn't pull free of him, but that wouldn't stop my magic. Calling to the world around me, to the winter air and every ounce of liquid, to the land itself and my connection to it, I crafted icicles. They formed like tiny needles above each of my fingers, their tips sharp and gleaming in the torchlight. With a single gesture, I sent them hurling toward Isolde, piercing her face, throat, and chest.

They went straight through her, and she collapsed in a growing pool of blood.

My ears rang. The storm inside was assuaged, but only a little. I was still surrounded by monsters, and neither Garrick nor I were free. Not yet.

"Guards!" Nerissa screamed, a vein popping in her forehead as she glared at me. "How dare you touch an immortal fae." She stomped toward me, slapping me across the cheek.

I laughed in her face, the sound coming out shrill. She thought *slapping me* would be enough to stop me?

But when I blinked, my cheek stinging, something about her face seemed all wrong. Her cheeks were hollow, her red eyes full of a dark threat. My stomach clenched in fear and revulsion.

Then the flickering torchlight changed, and I wondered if it had been a trick of the shadows, or fae glamour, even though their glamour wasn't supposed to be able to work on me.

The distraction provided enough time for guards to clamor forward from the deeper parts of the dungeons. I slumped with weariness. For all my magical power, I was spent. Paralyzing the underworld creature and stopping Isolde had drained me. I couldn't even pull free of Preston, let alone fend off half a dozen armed guards.

A pair of fae with gossamer wings, looking deceptively delicate and lovely, stomped over and clamped a set of forget-me-not shackles to my wrists. The pain and hollowness of losing my magic was instant, a fire tearing through me. I moaned and gritted my teeth to hold back the urge to scream.

"Just to be extra cautious..." Preston began behind me, and then something slammed into the back of my head and the world went dark.

Head pounding, I opened my eyes to find Preston leaning over me. My cheek smarted, and I scowled as my fuzzy thoughts gathered into one clear realization: he'd slapped me back to consciousness.

"At last," he snapped, pacing before the fireplace. I blinked, the cozy atmosphere at odds with the violent tumult I'd last endured when awake. The cushioned armchair I sat in was also more luxurious than the dungeons I would have expected, and my wrists were blissfully bare, as if being shackled had been nothing but a painful nightmare. Even my arm was bandaged, the cuts apparently tended to while I'd been lost to the world. "We need to talk."

I scanned the room, finding it was unfamiliar, though reminiscent of the inn room I'd occupied back when I'd dreamed of escaping. Back when I'd feared Garrick was my enemy.

Now, I'd killed for him. Again. I searched my heart, recalling the horror and remorse I'd experienced the first time I'd slain enemies in that unexpected avalanche. But I felt none, only the conviction that if Preston, Nerissa, or anyone else hurt him again—if anyone laid another finger on him—I'd kill to defend him. *They won't touch him again,* I vowed. Even if I feared their control on my magic with forget-me-nots would hold me back. I had to try. I couldn't watch Garrick suffer like that.

"Though you defied the rules by bringing a weapon to your test," Preston went on, jolting me from my thoughts, "your display did prove there is power in your blood." He paused, his form nothing but a silhouette against the crackling fire as he scanned me. "How powerful magic tolerates residing in your mere mortal vessel is beyond me."

I folded my hands in my lap, squeezing my fingers together.

"Therefore, despite your disrespect toward our time-honored traditions, there is no denying that one of the Silverfrosts debased themselves by being with a human and producing...you. We can only assume your mother, being utterly insignificant, escaped the slaughter at the castle when the Silverfrosts were killed in order to bear you in the mortal world."

Hot anger rose up my throat, but I swallowed it down. My memories of Mother were cloudy, but insignificant? Everything my stepfather had taught me about her made it clear she had loved with a fierceness few others had possessed. She'd been anything but insignificant.

Preston droned on, either heedless or—more likely—careless of my building fury. "The fact is, mortals do not rule in Silverfrost. Your kind is beneath us. Unlike other fae kingdoms, we don't stoop to marrying more fertile human women in hopes of continuing our lines. We don't mix immortal and mortal blood." He sniffed, stopping to stare at me as if I'd committed the aforementioned act, which he spoke of as if it were a crime. "But as there is no denying you are the last living being with Silverfrost blood, capable of sealing the underworld's entrance and dismissing the creatures that have already slipped into our world, it seems we are forced to adapt."

My stomach churned. I didn't like where this conversation was headed.

His bloody gaze latched onto my hands, where I clasped them tightly in my lap. "We have no choice but to wed."

I froze, barely breathing.

"We will announce our engagement tomorrow to the public, reassure them that the throne will continue to be occupied by immortals, while we use our magic to the fullest of its abilities. You will be my consort, satisfying what sliver of a claim you have to the crown and the people's need for a Silverfrost in a position of honor."

The room spun and spots flashed before my eyes. The anger growing inside me roared and broke free. I stood, meeting Preston's stare with a steady look. I refused to back down, refused to cower. "Never," I spat.

If I'd hoped for a reaction, Preston disappointed me. His expression remaining cool, he shrugged. "I expected resistance. Trust me, our union can't be any more distasteful to you as it is to me. But this is not a *proposal,* Snowflake. This is an order." He stepped closer, seizing my chin roughly and tilting my head back so he could glare into my eyes. "I own you. Tomorrow you will smile, you will be agreeable, and you will convince the people we are engaged. And when the time comes, we will wed. If not, I'll tie you to a chair and force you to watch me carve out that wolf shifter's heart. Slowly."

Ice trickled through my veins. Preston released me, and I staggered back, nearly falling into my chair.

Striding carelessly toward the door, Preston snapped his fingers. Guards entered the room, their faces impassive. "Lead us to the dungeons."

All words were trapped in my tightening chest as I followed Preston and the guards, my temples throbbing while my mind raced. Down a stark hallway lined with torches, we turned toward a heavily barred door. Another set of guards unlatched it for us and stepped aside for us to descend an endless stone staircase. The walls were narrow and the steps steep, giving me a sense that the walls were closing in and a growing fear that I'd slip and fall into nothingness. Though additional torches lit the way, they seemed to cast more smoke than light, making me cough as we walked down, down, down.

My legs burned. Preston said nothing. He let my own thoughts be my torment.

Eventually, sounds drifted toward us from below. Scraping. Hissing. Whimpering. A scream.

Gooseflesh rose along my arms. That feeling of evil swept over me again, the same dread and wrongness I'd sensed first entering this fortress and again when facing the underworld being.

By the time we struck the bottom, I was trembling. A narrow corridor with scarcely enough light to see more than vague shapes stretched before us. Cells lined either side, though it was too dark for me to make out their occupants. The sounds grew louder. Someone was sobbing.

"When we deal with criminals and disobedient subjects," Preston murmured at last, shooting me a sidelong look I couldn't read in the blackness, "this is where most are sent. Some are given to the underworld creatures—might as well make the demons useful and let them torment the worst of us while they're here."

I shuddered.

"Others we deal with ourselves."

My head pounded as Preston turned a corner. This one was brighter, with more torches spitting flames and painting the stonework a warning shade of red. My eyes darted to a cell on my left, where guards gathered around a fae man chained to the wall. He was marred by grime, blood, and scars to the point that he barely looked like a living being, but his cries made it clear he was still alive to suffer. One guard was using a wicked-looking tool to systematically break the man's fingers. Snap. A shriek. A sob for mercy.

Bile rose to my throat, and I seized Preston's arm. "*This* makes you no better than the demons you seek to dismiss!" I cried. "You're a monster—"

Face expressionless, Preston turned, slapping me across the cheek. I reeled back from the force, almost collapsing. One of the guards behind us slammed a fist into my back, shoving me upright. I bit back a groan as Preston clutched my hand and dragged me forward.

"This is who I wanted you to see," he said, pausing several cells down and gesturing like he was showing off a fine new exhibit.

"Garrick," I choked out.

Wrists shackled, Garrick hung by his arms from chains extending from the ceiling of his cell, his feet brushing the stained stone floor. His face was beaten and bloody, one of his eyes swollen shut. At his side, Queen Nerissa looked startlingly pristine, her dark hair gleaming in the torchlight as she ran a dagger along his skin. She moved it with such gentleness, it looked deceptively like a caress but for the flash of steel and the trickle of blood leaking from each new cut. She was carefully tracing small incisions into his arms and chest. Not enough to seriously harm him—only enough to hurt him. To draw out his suffering.

"Let him go." My voice sounded brittle in my ears. I knew that was the reaction Preston and Nerissa wanted from me, but I couldn't help it. The sight broke something in my chest. My earlier promise to myself echoed in my ears: *They won't touch him again.*

I let my emotions scream through me, releasing the building storm in my soul. Ice crackled, materializing in a shimmering rain of fatally sharp icicles. They soared through the air, flying toward Nerissa in a relentless assault.

But before they could touch her, one of the guards stepped forward, taking me by surprise as the fierce pain inflicted by forget-me-not shackles pummeled into me. The instant the cuffs clicked around my wrists and agony ignited in my veins, the ice I'd conjured crashed to the dungeon floor and melted into harmless puddles.

Nerissa laughed aloud, turning so I could more clearly see her blade and the mixture of blood and something tinted green shimmering on its edge. My stomach churned. What was she doing to Garrick? "He knows the price he must pay for disobedience." Her deep red eyes gleamed with brutal delight. "And now, so do you."

I gasped for air as both resignation and self-loathing washed over me. I had no other choice—not now, anyway. My pain was mounting, making it difficult to even think clearly. "Very well." Sweat beading on my brow, I faced Preston, shoving my disgust deep down. "I accept your proposal. I'll marry you."

CHAPTER SEVENTEEN

I protested the entire time Preston dragged me out of the dungeons and back to my room.

"Release him! You have what you wanted: my agreement!"

"And he must pay for defying us by slipping you that knife," Preston hissed in my ear when we stopped outside my door. Once he'd ordered the guards who'd trailed us to unshackle me, he opened the door and shoved me in unceremoniously. "We'll make an official announcement tomorrow. Sleep well, Fiancée." He sneered before slamming the door in my face.

Motionless, I waited several seconds for his footsteps and those of our escort guards to fade away. Blood pounded in my ears. Yet just as I'd feared, when I tried the door, I found it locked.

I lost track of time as I slid to the floor, burying my face in my arms and dissolving into tears. Helplessness consumed me, and I hated it. Hated that I was trapped in this room while Garrick suffered. Hated that I couldn't stop it. Hated that I was a prisoner to these fae, forced to obey their cruel whims. Hated that I'd been powerful enough to defend Garrick and slay Isolde, only for Preston and Nerissa to force me back into a corner where I was weak and trapped again.

They won't win, I promised myself, curling my fingers into fists. Though I wasn't sure how when they'd all but stripped me of my power, I would find a way to win my freedom.

Wiping my face, I stood, seizing one of the blankets from the bed and wrapping it around myself as I sank into the chair before the fire. After facing the underworld creature, I knew in my bones I was meant to be in Silverfrost, meant to protect this kingdom—and the rest of the world—from those demons slipping into our realm and harming us.

That meant running was no longer an option.

My mind whirled, but in this unfamiliar place, where I was surrounded by magical fae who'd been wielding their power far longer than I had, I wasn't sure how I could fight back. I'd have to bide my time, patient and observant as I awaited an opportunity.

At some point, exhaustion from my earlier fight and my tears took over and I nodded off. The creak of the door and then a slam jolted me awake. Startling, I jerked upright in my chair, blinking against the dim light of the low-burning fire.

Garrick leaned against the door, his shoulders slumped. His loose shirt was only half buttoned, giving me a glimpse of countless bandages stretching across his chest. He stared at me with glazed eyes, appearing as bleary as I felt, but neither were swollen shut, so a healer must have tended to him since he'd been released from his cell. But that realization was only a small relief.

"Garrick," I whispered, abandoning my chair to run to him. "Are you all right?"

I reached for his arm, but he wrenched away, hissing like he expected my touch to burn. Biting back my frown, I pulled away.

"You can't touch me," he said, his voice a low rumble, his golden eyes fixed on the floor. "They'll know."

"I don't understand."

Garrick lifted his face to meet my gaze, his expression pained. "They prey on weaknesses. They'll always use us against each other, Starlight. If you touch my skin, Nerissa will smell you on me. The scent will be too strong that way. And then she'll punish me by hurting you." He barely resisted a shudder. "And if I touch your skin? The same."

"Why?"

Garrick's expression was hollow, his eyes haunted. "They love to play games like this. They forced me to come here and guard you, knowing..." He trailed off, shaking his head. "Knowing that because of your royal blood, you have my deepest loyalty, and I'd naturally want to serve you. If I try to tend to those scratches of yours" -his eyes flicked to the bandages covering the claw marks on my arm- "they will know. It's a sick way for them to force us to not show basic kindness or companionship toward one another. A way to make us feel divided and alone and hopeless."

I swallowed. "They're monsters."

"I belong to them. I belong to her." He raked a hand through his hair, mussing the white-blond strands. "Just like you belong to him."

My stomach clenched. "You're engaged to Queen Nerissa?"

He flinched. "Not as if they'd ever let me rule, just as they won't let you. She simply loves to know she owns me, her prized hunter." Garrick's tone turned low and guttural. Hateful. "Her dog." His eyes flicked back to me. "She doesn't care for my affection, only my obedience and service in tracking down whoever she needs. But that doesn't mean she isn't possessive. Especially now that she knows—they both know—how to control us both."

I sucked in a breath. "You shouldn't have done it, Garrick. You knew giving me the knife was breaking a rule. It was too recognizable, too dangerous. Why did you do it?"

His eyes were like molten gold, burning into me with an intensity that reminded me of his wolfish nature. "There's no doubt you're a Silverfrost, and I could tell..." He cleared his throat, clearly struggling with words. "They were...affecting your magic somehow." I wondered if his oath to the siblings made it so he couldn't openly speak ill of them. "As your rightful subject, my loyalty belongs to you."

I let the proclamation warm my heart, even if I wished he'd been saying he was loyal to me for other, more sentimental reasons. "Did Nerissa poison you?" I ventured.

Garrick shook his head, pushing off the door to pace the floor. "It's a toxin without lingering effects." It didn't miss my notice that he didn't expound on what those effects were. "I don't regret what I did." He whirled toward me. "You need to leave. Run. I know their orders will force me to pursue you, but you're powerful and clever. You can invade me. You'll find a way. Anything is better than this. Forget the risks I mentioned, forget everything."

"No."

Garrick's eyes widened. "You have no reason to stay."

"I'm not leaving these people to be tormented by underworld creatures. I'm not risking that more escape into our world. There won't be a safe corner of the earth if they overrun us." I crossed my arms. "And I'm not leaving *you*."

Garrick stepped closer, his eyes glinting in the firelight. Earnest. Hurt. Pleading. "You owe Silverfrost nothing. You owe *me* nothing. It's my fault you're here. I'm already lost, but you can still save yourself."

Tears burned my throat. "No, Garrick. I'm going to save you too."

He scrubbed his hand over his face, turning away and shaking his head. "I'm too far gone," he muttered.

"I refuse to believe that," I insisted. My hand hovered over his shoulder before I remembered his warning and dropped it. I didn't want to see him hanging in chains again, suffering because of the siblings' cruel need to hurt us both. "Don't try to talk me out of what I know is right. Staying is the right thing to do. Running would only delay the inevitable, and knowing others were suffering because of me—I would never know peace again, Garrick."

Garrick's shoulders slumped. "I know," he said, resigned. He turned back to me, eyes scanning my face almost reverently. "You're *good*, Starlight. Pure and courageous and powerful in ways most of these fae cannot begin to fathom. Selfishly, I wish you were a little less so and would leave for my sake, but I can't ask you to be anything less than what you are."

My heart skipped a beat, wanting that look and those words to mean more than they did. He cared for me as a friend, as his potential queen—nothing more.

And even if there *were* deeper feelings, I told myself it didn't matter. We both belonged to others, whether we wanted to or not. Even our own hearts weren't free.

I glanced away so Garrick couldn't see the heat flooding my cheeks. "Then it's settled. You know I have to stay." Sighing, I dared to study him again. "And you really *are* all right?"

Garrick swallowed, his smile bitter. "As all right as I can ever be." He sighed. "You must be exhausted. That fight with..." He shook his head. "It was brutal to watch, even if I knew you would win in the end. You should get some rest." His eyes flicked to the bed.

Discomfort squirmed in my stomach. It wasn't the first time we'd occupied a small space, but I was far more aware of it—of *him*—than I was even before. "You need to sleep too."

"I'll take the chair," he said, nodding toward where I'd left my blanket before the fire.

I opened my mouth as if to protest, though I wasn't sure what I'd argue. It wasn't as if we could share the bed. Surely Nerissa and Preston would know if we were in such close proximity to one another. Not to mention, that would be a different sort of torment for me to endure, longing for his touch while knowing I couldn't and shouldn't have it. Instead, I bit my lip and nodded.

Without anything to change into, I unlaced my boots and set them beside my bed. My leggings and tunic weren't the cleanest after my encounter with the demon. Some of the fabric was spattered with my own dried blood, but there was no tub to bathe in this room. As I settled under the blankets, grateful we were high enough above the dungeons not to hear the prisoners or creatures residing there, I relished the warmth. Despite the earlier horrors I'd witnessed, having Garrick nearby comforted me. My eyes traced the dancing shadows cast by the glowing embers of the fire.

After a long moment, Garrick's voice rumbled toward me. "Don't fret too much, Starlight. At least the king and queen's propensity to assign me as your guard is as comforting as it is tormenting," he joked.

I blinked at his form in the dimness. "What?"

"I mean," he continued, his voice still laced with humor, "if we must suffer, at least we don't also have to be lonely. I've grown fond of your company."

My face warmed, even if I knew it was only a friendly statement, not some declaration of love. "I'm not surprised you'd try to find some good in our circumstances, even now. Goodnight, Garrick," I whispered.

"Goodnight."

The underworld creature was staring at me, as if it could see straight into my soul despite the black smudges where its eyes should have been. Its horned skull leered over me, wreathed in darkness, and every muscle in my body drew taut. Iciness flooded my veins, nothing like the power I felt from my magic.

This was like an absence. A warmth and life-stealing void. My bones turned leaden, and my mouth tasted of ash as my lungs seized. I couldn't breathe. Couldn't move. Even my tears froze on my lashes.

The creature leaned closer, its cold breath ruffling my hair and causing my body to spasm with shivers. Pain. Terror. Despair. I was overwhelmed and lost in the darkness, trapped forever in this hopeless place.

And the creature whispered in my head:

Quiet and powerless. Little Snowflake, you will never be free.

I choked on my scream, because I couldn't force any sound out at all when there was no breathe in my lungs.

When I blinked, the darkness and the demon were gone, but the horror remained. I was in the dungeons again, listening to the restless pacing of unseen creatures, their claws running along stone. Whimpers and moans echoed in the damp air. Ahead, the only flickering torches in the whole space bathed a single cell in orange light. Within, Preston and Nerissa were laughing as they carved into Garrick's flesh. Chained to the ceiling as he was, he could do nothing but scream and flail as they mangled his body into something bloody, nightmarish, unrecognizable.

I screamed. I beat against the bars of the cell. I reached for magic that wouldn't come. But nothing I did stopped the cruel siblings; nothing could save the wolf shifter I cared for.

Garrick's gold eyes flashed open one last time, even though his body had stilled, and I had been certain he was dead. His voice was guttural. *You should have run, Starlight.*

My throat was raw from my screams as I jolted awake. Tears wet my cheeks and my legs were tangled in the bed clothes.

"You're safe." Arms enveloped me, helping to calm my racing heart. "Starlight, it's all right. It was only a nightmare. I'm here."

More tears traced a path down my jaw. My chest was so tight that it took a concentrated effort to steady my shallow breaths into deeper, more fortifying drags of air. I let myself relax against Garrick's chest, relishing the wall of solid muscle and the rhythm of his heartbeat and the way they grounded me. In his arms, I was safe.

But...

Renewed fear froze my insides.

"Garrick," I managed, wiping at my cheeks. "*You're* not safe." I nearly sobbed again as the images from my dream seared my memory.

"It was a dream, Starlight," Garrick insisted, running his fingers through my hair.

I closed my eyes, trying to soak in this moment and reassure myself. He was here. Alive. Holding me. He cared.

Warmth filled me as he pulled me closer, tucking me against him as one hand held my waist securely and the other traced lazy patterns down the back of my neck. Each touch sent trails of fire down my skin. Was this the comforting touch of a friend? Of a man loyal to the death to the woman he believed was his rightful queen?

Or was he feeling what I did with our nearness? Every brush of his breath against my neck had me resisting the urge to shiver, and each caress from his fingers made me feel emboldened in a way I never had before. Suddenly, I was thinking of twisting in his arms, of facing him and pressing my lips to his. I was lost in a daydream, wondering what he would taste like. Wondering what it would feel like to be pressed against him.

What had seemed so scandalous before now only carried with it a sense of security and belonging. I knew Garrick wouldn't touch me inappropriately; he had always been a gentleman, and our proximity comforted me.

But...

He was still *touching* me.

"Garrick," I said again, more urgently. I wrenched away so abruptly that his hand fell from my waist. Chill air licked at my skin as I sat up, away from Garrick's warmth. "You can't be here. You can't—" My voice cracked as I turned to him.

He was already sitting up, and my stomach leapt when I realized he'd removed his shirt to sleep. Though the embers had almost completely burnt out in the hours since I'd fallen asleep, there was just enough golden light to burnish his skin, accentuating the outlines of countless muscles. Cheeks heating, I dragged my eyes up to his face.

"I thought you were going to hurt yourself," Garrick murmured, his face solemn.

Fresh tears burned my eyes. "But they'll hurt you for touching me."

A muscle jumped in his jaw as he swiped a hand through his hair, standing some of the white-blond strands on end. One fell across his forehead, and I had to curl my fingers into my palm to keep myself from reaching out and brushing it out of his face. "More likely, they would harm you to make me suffer," he said, his eyes dark with loathing. He swallowed, his throat working. "They've wanted me to serve as both your captor and your bodyguard. Maybe we can convince them you were trying to escape. I can pretend I was only here to keep you in your bed." His lips twitched in a humorless smile. "We can behave as if I was only being their faithful dog."

Garrick rose from the bed, pacing across the floor.

"You can't lie," I whispered. I couldn't banish the images of a bloody, tortured Garrick from my mind, and I didn't want to find out what Preston and Nerissa would do to him if they found him holding me, sharing my bed.

His expression was tormented as he raked his fingers though his hair again. "Maybe you should leave—"

"*No.* We already went over this," I said firmly.

"They'll torture you." Garrick's voice was ragged. "That's how they'll punish me. And it's my fault. I was the fool who held you—"

I lifted my chin, once again cutting him off. "Well, they can't do much to me if Preston is to announce our engagement soon. They need me alive, and they can't do anything to obviously mar my appearance, either, or the citizens will see and know."

"Starlight..."

"I'll be fine," I insisted. "Go back to sleep." I lay back against the pillows and pulled the sheets over myself, pretending that I was about to fall asleep myself.

We spent the rest of the night in tormented silence, each trying to fool the other into thinking we were fine. Asleep and unafraid.

Occasionally, I heard faint shrieks from deep in the bowels of the fortress, down in those awful dungeons. I squeezed my eyes shut, telling myself at least it wasn't Garrick. And it wouldn't be him tomorrow, either.

Better me than him, I thought.

CHAPTER EIGHTEEN

Garrick was on his feet, hunting knife in hand, before the door even swung open that morning. I was moved by Garrick's protective gesture even if we both knew it was futile. But it wasn't Nerissa or Preston—at least, not at first. A guard entered with a tray of food, leaving it wordlessly on the bed beside me.

My stomach churned.

"You should eat," Garrick said. "Restore your strength after fighting that demon."

"What about you?"

Hesitating, Garrick sat on the edge of the bed, keeping plenty of distance between us. "I'm not hungry."

I wasn't either, and despite my efforts, I couldn't manage to do more than pick at the food.

When footsteps approached again, Garrick leapt to his feet, knife firm in his grip.

The door swung inward, and Preston's piercing eyes immediately darted between Garrick and me. A derisive grin overtook his features. He stalked into the room, sniffing. "Garrick, you stink of human—and mortal, you smell of *him*." He shook his head. "The fact that you can even bear to touch her..." He trailed off, flicking his fingers without even sparing Garrick another glance.

Stiffening, the wolf shifter lowered his weapon, his expression melting from fury to cool indifference. I sucked in a shaky breath. He was under Preston's control now.

"You should know better, Fiancée," Preston continued, stepping even closer to me, his presence looming. Though my heartbeat picked up, I refused to let my growing fear show on my face, instead setting my jaw and forcing a mask of calm in place. "No one touches what is *mine*."

"I don't belong to you," I said, standing slowly. "I don't belong to anyone."

"Garrick," Preston snapped. A single gesture from the king had Garrick reaching to gather his hunting knife and stalking toward me. There was no sign of the man I knew. He seemed like a mere husk, a puppet forced to do Preston's bidding, as he seized my wrist and twisted me around until my back was to both men.

My heart twinged. I'd expected Preston to inflict some sort of hurt on me—I hadn't anticipated him using Garrick to harm me.

Still, I didn't resist, didn't cry out. I couldn't let Preston know he was winning, couldn't let him gain a single more ounce of pleasure out of my suffering. He could enjoy watching Garrick harm me with his knife, but he wouldn't hear me sniffle or beg.

I fought the urge to tremble as cool metal pressed against the skin at the base of my neck, hesitating before slicing downward through my tunic. The sound of tearing fabric rang out in my ears too loudly in the quiet, and cool air nipped against my back. I ground my teeth together at the first press of the tip of Garrick's knife, the first well of warm blood, the first sting of breaking flesh. Tears burned the back of my throat as he worked slowly, methodically, one firm hand on my waist.

This isn't him. This isn't him.

Closing my eyes, I reminded myself of the ways I'd pretended back home when the cutting words of others had hurt, and I'd refused to let them see. The complacency I'd settled on my face. The distant places I'd let my mind wander. Once, I'd gone back to times when my stepfather had been alive and home had felt safe and loving, or I'd daydreamed about the next dress I'd create.

This time, I was back in Garrick's arms, cradled against his chest and listening to his heartbeat as we huddled together for warmth in that cave, back when we'd still been on the run from Preston and Nerissa. I was under the stars again, studying the constellations, listening to Garrick share their stories. I was training with him, learning how to defend myself while silently appreciating his smooth, graceful movements, all the while knowing that as long as I was near him, I was safe.

I tensed every muscle in my body against the pain growing in my back, not wanting Preston to see me tremble or flinch away. More blood trickled down my back, wetting the end of my ruined tunic. I counted breaths, trying to keep the memories in the forefront of my mind, warm and soothing and vivid. *Someday those memories will be my life again,* I vowed.

At last, Garrick released me, and I turned, holding my tunic to keep it from falling off my shoulders as I peered at Preston defiantly. I couldn't tell from the look in his cold eyes if he was satisfied or angry at my lack of reaction. Out of the corner of my eye, Garrick breathed heavily as the bloody knife and his shoulders slumped forward. I refused to glance at him to gauge his reaction or see if Preston still controlled him. Devastation or indifference—I wasn't sure I could bear either expression in that moment.

After a long, silent moment, Preston narrowed his eyes. "I'll send Aspen to help you clean up. Hurry. We will return to Northelm to announce our engagement. There's no time to waste."

Back throbbing, I didn't respond or even move my head. I simply stared at him, praying he could read the silent challenge in my glare. But if he saw it, he didn't react at all.

"Come, Garrick," Preston snapped, and he swept out of the room, Garrick trailing rigidly.

The door slammed behind them, and I was left for a few minutes in blissful silence, able to sink on my bed and breathe deeply, forcing back my tears. Unfortunately, my solitude didn't last long, and a knock on the door forced me to stand and shuffle forward to cautiously pull it open.

Aspen was perched on a guard's shoulder, her arms crossed and her expression crinkled. There was a heavy bag hanging from one shoulder, though I couldn't possibly fathom how something small enough for a pixie to carry could hold anything that would help me.

As soon as her dark eyes noticed my disheveled appearance, she stood hastily, the weight of her swinging bag making her stumble a little. "Would you let me in, Your Majesty?" she asked, gesturing toward my hand.

With one still awkwardly holding the back of my tunic together, I extended my free hand and let Aspen drop down into it. She stood there for a moment, blinking up at me, before shooing me forward. "Get inside, close the door. We have work to do, Florentia Silverfrost!"

I hastened to obey her command, kicking the door shut with my foot. "Ren."

"What?" she asked.

"Please call me Ren."

The pixie smiled up at me. "Very well, Ren."

As soon as I'd settled onto the bed, Aspen hopped out of my hand and onto the covers, tugging the bag off her shoulder. "You might want to slide over a little," she said without any preamble.

Frowning in confusion—the tiny pixie had plenty of space—I did as she asked, moving closer to the edge of the bed.

In a blink, the pixie I'd been studying vanished, and a full-grown woman sat beside me in her place. She appeared exactly like Aspen—smooth, dark skin, glittering eyes, and bouncy curls. Even the bag she'd been holding had grown, now resting in her lap.

I gaped. "How—what—I don't understand," I spluttered.

Aspen laughed, the sound light and airy. "Have you never heard about pixies' ability to shapeshift?"

"Then why do you spend so much time in a little body, being carried to and fro?"

Aspen fluttered her lashes. "If you could be ferried about all day like royalty, wouldn't you choose to be?" When I merely continued to frown, she waved a hand and laughed again. "My smaller form is my *natural* one. Being pixie-sized is most comfortable for me." Her expression grew solemn. "Now, turn and let me see your back."

"I figured you would hate me," I choked out. "You're only doing this at the king's bidding, aren't you?"

Aspen shook her head. "If you mean because of what you did to Isolde..." She rolled her eyes. "She wasn't my friend. She was a notorious court gossip, and with her access to every corner of the palace because of her healing magic, she was a useful informant. But truthfully, I tolerated her. She didn't have an unselfish bone in her body, and her cruelty goes against a healer's nature."

I raised my eyebrows in surprise, but Aspen gestured impatiently for me to move.

Turning to the side, I allowed her gentle fingers to pull my ruined tunic away from my body. A sharp intake of breath told me that she was horrified by whatever she saw.

"King Preston is a wretch," she practically snarled, the most hostile I'd ever heard the pixie's sweet voice turn. "Why did he do this?"

"I—" I hesitated, swallowing. If Aspen had no qualms about speaking ill of the king, then surely I could trust her. Right? "He promised if he could smell Garrick on me, there would be punishment. Garrick was tasked with spending the night here as my guard, and I woke him when I had a nightmare. He came to comfort me, and..."

"And this was the king's sadistic retaliation," Aspen muttered. "He and Nerissa set this up in order to entrap you. They expected this to happen. They love to play mind games and set the board so their victims always lose. And then he *carved into* you."

"He forced Garrick to do it," I breathed.

Aspen hissed words under her breath that sounded like they were in another language, but her harsh tone told me they were likely a string of foul curses. "It's the Stormclaw emblem—*their* emblem. Claws and snow."

"Stormclaw? Was that their name before they took Silverfrost and ruled for the dead family?"

I heard Aspen rummage through her bag as she hummed her assent. "He's essentially marked you as his," she practically spat.

I stiffened, imagining the bloody cuts on my mid-back and what they represented. It was as vile as if the king had forced Garrick to carve *Preston* into my flesh. "I don't belong to him," I said, echoing my earlier claim before the royal had hurt me.

"No, but as long as he thinks you do, he will make your life a living hell." Aspen paused. "This may sting. I'm going to clean your wound first, and then I'll use a concoction my people swear by. It won't be enough to prevent scarring, but you'll feel relief instantly."

I was quiet as the pixie worked, cleaning the blood off my skin and then applying something cool and sticky to my wound. "That smells like...honey."

"Because it's made with honey. It's mixed with plenty of natural ingredients found in our land—which is the source of our magic, after all—and then it's pixie-blessed. Or, that's what we like to say. Pixies don't technically have magic beyond shifting. I suppose the gods thought changing our forms at will was enough power. We can't use glamour either. Really, we are just another type of fae shifter, like your hunter."

"He isn't *my* hunter," I protested, as the pixie reached for the sleeve of my tunic, pushing it up to reveal my bandaged arm.

As she unbound the gauze and cleaned the cuts, a coy tone seeped into Aspen's words. "Isn't he? Transforming into his wolf form and killing the humans attacking you in the arena. Slipping you a forbidden knife for your encounter with that underworld creature. And holding you when you were troubled by a nightmare?"

While Aspen finished rebandaging my arm, I picked at a loose thread in my leggings with my other hand, feeling heat rush to my cheeks. "And through all of that, he's never indicated his feelings go beyond friendship and loyalty to someone he believes is his true queen. Besides, no fae in Silverfrost seems to view humans *that* way. And he belongs to Nerissa."

Standing, Aspen withdrew a fresh tunic from her bag and set it in my lap. "Change out of that bloody tunic so I can burn it," she ordered.

As I obeyed, tossing her the destroyed one before slipping the new one over my head, Aspen crept toward the hearth, adding fresh logs and stoking the fire back into a steady flame. "He belongs to Queen Nerissa in the way you belong to King Preston—which is to say, he doesn't love her, and he never will. You know that as well as I. He is as much a prisoner as you or any of the human slaves they keep at the castle." She fed my old tunic into the fire and then turned, crossing her arms. "As for fae loving humans...how else do you think you came into existence?" A smirk tugged on her lips.

I shrugged. "Somehow a Silverfrost and my mother must have met, but it all seems to be a mystery to everyone."

Aspen's eyes glittered. "I need to shift. If you let me sit on your shoulder while we still have time, I can share what I know of your story."

As I settled into the armchair by the fire, Aspen transformed into her pixie form. She hopped into my palm, allowing me to set her on my shoulder.

"I was a servant in the palace before the Silverfrost family was massacred," Aspen explained, "and I attended both your father and mother. I know more of their story than anyone else left alive, it seems."

She leaned back, her eyes growing distant as if seeing images from moments long since passed. "Your father was Ashton Silverfrost, beloved second-born to the king and queen, and promised to a fae woman at court. But your father had a rebellious streak and a romantic heart. He dreamed of a love match rather than a political one, and he had a tender spot toward the humans enslaved in Silverfrost. He was one of the few who disagreed with the ways humans were mistreated and looked down upon as inferior, and in fact...he secretly helped many of the humans in the castle escape. It was on one such excursion, returning some mortals to the human world, that he met your mother.

"I'll never forget how he spoke of her when he returned. I was his confidante, for he knew I alone sympathized with his views and did what I could to help the humans. I'm not sure what gave the prince such a tender, kind heart when so many of his kin were vicious and proud and cruel. Unlike shifters such as Garrick and me, who understand what it's like to be viewed as weak and inferior, he had powerful magic and glamour. He was beloved among the people of Silverfrost and renowned for his magic. He could call upon the earth itself, shifting it and causing dangerous earthquakes and rockslides. He could snuff out all light with a single breath, immersing his victims in darkness.

"And yet, he had no stomach for war and conquest except when forced into it to protect his people. While his parents plotted ways they could use his powers to claim the other kingdoms of Brytwilde for Silverfrost, your father only dreamt of ways he could leave his responsibilities behind. He even spoke of abandoning the fae world and glamouring himself as a human to live among mortals.

"I think, had things not happened as they did, that's what he would have done. He and your mother would have happily raised you in a quiet mortal town."

"But that's not what happened," I said sadly.

Aspen shook her head. "Your parents continued to see each other in secret. They pledged themselves to one another, even though your father was betrothed to someone else and your mother's family was so terrified of fae she dared not even introduce her sweetheart to them. They bound themselves to one another not in a traditional marriage, but in the only sort of way they could, speaking their own vows in solitude and promising themselves to each other.

"Your mother feared scandal when your father sent me secretly to her town to see to her, and I told her she was with child. Her townspeople wouldn't understand—they thought of her as a single woman, and her pregnancy would have ruined her reputation and cast her out from her family home. So your father and I made plans...plans for both your parents to escape their lives."

Aspen sighed. "Sometimes, your parents were a little reckless in love. Your mother ventured into fae territory and was visiting your father when the attack happened. To this day, I don't know who opened the entrance to the underworld, though I have a suspicion it was Ivy Stormclaw, a woman who'd been betrothed to your father, and a relative of Preston and Nerissa, no less. Your mother confessed to me that she believed Ivy had spied the two of them together. Somehow, I think she manipulated your father into opening the door, threatening someone he loved. What she thought would happen or how she believed she herself would survive an onslaught of demons is anyone's guess, but jealousy is an ugly thing that doesn't always know reason. She didn't survive to share the details of what happened."

Aspen swallowed. "Your father stayed behind to fight with your family, to ensure we had time to escape, while he tasked me with helping your mother to safety. I traveled with her all the way to the border between fae and mortal lands, and there we said our goodbyes. But I returned to nothing but bloodshed and horror. The underworld creatures killed every last member of your family. I arrived just in time to see the Stormclaw siblings enter the castle and rally the remaining survivors, subduing the demons. By then, all the Silverfrosts, including your father, were dead."

Bitter tears burned my eyes for the courageous man I'd never met.

"Before they all died, one of the Silverfrosts must have managed to partially close the door. But it wasn't enough—not when we've watched the entrance weaken for over two decades' worth of winter solstices. Without a surviving member of the family to seal it each year, it continues to open wider, letting more and more creatures into our world."

I heaved a sigh. "And then, once they swept in to secure the demons, Preston and Nerissa were hailed as heroes."

"It's still a mystery to me how they overpowered the demons alone when the entire Silverfrost family failed." Aspen's eyes were dim with sorrow. "But their magic is quite strong...a sort that I suppose is a worthy match against an underworld creature's powers. Their magic is, quite literally, *death*. I've seen them peel the skin off a victim's bones with a simple touch."

My heart throbbed in my temples. "They don't use it often, do they?"

Aspen shook her head, mouth tightening into a firm line. "They prefer to slowly torment the ones they want to punish rather than give them swift deaths." She gestured to me. "It's why they'll taunt you, play mind games with you, treat you like their plaything, and use others to hurt you long before they'd ever use their own magic against you."

I swallowed thickly. "And yet, you're here—serving them?"

Aspen glanced down at her swinging legs. "At first, I thought they were the heroes everyone claimed they were. But as the years passed, I saw their cruelty against humans and fae alike. They're bloodthirsty and selfish, but you already know that. I've stayed as a spy, trying to help the mortals enslaved here like your father once did, and hoping to gather information to use against them. To condemn them so even the Silverfrost citizens would agree the siblings must be dethroned. But Preston and Nerissa have also mistreated the fae here, and a growing number of citizens are becoming more and more dissatisfied. It's made my mission of gathering rebels together quite simple over the years. We have amassed numbers in your absence, biding our time in hopes we can organize a coup." She studied me, eyes piercing. "I was also waiting for you."

"Waiting for me? When we first met, you said I was a weak human you didn't think could be a Silverfrost."

Aspen shook her head. "I said that *some* people thought that, for Isolde's benefit. I didn't want anyone to know my allegiance was with you and not King Preston and Queen Nerissa. Anyway, I tried to search for you on my own, but I can't remain in any form but my natural one for very long. And a tiny pixie can't travel far distances in secret all that well. Instead, I started to send Garrick out to nearby human towns to search for you. Not to tell you who you were or bring you to Silverfrost, but more to ensure you were all right, safely away from the fae...at least until we rebels were ready to talk to you about your origins."

I recalled the way Garrick's eyes had latched onto me that first night across the ballroom, the way he'd seemed enthralled by my unusual hair. He'd known. He'd known who I was all along.

"He didn't tell me," I said. "Why didn't he tell me?"

"Well, he wouldn't have been sure who you were, not right away. And then everything went wrong," Aspen said, wringing her hands. "We'd hoped to eventually share information with you while you remained safely in the human world, but the night Garrick met you, when your brother gave you to the king and queen..."

I cringed. "I was brought to Silverfrost before I was ready."

"Garrick did what I would have wanted him to do—tried to take you to the sanctuary of another, kinder fae kingdom. You could have hidden in Ashwood for years, if needed, until we had a solid plan and were ready to reveal you to Silverfrost as our true queen. But unfortunately, the royal siblings control him. Because of this, Garrick was never supposed to travel with you...only to find you, simply because he's our best hunter. We'd agreed that when the time came for you to leave the mortal world, we would send someone who couldn't be controlled to bring you to our kingdom."

"How did that happen? Preston and Nerissa's ability to control Garrick, I mean?"

"In those early days, Garrick—like me—thought Preston and Nerissa were heroes. Garrick's entire family had been visiting the castle the night of the slaughter. They died alongside the Silverfrosts. Garrick was only a boy, and he felt it was his duty to his family to pledge himself to our new king and queen, as if serving them was the best way to avenge his family's deaths, since the demons can't ever be killed, and can only be banished back to the underworld without Silverfrost blood."

I sucked in a sharp breath. "That's why they can control him without glamour."

Aspen nodded slowly. "It is a blood oath, the most powerful oath one fae can make to another. He gave them his life—quite literally. Whenever he's in close enough proximity to either of them, they can control his body, even his words. His vow to them can only be broken in death."

My mind whirled. No wonder Garrick had said I couldn't save him, that he was doomed to serve them forever. "There's no other way out?"

She shook her head sadly. Regretfully.

"There's something else you should know," the pixie added, casting a glance across the room, toward my bed where my tray of food rested. "In food, forget-me-nots don't affect you the same way. You can consume a small amount of the flowers without feeling pain, but once digested, they destroy your ability to access your magic, the same way they do if they touch your skin. Preston and Nerissa have been drugging you."

My eyes widened. "How do you know this?"

"I tasted a bite of your food when I was in your room back when Isolde healed you. I couldn't shift for hours. Unfortunately, I don't always have access to your rooms, and the king and queen only allow certain servants to bring your food. I can try to sneak some food to you from the kitchens, but when I can't, you'll still need to keep up your strength."

I frowned contemplatively. "I've managed to access my magic sometimes even while eating their food."

Aspen nodded. "We'll find a way to overcome them. I think—"

A sharp knock interrupted us, and Aspen scowled.

"It's time," the muffled voice of a guard said from the other side of the door. "The king and queen are returning to the castle, and they've summoned you to leave immediately with them."

CHAPTER NINETEEN

After I pulled on my coat and Aspen gathered her bag, I lifted her in my hand and looked at her frantically. "How?" I asked helplessly, and I could tell by the way she smiled softly at me that she knew what I was really asking, what I didn't even have the words to voice aloud. I sat to pull on and lace my boots, my fingers feeling clumsy as I worked.

"I will see you later today," Aspen whispered. "I'll need to reapply the ointment to your wound, and we'll discuss plans. In the meantime, continue as you have been. We'll let them grow ever bolder in their belief that they own us. But they will never own us. Stay strong, Your Majesty. We *will* be free."

When I opened the door, the impatient guard huffed as he extended a hand to accept the pixie. "Are you quite ready?"

There was no deference in his tone, no respect in his expression. It was clear that *he* wasn't one who believed the throne was rightfully mine. Like Preston and Nerissa, he likely thought I was a lowly, disgusting human.

Straightening my spine, I nodded. I'd brought no belongings with me but the hunting knife that had been taken from me—and then used to carve the mark on my back. Wearing the clothes I'd arrived in, I trailed the guard out of the room and through countless windowless halls, where only the torchlight dancing off the stone provided any light. In this harsh space, time had no meaning, and it could have just as easily been midnight outside as daylight.

When we at last exited the fortress, the icy air was the first to greet me. Harsh daylight glinted off every flake of snow and bit of frost dusting the ramparts and crusting the courtyard cobblestones. My eyes watered from the sharp contrast after the dimness of the fortress.

"At last," Queen Nerissa said from her mount, studying me with annoyance as if I'd spent hours rather than minutes leaving my room after the guard had knocked.

My eyes snagged on Garrick, seated on a horse behind her, but his expressionless mask told me he was in the siblings' grip. I chewed on my inner cheek, fuming silently.

Nerissa waved toward where Preston stood beside his stallion, his blood-red eyes piercing my soul. "You'll ride with me," he declared. "Hurry."

I swallowed down my disgust and forced my legs to move toward him, accepting his gloved hand as he practically shoved me onto the horse and then swung up behind me. The difference between sharing a horse with Garrick and sharing one with Preston was jolting—where before I'd relished the warmth emanating from the wolf shifter, had blushed at our proximity and the woodsy scent surrounding him, now I had to struggle not to gag. The air around Preston felt somehow even chillier than the icy breeze clawing through my hair as our company trotted out of the courtyard.

"Today, I will announce our engagement at a feast," Preston murmured as we followed a path along the outskirts of Northelm. "You will be the picture of grace and obedience."

I didn't respond, my chest tightening at the firmness in his words. He didn't need to add a threat.

"Garrick will be your guard."

I wondered if Garrick would be under their control, or if his presence would be yet another test.

"You will dance, you will laugh, you will be pleasant. You will play the role of a besotted, soon-to-be consort and their heroine. And then you will prepare, for your real work begins on the winter solstice. Then, you will prove yourself one final time by using the power of your blood on the entrance to the underworld the night it is most fragile."

"And send back the demons that have been imprisoned here?" I questioned, not turning around to meet his gaze.

"Yes."

My mouth tasted sour as I thought of my impending engagement announcement, but I drew a calming breath, forcing my mind to think. There wasn't much time left before winter began. My calculations—if I hadn't lost track of time in this awful realm—told me there was only a week left until the solstice. Somehow, I was determined to free myself of Preston and Nerissa before then. That meant I had one week to formulate a plan with Aspen to save Garrick and myself. One week to end the siblings' awful reign. One week to take back my life.

And, despite the restrictions the siblings had put on my magic by spelling my quarters and using forget-me-nots against me, my magic would also be at the height of its power once winter began in earnest. That could only work in my favor. I hoped.

Back at the castle, Preston himself escorted me to my rooms and left me with maids already waiting—both glamoured humans that made bile rise in my throat just to look at them. As soon as the king closed the door behind me, the two women set to work wordlessly, one drawing a steaming bath in the washroom while the other ushered me toward a side table where a tray laden with food and tea was already set out.

My heart climbed up my throat at the sight of the food as I remembered Aspen's words. Despite my hunger—a quick glance out the window told me it was past noon by now—I knew what eating or drinking anything brought to me would cost. Unfortunately, I also knew that maintaining my strength was crucial. If I wasted away, my magic would be almost as useless as the forget-me-nots rendered it.

If Aspen wasn't confident she could bring me a regular supply of uncontaminated food, I'd have to eat what I was given. I poured myself a cup of tea and picked at the fresh fruit on a platter.

What if I can grow accustomed to constant exposure to forget-me-nots? I wondered, sweet flavor bursting on my tongue as I bit into a strawberry. If the fae avoided the flower so religiously, did they know what would happen if I was continuously dosed with it? I'd heard tales of dedicated servants to our king back home building immunity to poisons, sometimes even assisting members of the royal family in the ability. If their mortal bodies could manage such a feat for survival, what more could mine accomplish, when I carried magic in my veins and was part fae? What if I found a way to increase my exposure to the forget-me-nots until I could learn to push past their influence and grasp stronger tendrils of my magic?

I drew a slow breath as the mortals shuffled about behind me, laying out cosmetics and other accessories for my hair. If I could regain my power, I would become someone the king and queen would fear. Someone who might be able to gather enough allegiance from the courtiers and Aspen's rebels to assemble a resistance against them that would help me ascend my throne. Someone who might be able to end their bloody reign.

And then you'll be queen, in a land full of immortals who think you're lesser. In a strange, cruel world that you hardly understand. I forced down my fear. With Garrick and Aspen at my side, surely I could manage.

It was that, or abandon Silverfrost and the underworld entrance, condemning not only this land but also the entire world to eventually being overrun by demons and monsters.

That wasn't a choice.

"Your bath is ready, my lady," one of the women murmured.

I glanced over my shoulder to meet her glazed blue eyes. My stomach clenched at the sight, and suddenly, my appetite was gone. I set down my teacup and rose.

Despite its futility, I tried to engage her in conversation as I followed her across the room. "What is your name?"

The girl paused, blinking. "Excuse me? Is there something else you desire?"

"Your name."

She stared at me emptily. "I am your humble maid. What else can I do for you?"

"But what are you called?"

She blinked again. "Servant." She turned away toward the washroom.

A bang on the door to my quarters interrupted us, and I jumped. The two maids didn't seem fazed. One waited at the entrance to the washroom while the other strode toward the door and opened it. Before she could speak, Garrick shoved past her, forcing his way in.

"Starlight," he breathed, his chest heaving as if he'd run the whole way here. His gold eyes were full of pain, his face haunted in a way that stole my own breath.

"Garrick?" I crossed the floor to him, terrified the siblings had wreaked some new havoc.

"Leave us," he growled to the two women, sending them scurrying without protest from my room. They only knew how to obey.

There was a wolfish way about Garrick as he stalked closer, shaking his head. "I need to see." His voice trembled.

"Garrick..."

"Did Aspen tend to you?"

"I'm fine," I said, but Garrick grasped my shoulders, ducking his head to peer into my eyes fervently.

"Let me see, Starlight," he pled.

"They'll smell you on my skin," I insisted faintly, glancing at where his hands grasped my shoulders still, his thumb brushing against my collarbone.

He shook his head. "You'll bathe and change. And I will too, before the feast. They'll never know." He cupped my face with a scarred hand, and I couldn't help myself from leaning into his touch. My heart quivered. Before I could wonder if maybe this was the tender touch of someone who cared for me as more than a friend, more than his sovereign, Garrick spoke again. "Please."

Biting my lip, I turned around, letting him use shaking hands to unbutton my tunic far enough for him to see the bandage Aspen had used to cover my wound. Garrick sucked in a sharp breath as he cautiously peeled it back. He cursed.

"*I* did this to you."

I turned, clasping one hand to the front of my tunic to hold it up. When I met Garrick's expression, the raw devastation in it cut me to the core.

He dropped to his knees, tears shimmering in his eyes. "Forgive me." He shook his head again, as if he could wish away the marks marring my skin.

He wrapped his arms about my waist and pulled me to him, burying his head against my stomach as he wept.

"There's nothing to forgive. You didn't do this," I said firmly. I gathered my courage and ran my fingers through the white-blond locks of his hair. They were silky to the touch, and the act felt so intimate I couldn't stop the blood from rushing to my cheeks. "*Preston* did it." I injected venom into my words. "As surely as if he'd lifted the blade himself. But like a coward, he forced you to do it. It's not your fault. It's *his* crime. *His* mark. And *he* will pay."

Garrick drew back enough to look up into my face. "He's already forced us both to pay the price," he said. "Every time I see you, I'll know I failed you. You, my rightful queen. The starlight to my darkness."

"Never," I bit out, slowly kneeling until we were face-to-face. "When you look at me, I will wear this mark as a badge of honor. A sign of what we've both survived and will overcome. I promise you, Garrick."

My words calmed him at last. He blinked, nodding as he searched my face, as if he could read my every thought and plan. Lifting a hand, he swept it through my hair, each brush achingly tender. "Aspen spoke to you?"

"Yes."

A slow smile spread across his face, the first sign of hope I'd seen in him in far too long. "She'll help us. We'll make them both pay."

He leaned forward until our foreheads touched, until we breathed the same air. My chest tightened at his proximity, at my sudden desire to confess to him how deep my feelings truly went. But he called me his queen. Did he only see in me what all his people saw—a savior? Or did he care about more than what I could be—did he care for *who* I was? Even if we defeated Preston and Nerissa, freeing him from their control, would he ever want me the way I wanted him?

Before either of us could speak another word, a soft knock echoed on my door. We jolted apart, terror coursing through my being. What if Preston or Nerissa found us out before we'd had a chance to hide the fact that we'd touched? What new horrors would they force us to inflict on one another?

"Your Majesty, time is short. We must prepare you now. Please allow us to enter."

My breath left me in a relieved whoosh at the maid's voice.

Solemnly, Garrick grasped my free hand and pressed his warm lips to my palm. I swallowed when my mouth ran dry. *Just the touch of a man loyal to his queen? Or...?*

"I'll see you at the feast, Starlight," he promised, and then rose, striding to the door and letting the maids back in.

The glamoured girls didn't react to the way I knelt on the floor, my half-unbuttoned tunic hanging loosely from my frame. They didn't notice the way Garrick and I stared at one another for one last, long moment, silently making promises of helping one another to freedom, *somehow*, before he ducked out of the room. They simply escorted me to the tub, waiting with their eerily blank expressions as I scrubbed myself clean, rinsing away Garrick's scent from my body even as my skin continued to tingle from his every touch.

CHAPTER TWENTY

As soon as the maids turned me to peer into the mirror, I gasped. I'd scarcely paid attention to the dress when it had been laid out, and my mind had wandered as the women laced me into a fae corset and pulled layers of fabric over my head. Now, I found myself staring at a woman dressed all in white lace, adorned in silver beading. I cringed. I was dressed like a bride. Like a snowflake. Silver glitter even dusted my cheeks and eyelids.

A knock sounded at the door.

One of the maids went to open it, and I silently begged that it wasn't Preston on the other side of the door. To my relief, Garrick waited for me in the hall.

"Ready?" he asked. "His Royal Majesty requested I personally see you safely to the feast."

I glanced toward the window, surprised to find late afternoon light gilding the snow outside. Time had passed quickly, and now that I knew what horrors of the underworld escaped at night, I realized our time for an evening feast was short.

Garrick stepped inside, leaning back against the closed door as both maids fluttered about me, tugging my dress this way and that in final touch-ups.

I turned toward Garrick when the women finally moved back, but froze when I caught his assessing glance burning into me. Heat flooded my cheeks. Was it my imagination, or were his eyes trailing me up and down?

His gaze latched onto mine, and he grinned. The warmth in my face sank down into my chest, and I returned his smile.

"I know this isn't the color you'd prefer to wear," he said, his smile turning forced, "but you still look lovely."

Clothed in leathers and fur and wearing his knives strapped to his belt, Garrick looked like the hunter he was. But the outfit suited him more than formal attire would have. The cut of his clothes emphasized the muscles hidden beneath, and the rugged look made his gold eyes shine even brighter.

Feeling daring, I lifted my chin. "You look rather handsome yourself."

His mouth curved upward in a crooked smile. "It's nice to hear you admit it out loud."

I flushed. "What?"

"You heard me. I've seen the way you look at me, Starlight."

Quickly averting my gaze from his, I quipped, "That sounds awfully arrogant." It was nice to hear him flirt like his usual self, though I didn't dare read into it. Instead, I strode across the room, looking at the arm Garrick had offered me.

"You can touch my sleeve," Garrick reminded me, reading my tumultuous thoughts. "They'll expect me to escort you properly. Your scent on my clothes won't bring any punishments. Only skin."

Slowly, I slid my arm through his. "He's dressed me to look like his bride," I whispered despairingly as he escorted me out the door and down the hall.

Garrick's grasp tightened. "It won't come true," he said, his voice lowered. "They'll take control of me as soon as we enter the hall where the feast is to take place, but Aspen will be there. She has a plan."

"So do I," I murmured.

A few guards pulled away from the walls to escort us, preventing further conversation about plans. Instead, I tossed Garrick a questioning look.

"You have extra guards because the king and queen want to ensure your safety, especially once your engagement is announced," he explained wryly. "Despite your heritage and your magic, it's possible the fact that you're human will turn some against you and this union." He cast me a piercing look. "Nothing will happen to you though; I'll make sure of that."

My heart warmed at his words.

At last, we rounded a final turn in one of the endless stone hallways and approached a set of open double doors leading into an enormous room. Music, talk, laughter, and warmth all poured from within, along with the tantalizing scents of endless mouthwatering foods. Beneath banners emblazoned with the Silverfrost sigil—crossed silver swords on a backdrop of blue—and intricate tapestries, long tables laden with the feast rested against one wall. On the opposite side were more tables and chairs, full of chattering fae of all appearances, some dressed as formally as I was, others clothed more for battle or hunting like Garrick, and a few so scantily clad that I had to avert my eyes. Nearby, a roaring fire filled a huge hearth. The middle of the room was wide and open, likely for dancing to the songs musicians serenaded us with.

Beyond all of this, on the far end of the room, was a stone dais. More banners hung from the ceiling, and an impressively large window bathed the space in the glow of the sun's last rays. Sitting in that glow, like angelic beings gracing us with their powerful presence, were King Preston and Queen Nerissa. Each occupied intricately carved wood thrones. While Preston was adorned all in black, emphasizing his dark eyes and every sharp angle of his harsh face, Nerissa wore rich blue and silver, making her appear every inch the cold, foreboding winter queen. Both wore their silver crowns and matching arrogant grins.

Preston's gaze snagged on mine, and the breath froze in my lungs. There was a taunting look on his face, like he was daring me to complain about my dress or about the mark I bore on my back. I was trapped in his sick game, and he was enjoying my misery.

While the guards trailing us found positions along the walls, Garrick drew me into the room, past the tables. Talk and laughter ceased as fae studied me, some with respectful dips of their heads, a few with uncertainty, and still others with outright scorn. Behind the tables, rows of empty-eyed human servants stood against the wall, waiting to serve the fae. The sight made me want to scream.

I scanned the gathered fae fruitlessly, wondering which shoulder my pixie friend might be perched upon, hoping I'd find her soon. In a sea of strangers and enemies, with Garrick stiff and stone-faced at my side—already lost to the siblings' control—I longed for the comforting sight of an ally still in possession of her free will.

A troll bared its teeth as we drew close, and Garrick set his free hand on the hilt of one of his knives in a silent warning. The creature lumbered away, but I didn't miss the resentment burning in its pale yellow eyes.

When we neared the dais, Garrick dipped into a low bow, but I stood rigidly to await Preston as he rose and strode slowly down the steps. The twisted smile he wore made my stomach spasm in response. "Snowflake. How good to see you looking...almost as well as the rest of us." He chuckled at his jab.

Nerissa followed him, waving a bored hand to signal Garrick to rise and come stand at her side. Eyes locked on me, she snaked her arm around his waist and pulled him against her, pressing her lips to his. I turned away, staring toward the window and swallowing the bile rising in my throat.

"Never fear," Preston muttered at my side, his expression cold as he surveyed his court, "I have no desire to taint myself in such a way with you, human."

But what about when he would need heirs? The thought made my stomach churn; he might not desire to touch me, but he'd probably *need* to. I shook the worry away, not letting it linger. I wasn't going to marry him, which meant that I'd never have to concern myself with such things.

Grasping my arm, he turned me to face the crowd. My gown rustled and the room seemed to spin as I tried to look unafraid while searching the countless unfriendly faces.

"Citizens of Silverfrost," King Preston began, "loyal members of our court. We bid you enjoy our celebration as we welcome Florentia Silverfrost to our kingdom."

My pulse throbbed in my temples. Somehow, I'd imagined there would be more time before he made this announcement. But here it was, happening immediately, and I could feel the walls closing in.

As I forced myself to concentrate, I realized Preston had been speaking the whole time, while I'd stood statue-still with a smile plastered to my mouth. "And it is my great honor to announce that Miss Silverfrost, our hope in these difficult times, has agreed to join with me in matrimony and be my revered consort. Please give her the respect she deserves as my future bride and our kingdom's future security."

The applause that erupted was mixed: some courtiers seemed genuinely pleased, either thrilled to honor me as their hoped-for savior, or content to know I would not rule, only stand beside their immortal rulers as a figurehead. Others' expressions made it clear they loathed the thought of a human marrying one of their kind at all. They fought disgust as they forced themselves to cheer at their sovereign's bidding.

I'd scarcely had time to shake the echo of Preston's announcement from my ears before he seized my arm and nearly dragged me toward the nearest table, where seats had been reserved for us, Nerissa, and Garrick. As we settled into our chairs, Nerissa clapped her hands and servants rushed to the side tables, filling trays with food and then making rounds, offering the fae their pick of food with which to fill their plates.

I tried not to look too closely at the mortal man's blank face as he stepped up behind me, holding out his tray for Preston and me to peruse. I selected an assortment of cheeses and fruits, a slice of bread, and braised beef in gravy. Despite my lack of appetite, I knew how important it was to keep up my strength—especially considering this food wouldn't be laced with forget-me-nots. As much as I wanted to build up my immunity, I knew eating untainted food would be wise, a way for me to remain powerful and wield a little bit of control over my doses of the flowers.

Between chewing bites of food, avoiding glancing toward the servants or Garrick and the way they all resembled puppets on strings, and pretending to smile and laugh when courtiers introduced themselves and offered false congratulations and praise, time inched by miserably. On my right, Nerissa ignored me in favor of her wolf shifter, leaning over to whisper in his ear and trail lecherous fingers down his chest. My stomach was in a constant knot. The one blessing of the meal was that Preston hardly spared me another glance. As promised, he didn't try to touch me. Didn't attempt to pretend to be a doting fiancé.

At long last, the music swelled, and servants began clearing empty plates. Couples started to rise from the tables and swirl and sway together across the open floor. Preston left to mingle with courtiers further down the table, and I drew my first deep breath of the evening, feeling free at last to stand and hunt for Aspen.

My heart leapt when I spotted her two tables down, sitting cross-legged on the tabletop with an empty pixie-sized plate before her and a glass of gold fae wine in her hand. Her emerald dress set off her brown skin, its skirts pooling around her legs as she giggled at something the woman at her side had said. As soon as Aspen's eyes met mine, her grin turned saucy, and she lifted her glass in a toast. "A hearty congratulations! You are a vision, Your Majesty."

As Aspen took a deep gulp of her wine, staining her lips gold, the other woman shot her a questioning glance. I had a feeling she didn't appreciate the fact that Aspen had called me *Your Majesty*.

I cleared my throat. "Aspen, may I have a word?"

She stood, nodding until her curls bounced.

When I offered a hand, she strolled across my palm and up my dress sleeve until she reached my shoulder. "Walk about the room, could you?" she asked as she settled in a seat, kicking her legs and sipping at her wine.

With a silent dip of my head to the stranger, who continued to watch us both warily, I began to circle the room leisurely, doing my best to dodge anyone who wanted to speak to me.

"Go to the tables and fetch a glass of wine," Aspen prodded before I could tell her about my idea of building an immunity against the forget-me-nots.

I blinked. "What?"

"You have fae blood running through your veins, Ren. A little wine won't harm you, but it *will* remind these arrogant members of court just who you are. You are no mere mortal. You're our rightful queen, and you alone bear powerful Silverfrost magic."

My scalp tingled at the thought. It was a bold move, but it was smart. A little wine shouldn't affect me like it would other humans—a lot would likely be an issue. Straightening my spine, I skirted the dance floor as I made my way toward the tables, eyeing the rows of glasses full of glistening liquid. As I seized the stem of the nearest wineglass, I turned to face the room. With most of the fae either dancing or sitting with their drinks already, I drew many eyes. Even beneath the steady rhythm of the lively tune the musicians had taken up, a steady murmur rippled through the courtiers. Men and women turned and whispered to one another. Eyes filled with curiosity or glee, eager to watch me make a fool of myself.

"Smile," Aspen urged, lifting her own glass toward her lips as if we were toasting.

Forcing my lips to curl, I matched her gesture and then took a long pull of the wine. It tasted of honey, sweet and light on my tongue, and it filled my chest with a burst of warmth as I swallowed it down. "Delicious," I told Aspen.

"I told you," she said proudly. "If it was going to affect you like other humans, it would taste rotten and wrong, but you would be compelled to keep drinking anyway. It would make anyone, with or without glamour, easily able to constrain you to do whatever they wanted. Even harm yourself."

I repressed a shudder.

"But they can see you're enjoying the wine, not grimacing. It's a silent but significant reminder."

"Speaking of," I said, glancing about to ensure none of the dancing couples were too close to us, "Garrick said you had a plan?"

"Working on one," Aspen murmured, "but these shows of yours when you're before the court are all integral to it. We want to gather allies."

I nodded my assent. "I have an idea to regain my magic."

"You can't starve yourself," Aspen said.

"No, but what if I exposed myself to more forget-me-nots? What if, just as some learn to build an immunity to poisons through exposure, I let my body grow accustomed to their influence? Do you think that's possible?"

Aspen swirled the remaining wine in her glass, contemplating. "Considering you've already drawn on your magic in times of need despite the forget-me-nots you've been steadily fed since your arrival? I'd say it's entirely possible. I just hope we have enough time, with the winter solstice being so near. But I think, if anyone can, it would be you. Winter will begin in earnest, and you're on Silverfrost land with the strongest magical bloodline our kingdom has ever had. And the power you've already displayed? It's significant. Perhaps more powerful than many of the full-blooded fae in your ancestry possessed."

I drew a deep breath, letting her words wash over me, dousing me in renewed hope.

Before either of us could say more, I noticed Preston approaching out of the corner of my eye. He circled the dance floor, but his eyes were locked on me. My stomach turned, and I wasn't sure even the cheering effects of the wine could help me pretend to be anything but revolted.

On my shoulder, Aspen went silent, but I could feel the stiff way she sat.

On the far side of the ballroom, the doors creaked open and one of the guards hurried forward, her violet eyes wide with discomfort as she bowed to her king and queen. Silence descended as everyone turned to see why a guard had barged in during the festivities. "Your Majesties, I'm so sorry to interrupt—"

"Are you?" Queen Nerissa cut in, lifting a brow as she strode forward to meet the guard near the entrance. "Because it seems you're not that sorry if you chose to interrupt anyway."

At my side, Preston sneered, refusing to even move or acknowledge the woman. Instead, he looked impatient.

"There's a-a...well, a messenger from the warfront," the woman stammered.

Nerissa waved her hand. "My brother is occupied. Lead me to this messenger."

Bowing in acknowledgement, the guard guided Nerissa from the ballroom, and the music resumed.

"Come," Preston said, turning to me without preamble. "It is tradition for a newly betrothed couple to dance at their own celebration."

"Are you not concerned about the state of the war?"

"My sister is capable of handling those concerns. Today, my concern is our arrangement." His eyes bored into me.

"Of course." I set my glass down on the table, trying not to grit my teeth or flinch back from him. It wouldn't help my image before the court, where I needed to look strong and capable, if I cowered away from the man I needed to overthrow.

Preston's gaze flicked to Aspen. "Couldn't you shape shift and leave us?" he asked irritably.

Silently, Aspen hopped down, standing as tall as me before her slippers even hit the floor. The effect was dizzying, and I wasn't sure I'd ever grow used to it. She dipped into a swift curtsey, clutching her glass as she swept away.

I forced a smile as Preston's cold hand grasped mine and led me onto the floor. That smile remained firmly in place as he set his other on my waist and I forced myself to step closer, glancing to the other couples to see how this fae dance went. Unlike back home, where we never stood so near to one another in a dance, this one seemed to require me to be face-to-face with the king, keeping one hand in his and the other on his shoulder.

Aspen's words echoed in my mind: *Their magic is, quite literally,* death. *I've seen them peel the skin off a victim's bones with a simple touch.*

With Preston's icy hand in mine, I glanced demurely down, pretending I was shy rather than too horrified to look into his eyes. Maybe the burden of carrying death magic was to forever have the likeness of death, with his pale skin, bony hands, and bloody eyes.

"Enjoyed your wine?" Preston asked. "I've always heard that to mortal tongues, it tastes of ashes."

"It was quite delicious," I answered tightly, forcing myself to lift my chin and briefly meet his eyes. I didn't want him to think I was afraid. I was only disgusted.

He snorted, as if he didn't believe me.

"I suppose I have my Silverfrost blood to thank for that," I went on, emboldened. Let him be reminded of who I was too. Let him feel the threat to his throne.

For a moment, he stared at me silently, and in that wordless glare, I thought maybe he understood what words ran through my mind. *You can't trap me forever. You can't cage my magic by drugging me. You can't deny my heritage when I can flaunt it with my power.*

"I suppose it must be nice for a mortal to have the chance to feel significant," he said at last, dismissively. "To be able to taste the wine and magic of immortals. How colorful it must make your drab, brief existence."

Ignoring his jab, I focused on the steps of the dance as we spun across the floor. I tried to ignore the eyes on us both, assessing, critical, interested. I tried not to notice Garrick's impassive expression as he watched us from his seat on the other side of the room. And I especially tried to pretend I wasn't dancing with a man who made my skin crawl.

Instead, I pretended I was dancing under a starry sky in Garrick's arms. Imagined we were free and safe. Daydreamed I was anywhere but here.

Startled shrieks and the twang of a string jolted me from my reverie. The musicians' song crashed to a discordant halt. An arrow slammed into Preston's shoulder, knocking him backward and out of my arms.

I choked on my cry as courtiers dashed off the dance floor and guards rushed to Preston's side. Pure rage hardened his features, turning his eyes a brighter red as he lifted his face toward the wooden beams of the ceiling high above us. I turned and followed his gaze to find an archer perched on one of the beams, a heavy bow clutched in his arms. He was already stringing another arrow, perhaps realizing he was caught and doomed but determined to take his victim down with him.

Preston lifted an arm and twisted his hand in a strange motion. There was an awful cracking sound, and the man screamed as his arm fell limp and twisted at his side. He dropped the bow, the arrow collapsing to my feet before the weapon crashed to the polished floor after it. And then the assassin himself lost his balance, teetering and falling.

Heart in my throat, I staggered backward to avoid him.

"Seize him!" Preston shouted, and several guards surged forward, catching the man before he could strike the floor. "Take him to the dungeons."

As the guards filed out with their captive, Preston settled a hand on my arm. Startling, I turned back in time to watch him lift his free hand and carelessly wrench the arrow from his shoulder. The arrow bounced across the floor, the sound loud in the all-consuming stillness that had overtaken the room. Everyone was still, lost in shock, in horror. Blood soaked Preston's torn sleeve before men and women that I assumed were gifted in healing converged upon him, wasting no time in pulling gauze from the bags they carried and binding his wound to staunch the flow.

And then Preston was moving, shoving his attendants away as if the injury was a mere nuisance. "Come with me," he snapped, his fingers curling painfully around my upper arm as he dragged me from the room.

CHAPTER TWENTY-ONE

The castle dungeon was similar to the one in the bowels of the fortress. Torchlight flickered eerily off damp stone walls, and a permanent stench of decay, blood, human waste, and despair filled the air. Rusty stains that looked suspiciously like old blood decorated many of the uninhabited cells we passed, while distant moans and whimpered pleas haunted me with every step.

Not far behind us, Nerissa trailed with Garrick on her arm, his eyes vacant.

Bile soured my mouth as I recalled the torment she'd inflicted on Garrick, and I feared I was about to witness something equally as vile enacted on the would-be assassin. Worse still, I was terrified that Preston blamed *me* for the failed attempt somehow. That Garrick and I would soon be suffering down here as well.

Preston drew me to a halt before a cell just as the guards were throwing the prisoner inside and locking the door. "Leave us," he snapped, and the guards dispersed with quick salutes.

I frowned, surprised he hadn't demanded the keys. Was he going to interrogate and torment the man from outside his cell?

Nerissa stalked closer, her red lips stretched wide in a gloating smile. "This should be entertaining," she said, casting her brother a sideways glance. Garrick stayed behind, watching the prisoner blankly, almost as if he didn't see the man at all.

Preston sneered and stepped up to the cell, clutching the bars. "Who are you?"

The prisoner, seated on the floor where he'd been thrown, lifted his face to reveal a defiant smirk. Clothed in a cloak, the hood of which had fallen back, he had horns protruding from his shaggy brown hair. His dark eyes didn't seem quite human, with overly large pupils. But even stripped of his weapons, imprisoned in this awful place, and cradling his broken arm in his lap, he had an aura of fearlessness about him. "Someone who despises usurpers."

Muscles worked in Preston's throat as he swallowed, perhaps forcing down the first angry retort that came to mind. "My sister and I are from the Stormclaw family, distant relations of the Silverfrosts. Once that line ended and we entrapped the demons and creatures overtaking our kingdom, citizens like you agreed to crown us as your leaders to keep you safe."

The horned man snorted. "Stormclaw, eh? Even if that is true—and whispers on the street say your magic isn't right for that line, that *that* family all died out decades ago too—you have a true heir now." He jerked his head toward me, and ice filled my veins. He'd tried to kill Preston for *my* sake? Preston and Nerissa would surely retaliate against me now.

"Our rightful queen stands beside you," the prisoner went on, "yet you don't abdicate your throne for her? She's revealed her magic. Her blood will save us all. And you want to make her your *consort?*"

Nerissa's laughter came out harsh and shrill. I shrank away from its assault on my ears. "What miserable excuse of an immortal are *you*, to think a lowly mortal deserves to rule over us? Pathetic! We have given her a place of honor. Marriage to my brother is more than a human is worthy of, but because of her magic and blood, we are permitting what has never been done before. A human standing beside a Silverfrost king is unheard of!"

"She deserves it more than you," the man said, his large pupils expanding as his voice pitched low with rage. "You torment more than humans. You harm our own with your selfishness and greed. You send our families to battle against the other kingdoms of Brytwilde without riding out among our soldiers yourselves, and you misuse the Silverfrost coffers. While our citizens hunger and die, you feast on delicacies and host parties. While demons slip from the underworld and devour our people."

"Fool!" Preston slammed his fist against the cell bars, rattling them. "We entrap those demons."

"And then host endless revels in your own honor while we mourn." The man snorted again. "You are ill-suited for the throne. You've never cared about us."

Nerissa stepped forward, tilting her head to the side as she studied the prisoner. "I take it that you come from that band of rebels that loves to slander us? Yet they sent you alone on this assassination mission?"

The horned man smiled, showing sharp teeth. "Torture me all you want. You won't learn anything from me."

"Thank you," Preston murmured, his tone full of deadly calm. "Then we won't waste our time." He lifted his hand, and a sense of wrongness crawled over my skin. The temperature dropped and the torchlight sputtered, casting eerie shadows across the prisoner's cell.

With a snap of his fingers, Preston unleashed magic unlike anything I'd ever witnessed. The tang of death consumed the air, and the assassin's cocky demeanor fell away as he dissolved into screams, collapsing to the floor and writhing in agony. His flesh peeled off his bones—skin, blood, muscle, tendon—it all sloughed away as if he were nothing but a melting candle.

And then, he lay still, a puddle of gore beside his contorted skeleton.

I vomited across the stone floor.

Nerissa turned, her taunting laughter echoing. "Does that upset your weak mortal stomach? He deserved worse. A slow death. One we could savor." She licked her lips, and a shudder of horror I couldn't repress wracked my body.

Preston whirled on me, his expression as cold as if it had been etched from stone. "Who have you spoken to?" He clutched my arms, shaking me until my teeth rattled together. "He spoke of allegiance to *you*. Are you spreading blasphemy?"

I scoffed. "How would I, when I haven't been permitted to leave these castle walls without a whole host accompanying me? When most fae despise me? Where would I find friends?"

But all the while, my blood thrummed in my veins with my mounting fear. What if the assassin had been part of Aspen's plan? What if she had been gathering loyalists like that man for years, awaiting my return? How large was this rebellion the man had been a part of? Were there more assassins? I didn't know whether to be glad for these allies or terrified that more failed assassination attempts could doom me to suffering. Or worse, condemn Garrick in order to make me hurt for him.

But for now, Preston and Nerissa seemed satisfied. After all, they knew I spoke the truth. I'd only interacted with Silverfrost citizens in their or Garrick's presence since my arrival at the castle. Perhaps this wasn't the first attempt on one of their lives, if the discontent and hunger the horned man spoke of was true.

"Very well," Preston muttered, waving a hand. "Our evening of frivolity is over. I'll announce that we are hosting a ball for all of Silverfrost the evening before the solstice. It'll be an official celebration of our engagement."

I bit my inner lip, frustrated. Hadn't this afternoon's feast been enough? I hoped, with Aspen's help, the ball would never occur, but if we needed more time, it would be another night where instead of planning to overthrow the king and queen, I'd be forced to pretend.

"You seem to enjoy tempting the demons that escape," I said. "Even if you clear out the castle before nightfall, that seems foolish. Why not take me to the underworld to defend the entrance at night? Spare your guards and let me incapacitate the creatures I'm already supposed to stop. Let me prepare for the night of solstice so I don't fail."

Preston shook his head sharply. "You won't fail the night of solstice." The words sounded more like a threat than encouragement. "And we can't afford to risk your weak mortal body beforehand."

"But—"

Nerissa stalked closer, glaring at me. "What was that, little Snowflake? Do you think you know better than us? Do you want to risk our wrath?" Her eyes flicked toward the prisoner's remains in the cell, a silent reminder that made me queasy.

"No," I managed to grit out. I drew a deep breath. "When do King Preston and I wed?"

Nerissa and Preston shared a smug look. "The next morning!" Nerissa said. "Your reward for your usefulness."

I swallowed. *That won't be happening,* I promised myself. By solstice, I had to have the crown, or at least some temporary haven away from the castle in which to hide and plot with allies. Anything but a wedding.

"Garrick." Nerissa tossed her dark hair over one shoulder and snapped her fingers as if summoning a pet. "Escort little Florentia to her rooms and ensure she's well-guarded."

While the siblings swept down the hall, Garrick blinked and shook himself, as if coming to. When his eyes met mine, they were his again, full of compassion. "Starlight, I'm sorry they forced you to witness this."

Keeping my gaze carefully averted from the cell, I sighed. "Take me back to my rooms like they ordered," I said wearily. My back ached beneath my bandage, reminding me of my wound. "And could you send for Aspen?"

Offering me his arm—the only touch we could share with layers of fabric between our skin—Garrick led me out of the dungeons and through the long corridors and stairwells to my quarters.

Outside my chamber door, I inhaled deeply. Once inside, the enchantments placed upon my rooms would make it impossible for me to use my magic. But here, after a meal without forget-me-nots, I was free to draw on the brittle threads of power stirring in my veins.

Garrick glanced at me, but either not wanting to speak when the guards posted outside my rooms were near or when he saw such concentration etched on my face, he remained silent.

Uncertainty wound through my mind. *What if I'm wrong, and more exposure to the flowers can never be overcome?* I gritted my teeth. It would have to work. Lifting my hand, I made frost form, glistening in lovely, intricate patterns, across my palm.

I made myself memorize the feeling—the way I was connected to the land. The rush of joy that came from using my power. The sensation of strength.

"Light in the darkness," Garrick muttered, and I smiled at the way my magic made my hand sparkle in the dim hallway.

When I closed my eyes, I was under a velvet sky again, peering at shimmering constellations. *Starlight.* Garrick said I was light to his darkness, the same way I was hope to a despairing kingdom. Painful brightness to shadowy underworld creatures. And that was what my magic was to me—my hope, my shining guide in this treacherous world.

Holding onto those thoughts, onto the image of starlight and the feeling of Garrick nearby, offering companionship and safety, I let warmth fill my chest. Those were the memories and feelings I could recall each time I wanted to remember my magic as the forget-me-nots' influence gripped me. Something tangible when I forgot how my magic felt. Something that, maybe, I could use to ground myself despite Preston and Nerissa's best efforts to render me ineffective.

Twisting the knob to my rooms, I stepped inside and Garrick followed, doing a quick scan of my chambers as if he thought more assassins might be lying in wait, prepared to murder me. I supposed that wasn't a far-fetched idea. There were probably as many fae that hated me as there were that hated Preston and Nerissa—perhaps more.

"I'll fetch Aspen," Garrick said.

For a moment, we looked at one another, unspoken words passing between us. I wondered if he wanted to reach for me, to comfort me with an embrace after the horror I had witnessed. Then he turned on his heel and vanished out the door.

Alone in my room, I shoved the awful images from my brain, trying not to fixate on how Preston's death magic had peeled the bones off his victim. No wonder he and his sister had fended off a horde of demons. No wonder they'd been hailed as heroes and protectors of this kingdom in the absence of Silverfrost magic. No wonder they wielded such power, even when rebels were amassing and angry.

But as terrifying as their magic was, as much as I feared I couldn't stand against them no matter how many allies Aspen had gathered for me, one thought kept echoing in my head. One steadying piece of comfort. If they were drugging me and enchanting my rooms, the siblings were threatened.

They feared what I could do with my magic.

CHAPTER TWENTY-TWO

Aspen tended to my wounds on my back and arm again while we discussed what had happened that night. I explained to her the awful encounter I'd had with the rebel in the dungeons, what he'd said, and how Preston had slain him.

"Did you send that assassin?" I asked as I stretched out on my stomach on my bed, allowing her to work on the Stormclaw mark on my back.

Hovering behind me in her high fae size, Aspen scoffed. "Not at all. It was a foolhardy move, doomed to fail. But it's a powerful reminder that more citizens grow weary of the siblings' reign. There are reports that Ashwood's army is pressing toward the capital, even now, yet you've seen how they don't let the messengers speak before their court. They distract with extravagant parties. And we have men and women dying for Preston and Nerissa's greedy aspirations all while we're in danger from escaping demons at home. It's costly enough to build caged wagons to transport demons to the fortress and to hire guards who are willing to risk monitoring the fortress dungeons. It's also expensive to wage war. Yet instead of being frugal, Preston and Nerissa continue to host feasts."

I swallowed. "And the death magic..."

"It is terrible," Aspen agreed.

"Yet they fear *my* power."

"Firstly, you're the only one who can send the demons back and seal the underworld's entrance. You are the hero to our people that they can never be, and it's unsurprising they'd envy that. And your winter magic *is* strong. Unleashing an avalanche? Crafting a sword of ice in seconds to stab your enemy? Your abilities will only grow as winter begins in earnest and you have more time to practice your magic."

"Which they are ensuring I don't have," I said bitterly.

"I think your theory about gaining immunity to the forget-me-nots is possible though." The pixie finished applying a fresh bandage to my back and buttoned up the tunic I'd donned before she arrived. "After all, the flower only affects fae, by making us forget how to even wield our magic. Sometimes, that we even possess any. But you are part human. I imagine there's a part of you that's unaffected. That part of you can help you remember."

I nodded slowly. "I think I have some memories I can cling to that will help me."

Aspen squeezed my arm. "As often as I'm permitted to visit, I will. I have so much more to share with you, but first...you need rest." She shot me a look. "I'm going to contrive a way for you to leave the castle and meet with some of our rebels. Or, better yet, I'll find a way to let you visit some of the wounded returning from our battles with Ashwood and let rebels and non-converts witness your compassion. It'll instill further belief in those on our side and gather more to our numbers. Gods know King Preston and Queen Nerissa haven't deigned to visit their suffering soldiers or any of the bereaved family after sending their own to fight for them." She scowled.

With that, Aspen had left me with a leather satchel of dried forget-me-nots she'd pilfered from the castle's storage room within the armory, where the king and queen horded many of the flowers to use against their enemies.

But I couldn't use them here, in these enchanted rooms. Glancing out the window, I surveyed the blood-red sky. There wasn't much daylight left, but perhaps it would be enough before there came a risk of demons escaping the underworld and stalking the halls.

When I poked my head out the door, I studied the guards posted outside my rooms. I decided to feign boldness, like I was confident in what I was doing and where I was going, and I stepped outside. No one stopped me.

Realizing I wasn't trapped in my chambers—only the castle, it seemed—I crept down the hall and toward the staircase. Garrick stood from a bench against one wall, where he'd been reclining in the shadows, sharpening one of his knives. He was fully armed, even with a sword strapped to his back, which reminded me that Silverfrost wasn't safe at night with the underworld creatures that were regularly escaping.

"What are you doing?" Garrick's gold eyes studied me almost warily.

My heart slammed painfully against my ribcage. Maybe he'd been ordered to stop me if I left my rooms. Maybe his blood oath would compel him to work against me, whether he wanted to or not. His expression was his own, but just because the siblings weren't controlling him now didn't mean he wasn't bound to their long-term orders.

I stepped forward cautiously, the satchel swinging from the belt I'd fastened around my waist. "I want to practice," I whispered, conscious of the guards posted not far away.

Garrick raised an eyebrow in question, as if silently asking: *When the king and queen have suppressed your magic?*

"I have to try."

"All right." Garrick frowned thoughtfully. "I know a place we can go, but we can't linger long." He cast a glance over his shoulder out the nearest window.

I nodded in understanding. Without another word, Garrick proceeded toward a different set of steps, waving for me to follow him.

At the top of a winding, narrow staircase, Garrick shoved open a door and we stepped out into the chilly evening. I gazed about in wonder. We were at the pinnacle of the castle's tallest tower, surrounded by a stunning view of snowy mountaintops bathed in red and gold as the sun sank in the west. "Beautiful," I murmured.

Icy air plucked at my loose hair and made gooseflesh rise on my bare arms.

Garrick's arms snaked around me, enveloped in the warmth of his furs. Though his hands never touched my bare skin, it still felt intimate to be in his embrace. I swallowed my gasp of surprise and delight. The warmth of his coat dashed away the cold, and his earthy scent surrounded me.

For a moment, he didn't move. I could feel his breath on the back of my neck. So close, yet so far. I ached to turn and wind my arms around him. To taste his lips on mine.

Would he welcome the advance, if we could risk it?

Too soon, he pulled away. My hazy thoughts cleared, and with it, the reminder that now wasn't the time to profess feelings. I had limited time to learn to wield my magic. The daylight would vanish far too soon.

As if sensing my nerves, Garrick murmured, "Remember, you are powerful, Starlight. You were made for this. The land knows you. Its magic is yours."

Steeling myself, I plucked a few forget-me-nots from within my satchel, holding them in my palm despite the pain and despair that flooded me as my magic seemingly snuffed out. Closing my eyes, I tried to picture pinpricks of light in a dark sky, the silver glow bathing Garrick's face when he'd studied the constellations with me. I thought about the way magic flooded my veins with power, igniting a strength in me I'd never known I'd possessed before.

Human. I squeezed the petals in my hand, not tightly enough to damage the brittle flowers but enough to embrace the pain they brought. I pictured my power unleashing, snow howling through the air and tiny shards of ice stinging my cheeks. The roar of an avalanche. The cold of a sword made of ice in my palm. The beauty of a pattern of frost.

For an instant, a familiar chill filled me. Not the cold of terror or discomfort, but the gentle touch of my magic. I could almost hear ice crackling and forming around me. Almost sense the fresh, wet scent of snow lingering in the air.

But when I opened my eyes, everything was as it had been before.

"Try again," Garrick urged. He stepped nearer, his eyes gentle, and my stomach clenched with the desire to take his hands in mine.

This time, I didn't close my eyes. I thought of the frost I'd summoned outside my chambers earlier. I could do that again, surely. With the petals clutched in one hand, I held out the other, palm upward, and concentrated on tracing frosty patterns along my skin. I thought of the power and joy my magic brought me. I thought of Garrick's confidence in me, and leaned into it, wrapping myself in it until my own belief swelled.

Frost crackled, coating my hand in its silver shimmer and then racing outward until the entire tower roof was glistening in a thin sheet of ice.

Eyes wide, I turned to Garrick. "I did it," I breathed.

"Of course you did," he said, beaming.

I wanted to throw my arms around him, but I shoved the urge down deep.

"Try again," he repeated.

I called upon more frost, thickening the ice around us until, with a laugh, I took a step, letting my slippers slide across the slick surface.

"Careful." Garrick caught me, his hand swerving at the last second to avoid my skin and catch my forearm, covered in his furs.

The air froze in my throat as he gently drew me closer, setting his other hand on my waist to balance me. His face was inches from mine, our steaming breaths mingling.

"Thank you," I whispered.

There was a moment, when his eyes dipped to my mouth, that I thought he felt the same desire, the same longing. A confession lingered on my tongue. But as beautiful as the words sounded in my mind, they also were painful. If Garrick felt the same way, wouldn't I only be driving a dagger into his heart? We couldn't even touch. We were both bound unwillingly to others. If we didn't win our freedom, we could never be.

Before I could decide, Garrick's mouth curved in a crooked smile. "It is my honor, my queen." His hand dropped from my waist and his fingers loosened from my wrist. He stepped back, and the space between us had never seemed vaster. Even his choice of words—*my queen*—emphasized distance, like he was only my loyal subject. My heart ached, wishing he'd used my nickname instead.

"Aspen says she has rebels willing to help me," I said, desperate to change the subject. "Do you know of them?"

Garrick nodded. "I don't meet with them though. With my blood oath, few trust me." He shrugged. "They're right not to. Even Aspen is cautious about how she speaks with me. Any suspected treachery, and Preston or Nerissa could force confessions from my lips. I'd withhold nothing."

"But—"

"You can't trust me with every detail of your plans either, Starlight," he said, his voice low, his eyes sorrowful.

"It's not your fault."

He shook his head. "The results would be the same. I don't know the location of the rebels' meeting places. I don't know their strategies. And I don't want to know any details about what you and Aspen choose to do. Nerissa uses me as her hunter, but also as her spy, when she believes someone to be plotting. She'll make me share everything, if she thinks you have a plan."

The question was out of my mouth before I thought it through, my words bitter. "Does she also force you to share...other things?" My cheeks flushed. "She kisses you as if she owns you. Does she...do more?"

Garrick closed his eyes, and instant regret crashed into me. What sort of heartless question was that? But his tone was relieved as he said, "No. I think she sees me as a pet—handsome, but to do more than kiss me would be...appalling to her. I am little better than a human. Disgustingly weak with my inability to glamour others or wield magic outside of shifting or putting others to sleep."

"And yet those skills are so valuable for her when it comes to catching her prey."

"There isn't even a wedding date set or discussed. I think she announced our betrothal for some of the same reasons Preston chose to bind himself to you. If she can claim me as hers—her pet, her hunter, her fiancé—then no one else can view me as...available. And it reminds me I have no hope to bind myself to another in any way, body, heart, or soul."

My mouth tasted sour.

The wind ruffled through Garrick's white-blond hair as he crossed his arms, his smile mirthless as he studied the gathering twilight. "Don't look at me like that. I chose my own fate when I made my blood oath."

"You didn't know what they were."

"I should have been more cautious."

"Garrick, you were a *child*."

His tone was bitter. "And a fool. I must live with the consequences of my choices."

Before I could try to protest more, Garrick's gold eyes hardened. "It's growing darker, Starlight. You need to return to your rooms."

Powerful blood or not, I winced at the thought of encountering another demon so soon. "You're right," I murmured.

Grasping me by the elbow to help me navigate the icy rooftop in my slippers, Garrick led me back to the door.

We were down the stairs and in the first corridor when the sound of claws scraping against stone echoed off the walls.

CHAPTER TWENTY-THREE

Garrick had one knife in his palm instantly, shoving another into my hand. His voice was a low warning growl. "It's not yet fully dark, but…"

I nodded. There was no mistaking the sound of demon claws, or the creeping feeling of dread consuming me. But I was also the one whose magic could resist such a creature, and whose blood could disarm one. Steeling myself, I pushed forward past Garrick.

"Starlight…"

Ignoring him, I reached the nearest corner, pressing myself against the wall to peer around the bend and into the next hallway. My stomach lurched, and I had to fight not to lose its contents right then and there. The scent of blood assaulted me first, and then the horrific sight: a hunched creature with countless inhuman eyes and a gaping, bloody maw tearing into a fae's ruined corpse. Gore and innards spilled across the plush carpet as the creature feasted. Its pincered limbs, ending in enormous pointed claws, reached out to claw along the exposed stone of the hallway. *Scrape, scrape, scrape.*

Garrick's hand brushed against my arm, the warmth seeping through my shirtsleeve. Blinking dazedly, I glanced over my shoulder at him, trying to clear my thoughts when raw terror threatened to drag me under. He leaned so close to me his breath tickled my ear, his mouth almost brushing against my lobe. "Demons like this one don't behave like the one you fought. They often escape and work in groups. This one may be baiting us while another lies in wait."

I drew back. A new emotion was consuming me, swiftly overtaking my nerves. Fury. I didn't know the demon's victim, and most of the fae in Silverfrost were strangers to me. Some would gladly see me killed or imprisoned. I owed them no allegiance, no love. And yet, seeing the horror this underworld creature was inflicting, with Preston and Nerissa nowhere near to stop it, made my blood heat. Maybe they'd been hailed as heroes when they'd first rescued this kingdom, but they seemed rather careless about protecting it now. Whatever most of this land's inhabitants thought of me, there were some who cared. Some, like Aspen, who were good. Who had waited for me, loyal and determined.

And for these people to be preyed upon like this? Slaughtered in the most vicious, awful of ways? It wasn't *right*.

I set my jaw, palming the knife Garrick had given me. "Then I'll give them my own distraction." Worry flickered in Garrick's gold eyes, but before he could protest, I added, "Do you have my back?"

He dipped his head. "Until I draw my final breath."

Pressing the tip of the blade into my palm, I sliced a shallow cut and stepped into the corridor where the demon was. Squeezing my hand into a fist and lifting it into the air, I let my blood spill in droplets along the carpet.

Sniffing, the demon straightened, turning slowly so its countless eyes—black and beady and soulless—glared at me. Gore dripped from its open maw, full of endless rows of razor-sharp teeth. My stomach roiled, but I held my ground, letting the creature scent my blood.

Its pupils dilated, darkening its eyes even further, but a crash behind me warned me a second demon was emerging, charging with impossible speed from another room. I didn't turn, didn't waver. Just before the new demon could leap upon me, a wolf's snarl pierced the air. A flash of white darted in my peripheral as Garrick collided with the monster, snapping his teeth mercilessly.

With an enraged roar, the demon before me charged, claws slamming into the carpet. The floor shuddered.

I wondered where the guards were, where Preston and Nerissa were. The castle had never seemed so quiet—as if everyone else had hidden or evacuated, leaving these creatures to sew their chaos.

Gritting my teeth, I sent ice crackling beneath the creature's feet. Its claws scrabbled for purchase on the slick surface, scraping in a high-pitched whine that made my ears ache. As it lost control, sliding straight for me, I sidestepped, only extending my bloody palm over it.

It wasn't a lot of blood, only a drop, but as it splattered across the demon's hideous face, a burst of light flared and it squealed in pain. Feeling victorious, I lifted my knife to slam it into one of its eyes, but the beast swiped out with one of its long limbs. Not slicing with its claws, but pommeling me with the blunt side of its leg, knocking me off my feet. The knife flew from my grasp, sliding across the carpet.

Breath knocked out of me, I reeled, struggling for air. The demon darted forward, hemming me in with its claws stabbing into the floor on either side of me. I choked as it loomed above me, maw dripping hot blood across the front of my dress. The stench of copper and rot consumed me as I finally heaved in air, my lungs burning.

Trapped again, crowed the creature inside my mind, its words low and slippery. The invasion was uncomfortable, sending spikes of pain through my head. *Poor little human.*

As it spoke, the world shifted, until instead of the castle ceiling high overhead, cloaked in shadow, I saw the bars of a rusty cage climbing around me. It had no doors, and the surface I stood upon was littered with broken, yellowed bones that crunched beneath my feet.

My chest tightened in panic.

Your freedom is forever out of reach.

Distantly, as if he spoke through a wall, Garrick's voice sounded. "Starlight! It's a trick! *Ren!* It's not real!"

Though my head understood what was actually happening—the demon had locked me in a vision displaying one of my nightmares—I couldn't dispel it. Couldn't fully convince my mind that what looked and felt so real beneath my palms was a lie. The cool metal was unyielding, the rough edges of rust scraping at my skin.

Beyond my cage, Preston stood, surveying me with a gloating expression, his red eyes piercing. He opened his mouth, filling the air with the reek of death. *I own you.*

"Ren!" Garrick's tone was desperate. Pleading.

It made me tear my gaze from Preston, choosing by some instinct to look up instead. The bars of my cage extended on and on, but overhead, there was a window letting in the cold light of a winter's night. My thoughts snagged on this realization as I stared at countless silver stars. *Stars.*

Squeezing my eyes shut, I poured every ounce of my energy into visualizing my magic pouring out of me. Into imagining the power and light that resided in my very blood repulsing these creatures that tried to prey on me. With a cry, I opened my eyes and the demon was before me once more, leaning forward to tear into my throat with its wicked teeth.

I slammed my bleeding palm against its eyes. Again and again. Light flashed, almost blinding in the dim corridor. Screeching, the monster reeled backward, writhing in misery.

Lurching to my feet, I found Garrick back in his fae form and already at my side, my lost, bloodied knife in his hand. Behind us, the other demon hissed and struggled on the floor, pinned by its throat with Garrick's other blade. I called on my magic again as the demon before us gathered itself, preparing to launch. *Ice,* I thought, pleading for the weak threads of my power to conjure something more than frost. Thick, black ice that would encapsulate the demon and root it to the spot.

But the ice that formed at its clawed legs cracked and shattered almost instantly, brittle as glass. The demon jumped—higher than two men were tall—and Garrick seized my arm, forcing me back with him as he hurled his knife for its open maw. His blade struck true, but as the creature landed, it growled and lunged again, barely slowed by the pain.

Steel screamed as Garrick drew the sword strapped to his back. He moved with grace and strength, parrying the clawed strikes from the demon in a deadly dance while I focused on my magic again, trying to find a way to slow the monster—at least enough that I could draw close and use my blood against it.

But my thoughts distracted me. I didn't hear the second demon finally pry itself free, the knife squelching from its ruined throat. Not until it was too late. A shock of pain lanced along my back as it sliced its claws through the back of my tunic and into flesh.

I screamed, sprawling across the floor. Blackness danced along my vision.

And then—the sound of snapping bones. The sickly-sweet stench of decay. The low, careless laughter that always made disgust skitter across my skin like countless invisible insects.

"Couldn't even overcome two little demons?" Preston taunted.

I lifted my head, back burning. My vision was blurred, my eyes watering from the pain and obscuring my view of the pale-faced king as he stalked forward. With a snap of his fingers, guards emerged from the shadows, restraining and shackling the demon Preston's death magic had immobilized with countless broken bones. Others released Garrick from his solitary struggle with the second, chaining it too.

"Pathetic, but what else would I expect from a mortal and a dog?"

Garrick wasn't under Preston's control, for he stepped forward, slamming his fist into Preston's face. The king stepped back, blood trickling from his split lip. Horrified to see what sort of retaliation he'd inflict on Garrick, I opened my mouth to distract him, but Preston only laughed.

With a jerk of his chin, he turned Garrick's attention to me. "You were supposed to ensure the mortal didn't needlessly spill her blood."

"Starlight," Garrick breathed as he whirled around, taking in my injuries. He rushed to my side, crouching and cradling me in his arms despite being in Preston's presence. "Where's Aspen?" he demanded, his tone laced with a threat he unfortunately couldn't inflict. "Send for her at once."

Preston rolled his eyes. "So dramatic. Florentia won't die, fragile as humans are. I'll escort her to her rooms. *You* find Aspen."

Garrick's arms tightened around me before abruptly going slack. I knew in that moment, without turning my head to study his expression, that Garrick was locked under Preston's control. He couldn't stay by my side no matter how much he willed it. Standing stiffly, he bowed and trudged off, leaving me alone with the foul king.

My heart throbbed in my throat as I forced myself to stand, the world shifting around me. Cool air teased my bare back, a sharp contrast to the hot blood soaking the shredded fabric of my dress.

Preston snapped his fingers again as if I were another of his guards to be ordered about. "This way. It's unlikely there are more demons, but this close to solstice, one can't be too sure. Especially since the ones roaming this far from the entrance prove our guards were killed again. We've had to replace them so many times."

I scowled as I staggered behind him, struggling to keep up. But my voice was strong. "Where were *you*? If this happens often, if these creatures kill your own people this regularly, then surely you, one of the heroes of Silverfrost, should be guarding the entrance yourself all night long."

Faster than I could blink, Preston had turned on me, shoving me against the wall. I choked on a feeble cry as my wounds came into contact with the rough tapestry behind me, staining it with my blood. "Do kings toil as slaves? Do gods stoop to work as servants?"

I slammed my teeth together to keep them from chattering, either from shock setting in or my fear.

Without waiting for an answer I would not give, Preston went on. "No, my fiancée. They do not, and neither do my sister and I."

As he released me, I trailed after him, slowly ascending a flight of steps. Each movement sent more stabs of pain through my body. My back throbbed. For one delirious moment, I nearly dissolved into laughter as I wondered if these new wounds had peeled away the bandage covering my old one. If these fresh claw marks would ruin the mark Preston had so diligently forced Garrick to carve into me. If so, what a strange sort of victory that would be over this disgusting excuse of a man. Of a king.

Somehow, despite my fear of him and my mounting pain, the fire in my blood wouldn't be quenched. Once I'd easily curbed myself, remaining silent and meek to avoid notice whenever I could. Now I was struggling to be quiet. The injustice of Preston and Nerissa's reign was eating me alive, and a newfound passion was growing in me for this land. Perhaps not for its people, little more than strangers to me, but for the magic that bound me to it and to them. For the memory of the family I'd never met; for the fae father who'd fallen in love with a mortal woman and died saving both her and me. And for right to win over all the wrongdoings the siblings had committed over the years.

It burned and burned until we were outside my door. The posted guards saluted Preston, and the action set my teeth on edge. He didn't deserve it.

I couldn't stop my tongue. "You think yourself so much better than the people you send off to die in battle, or the guards you post to protect this very castle? But what would you be without them? King over nothing. You have not earned their loyalty, not with your mistreatment of them. No wonder that archer tried to kill you. You are nothing but a coward."

Preston cocked his head, and in the dimness, with nothing but flickering candlelight from the sconces on the walls to cast a glow across his face, his sharp features made him look nearly skeletal. "I suppose you think that offends me." He stepped closer. "You think insults from a feeble human, one who will die and be forgotten while I continue on for endless ages, will trouble me? You, who nearly perished tonight trying to fend off that demon?" His smirk was cruel. "The undead of the underworld love to feed on life, to taste it, to claim a bit for themselves. But I wonder if, had that demon tasted you, it would have realized you were hardly more alive than it to begin with?" He reached around, miming the act of tracing a finger through the blood soaking my back. When he lifted that finger to his lips, pretending to lick it clean, my stomach roiled. The mere idea of him tasting my blood disgusted me. Preston sneered. "Your mortal blood is entirely revolting."

Without another word, he yanked open the door to my rooms and shoved me inside.

"Hopefully Aspen can cure your mortal body enough to function through the work you have ahead of you in a few days," he went on. "Though I suppose all we truly need is your blood. Oh, and clean yourself up. You stink of dog."

"You stink of death," I retorted.

Preston merely laughed, the sound echoing in the corridor as he slammed my door shut.

CHAPTER TWENTY-FOUR

Garrick barged into my quarters a few minutes later, Aspen perched on his shoulder with her bag. Once they were within my rooms, she hopped down, shifting into her larger form. Seated on the edge of the bed, I blinked at them blearily, half-consumed with pain. Despite Preston's insults, bathing was the last thing on my mind. I wasn't worried he'd punish Garrick for touching me tonight, not when he'd been trying to protect me—I feared it was more likely Preston would hurt him for failing to prevent a demon from injuring me.

Instead, I'd tried to focus, tried to clear my thoughts. Perhaps there was some way I could prevent him or Nerissa from hurting Garrick. Some way I could convince them it wouldn't be worth it. But my thoughts felt sluggish and my head light. I wondered vaguely how much blood I'd lost. Not enough to threaten my life, but enough to make me weak.

When I glanced up to see my friends, Aspen looked stern while Garrick seemed frantic, his brow creased with worry.

"Lay on your stomach," Aspen said without preamble.

I stretched out across the bed as she'd ordered. The mattress bounced lightly as she tossed her bag down, reaching in for something. A moment later, I heard her slicing through my shredded tunic. Garrick positioned himself on the other side of the bed, leaning over to cradle my head in his calloused hands.

Aspen worked silently, not remarking on the state of my injuries as she applied something that stung fiercely. I bit back a groan, and Garrick brushed a tender thumb across my cheek, lifting my head so I could meet his golden gaze, soft and focused. "It'll be over soon," he murmured.

Once the pixie had finished cleaning the wounds, she set to work stitching the skin closed. Each pull of the thread had me hissing through clenched teeth. I tried to keep my eyes only on Garrick, letting his soothing words wash over me. "You're all right, Starlight. Look at me. Think of your magic, what you succeeded in doing tonight. It was incredible."

What he didn't know was that I was concentrating not on the ice I'd conjured on the rooftop or the light that had flared from my blood when I'd fended off the demons, but on him. On the warmth of his arms when they'd encircled me on the rooftop. On the familiar rumble of his voice. On the achingly sweet touches he granted me now as he threaded his fingers through my hair, brushing it behind my ears, or as he ran his thumbs across my cheeks, catching stray tears that slipped out. On his eyes, bright and beautiful and full of an emotion I was sure I could name. It was on the tip of my tongue.

"Your plan worked?" Aspen asked at last, when she'd finished wrapping bandages around my torso. "You already saw results?"

As I sat up, cautiously clinging to the front of my tunic, she tossed me a fresh one from the wardrobe. Garrick turned his back to me without a word, offering me privacy as I shed the ruined garment and tugged the new one over my head. "Yes. Garrick escorted me so I could practice on a rooftop alone. It wasn't much—but it was something."

Garrick, who'd turned back to us, leaned against the headboard of my bed, a smile tugging at his lips. "It was more than something. Tell her what you did."

I described the ice I'd managed to form across the roof floor, and Aspen grinned. "And they think your mortal side is a weakness. Look what a strength it has turned out to be, making you more resistant to for-get-me-nots than any fae could ever hope to be."

"I'm afraid it was one time when I probably shouldn't have been her escort, though," Garrick said, his expression sobering. "Not that I expect Preston or Nerissa would question me about Ren's use of magic. Unless she's been under threat of death, like tonight, they have no reason to think she can wield her power while they're drugging her with forget-me-nots."

"You're right," Aspen said. "We can only hope they won't have any reason to suspect she can resist the flowers' influence. And I assume they ordered you to escort and guard Ren anywhere she goes within the castle?"

Garrick gave a single nod.

"Then we will just have to manage. I never thought I'd say this, but thankfully, we only have a few days left to keep our secrets." Aspen studied Garrick thoughtfully. "As for tonight...Ren and I could take advantage of this time to plan, unless you were ordered to remain here?"

Garrick sank his hands into his trouser pockets. "No, I was not." I could see the reluctance painted across his face, even if he knew—probably better than Aspen or me—how important it was for him not to know every detail of our plans.

Crossing over to me, he grasped my face in his hands again, drew a deep breath, opened his mouth, and...shook his head. Without a word, he slipped from the room. I gritted my teeth, a mingling sense of desperation and loss coiled in my chest. Was he holding back the words I hoped he was? Did he worry they were futile, impossible?

Aspen's dark eyes darted between Garrick's retreating form as he closed the door and back to me. "We will win," she promised, and I wasn't sure if she was saying that to comfort me and give me hope for Garrick and me, or to refocus my thoughts on our mission.

Aspen had an entire kingdom to save. And while I didn't want to see anyone suffer needlessly either—while I longed to do what was right—the reason I ached for a victory, for freedom, was for the chance at a future with Garrick. Or, if he didn't want me, at least to see him also free and happy.

Settling on the bed, Aspen sighed. In a blink, she was her usual pixie size, relaxing cross-legged on the coverlet. I settled beside her, already feeling blessed relief from the pain-numbing salve she'd massaged into the wounds across my back. "Will they cover the Stormclaw mark?" I asked, gesturing vaguely toward my back.

When Aspen shook her head, her curls bounced around her shoulders. "I'm afraid not."

I shrugged. "Then we can use it to our advantage."

Aspen tilted her head to one side. "How so?"

"At the ball, the night before winter solstice, I can wear a dress with a low-cut back," I mused. "Anyone present who is questioning their loyalty to the king and queen can see what they did to me, a Silverfrost by blood. And I suppose the claw marks will also be a reminder of what I've survived while facing demons."

Aspen's lips curled into a slow smile. "I like it. But do you think you can convince the seamstresses to make a ballgown to your specifications? They're to come to your room tomorrow to measure you and have you try on fabrics. I assume Preston and Nerissa already gave them instructions about the sort of attire you're supposed to wear." She rolled her eyes.

"Back home," I said, studying my hands, "I made my own dresses. Our human fashions are much simpler than the dresses fae wear—I would never have been caught wearing a dress that exposed my back at home—" -a soft laugh escaped my lips, an ache tugging on my heart for a place that would never be home again- "but surely, I could make a ballgown fit for the Silverfrost court. I would use finer fabrics."

Aspen tapped her chin thoughtfully. "I suppose they'd assume you'd want to wear something simple and human-looking. I can't think of a reason why they'd refuse you."

"I have great plans for it," I said, my excitement mounting.

Aspen tossed me a sidelong glance, but didn't press for details. "This would be perfect," she mused. "I'll speak with them, ask if I can be your escort into Northelm to purchase fabric. I'm sure they'll send Garrick along too. They'll order him to not let you escape. But this provides a chance for you to visit the wounded while we're there. There are rebels there already, tending to our injured. It'll be an opportunity to bolster their confidence in you, while also letting the wounded soldiers see what a better leader you would make. A way to draw even more to our side." She fidgeted with the ties of her bag, its size now proportionate to hers. "As for the ball itself, we have been planning to make a move then..."

She launched into the details her rebel group had planned out. A lot of our success would rely not only on our growing numbers, but also on the hope that my powers would be at full strength then, enough to combat the might of the siblings' death magic. If my magic wasn't ready then, the resistance could turn into a bloodbath.

"During the ball, you'll act normal. Drink more wine and let your scars be seen—if those actions sway more toward our cause, we may gain additional numbers when the fighting ensues. And watch and wait for the signal. Of course," Aspen finished, "everything could change at a mo-ments' notice. Scouts are reporting that the Ashwood forces are pressing ever closer. If we're dealing with a foreign invasion by then, we may have other problems to worry about."

"What if I'm not ready?" I asked. "Would you wait?" I bit my lip. While I had the looming deadline of the morning after solstice threatening me—the idea of binding myself to Preston in marriage made my stomach curdle—the rebels had no such restriction.

"Unfortunately, we cannot wait. There's something I haven't told you," Aspen said, her brow furrowing. "In Silverfrost, marriage works a bit differently than it does in the mortal world. It's a requirement among royals that magical power is exchanged through blood. I fear Preston hopes to not only use you as a pawn and figurehead, but also to steal your power. And if he does? If he can seal the door to the underworld himself? I wouldn't be surprised if he also killed you on your wedding night."

I sat back, stunned. I had no choice but to be ready in only a few days.

Aspen stood, walking across the bed to set a small hand on my arm. "And you're already drawing on your magic, Ren. I believe in you. You'll be ready. You're *meant* to be our queen. You can't fail."

After a reminder to rest, she bid me goodnight, shifting again into her larger form to more efficiently walk the castle halls.

"Be safe," I murmured, thinking of the demons who'd attacked Garrick and me not long ago.

Aspen smiled, withdrawing a dagger from a sheath at her thigh, tucked beneath her dress. "I'm as prepared as I can be, but considering there was already one attack tonight, it's unlikely more will slip out until tomorrow."

As she left, I settled back in bed, pulling the covers up and trying to settle my whirling mind. But when I slipped into dreams, I was plagued with memories of Preston's sharp features as he stood before me, pretending to lick my blood off his finger.

My heart pounded with anticipation as Aspen, Garrick, and I trotted into Northelm under the watery light of late morning. Nerissa had given Aspen her approval to take me to select fabrics, and according to the pixie, had laughed and waved her hand carelessly at my "human desire to make a mockery of myself."

Remembering that now as we rode along the main city street, women, men, and children stopping to bow or curtsey in respect when they saw me, I couldn't help the smug smile that danced across my lips. Little did Nerissa know that I'd be making a mockery of *her*.

I waved as the people bowed, nodding and smiling my thanks at their recognition. It was impossible to tell how many truly respected me and how many only displayed outward signs of submission because they feared repercussions if word got back that King Preston's future consort had been insulted. All I could hope was that more fae than not would want to join our side when they attended the ball.

Still, it was an encouraging sight. Between their warm welcome, last night's success with my magic, and my wounds feeling significantly improved after Aspen's ministrations both yesterday and early this morning, my spirits were hopeful. Our hoped-for coup felt *possible*.

"This way," Aspen murmured, pointing down a side street from where she lounged between my horse's ears. I led my mount in the direction the pixie had indicated.

Garrick, stoic and quiet, waited before tailing me. Though I'd frequently felt his eyes on me throughout our ride into Northelm, he'd hardly spoken a word to Aspen or me the entire time. He didn't seem to be under Preston and Nerissa's control, but I wasn't naïve enough to assume they hadn't tasked him with strict orders.

We tied our horses outside an unassuming shop halfway down the road. A welcoming plume of smoke curled forth from its chimney, and in windows reflecting the glow of warm candlelight, mannequins displayed fabrics ranging from thick and practical to sheer and scandalous. When Aspen shifted into her high fae size and tugged open the door, a bell chimed merrily.

Garrick's presence was solid and reassuring behind me, though as I stepped inside the shop, I studiously avoided glancing back at him. I hated to see the distant, hopeless look in his eyes. The way he saw himself as an enemy, a threat to Aspen's and my cause, because of the pawn Nerissa and Preston had turned him into.

"Welcome!" called a clear voice, as bright and musical as the ring of the bell. It took a moment for me to identify its source—the shop was full of crowded racks and shelves, full of everything from completed outfits to mannequins clothed in half-finished attire decorated with the pins holding them in place, to swaths of richly colored fabric. At last, I spied a counter in one corner, where a plump fae woman with sparkling eyes as vivid as amber and pale blue skin was cutting and sorting through piles of fabrics. When she set down her scissors to wade past the shelves and racks to approach us, I realized there were twigs and leaves in her dark curls, and they didn't appear to be decorative. They seemed to be a part of her, growing from her scalp as surely as her hair was. "Oh, Aspen, it's good to see you." Her eyes darted to me, her mouth forming a small *O* of surprise before she dipped into a pretty curtsey, her whimsical patchwork skirt drawing my eye.

"It's good to see you too, Juniper. We need to purchase material suitable for Her Majesty's ballgown for the upcoming celebration," Aspen said.

Juniper's eyes widened eagerly, and she ushered Aspen and me forward, talking quickly as she guided her to her counter and started displaying various fabrics for her. Meanwhile, Garrick stationed himself near the door, arms crossed and face as expressionless as if he were a guard stationed at the castle.

The sight of so many fabrics, threads, ribbons, and other sewing necessities filled my heart with a sense of joy and familiarity. After a little while, I excused myself from the counter and left Aspen and Juniper to chat alone so I could wander among the shelves. I brushed my fingers along different swatches of fabric to test every texture and admired the numerous different colors and patterns. As I scanned the shop, I allowed myself to imagine a future in which we succeeded. In which Preston and Nerissa abdicated the throne and I was free, able to pursue what I wanted. Able to dream again. I didn't fool myself into thinking my new life would be easy—I had no idea how to run a kingdom, and I knew many fae would remain opposed to me as queen. But in that moment, I could envision a world in which I was able to sew to my heart's content without fear of being controlled or threatened. In which I could create a haven out of the castle I now so abhorred, and slowly assemble a court I trusted. One that I hoped included Garrick and Aspen.

A flash of glistening silver against velvety black caught my eye as I strolled past one of the shelves. I paused, lifting the fabric to watch it shift and shimmer in the light from a nearby candelabra. Traces of blues in varying shades flashed in the material as I moved it. It was like a beautiful night sky adorned in stars. It was perfect.

Preparing to gather the roll of fabric and take it to Juniper's counter, I paused when I heard voices nearby. I lifted my head, noticing two figures a few shelves over muttering together. The shop was so large I hadn't realized there were other customers present.

One of the forms sauntered in my direction, and when he lifted his head, revealing a scarred face and sharp green eyes, nerves stirred in my stomach. I moved to walk away, but unfortunately, fae were impossibly fast, and I hadn't made it out of my aisle before he turned into it. "What a pleasure to run into you, *Your Majesty,*" he said, his tone mocking.

I straightened warily. There was no deference in his posture, nothing but hostility. "What do you want?"

He was in front of me in a blink, making my blood run cold. He was too fast. Too muscular. His hulking form dwarfed me, making me wonder if his high fae blood was mixed with that of a troll or giant. He was powerful, and my magic—when I reached for it—was still an echo of what it should have been.

"I want to see you put in your place," he snarled, hot breath washing over my face as he leered at me. "A lowly human has no place near the throne or married to a fae king. No matter your blood. And we *don't* need you alive to use your blood."

"Actually, you do," I retorted. "Even if someone else can use my blood to close the entrance, once I'm dead, there won't be anyone else to continue to seal it for the years to come. Why would you doom your kingd—"

A meaty hand latched around my neck, squeezing. I choked in vain for air, my hands beating against his to no effect. My mind scrambled to concentrate and wield my magic, but after a breakfast laced with forget-me-nots, trying to grasp for my power seemed more like reaching for single grains of sand.

"Pity for you that you're all alone," he taunted.

Dark spots danced across my vision. I couldn't even think straight anymore, let alone try to conjure my magic.

The man laughed cruelly. "What can your guard dog do now?" His fingers dug into my throat, trying to crush my windpipe.

A low voice rumbled behind him. "Kill you."

I hadn't even heard Garrick approaching—hadn't noticed him sneak up behind the man. Not until he sidestepped him and seized the brute by the neck. Even though the stranger towered over him, Garrick's motions were effortless. His pupils were blown wide in his gold eyes, dilated so much he looked more wolf than man.

The man released me to reach for a dagger strapped to his waist, and I stumbled back, clutching my aching throat and gulping down stinging lungfuls of air. He didn't have time to even unsheathe his weapon before Garrick's wrist twisted. There was a sickening crunch, and I turned away as my attacker's neck snapped, his bulky form crashing to the floor.

Tears stinging my eyes, I scanned the shop, but the brute's companion was nowhere to be seen. Garrick was in front of me in a moment, the wolfish bloodlust in his eyes melting into concern. He grasped my chin with the same scarred hand he'd used to kill only a second ago, but this time his touch was impossibly tender as he tilted my face upward and inspected my throat. *You can't touch me,* I thought feebly, but I wasn't sure I could form the words. Maybe Preston and Nerissa would forgive him like they had last night, since he was only protecting me, just like they'd ordered him to.

Garrick hissed a curse at the sight of the bruises I imagined were forming on my skin. "Don't speak," he said. "I'm going to talk to Juniper."

Gently grasping my arm, Garrick led me past the rows of shelves and mannequins to the counter, where Aspen and Juniper froze mid-conversation at the sight of me.

"What happened?" Aspen demanded, rushing to my side and clutching my free hand as her eyes roved over my neck.

"A bloody man attacked her, right here in your store," Garrick growled, his eyes snapping to Juniper.

Juniper blinked in horror before collecting herself. "Is he still here?"

"I disposed of him, but you'll want to clean up the body," Garrick said coldly.

Juniper nodded sharply, as if she'd expected no less. "I'm closing the shop immediately." She glanced at me. "I'm so sorry, Your Majesty. I never would have imagined anyone would be so bold as to harm you here in public, in the middle of my own shop." She lowered her voice. "Aspen told me of your other plans while you're in Northelm. I will lead you to the infirmary myself, and ensure a healer sees to you immediately."

As she scurried off to check that her shop was empty of other customers, blow out candles, turn her sign, and bolt the door, Aspen squeezed my hand reassuringly. "She's a fellow rebel and integral to our movement," she whispered. "You can trust her, despite what happened here. I'm so sorry." She glanced toward Garrick. "Remember, stay out of the way. The rebels don't fully trust you."

"Rightfully so," Garrick muttered.

Juniper guided us through a back room and out another door, taking side streets and alleys to reach an abandoned shop. The building was long and low. Its door creaked on rusty hinges as she pushed it inward.

Aspen shifted back into her pixie form, and I settled her onto my shoulder.

The scents of blood and infection reached my nose and I forced myself not to cringe as I stepped inside after the shop owner. Garrick lingered outside where he wouldn't be seen. Within was a single long room, dimly lit by curtained windows lining the walls. Countless cots occupied by wounded fae filled every available space, while healers walked among them, tirelessly working their magic.

"There are more wounded than the last time I visited," Aspen muttered from her place on my shoulder.

"Can the healers' magic can't save them all?" I whispered back.

"Not always. Some wounds are too grievous. Even immortals can die." The pixie's voice was heavy with her sadness.

Hands shaking, I listened as Juniper murmured something to one of the nearest healers, who nodded in understanding before lifting her gaze to my face, awe in her expression. She dipped into a curtsey. "Could I tend to you, Your Majesty?"

At my nod, she strode forward, placing gentle, cool fingers on my neck. There was a flare of pain before a wave of weariness struck me. Slowly, the discomfort of my swollen throat eased. Then, she circled me, her fingers cautiously skating over my back. Her power must have been great, for even through the fabric of my tunic, I could sense the effects of her magic binding my skin, stealing the sting from both my Stormclaw mark and the demon scratches.

"How did you know?" I asked.

"I can sense injuries as well as heal them, my queen," the woman said as she walked around to face me again. "The marks on your back will scar, but they shouldn't cause you any further pain."

"Thank you."

She grinned widely, her pink eyes sparkling. "My pleasure." She glanced about the room. "Feel free to walk among our injured and offer hope, Your Majesty. Thank you for taking the time to see us."

My stomach churned. This was a place of suffering, of death, so close to the castle where Nerissa and Preston hosted garish feasts and balls. No wonder a growing number of citizens were discontent with their rule, looking to me not only for salvation from the underworld creatures but also for hope and compassion.

Aspen stood on her tiptoes to hiss in my ear. "Remember, some of the healers are rebels, eager to see you prove yourself."

Not terrifying at all, I thought.

Rallying my courage, I forced myself to walk among the cots, asking names of the more coherent patients and murmuring encouraging words. Anything to let them know I saw them, that I cared. Some of the fae studied me uncertainly, but others reached for my hand and grasped me as if I were their lifeline. As if my touch could heal.

All the while, I was conscious of the healers pausing their work, watching me with cautious curiosity. It was a constant reminder that even among the rebels who'd been waiting for me for years, I hadn't proven myself yet. I had a reputation to withhold, and decades of hope and dreams to fulfill for them. I could only pray I lived up to their expectations and secured their loyalty and confidence.

"Address the room," Aspen encouraged in her soft voice. "Give them a speech worthy of a queen. Their true leader."

Exhaustion from the healer's magic beckoned to me, but I knew Aspen was right. I needed to say something for the rebels to overhear. I needed to convince them I could lead—even if I was untrained and uncertain. I needed to at least appear willing to learn and try.

Swallowing thickly, I scanned the room, at first seeking the healers' faces before glancing back to the wounded. Even though the rebels would be the ones to fight for me first, the patients, soldiers sent to suffer in a war the siblings had needlessly caused, held my attention. They were the ones who needed me most in this moment, the ones I hoped would recover and remember me later. They were as much my people as the rebels were.

"By now, I know word has spread of my engagement," I began. Inwardly, I cringed. That wasn't how I should have started. "I..." I cleared my throat, fumbling for words. Back in Altidvale, I had never been expected to address an entire crowd of people. I'd been trained to be a quiet, amiable woman and to communicate well at parties and other frivolous events. I'd never been taught how to soothe wounded soldiers or instill bravery in men and women I needed to fight for me.

"You can do this," Aspen urged. "You're their queen, Ren. Tell them who you are."

I tried to start afresh. "That is, I know I may be human, and it's true much of this world is strange to me..."

One of the healers, a man with antlers twisting behind his ears, turned away, shaking his head. Unimpressed.

My mouth was dry, and whatever I'd intended to say vanished from my mind. "I..."

"Who do you think you are?" one of the patients croaked from her cot. Another scoffed. "Nobody."

Murmurs broke out, doubt swiftly overtaking the room. Sweat beaded on my brow, and my weariness made me sway on my feet. I wasn't strong. I wasn't a leader. I was failing already. They'd never help overthrow Preston and Nerissa, and Aspen and I would lose.

The sound of the door creaking open shattered the growing conversations around the room. Garrick's form hovered in the entrance, his eyes burning with unmasked fury. "Who is she? She is Ren Silverfrost, daughter of Prince Ashton and only surviving member of our royal family. She is your rightful queen, and she sees your suffering and refuses to sit idly by. She's here to fight for you, and she is worthy of your allegiance and respect."

Stillness settled over the room as patients and healers stared at Garrick. And then, the silence was broken as more talk erupted. One of the healers, the burly antlered man, stalked forward until he was chest-to-chest with Garrick. "You're the imposter Nerissa's lackey," he accused. "Why would we listen to a word you say, when you love to run about doing *her* bidding?"

Apparently he had no fear of insulting the siblings here, with other rebels nearby. The only ones who might be loyal to Preston and Nerissa were likely the injured, though I doubted many of them held the royals in high esteem after being left, forgotten, first at the border and now here in the castle's very shadow.

Garrick stiffened, and without warning, the antlered man shoved him, hard.

My anger flared. "Stop," I commanded.

"You worthless, traitorous dog," the man snarled. "You're the reason my brother is dead. You hunted him for them like the mindless puppet you are." Something silver flashed in his hand—a hidden blade—as he swung a fist at Garrick. The hunter dodged but didn't draw one of his own weapons.

"Don't you dare touch him," I warned.

The man only snarled at me before lunging for Garrick again.

I didn't think, only reacted. A whirlwind of snow and black daggers of ice tore through the building, slamming into Garrick's attacker. It was over in seconds, shards of glistening ice stained red with the man's blood as he gaped and then collapsed. Still. Dead.

No one moved. I could scarcely breathe. "Garrick Darkgrove is loyal to me, and is here as my subject," I announced, forcing my voice to be steady. "Does anyone else wish to threaten him or defy my orders?"

Silence answered me.

And then, the first of the healers stepped forward, her eyes wide with wonder and terror as she dropped into a kneel. Throughout the building the rest followed, joining her as she spoke:

"All hail Queen Ren Silverfrost."

CHAPTER TWENTY-FIVE

The following days were a whirlwind of preparation. King Preston and Queen Nerissa gave me permission to order their seamstresses about, calling on them for any materials I needed. I worked cloistered in my chambers, utilizing a mannequin provided by a seamstress to hold my work-in-progress and a screen set in the corner of my bedroom to conceal it from view. In between communicating in secret with the rebels and tending to various tasks the king and queen gave her to help prepare for the ball—mostly, concocting various potions and tinctures that only a pixie could make—Aspen would visit with me or bring me untainted food.

In free moments, Aspen and Garrick each took turns escorting me to private areas of the castle where I could practice my magic undisturbed. Neither let me wander in the evenings anymore, not wanting to risk a chance encounter with a demon. The creatures were escaping earlier each night we drew closer to the solstice. More than once my sleep had been interrupted by the sounds of claws scraping along a stone corridor and shouts from guards fighting to subdue the creature.

Despite the power in my blood, Preston and Nerissa never called on me. Instead, they'd started commanding the guards to lock me in my rooms at night. The first evening I'd tested my doorknob, fury had burned in my chest, followed by worry. Did they know I was sneaking out to practice magic? Did they suspect Aspen and I were plotting? Or were they only being overprotective, ensuring their precious tool wasn't injured or killed before the solstice?

If they did suspect us of anything, they made no accusations. At every dinner feast, Preston made a show of having me sit at his side, his willing possession. His trophy to display on his arm.

He and Nerissa didn't tempt Garrick and me again either by sending the wolf shifter to my rooms to guard me. And they didn't punish him for touching me either time I'd been attacked—not by demons and not by the fae in Northelm. But I didn't fool myself for a moment into thinking the siblings' lack of playing games with the two of us, their sudden disinterest in tormenting us, was a good thing. Instead, I knew it meant they were busy in preparations for the ball, solstice, and the coming wedding.

Each day, new items were delivered to my rooms. A wispy fae gown in shades of silver and black that was declared to be my wedding dress and was stored carefully in my wardrobe. A delicate silver tiara in a carved wooden case—one I knew was all for show, for I was to be a consort, not a ruler. A pair of flimsy black slippers to wear with my dress. Every time, maids with glazed eyes dropped off the items, leaving my stomach in knots at the way they avoided my questions about their personal lives or stared at me blankly.

I had to free them. I had to free us *all*.

The day of the ball dawned frigid, with billowing grey clouds gathering on the horizon, threatening a snowstorm. My stomach was a tangled ball of nerves as my maids brought me my breakfast, one I knew was laced with forget-me-nots, like always. After my days of exposure to the flowers and practice with my power, I felt more confident, though not nearly as confident as I'd hoped. I'd managed to conjure an ice blade on one occasion, but that was all. Anything beyond that or toying with frost and ice that I could dismiss with a flick of my hand had been impossible. It wasn't as if I could have called on a snowstorm within the castle walls without giving myself away.

As I cradled my steaming mug of tea and gazed out the window, studying the clouds and wondering what the weather would bring, I tried to assure myself that the land was on my side. It knew my magic, my blood. It was connected to me, and I with it. I was *meant* to be here, meant to rule. Meant to protect this land from the undead souls and demons slipping through the entrance to the underworld.

The door creaked open, and Aspen, settled in a guard's hand, dismissed the servants with a few whispered words before ordering the man to deposit her on my bed and leave. Once the door closed behind him, she sat cross-legged on the covers and studied me thoughtfully. "When the time comes, you'll know what to do," she said, as if reading my mind.

"A little magic isn't the same as the power I need to wield." I glanced down at the steam rising from my cup, enjoying the way it warmed my cheeks. "Coating the floor with ice so Preston and Nerissa might slip isn't going to stop their death magic from wreaking havoc on our people."

Aspen dipped her head. "True, but the fact that you can command a little power now even when in contact with the forget-me-nots is unheard of for pure-blooded fae. Before, you managed to wield powerful magic when your life was under threat, and you hadn't consumed or been in contact with the flowers for several hours. Imagine what you'll do today—not only with the message you'll send in that gown—but also with the need to strike back and save lives."

I traced the lip of my mug with one finger. Aspen and I had discussed many outcomes before, yet I still couldn't help but ask the question again. "Do you think Preston and Nerissa would ever abdicate, or will we be forced to kill them?"

When I glanced at her, Aspen's expression was tight. "Don't feel any remorse or guilt for them, Ren. If they force us to end their bloody reign with more death, then so be it. They have killed so many. They have done so much to hurt *you*."

I lifted my chin. "I'm not afraid. I've killed to protect Garrick, and I'd kill to save you too. You're a good friend, Aspen. And I'd kill to save any other innocent person they tried to attack. I won't hesitate if it comes to that. I just..." I frowned. "I wonder if killing them will make our future path much harder. The fae that support their rule will hate us even more if we slay their king and queen."

"I'm afraid you'll have resistance no matter what you do, with Silverfrost prejudice against humans ingrained so deeply. But you won't be alone. I'll be happy to stay by your side as an advisor, as long as you need me, and all my rebels would be proud to serve you."

"Thank you." I swallowed. "I suppose this is it then. The beginning." *And not an end,* I prayed.

Aspen's smile was radiant. "A wonderful beginning."

Though it was only midday, the clouds had gathered in a thick blanket to stifle the sunlight and make it as dark as a gloomy evening. I sat quietly before my vanity, trying to ignore the glazed look in my maid's eyes as she brushed through the long strands of my hair, leaving it to hang loose over my shoulders.

When she stepped back at last, I drew a deep breath and rose, crossing over to the full-length mirror in the corner of my room. I stared, taking in the effect of the ballgown gracing my form for the first time. Silver glitter dusted my eyelids, matching both my hair and the glistening strands in my dress. The sleeves were long and delicate, while the neckline dipped below my collarbones in a fae style without feeling immodest by human fashion standards. The skirts and bodice were full of stunning details, crafted with the fabric I'd found in Juniper's shop and rippling with veins of silver and blue and violet, as well as bits of decorative black lace. And over all of it, enchanted with an elixir Aspen had concocted so their brittle, dried petals would not disintegrate and scatter, were sewn forget-me-nots.

From my sleeves to my bodice to my skirts, the blue flashed proudly everywhere. Stunning. Elegant. And the perfect message to Preston and Nerissa as well as the rest of the court and every ball attendee from Northelm: I would not be controlled, and my magic would not be contained. I was powerful, strong enough to withstand the forget-me-nots' influence. Strong enough to withstand *them*.

Turning, I glanced over my shoulder to study the low dip of my dress in the back, revealing the Stormclaw emblem carved into my skin as well as the scars from the demon attack.

I couldn't help the grin that curved my lips. I was ready.

A knock on the door had me turning, my pulse racing with anticipation. I couldn't help it. Knowing Garrick was my usual escort and guard, I couldn't wait to see his reaction to my gown. Couldn't wait to have even a few minutes alone with him. Even if his mind wasn't his own and the siblings controlled him, I knew I would draw comfort from his steady presence. I knew even if they forced him to fight on their side today, he was with Aspen and me.

After today, if all went well, he would be free of them. Never forced to be someone else's pawn again.

When I turned, I was surprised to find I'd been so consumed in studying my dress that I hadn't even heard the maids file out, leaving me alone. I stepped forward hopefully as I watched the knob turn.

Yet when the door opened, it wasn't Garrick, but Preston who stepped inside. My stomach soured as his red eyes scanned me from head to toe, his nostrils flaring with annoyance.

"What is this?" he asked, his voice deadly quiet.

I lifted my chin defiantly. "My ballgown." Ignoring the way my blood throbbed in my ears, I swept toward the door, eager to leave my chambers and avoid being alone with the king for a moment longer.

As I tried to push past him, Preston reached for my arm, pulling back at the last moment with a hiss when he realized he couldn't grasp me without touching the forget-me-nots gracing my sleeve. I resisted the urge to grin in triumph as I opened the door and slipped out into the hall. The guards saluted as Preston trailed me.

He cornered me halfway down the hall, seizing me by the hair, where there was no danger of brushing against a petal, and roughly shoving me into a dark alcove. A marble statue of an old fae queen, her smile cruel and arrogant, leered down at us. "Your presence at this ball is meant to rally confidence in your magical abilities," Preston snapped. "So what is this foolish display? Why would you cripple yourself?"

My eyes watered as I struggled against him, trying to wrench my hair free. "Don't you know?" I gritted out. "Human blood isn't affected by the flowers the way fae blood is."

Preston's eyes narrowed as he jerked my head back, forcing me to meet his gaze. "If you don't obey..."

I swallowed, my words coming out bitter. "I know, you'll punish me, because I 'belong to you.'"

"No," Preston snapped, leaning closer. Cold air enveloped me. When he ran an icy finger down my face, I shuddered. "I'll punish your wolf."

He released me abruptly, causing me to stumble. "Let's go." He stormed down the hallway, and I did my best to keep up.

Strains of music as instruments were tuned and the gentle rumble of conversation and laughter hit me before we rounded the final corner to the ballroom entrance. Beyond the double doors, servants milled about on a balcony overlooking the space, where countless candles flickering in chandeliers and candelabras cast a warm glow on everything. A wide staircase carpeted in blue and silver stretched down to the polished ballroom floor. Tiny sprites darted above the larger fae guests, their lights adding to the magical radiance of the night as they twirled through the air, moving to their own silent music. Glittering silver garlands, blue ribbons, and stunning bouquets of fresh white roses—gathered from I-knew-not-where—all added to the warmth of the party. It was a little jolting to take in, given the circumstances. Preston and Nerissa were the last people I would imagine hosting such an inviting party, but then again, hadn't the would-be assassin accused them of extravagance and waste?

Perhaps this wasn't only a way for them to enjoy excess, but also a means of providing a distraction. A garish celebration to celebrate me, Silverfrost's savior, and to lull both the court and citizens from Northelm into a false sense of security, even as men and women were dying in battle against Ashwood. Even as Ashwood was invading our kingdom, pressing ever closer to the capital.

One of the servants posted near the doors dipped into a low bow at the sight of Preston and me before announcing us. "King Preston and his fiancée, Florentia Silverfrost!"

I forced a smile on my face as I stepped forward at Preston's side. He refused to take my arm to escort me, avoiding the forget-me-nots. Instead, he seized my hand, his grip sharp and painful as he guided me toward the steps. My eyes swept the ballroom below, snagging on Nerissa, who was clothed in frothy layers of silver and blue, and then finding Garrick standing stiffly nearby. As at the last celebration, he was clothed in leather and a fur-lined vest, as if Nerissa refused to let him wear finer attire. Despite his status as her betrothed, it seemed she wanted everyone to forever remember that he was beneath her, a servant. Her hunter. And yet, the leather and fur complimented him perhaps better than anything else could. In the glow of the candles and the sprites' flashing lights, his gold eyes were rich and warm and striking. His muscular figure might have been tall and imposing to others, but to me, the mere sight of him was a reminder of the reassurance and safety he offered me.

As Preston and I descended the stairs, the loud conversation and laughter ceased, guests quieting as they took in my dress. Heads dipped toward one another as winged women and horned men whispered to each other, speculating. I kept my demure smile firmly in place. Once I would have shunned such attention, seeking solitude in the human world, where anyone talking about me only meant shameful rumors and being rejected or mocked. But here? I wanted them to look. Let them fear and avoid me, or let them respect and follow me. Let them know I was not to be controlled or trifled with—that I was not meant to be a mere consort, but their queen.

I lifted my eyes again toward Garrick as Preston and I neared the last step and the crowd surged backward, parting to give us plenty of room. Normally, I would have assumed it was a sign of respect, but I knew better this time. This time, they were afraid, granting me a wide berth so as to avoid their skin accidentally brushing against my forget-me-nots. Garrick's expression told me he wasn't under Nerissa's control, not yet at least. His eyes were locked on me, all-consuming. Heat licked at my cheeks as I returned his stare. I couldn't read his expression, but I sensed he wished he could silently communicate something to me across the ballroom. That he was on my side? That he found me beautiful?

I was tired of unspoken words between us, of wishful thinking and hopes. After today, we would be free. And I ached to tell him how I felt, to see if there was even the chance of a future for us beyond friendship.

"Stay with me," Preston muttered out of the corner of his mouth as the musicians began to play and conversations slowly resumed in earnest. Everyone we passed bowed or curtsied respectfully, their eyes barely lingering on their king before latching on me, tracing the petals gracing me from head to toe. I felt eyes burn into my back when I walked by and they glimpsed every scar carved into my skin. While the demon claw marks were a sign of what I'd survived, I wondered what their reactions were to the Stormclaw emblem. Did most think it was Preston's right to mark me as his, lowly human that I was? Or were they repulsed by such an open display of his violence and cruelty?

I could only hope most thought the latter.

Time passed slowly as Preston escorted me in a slow circuit about the room, engaging in meaningless chatter with countless courtiers who studied me warily, offering backhanded compliments or honeyed words meant to flatter and win them my favor. I scanned the room surreptitiously any chance I had, taking note of where Aspen was perched on Juniper's shoulder, chatting animatedly. Other rebels I recognized from the makeshift infirmary were posted about the room, looking for all the world like casual guests deep in their enjoyment of fae wine, rich food from the wide array laid out on the side tables, conversation, and dancing.

It took numerous conversations before anyone broached the topic of the flowers covering my dress. "I don't understand the forget-me-nots," a woman with slitted pupils that reminded me of those of a snake murmured. She flicked her gaze up and down, her lip curling in disgust. "I thought your power was supposed to dismiss the creatures back to the underworld."

"The power in her blood will send them back and seal the entrance," Preston cut in sharply before I could say anything. "Don't fret about the forget-me-nots; they're a silly human choice of hers. She knows the heavy price if she fails to close the door to the underworld." He cast a sidelong glance at me, his eyes burning with a threat. Challenging me to dare to deny him.

I itched to show him what little effect the flowers now had on me. I longed to see the fear in his eyes when he saw his and Nerissa's efforts had no longer leashed my power. But I wanted to wait for a moment when more of the court could see me, not here when we were in a corner of the room.

The woman sniffed, stepping back from the hem of my gown, apparently choosing to see my display as proof I was nothing but a weak human with pitiful magic. Not evidence I could overcome the flowers' influence.

As Preston seized my elbow and led me away, the musicians launched into a new song. "Time to dance," he muttered, and my one comfort was that he appeared as repulsed by the idea as I was.

While one of his cold hands latched onto my waist, the other grasped my hand, pulling me out onto the dance floor. I couldn't help but wish that, like last time, someone would shoot an arrow at him and cut short this miserable show of ours. As we wove around other couples, nearing the center of the dance floor and drawing more eyes toward us, I drew a deep breath and concentrated. I pulled away from Preston, and before he could react, lifted a hand and directed icicles to form on the garland stretched overhead. They sparkled golden in the flickering light, drawing countless stares and inducing scattered gasps and whispers throughout the crowd.

Preston froze, his eyes widening with fear before narrowing in fury. He seized my wrist, yanking me toward him until I was uncomfortably close. "You've made your point, Snowflake," he hissed. "Now dismiss the ice."

I had countless rebels on my side and a plan to fight back today. I wasn't afraid of him. "Why?" I asked. "Afraid my showy magic will prove to your court that I'm even more powerful than they've been led to believe?"

Preston scowled. We ended our dance in silence, and without another word, he slunk off the floor toward his sister, leaving me free to approach the tables. Per Aspen's advice, I selected a glass of fae wine, sipping it as I dodged the courtiers who tried to approach me with questions. If they were on my side now, they would join the rebels and me later. Otherwise, I was in no mood for more shallow conversations and false politeness.

Slowly, I edged my way toward a shadowy corner, ducking behind one of the stone pillars stretching toward the ceiling. Here, I breathed a sigh of relief as I studied the crowd, awaiting Aspen's signal. It felt like hours had dragged by already, and I was growing more anxious as time passed.

Downing the last of the wine in my glass, I froze when I noticed a fae servant slip through the crowd, approach the queen, and dip his head to whisper. Nerissa stiffened, spoke briefly to her brother, and then quietly vanished through one of the doors with the servant. I frowned, wondering what news she'd been given. Did anyone suspect the rebels' plans, or did it have to do with the war? Preston made his way through the crowd, playing the role of charismatic host as if he wanted to do everything he could to distract his guests from noticing his sister's absence.

And Garrick was nowhere to be seen. I set my empty glass down on the floor behind the pillar and sank against the wall, letting the chill emanating from the stone seep through my dress and cool my heated skin.

"I suppose you can learn all you need to know about a party if the guest of honor is hiding," a low voice said at my side.

I startled, turning to see Garrick leaning against the wall nearby, his gold eyes luminescent in the shadow cast by the pillar. "You managed to slip away too," I said, grinning.

"You look…" Garrick hesitated, tipping his head as he scanned my form, as if he hadn't already stared at me the entire time I'd entered the ball. "Ethereal."

Hoping he couldn't see the blush staining my cheeks, I settled back against the wall, turning my tone playful. "Ethereal? Whatever do you mean?"

Garrick stepped closer, his voice pitching lower. "I think you know, Starlight."

My heart slammed into my chest as wild and hopeful thoughts spun through my head. "Garrick," I whispered, "will you dance with me?"

Regret flashed in his gaze. "I can't."

My eyes darted about our concealed space. "Then not out there. Here."

Garrick shook his head. "It's not that." He shoved his hands into his pockets and leaned against the wall, keeping a careful distance between us. "They forbade me to touch you at all. Even if I only touched your sleeve or put my hand on your waist." His throat worked as he swallowed. "It's another test of my obedience when I have free will, and you know what they'd do if I failed it. I can't be the one to hurt you again."

My heart sank. Of course Preston and Nerissa were still playing their sick games, making the rules even stricter when they suspected I would be more tempted than ever to touch Garrick. "Then let's dance like we would in the mortal world, only never holding hands." I stepped forward, turning to the side and pulling my arm close against my hip.

He blinked, as if recalling some of the dances he'd witnessed at the ball in my hometown, the night we first met. How did it already feel so long ago, when only days had passed? He mimicked my stance, stepping up beside me and keeping his own hand held carefully away so it wouldn't graze mine accidentally. We moved slowly to the music, circling one another and then reaching out our hands as we spun together—never holding hands, never even letting them brush. Our bodies never collided as we stepped near enough that I could feel his warmth, but stayed far enough apart that I could only dream of him pulling me in, dancing with me as Preston had.

"See?" I said with a grin as we paused across from one another, the song coming to an end. "We can still dance as friends."

Something flared in Garrick's eyes as a new song began. In a blink, he'd stepped so close to me I was forced to move away, my back striking the stone wall. "What?" His eyes burned.

"I said we can still dance as friends," I managed, scanning his expression, trying to read the look on his face.

"Friends." The word came out husky as he pressed his hands on either side of my body, hemming me in without touching me. He dipped his head to meet my gaze, trapping me in the molten gold of his eyes. "If I could touch you, Starlight, I would not be dancing with you as a friend. I wouldn't touch you as a *friend*." I couldn't move as he leaned closer, his breath caressing my face. Out of the corner of my eye, I watched his fingers flex against the wall, as if it took every ounce of his strength to hold himself back from touching me. "If I could," he went on, "I would ensure every touch I gave you was searing. I would kiss you until your knees went weak." He pulled back, inhaling sharply as if he'd been struggling for air too. There was a desperate look on his face, a heart-wrenching tangle of hope and despair, desire and adoration. "Because...I might never deserve you—and I might be forced to obey *them*, my very body belonging to them to control—but every piece of my heart belongs to you, my Starlight. Gods have mercy on me, but you've captivated me from the first moment I saw you, and you've enchanted me every moment since. I shouldn't even dare to think the words, and they don't feel like enough...but I love you. So don't call me a friend, I beg of you. Even if you don't feel the same, please spare me that. I already have to watch him touch you and claim you, and it's the worst sort of torment."

My thoughts were wild, my heart light. He *loved* me. No matter what today brought, I could cling to that. It was his freedom I fought for. Our future. Our love. For that, I could win. I *would* win.

"You…love me?" My voice came out strangled. I shook my head to clear it, my thoughts racing. "But they cannot own you after this evening, and Preston won't be able to pretend I'm his. We can't let them dictate what we do anymore. They won't hurt us again, Garrick." I studied his face—the white-blond lock of hair across his brow, the beautiful gold of his eyes, the stubble dotting his jaw—and gathered my courage. "Kiss me."

Garrick's eyes widened, his breaths turning uneven. "What?"

I lifted my head the smallest bit, desperate to close the gap between us but also not wanting to risk something he wasn't willing to chance as well. "Kiss. Me."

Those two words were all it took to snap the last of Garrick's restraint. His hands moved immediately, cradling my face as he lifted my chin and closed the remaining space between us. His body molded to mine, and his mouth consumed me. There was so much want, so much *need*, between us, every caress of our lips sharing the words we'd left unspoken for so long, making vows of a future I finally dared to believe was within our reach. He ran his thumbs along my jaw, tangled his fingers in my hair, dropped his other hand to my waist and tugged me into his embrace. Just as he'd promised, his every touch was searing, as if his fingers could brand me, claiming me as his and undoing every unwanted touch and awful scar left by Preston. And his kiss was devouring yet tender, turning my head light and my knees wobbly.

When we broke apart at last, gasping, a glint of mischief flashed in Garrick's eyes. "This is where you ask me, Starlight."

"What?"

He flashed his teeth in a wide grin, his eyes darting to my lips. That was when I remembered the words he'd said the first night we met, and my heart jolted, but not unpleasantly. *I won't bite…unless you ask me to.*

I swallowed, a blush suffusing my cheeks. "I… Will you?"

"Close enough," Garrick said huskily, leaning forward to capture my mouth with his again. He took his time, as if he were savoring the feel and taste of me, and then he caught my bottom lip with his, nibbling it gently.

I couldn't help my giggle as he drew back, only to trace a path of whisper-soft kisses along my jaw and neck. My laughter died in my throat as he planted another over my pulse, and then moved upward, his teeth gently scraping against my earlobe. I let out an embarrassing gasp. "Maybe I knew I shouldn't flirt, shouldn't want you," he murmured against my neck, "but I've wanted to do that since the first night we met. Why else do you think I teased you so?"

Then, as suddenly as he'd lost his restraint, he sighed and straightened, pressing a gentle kiss to my forehead before pulling back enough to lay my head against his chest. His chin tucked against my hair, making me feel secure as I listened to the steady beat of his heart. But as I evened my breathing, I realized the arms that clung so tightly to me were shaking.

"Garrick?" I drew away, lifting my head to stare up into his face. Tears gleamed in his eyes.

"I shouldn't have done that. I fear what they could make me do to you again," he confessed. "I've held myself back, kept those words close to my heart, told myself I could never kiss you—wasn't worthy to even think of you—because I can't bear to see you suffer. And if *I'm* the cause?"

"You won't be," I cut in sharply. "I promise it." I settled a hand against his cheek, relishing the roughness of his stubble against my skin. "We're going to free you from them."

Movement over Garrick's shoulder caught my eye, and I paused. Was it the signal at last?

But instead, a pair of blood-red eyes peered at me as Preston leaned against the pillar, arms crossed. "How touching," he mocked. "Free the dog from the blood oath he *willingly* made? You truly think highly of yourself, don't you?"

CHAPTER TWENTY-SIX

My blood pounded in my ears, a heady mixture of terror and fury rushing though my entire body as I stared back at Preston. "He made his oath willingly because he thought you had some semblance of *honor*," I bit out.

Preston sneered, waving a careless hand. "What is honor worth? Power is all that matters, little Snowflake." His eyes snapped to Garrick. "Release her and leave us."

A chill swept over me as I met Garrick's eyes, watching fury flare and die in them as Preston took control. His expression shifting into blankness, the wolf shifter wrenched his arms from around me and strode away without a word or backward glance.

"Come, we need to talk, Fiancée," Preston said.

I fumed silently, refusing to move.

"Or I could punish Garrick immediately for disobeying my order and touching you." His mouth twitched downward in disgust.

Gritting my teeth, I forced myself to walk to Preston and fall into step beside him as he stalked away, not back toward the dance floor and the crowd of guests but to a far entrance. My stomach curdled, wondering what he planned to discuss—to do—in the less occupied parts of the castle.

As soon as we'd stepped out into a cool hallway, feeling dim and stale compared to the color and magnificence in the ballroom, Preston whirled on me, backing me up against the wall. "I know what you and Aspen are doing." His red eyes brimmed with murder.

My laughter rang out unconvincingly. "Becoming better acquainted? Beginning a friendship?"

Preston leaned closer, his putrid breath washing over me and making bile rise up the back of my throat. "She's a leader for the rebels, the same damn group that tried to shoot me. And you're planning with them, hoping to steal the throne."

My head whirled. What if this was it? Preston had me cornered. Maybe he would make good on his threat and murder me here, draining my body of blood and using that to seal the door. It would be a foolish move on his part—a temporary solution to Silverfrost's problem—but I had a growing suspicion he and Nerissa didn't care all that much for their kingdom. They certainly didn't seem to fear the underworld creatures themselves.

There was no point in denying Preston's claim. Perhaps he'd overheard us. In this castle, I could only imagine how many walls had ears. Instead, I narrowed my eyes and said, "It's impossible to steal what already belongs to you."

Preston grabbed a handful of hair and tugged viciously, making my scalp burn as he tipped my face toward the ceiling, too high above and cloaked in shadows to see. "A mortal has no right or claim to an immortal's station," he hissed.

With my neck so exposed, I had the terrifying sense he would draw a dagger and slit my throat right there. But instead he drew back, yanking on my hair to force me along with him as he stormed down the hall. Eyes burning and scalp smarting, I gritted my teeth to keep from crying out.

"There will be no rebellion today, no fights for freedom. You'll sit in our dungeon until it's time to drag you out for your blood, and then I care not what happens to you next."

I struggled against his grip, my wild thoughts wrestling to concentrate and draw on my magic. A blast of chill air gusted through the hallway, whipping the skirts of my dress around my legs and tangling them as ice crackled and hardened beneath our feet. Losing his hold on my hair, Preston slipped and caught himself, skidding to a stop. He turned toward me with searing rage in his gaze, but I was already armed with a blade of ice nestled in my palm.

I slammed it into his chest before he could react, plunging it deep into flesh. Stumbling back on the ice, I prepared to whirl and flee back to the ballroom, to notify Aspen and the other rebels that we only had to find

Nerissa. But Preston's face only twitched as he reached for the ice in his chest, yanking it out in one smooth movement. My feet locked in place, my shock rendering me immobile.

There was blood on the blade, blood gushing from the gaping hole in his finely embroidered tunic and the broken, pale flesh beneath it. But then it stopped, the wound stitching itself back together as if it had never existed. Preston stood, whole and unaffected. With air trapped in my lungs, I tried and failed to let out a strangled cry.

"All your clever planning, all of Aspen's attempts to spy and learn our weaknesses, and neither of you ever guessed?" Preston's laughter was cold as he tossed the ice blade aside. It didn't matter. The weapon was useless against him. "You know nothing of what we *really* want?"

"You're one of them," I choked out. "That's why you can't die."

"Not a demon," Preston said, stalking closer. In my shock and lack of focus on my magic, the ice had melted into nothingness, not even leaving a trace of water behind to dampen the floor. "My sister and I *were* fae once, and I suppose we still are. Our current forms are what we once were—mostly. Death tainted our magic and made it something new, though perhaps this is more powerful than ever. It's convenient, at least, that we can't die a second time." His lips curled in a wicked smile.

"If you're the dead souls of fae, why would you hate your own kingdom? Why subject its citizens to a war they are currently *losing*?"

"*Our* citizens?" Preston barked. He smirked. "It is said that the dead can show the living glimpses of their previous lives." Before I could jerk away, he seized my face with rough fingers. "It seems only right to reveal all now, on the eve of our victory. It's much more pleasant to let our victims know what is coming and quake in fear over what they cannot stop. Let me show you."

In a blink, the world around me had vanished, replaced by a thick forest of ancient, wide-trunked trees. By the brightness of the sun, the rich green of the leaves, and the flowers in full bloom scattered throughout the undergrowth, I gathered it was the height of summer. But the peace of nature was broken by the bloody sight before me: fae in Silverfrost colors of winter clashed in battle against other immortals clothed in shades of emerald and onyx. Based on the setting, I guessed the latter were fae of Ravenheart, the summer kingdom, fighting to protect their homeland.

At the forefront of the Ravenheart lines stood Preston and Nerissa, their skin less pale, full of color and life, and their eyes rich hues of blue-green rather than the blood-red they now bore.

One of the Silverfrost fae sauntered toward Preston. There was a silver circlet on his brow, and his sword dripped with the scarlet blood of Preston's people. His eyes were a striking shade of black, but his short hair was as bright and silver as mine. "If it's not the renowned Ravenheart warriors themselves," the man said grimly. "Preston Shadowfox and his sister Nerissa. If they sing songs of your glory now, imagine the stories they will chant about me, the one to finally slay you?"

"Ashton Silverfrost," Preston growled in return. *My father.* "Enough taunting; show me your mettle."

I blinked again and time seemed to move more quickly, skipping to the end of a long, brutal duel between the two men. It was clear the Ravenheart forces were outnumbered and weary. Even though their magic should have been strong, being on their own land during their most powerful season, too many of their soldiers were exhausted or wounded. The Silverfrosts were swiftly surrounding them, and even Preston's energy seemed to flag as Ashton cornered him against a tree. His death was swift—a fierce jab through his middle that left him choking and bleeding out on the forest floor as my father turned, shoving through the battle toward Nerissa.

The vision changed before showing Nerissa's death. Darkness enveloped everything, thick and consuming, so oppressive that even I, a mere witness, imagined my lungs would collapse for lack of air or from the sheer weight of the painful atmosphere if I lingered too long. Forms moved in the corners of my vision, shadowy figures that made my skin crawl and my mind scream at me to run. The same terror and despair that overwhelmed me when a demon was near.

But then—a light. An entrance into the living world, and a white-faced, scowling fae woman with a dagger to a silver-haired man's throat. He was restrained by a host of guards, while another silver-haired man—my father, Ashton—stood before the underworld's entrance, his expression etched into despair. I watched Preston and Nerissa shove through the narrow crack, exiting the endless darkness to stand on the other side of a carved stone door in the depths of a crypt. Their bodies were unlike what they'd been in life and even more terrible than they were now. They looked like corpses walking, their bloody eyes wild and cruel, their decaying flesh sagging off bones, and what was left of their teeth gnashing in their jaws.

"I've summoned you," the woman said, her voice shaking, "to enact my revenge on Ashton Silverfrost." She gestured to my father, whose jaw was taut with fury. "He was *my* betrothed, but he has chosen a mere mortal. He has taken everything from me. My life, my future. I want you to destroy him and everyone in this awful castle. Ruin the royal family. Win me back my future and my power."

"You said you would spare him if I listened—" My father began.

Ivy ignored him and waved a hand toward the other silver-haired man, who I guessed was Ashton's brother. "Fine. Guards, release him. Let him run away."

The guards' grips slackened obediently, though their faces looked so horrified at the sight of Nerissa and Preston, I wasn't sure if they would have lost their captive anyway. Unfortunately, despite my father's desperate pleas, his brother shook his head stubbornly, refusing to leave him behind. Refusing to save his own life.

Nerissa's voice came out in a hoarse whisper, grating on the ears. "Destroy everyone?"

Preston's skeletal face formed what I imagined was meant to be a smile. "Perfect. We've come for *our* revenge against the Silverfrosts."

They fell upon the woman first—the one I now realized was Ivy Stormclaw, my father's would-be bride—devouring her so quickly, she hardly had a chance to scream. Their bony, rotting hands snatched at her with strength she couldn't fend off. Their awful, gnashing teeth bit into her skin. Gagging, I had to cover my eyes, had to scream to try to block out the sound of tearing flesh.

When I dared to open them again, tears streaming down my face, nothing remained of Ivy—nothing but bones picked clean. Preston and Nerissa's skin looked more whole, parts of their skeletons covered completely by healthy flesh, as if by feeding upon a living creature, their undead forms gained back some of their previous life.

Before I could see what my father or the other fae did, the vision fell away, and I opened my eyes to meet Preston's bloody ones. It took every ounce of strength to fight the nausea crawling through my mouth and not lean over and vomit right there.

"Of course we want to see Silverfrost destroyed," Preston murmured, his rotten breath consuming me. "We died at their hands decades ago, all because they and Willowbark made a bloody alliance to destroy Ravenheart, to try to wipe us from the map. My sister and I were nobles in our kingdom. We fought proudly for our people, and we died defending them. Then we moldered away in the underworld, forced to pay for what the gods deemed as sinful lives. We'd always taken what we wanted, never worried about killing when it suited our needs. Apparently, that sends a soul to eternal punishment at the hands of demons. But *revenge*...revenge against your father freed us from the underworld, and revenge and the chance to taste life—half-lives that we are left with here—*that* is what keeps us fighting. Nightly, we collect the creatures that escape and store them in our fortress dungeon. Now that they see they can also taste life through immortal and mortal flesh, they are easy to win to our side. They are our own invincible army that, thanks to you, we can grow infinitely larger by flinging open the underworld entrance wide open at last. We can wipe out this whole damn kingdom. And the Silverfrost line will not only cease to exist, but will also be forgotten forever. And all the while? We will feed on as many of the living as we want and relish the way you grant us more life."

Clutching me by the neck, half-choking me, half-dragging me, Preston pressed further down the hallway as he continued. "The woman who helped let us out was a Stormclaw, a noble family that was distantly related to the Silverfrosts through marriage. She thought she was entitled to be joined with them again in another marriage." He laughed darkly. "Instead, she gave us our new name. It was easy enough for Nerissa and me to take the demons who escaped with us that first night to the Stormclaw residence and feed on any remaining souls who lived there. Their tragic end allowed us to step in as the new Stormclaws, supposed saviors of Silverfrost who easily subdued the escaped demons. The people of this land *begged* us to rule them. And Garrick, the only member of his family to survive the battle against the creatures in the castle, was so quick to pledge a blood oath to us in honor of his dead loved ones."

I couldn't even scream insults at him, not when my throat was constricting, my lungs burning. I dragged my feet to no avail. No one in the ballroom knew what was happening. And if no one could save me from Preston, who would save Silverfrost from the underworld? Who would stop him and Nerissa from forcing me to use my blood to fling the entrance open forever, and then destroy me so it could never be shut again?

Snow and wind roared around us to no effect. What could my magic do against a soul that was already dead?

There was a sudden halt to the distant strains of music still echoing from the ballroom. Screams broke out, forcing Preston to freeze. His grip didn't strengthen on me, giving me just enough air to survive, but it didn't lessen either. I clawed at his hands in vain, gasping on scraps of air as the corners of my vision filled with threatening black spots.

At first, I thought those spots had grown, that I was losing con-sciousness despite the air I fought to heave into my lungs. But as I blinked, the darkness grew clearer, moving as if it were alive. Billowing thunderclouds spiraled out from the ballroom and down the corri-dor, whispering through the air while flickering tongues of lightning sparked within them. The hairs on the back of my neck rose. It was unlike magic I'd ever seen before, and certainly not of Silverfrost.

Forked lightning lashed out toward Preston, and somehow, despite his hold on me, it didn't shock me. His body jerked, unable to die but apparently half-alive enough to react to pain. With his grip slackening, I was able to duck and break free, calling for ice, for snowstorms, for *anything* as I charged toward the ballroom. But as soon as I entered the churning clouds, darkness consumed me, and I couldn't see anything. Flashes of light sparked before my eyes, but rather than illuminating my path, they only blinded me until all I could see when I blinked was a dizzying display of shadow and light.

In the roiling storm clouds, thunder all but blotted out the distant cries coming from the ballroom. I had to get into that room, to the rebels. To Aspen. To Garrick.

It was clear to me now: Ashwood had arrived. While we'd plotted and hoped to tear Silverfrost apart from the inside, rebuilding it to our liking, our enemies had descended.

I reached for the magic within me, wondering if the same light that flared from my blood when it came into contact with demons could be summoned at any time. My mind conjured memories of distant starlight. I stretched out my hands, trying not to stumble into a wall, hoping I was still walking in the right direction. *Please, please,* I begged my magic.

But it was no use. The shadows enveloped me in a muggy embrace, tasting of early autumn days when the heat of summer hadn't fully relented. Electricity made my skin prickle.

Something struck the back of my head, and I was falling, falling into endless darkness.

CHAPTER TWENTY-SEVEN

I opened my eyes to the scent of woodsmoke and the sight of a fae man with shoulder-length auburn hair and piercing green eyes kneeling before me, his hands around my neck.

Pain crept up my throat and I panicked, lifting my arms to shove him away.

"Careful," he said, his voice low and soothing while he lifted his hands palms outward, as if indicating he meant no harm.

Heart throbbing in my temples, I heaved in a breath of air, noticing the swelling ache from Preston's fingers had vanished. He was a healer. Calming slightly, I scanned the area I was in. I was seated on a heap of blankets before a fire, surrounded by rustling canvas. Chilly, fresh air seeped in around us, but the pleasantly crackling fire combated the cold. An opening in the tent let the smoke swirl outside and granted a clear view to the starry night sky. The rest of the tent contained a wide cot and trunk in one corner, and a table laden with papers and maps and surrounded by chairs in another.

"Drink this," the healer said before I could formulate a question, lifting a canteen toward me.

I frowned at it before slowly taking it from him. If my captors wanted me dead, they could have killed me rather than dragging me here—which I assumed was an army campsite somewhere near Silverfrost's capital—and they certainly wouldn't have bothered with healing the bruising and swelling along my neck. While I swallowed down a few gulps of cool water, the healer stood and paced toward the tent opening.

I stiffened. Though I wasn't dead and I wasn't tied to the chair, I assumed there were guards posted outside. Kindness that healing me had been, I was still a prisoner. I wasn't sure I wanted the man with the soothing tone to leave, not when someone worse could take his place and begin an interrogation.

"Where am I?" I demanded.

The man paused, turning slowly. "I have a feeling you've already gathered you're in our camp."

"Far from the castle?"

Brow furrowed, his eyes dipped toward my neck before returning to my face. "Hate to be parted from your doting fiancé?"

"I hate to be kidnapped."

His lips twitched like he was holding back a smile. "We will be happy to answer your questions, but there are a few others who would like to be present. Let me tell them you're conscious and...feeling talkative."

I tensed nervously as the man slipped out of the tent. Sitting up straight in my chair, I felt the back of my head. No lump or ache. He must have healed that injury too. I stretched my mind toward my magic, wondering if there were enchantments placed on the camp that would prevent me from drawing on it. But before I could summon any ice or snow, the healer was back, trailed by three more people.

The first made my heart leap with momentary hope—a human woman, with long, black hair bound in a crown braid and intelligent blue-grey eyes. There wasn't a hint of that blank, glazed look the glamoured servants in Silverfrost possessed. But she was clothed in a finely embroidered tunic and trousers in shades of crimson, black, and gold—matching the attire the healer and the two others, both also fae men, wore. Perhaps the fact that she was human wouldn't endear me to her, not if she was apparently allied with the Ashwood kingdom closely enough to sport their colors.

Behind her, a tall man with a handsome face that looked carved from stone and inky hair studied me with sharp eyes. Something in his gaze made a chill creep over my skin that had nothing to do with the cool air gusting into the tent. He was not one to underestimate.

At his side, a shorter man with blond hair and warm brown eyes crossed his arms. A smile played about his face.

I wasn't sure which troubled me more—the emotionless look of the first man or the amused expression of the second. Did he find kidnapping women to be *amusing?*

"We're not here to hurt you," the blond man said, his tone friendly. His gaze snapped to where I held my hands before me, fingers curled into fists.

I glanced down and realized why he was grinning: I'd encased my hands entirely in ice. Cheeks heating, I lowered my hands and focused on retracting my magic, waiting for my fingers to thaw before tangling them in the skirts of my dress to warm them.

"Not unless you hurt us," the dark-haired man ground out.

Eyes flashing, the woman elbowed him. "That's not how you reassure a woman you've kidnapped," she snapped. Schooling her features into kindness, she stepped forward. "But Holden is right. We didn't bring you here to hurt you. My name is Elle Blackford, princess of Ashwood." She gestured to the cold-faced man. "This is my husband, Prince Fitz." The blond man moved closer. "That's his brother, Prince Holden." Lastly, she turned to the healer. "And this is Kinsey, a trusted friend...and, as you know, a healer."

Elle paused a few feet away from me. She waited a moment, as if hoping I'd supply my own name. When I didn't, she continued with her story. "We heard the rumors about a human being taken by the Silverfrosts—a woman with magic. But we had no idea what was true or even if you were betrothed to the king willingly until Fitz saw him attacking you. That was when we knew we had to get you out."

I watched her carefully. "If you meant me no harm, why knock me senseless and drag me out of there?"

Elle shot Holden a look, and he shuffled on his feet, rubbing the back of his neck bashfully. "I'm sorry about that. I don't see well in the storms Elle and Fitz wield, and while searching for you...well, I thought at first I'd come upon King Preston."

I folded my hands in my lap, listening to the logs snap in the fire as silence settled over us. Did they want an apology from me? A story about my life and who I was? Gratitude for carrying me unconscious out of the castle?

At last, I swallowed against the dryness in my throat. "What happened when you invaded? Were many of the guests killed? Did you slay Preston and Nerissa?" I frowned thoughtfully. "If the castle is now yours, wouldn't we be there?"

"As far as we know, the king and queen still live," Prince Fitz answered, his tone a low rumble. "Not enough of our forces have converged on the capital to launch a full-scale attack. We were too outnumbered. Instead, we settled for finding you." His gaze latched onto me pointedly.

As if they found me significant. Because they sympathized with humans, like Garrick had hinted? Or because they knew I was the true heir to the throne?

"And Preston got away," Holden muttered bitterly.

"There was infighting as we left," Kinsey interjected, and I turned to him, my attention rapt. The rebels must have chosen to make a move, perhaps thinking the chaos could be best used to their advantage. "But we didn't linger. I couldn't say who won the struggle, or how many perished in it."

I sucked in a breath, thinking of Preston's threats. If he and Nerissa lived, they knew of Aspen's plotting and would ensure she suffered for it.

"How long has it been?" I asked, glancing up at the hole in the tent, trying to catch a glimpse of the moon.

"A couple of hours at most," Elle said. "We had Kinsey heal your injuries as soon as we arrive."

I studied each of their faces, trying to determine if I could trust them. Despite what Garrick had told me about possibly finding safety in Ashwood, I knew better than to believe fae that claimed they'd rescued me out of the goodness of their hearts. Especially when Ashwood was at war with Silverfrost. I didn't know their motives, though I suspected taking me as a hostage could play to their advantage. What if they knew who I was, what value I possessed to the kingdom?

Even to Preston and Nerissa. They needed me alive for the solstice so I could open the entrance for them—that much was obvious, or they would have slain me long ago and filled a vial with my blood to use instead.

It was Kinsey who finally broke the silence, sliding a chair from the table over to the fire and sitting across from me. "I understand your hesitancy to trust us. But the only reason we are here fighting is because Silverfrost invaded our kingdom first. They've been slaying our people and causing problems for us all autumn, and we knew if we didn't press hard toward an advantage now, before winter sets in, we might lose our hope of any chance of victory at all."

"They're toying with you," I said. "Preston and Nerissa don't plan for their fae army to overtake Ashwood."

Prince Fitz and his brother shared a look before turning back to me. "What do you mean?" Fitz asked. "Why would they squander resources and soldiers on some...game?"

I leaned forward, resting my head in my hands. Though I felt no pain from the blow I'd sustained earlier, my mind was reeling. The information Preston had shared with me—the awful vision—wouldn't stop flashing through my thoughts. A heavy weariness settled in my bones as I considered the actual fight before me, not one against powerful fae, but against undead souls who feasted on the living to sustain themselves. Who wielded death magic. Who couldn't die again.

"I need to know," I said slowly, taking measured breaths to calm myself, "what your motive is regarding Silverfrost. Do you intend to take it for yourselves? Will you harm the people? The servants?"

When I glanced up, Elle's focus was intent on me. It was she, not Fitz or Holden, who answered, her grin conspiratorial. "We heard other rumors about you. That you wield magic because you're half-fae, the lost heir to the Silverfrost throne itself. We don't want your kingdom, Florentia Silverfrost. We want to help you take your throne."

"Why?" I blurted.

Elle quirked a brow. "Because something tells me that, especially after we offer you our help, you won't continue the war your predecessors began against our kingdom."

"And we grow tired of losing our people in a needless fight," Fitz cut in, his voice firm.

Before I could react, there was a cry outside the tent, followed by a feral growl. The hairs on my arms rose as everyone around me stiffened, hands flying to sword hilts. Storm clouds roiled in the tent corners, electricity tingling around us.

The four Ashwoods leapt for the tent entrance, and I threw myself from my chair to follow them. As they darted out into the cold night, I followed, scanning the few tents scattered nearby. Occupants were already spilling from their mouths, armed with daggers, bows, and swords. I caught a flash of white as a wolf charged from the shadows, mouth bloodied. Nearby, one of the guards stationed at the tent grimaced and pressed a hand to her bleeding shoulder.

Prince Fitz lifted his hands, clouds and lightning clashing in a powerful display as the storm gathered around us. Even outside Ashwood, with autumn breathing its last gasp, his magic was still formidable.

"Wait!" I shouted. "Please don't hurt him!"

Holden and Kinsey hesitated, their hands on sword hilts. Fitz scowled, but Elle seemed to understand before he did—or perhaps, as a human, she was more willing to trust me quickly. She seized his wrist, jolting his attention to her. With a sigh, he released his magic and the storm clouds disintegrated.

I spun toward the wolf, meeting his familiar gold eyes. "Garrick. It's all right. *I'm* all right."

There was a beat where my breath misted between us as I waited, fearing he wasn't under his own control and would continue to fight anyway. Feared how the Ashwoods would harm him if he lashed out against their own. But then, in a blink, Garrick was standing before us, clothed in the same leathers and fur vest he'd worn at the ball, though this time, he was dripping with knives and daggers fastened not only to his belt but also to leather bands strapped across his chest.

Eyes wary on the Ashwoods, he stepped toward me, his pace quickening until his hands settled on my shoulders. "Are you all right?" he demanded, scanning my body for injuries. His every muscle was taut, still poised to fight.

"Yes, they didn't want to hurt me. They took me from Preston when he was dragging me to the dungeons."

Garrick's eyes burned with cold fury. "Did *he* touch you?"

My hand flew to my neck, brushing my unbruised skin. "The Ashwood healer helped."

Garrick's chest heaved. "Curse this..." He shook his head, unable to speak plainly about his blood oath per whatever rules the siblings had bound him to. "This *restriction*. I need to tear his throat out."

Prince Fitz stepped forward, Elle at his side. "Who are you?" he demanded, studying Garrick warily. "Our people are at war, and you've invaded my camp and wounded one of my people. Tell me why I shouldn't kill you."

Garrick growled low in his throat, as if he were considering transforming back into a wolf any second.

Elle's eyes narrowed. "Fitz. Why not wait for our guest to explain who he is *before* you start making threats?" She turned to me, arching a brow in a way that warned me her patience was only a little greater than that of her husband.

"He's an ally," I said hurriedly, clutching Garrick's arm. "Garrick Darkgrove. He attacked only to rescue me."

Garrick cast me a sidelong glance. "You trust them?"

I gave a single nod. "They know who I am. They want to help me take the throne and end the war."

At Fitz's side, Holden broke into a warm grin. "Another ally? Welcome."

Fitz shot his brother a look, clearly still doubtful of Garrick's intentions, but Elle grasped his hand, threading her fingers through his, and the gesture seemed to calm him. "If you trust him," she told me smoothly, "then we do too."

Over her shoulder, I noticed Kinsey was already at the female guard's side, his hand pressed to the wolf bite in her arm. "I'm sorry about your guard."

Garrick ducked his head, looking sheepish. "I am as well." He glanced at the woman, who was flexing her arm, a healthy flush already returned to her cheeks thanks to Kinsey's ministrations.

"I suppose it was an honest enough mistake, when you thought you were rescuing the woman you love from danger," Prince Fitz murmured. "But we never meant her any harm."

"Starlight," Garrick murmured close to my ear, "they need to know. Preston and Nerissa sent me and could use—"

I squeezed his hand, silently cutting him off, noticing the way Elle was watching us. Had she and the others heard? I didn't want them to start doubting Garrick's loyalty, even if I understood his fears. They needed to know the whole story first. I bit the inside of my cheek, hesitating. "Could we return to the tent? We have much to discuss."

CHAPTER TWENTY-EIGHT

My heart hammered against my ribcage as Garrick, Kinsey, and I trekked through the snow, Garrick's gloves and fur coat shielding me against the freezing wind. Garrick claimed his body heat would be enough to warm him in the cold, though I knew that wasn't entirely true. He was warm-blooded, but even he could grow cold in the fierce mountain air. But I knew better than to argue. We'd also had to slice the hem of my ballgown higher so I could walk unimpeded through the snow, which unfortunately allowed for cold air to creep beneath the fabric. But I took comfort in the thick, woolen socks and leather boots we'd been gifted from the Ashwood camp so that I wasn't forced to walk in my flimsy slippers.

Pausing to catch my breath and study how close the castle was looming, I glanced at the sky. Snow clouds blotted out much of it, already spitting scattered flakes, but the sun gleamed harshly in a bare patch to the west. It was sinking slowly but steadily toward the horizon, reminding me that the night of solstice was fast approaching. Time was running out to seal the underworld entrance.

Preston and Nerissa would be impatient. But how did they expect to force me to fully open an entrance I was determined to close? That was the flaw in our plan, the strategy none of us had managed to guess at.

All last night and well into the late morning, Garrick and I had planned with the Ashwoods. At last, to prepare for the long evening ahead of us, we'd all retired. With Garrick still a bit on edge and wary of leaving me alone, the Ashwoods had graciously offered us our own tent. I'd blushed despite the many times Garrick and I had been forced into close quarters together, but with two separate cots, Garrick had given me the space I needed. Instead, he'd stretched out on his cot, lying parallel to mine. While I'd tried to rest despite the wild thoughts churning in my head and the daylight seeping through the canvas, Garrick had reached across the gap between us to brush soothing fingers through my hair until I'd fallen into a dreamless sleep.

Now, with only a few short hours' worth of rest and borrowed winter attire, I watched the snowflakes fall around Garrick, Kinsey, and me. Ahead, the hunter paused, his every muscle taut, his body alert. I watched him anxiously, already on edge. Already looking for any signs that our plan was about to fall apart, or that the trust we'd placed in the Ashwoods was about to go awry.

"We're almost in sight of the sentinels," Garrick announced, indicating that direction of the castle with a jerk of his head. My half-human eyes could only make out the parapets, and not the figures concealed and waiting behind them. If Garrick could pick them out with his keen wolf shifter gaze, then the fae posted there would surely be able to see us if we went any further. "It's time to prepare." His gaze flicked to me, even though this was possibly my easiest role to play in our plan. "Are you ready?"

Pressing my mouth into a hard line, I nodded.

"Now we can only hope the others are too." Kinsey plucked a pouch from where it was strapped to his belt, smiling wryly. "In all my years as the royal healer, I've never done something like this. Least of all to myself."

Hugging myself against the cold, I watched our Ashwood companion pluck several vials from his bag, downing each in swift gulps before returning the empty glasses to his pouch. With a wistful glance, he deposited the bag in the snow. He couldn't be caught with it on him later.

"How fast will they wo—" I began, the last word dying on my lips as Kinsey started to sway, blinking his eyes blearily.

Garrick stepped forward, catching the healer before he toppled into the snow. "Out cold," he murmured as he peered down at the slumped Ashwood. Garrick pressed two fingers to the man's neck, frowning in concentration. "And like he said, I can't even feel a pulse."

I gazed in morbid fascination at the way Kinsey's chest didn't move, as if he weren't even breathing. "How do we know he isn't *actually* dead?"

Garrick smirked. "He healed you well enough. I think he knows his medicines. Plus, he didn't strike me as the type to want to take his own life so young." He winked at me, but I was too nervous to grin at his dark humor.

Lowering the healer to the ground, Garrick drew one of his knives and, without preamble, sliced it cleanly across his left shoulder, cutting through his shirt. Blood bloomed, staining the torn fabric and dripping into the snow, coloring it crimson.

I grimaced, hating to see him hurt at all, even if I knew he'd been cautious, only injuring himself enough to make a bloody sight. He withdrew items stored in Kinsey's bag: a smaller pouch of herbs Garrick tucked into his pocket, and then a flask of blood—animal blood collected from a deer the Ashwoods had hunted for a meal. Enough for Garrick to pour over Kinsey, splattering it across his face, neck, and chest to make it appear as if the man truly had been fatally injured. Using the same knife he'd cut himself with, he sliced into Kinsey's coat in several places, tearing the fabric so it looked like claws might have torn into it.

With a final reassuring glance at me, Garrick slung Kinsey over one shoulder, and we resumed our journey toward the castle.

Shouts erupted at Garrick's and my approach, and the castle gates opened to usher us within the courtyard. Hurrying footsteps rang out on the cobblestones as guards and servants rushed to meet us, scowling at the bloody body Garrick carried and the gore staining his arm.

"Come, the king and queen will want to see you immediately," one of the guards said, leading us toward the entrance.

"Summon them now," Garrick ordered, his tone guttural. "King Preston will want to know his betrothed has returned safely."

My stomach turned over at those words, even if I knew it was all what they expected Garrick to say. It didn't detract from how nauseating it was to hear him call me Preston's.

Fae scattered to fulfill his order, but by the time Garrick and I neared the double doors, they burst open. Preston and Nerissa stood in the entrance, adorned in silver and blue with their crowns on for full effect, their eyes fiery. Their rage made my heart skip a beat, but I sauntered forward anyway, playing the role of a submissive girl relieved to be saved from her kidnappers.

As I ascended the steps leading to the entrance, Preston forced his mouth into a wide smile, opening his arms like he was overjoyed to see me safe. "Florentia Silverfrost! It is a relief to see you returned to us."

"Prepare her rooms," Nerissa barked at the nearby servants, who began to scatter. "It is the solstice, after all! We must prepare her." Her dark eyes flicked toward me, and I smiled demurely, as if I were content and ready for what came next. As if they really were preparing me for a heroic act, and not hoping to use me as a way to unleash destruction.

I stepped into the castle as all but the posted guards vanished, and Garrick halted behind me. Nerissa ordered the guards to close the doors, but as they thudded shut, Preston's attention shifted from me to Garrick. He reeled back, his expression marred with disgust. "You stupid mutt! Bleeding all over our entryway. And what is *that?*" He drew back, his face paling.

Garrick stepped beside me, shifting Kinsey's weight, who still hung, limp and unresponsive, from his shoulder. "One of Ren's kidnappers." His voice was cold, ruthless. "If you desire, you can use his body as a reminder that those who oppose your will receive no mercy." He dipped his head in deference.

My skin prickled. Even when Garrick wasn't under the siblings' control, he played his role well.

"And what do you expect me to do with a corpse?" Preston snarled. He whirled on Nerissa, who, though she'd schooled her features into a look of careful boredom, kept her distance from Garrick and his burden. "Why don't you keep a tighter leash on your pet? Tell him we have no use for the dead things he drags to us. Unlike him, we aren't *animals.*"

I bit my inner lip, temper flaring. I wanted to rebuke them, but now wasn't the time. Everything was going the way Garrick had anticipated it would, and my rage would only derail our plan.

Nerissa rubbed her temple before sighing and glancing at Garrick. "Dispose of the body." Her lip curled as she noted the blood staining his arm. "And get yourself cleaned up. I expect you to be present for our grand show." She lifted her head toward one of the high windows in the great hall, through which twilight's violet glow was shimmering. "You have one hour. By then, Florentia will be at the entrance, prepared to save us all." Her eyes flicked to me, silent laughter dancing in them as if daring me to refute her claim and call out her lie.

"Come, I'll escort you to your chambers myself," Preston said.

As Nerissa turned away, she tossed her hair over her shoulder. "Don't lose her again, brother." She sauntered off down the hall as Preston glowered, offering me his arm. Apparently he was in a good mood, ready to pretend to be an amiable fiancé. Maybe he was enjoying the game they were playing, up until its very end.

Behind me, Garrick turned and spoke to the guards, requesting they open the door for him once more. But I knew he wasn't going to take Kinsey's so-called corpse off the grounds. I wished I could linger and help, but my duty was to keep Preston distracted, so I settled my hand on his arm and let him lead me up the stairwell.

"Aspen won't be here to help you wreak havoc," Preston murmured as we passed the second floor and rounded a bend in the staircase, climbing higher.

"But you don't know where she is, do you?" I asked smugly.

It was only a hopeful guess, but I injected confidence into my tone, praying I was right. Despite Garrick's fear of being involved too heavily in any of the rebels' plans, he had known of one contact outside the castle. Last night, the Ashwoods had sent a messenger to that rebel, requesting he gather as many as he could that had escaped the ball and prepare them for tonight. None of us had any idea if Preston and Nerissa had restrained or hurt Aspen, or if she'd escaped in the chaos following the Ashwoods' invasion and my kidnapping.

Preston froze, seizing my arm in a painful grasp and whirling on me. "What do you know?" he bit out. "Did the Ashwoods take her too?"

I smirked. "She's safe from you. That's all I know."

Nostrils flaring, Preston drew a deep breath, visibly calming himself. He turned, dragging me up the steps behind him. "It doesn't matter. Prisoner or not, she can plot all she wants. Tonight, you'll fling the entrance to the underworld open wide and the demons will overtake everyone, including the Ashwoods and rebels. They won't matter anymore. The living souls will face our torment, and the dead will taste life's pleasures fully again."

"You can't force me to do your bidding," I protested, fighting against Preston enough that I forced him to a stop in the middle of the hall leading to my rooms. Anything to grant Garrick more time. "You can't glamour me, and you can't hold back my magic. I'll resist you, every step of the way."

Preston sneered. "Yes, I'm sure you will." He yanked me forward.

I dug the heels of my boots into the plush carpet. "And you won't win."

Preston's grasp on me tightened, making me ground my teeth against the sharp stab of pain from his bony fingers squeezing my wrist. "It takes more than idle threats to strike fear into a soul that's endured hell, Snowflake."

"But I know what can strike fear into your heart," I said quickly. "The knowledge that *I* have the power to send you back and close the door. That as long as I draw breath and this blood flows through my veins, I can continue to seal the entrance tightly shut, leaving you there to your eternal torment."

Preston tugged one more time, so hard I could no longer resist, and he forced my feet along after him. "This grows tiring. If you want, keep hurling your threats as we walk, but nothing will change your fate, mortal. Power has gone to your head, but yours will always be limited. Lesser."

I let his words roll off me, trailing him as we neared my door. All I could hope was that my delay had given Garrick and Kinsey the time they needed...and that Preston would descend the steps too distracted to notice anything was amiss.

When we reached my chambers, the king swung open the door, offering me a view of the glamoured humans already waiting for me, their blank eyes turning to study me without emotion. "They've been ordered to only dress you in what Nerissa and I gave them," Preston said, his sharp eyes dragging over my forget-me-not dress, half-concealed by Garrick's coat. "Arrive wearing anything else, and there will be consequences."

With that, he shoved me into my chambers and slammed the door.

My heart thundered in my chest. Had our walk taken enough time? Should I have tried to stall Preston further? I glanced out the window, looking at the moon already climbing in the darkening sky, and prayed all our careful plans wouldn't unravel.

CHAPTER TWENTY-NINE

I gazed into the mirror once the maids had finished dressing me, relieved to find Preston and Nerissa had ordered me to be clothed in leathers that reminded me of Garrick's hunting outfit or the attire of a fae warrior, not a flimsy dress fit for a sacrifice. It seemed they wanted to continue the farce of using me to be Silverfrost's savior until the last moment. In some twisted way, they were delighting in their deception, just like the other games they'd played.

While one of the women left to summon an escort for me, I considered the conversation I'd had with Garrick and the Ashwoods the previous night.

"They need more than my blood," I'd explained, "or else they would have killed me and drained it from me the moment they learned of my heritage. They need me alive to open the entrance. And yet, all this time, they've also feared me and suppressed my magic. I don't understand. If they've weakened me and I doubt my ability to command my power…how do they expect me to succeed?"

"It's possible the entrance is easier to open—especially since it's already ajar—than it is to close," Prince Fitz had mused. "It would likely take more effort to undo what has already begun. If it's already open, your presence and willingness to open it might be all that's required. But to close it? That could demand a lot of power."

"It always takes more power to hold the darkness back than to join it," Prince Holden agreed. "It's likely that you need to be at full magical strength to send back the demons and seal the entrance."

A knock at the door jolted me from my reverie, and I straightened as one of the maids opened the door for an escort of four guards. While the guards were likely a way to show the court that the king and queen wouldn't allow anyone to kidnap me again, I couldn't help but also see it as a sign of their fear of me, no matter what Preston said. They knew my magic was no longer locked away. Outside of my enchanted rooms, I was free to wield it as I pleased.

I could only pray it would be strong enough to do what I needed to.

Wordlessly, I filed out, letting a male and female guard each take the lead while two others flanked us. It was a long trek through the castle and down into its bowels, past the dungeons and through catacombs lit with flickering torches. Our footsteps echoed in the cramped space as we wound through countless tunnels, past silent tombs of Silverfrosts long dead. The air smelled dank and smoky, while the shadows were heavy. The same dread I'd experienced each time I neared underworld creatures settled in my chest, though this time it multiplied a hundred-fold.

At last, the sounds of people murmuring pierced the eerie silence. We rounded a final few bends in the catacombs before entering an open, well-lit space. The same one I'd seen in the vision Preston had given me, when he and Nerissa had first emerged from the underworld. Cobwebs clung to the edges of the ceiling, which was a little taller here, letting me feel like I could breathe freely after the cramped tunnels we'd exited. Three of the walls were smooth and bare, plain earth without any tombs or signs of disturbance. Just before us, King Preston and Queen Nerissa stood on a stone floor with a small group of heavily armed fae guards.

Ahead of the siblings, on the far wall, was the entrance to the under-world itself. If I'd thought the air had been oppressive before, it was now suffocating. The door was simple grey stone, carved with ancient markings in a forgotten language. One side was slightly ajar, offering a glimpse into nothing but blackness. Worse than blackness. It felt like a void, like endless nothingness and despair and misery.

I'd expected a larger crowd to witness this supposedly glorious mo-ment, but I supposed this was where the siblings' show ended. It didn't matter if anyone watched what happened next—perhaps they felt it would be easier to manipulate me if they didn't have others around who might interfere. Once the demons infiltrated our world, they would soon overrun the kingdom. Everyone would know of my failure.

It was a grave reminder that I *could not* fail. Too many innocent lives hung in the balance.

Foreboding raked its icy claws down my spine as my escort closed in about me, two of the guards seizing my arms. Here it was: the moment when the undead souls before me enacted whatever plan of manipulation they had in store. I could only hope that, while they were distracted, the rebels, Ashwoods, and Garrick could make it down here in time.

"Where are the demons I am to return to the underworld?" I asked, trying to sound confident as the guards dragged me toward Preston, Nerissa, and the waiting door. "Wouldn't they need to be present to be returned?"

Preston waved a careless hand. "There's no need to play pretend anymore, Snowflake."

My eyes darted back and forth between the guards, from those lined up beside the royals to the ones holding me in their iron clutches. I scowled. "How did you gain their assistance in destroying the world?"

Nerissa smiled contentedly as she stalked forward, her eyes piercing mine. "Their cooperation ensures their lives will be spared. Now, enough stalling. You have work to do." She drew a dagger from her belt, letting the naked blade reflect in the dim light of the lanterns as she raised it toward me.

I scoffed. "As if I'll open the entrance for you. My intention has always been to close it." My breath frosted between us as the air grew chillier, full of the threat of my building magic.

But Nerissa's gaze remained unafraid. Without drawing her eyes from me, she snapped her fingers.

Movement pulled my attention away from her, toward another row of guards, ones I hadn't seen before because they were carefully tucked behind the first. Bound and gagged between a pair of them, struggling in vain against their strong immortal grasps, was my half-brother.

My heart dropped. "Charles?"

Caught in my fight for freedom and survival in this cruel world, desperate to rescue Garrick and secure a better future for us, I'd scarcely spared my half-brother a thought since he'd so callously abandoned me to this fate.

One of the guards ripped the gag from Charles's mouth, and he gasped, his wild eyes meeting mine. His face was pale with fear; his dark hair tousled and greasy as if he hadn't had the opportunity to bathe in days. Dark circles rested beneath his eyes like bruises, and he trembled with fear. "Flor—ren— Ren," he choked out.

I didn't hate him. I couldn't. As much as his betrayal had cut me to my core, had made my heart ache and bleed, he was still the brother I'd grown up with. The boy I'd played chess with and teased. The one with my stepfather's chin and mannerisms, so dear in their familiarity. The one who, like me, shared our mother's eyes.

He'd betrayed me to this suffering, but that didn't mean I wanted him to experience the same cruel life.

"You and Aspen thought you were the only clever ones making plans, didn't you?" Nerissa crossed her arms, tucking her dagger against her chest, as her stare bored into mine and her voice went cold. "Open the entrance for us or watch him die."

My pulse raced. "Charlie," I breathed.

A guard kicked him to his knees, and he grunted in pain, grimacing as he crashed to the stone floor. The fae set a knife to my half-brother's throat, a silent promise. When Charles lifted his head, his eyes were shimmering with silver—tears he was trying desperately not to let fall. Did he still fear me? Did *he* hate me? Did he only see me as a way to survive, or did he feel remorse for what he'd condemned me to?

"I'm sorry, Ren," he said, his tone soft. I wondered when he'd last eaten, and how long Preston and Nerissa had held him in Silverfrost. How long had he been shut up here, either in these forsaken dungeons or in the hellish ones beneath the fortress? Had they tormented him? Left him to be leached of all hope by demons? My stomach churned as the images rose unbidden in my mind.

Pity rent my heart in two.

"You're better than any of us," he went on, blinking against his tears. "You always have been. The kindest, gentlest person in Altidvale. The most patient, despite all the unkind words we spoke about you. What I did was..." He trailed off, shaking his head.

"Unforgivable?" I supplied. Despite the ache in my chest, my tone was icy. For as much as I hated to see him suffer, I also hated to see him beg for mercy from the woman he'd shown none to. I couldn't help the bitterness that rose to meet my compassion.

Charles didn't deny it. "Yes," he said, even as he continued to tremble. He didn't avert his gaze, meeting mine unwaveringly. There wasn't fear or disgust in his eyes—at least, not of me. Now, I was his salvation. But was that all I was to him? "I could apologize a thousand times, yet it wouldn't be enough to atone for what I did—the pain I put you through, the way I cast you off."

I tried and failed to swallow the lump in my throat.

"Very touching," Preston cut in, jerking my attention to him. "But we aren't going to wait forever for you to make your choice. Open the door, or he dies."

The guard's hand tightened on the knife he held to Charles's neck, poised to strike. I knew it was all for show. I might be able to stop a guard with my magic and defend Charles, but the fae were truly holding him for Preston or Nerissa. And their magic—a simple flick of their wrist could end him. I didn't know how to stop that.

"And when I open the entrance to the underworld and all hell breaks free, Charles will be killed anyway," I protested.

Preston's smile was slow and cruel. "Oh no. Just like our bargains with the guards here, we will promise both yours and your half-brother's safety. Silverfrost may fall, but you can both escape to go live out your days in your human world."

And watch it fall around us as demons torment and murder our people, I thought darkly.

I turned to Charles again, heart thrashing in my chest. I was desperate, trembling. A tear broke free and trailed down his cheek, making him look so vulnerable and young. He was my little brother again, falling and scraping his knee on pebbles in the road, tearfully accepting my embrace as I helped him home and cleaned the wound.

I knew I couldn't trust Preston and Nerissa's word. As undead souls, they could lie.

"I forgive you," I choked out, my own tears blurring my vision as I met Charles's gaze. "Even if I'm unsure if you only beg my forgiveness now because you're afraid for your own life."

Charles made the smallest jerk of his head, all he could risk with the point of a blade pressed to his throat. "I love you, Ren. Don't open the door."

I gaped at him. He wanted me to watch him die?

But if I opened the entrance, countless lives would be lost. I would be sacrificing them for only one man. I thought of Garrick and Aspen, of the rebels who'd waited and placed their hope in me for years. I thought of the Ashwoods and their willingness to help me take my crown. I thought of the injured Silverfrost soldiers and the respect in their eyes when they saw how I took the time to notice and care for them. I thought of the healer who'd cared for me in Northelm and deferentially referred to me as her queen, and every citizen who had watched me with joy and welcome in their expressions, not seeing a human but their leader, their protector. And I thought of the people in my hometown, both those who'd treated me well and those who'd scorned me.

Countless fae and human lives were at stake, and whether some had wronged me or not, they didn't deserve the endless torture that awaited them if the underworld devoured the living one.

And yet...who would I be if I sacrificed my own half-brother?

It wouldn't be that simple, anyway. I knew that in my heart. If I stood by and let Preston and Nerissa order his death, they wouldn't let me walk away without manipulating me in some new way. They wouldn't rest until they could use me to exact their revenge. After Charles, perhaps it would be Aspen or Garrick. They'd find everyone I cared about, strip me of every person that made life worth living.

But if I could stall long enough for Garrick, the Ashwoods, and the rebels to arrive, perhaps we could rescue Charles together and subdue Preston and Nerissa, at least long enough for me to seal the door.

As if reading my thoughts, Preston strolled closer, a sneer across his face. He glanced back toward the catacombs, where a rumbling began as skeletons erupted from their coffins, spilling toward the entrance of our room. Cutting off any means of escape—or my reinforcements' route through. "I know why you try to stall," he said. "But whatever plans you think you've made...you're alone. No one is coming, Snowflake. It's just your little human self and your half-brother against us and our death magic. You can't kill us." The rotten stench of his breath enveloped me like a cage.

I stared at the skeletons standing like sentinels, prepared to fight and hold back anyone who tried to come to us. The hairs on the back of my neck stood on end at the unnatural sight. Countless empty eye sockets and gaping jaws grinned back at me, their finger bones clinking together as they fisted their hands.

My stomach sank. There would never be enough time then, not for Charles. I had only one choice.

"I love you, Charlie," I said, and then I stepped forward. Stale air from the underworld filled my lungs as I approached its door. I could taste it on my tongue: coppery with the scent of blood and despair. Terror made my knees tremble as I held out my hand toward Nerissa, prepared to accept the dagger she clutched.

She gave me a smile that was all teeth. "You don't need to spill your blood to open it, not when you live. It's there, inside of you. *This* was merely for if you didn't cooperate."

I frowned, absorbing her words. When I'd fought off underworld creatures in the past, I'd had to use my blood to repel them, but perhaps that was because my magic had been frail from forget-me-nots and little practice. All along, I hadn't needed to weaken myself.

Inhaling sharply, I pressed my palm against the door, feeling the scrape of rough stone against my skin. It was cold—colder than the frost and ice and snow my magic could summon. Colder than death. The sensation sank all the way to my bones, a sharp ache of pain from the shock of such a loss of warmth in my body. I shuddered, squeezing my eyes shut as I attempted to concentrate.

Open, I thought. My body quaked, muscles spasming with cold and fear and overcoming despair. Every ounce of me rebelled, instinctively knowing that nothing good could come out from behind the door.

Gritting my teeth, I thought of the light that flared from my very blood. *Starlight.* But I wasn't trying to repel the demons this time; I needed to force the door to harken to my will. There was power flowing through my veins that could command this entrance, could determine the fate of the world itself. I mustered every ounce of authority, every piece of me that ached to protect Charles.

"Open," I ordered, and my voice didn't even seem like my own anymore. It was that of an uncompromising queen, confident in her power and her strength. It was low and yet loud, echoing in the chamber.

With an anticlimactic creak, the entrance swung further and further inward, until I stood before nothing but gaping blackness. The scents of decay and blood poured forth, as if welcoming me into an icy embrace. And then—approaching sounds filled the air. The rattling of bones, the scraping of claws, the snapping of teeth.

The creatures of the underworld were coming.

CHAPTER THIRTY

Everything happened at once. Cries erupted behind us as my friends and allies collided with the skeleton army Preston had summoned. I spun toward Charles, finding that the guards who'd been restraining him were already retreating on shaking legs, overwhelmed by terror at the noise of demons approaching. Apparently, when danger was actually nearing, their trust in the siblings' protection was fragile, too.

A long, pincer-like limb lashed out through the yawning entrance, and I leapt back just as one of the guards hurled a dagger at the creature.

"Traitor," Nerissa snapped, and with a single gesture, she yanked the flesh off the screaming man's bones.

Charles vomited, but I had already seen such horrors, and my mind was preoccupied with survival. The creature lurched forth from the underworld, same as the type Garrick and I had fought only a few nights ago in the castle halls. It swung one of its claws for me, and I ducked, trying to concentrate on the power in my blood. All I needed was to draw close enough to risk one touch, and I should be able to repel it. Perhaps I could force it back into the underworld, force all the demons back before they could rip the kingdom to shreds.

With ear-splitting shrieks, more creatures burst through the entryway, shattering my hope. One bore the skeletal head of the demon I'd faced in the bowels of the fortress, its empty eye sockets stirring terror and despair as soon as it turned its head in my direction. Others varied, but were no less terrifying: a monster with fangs too large for its jaws and eyes too large for its head thundered forward, shaking the floor. One of the guards attempted to meet it with a sword, only to be pummeled with its fist and then, in a single bite, lose his head. Another creature didn't look quite corporeal, flitting through bodies and objects only to take its victims by surprise, sinking teeth into throats or tightening long, slender fingers around necks to snap them.

I screamed, unleashing a blast of cold air and hail that formed at a mere thought, reacting to the riot of emotions churning inside me. The ice pelted against the demons, slowing but not stopping them.

"I knew you'd break your bargain," Preston said, startling me with how near he was.

Spinning, I found him behind me, grasping Charlie with one strong hand while the other hung loosely at his side, free for him to do whatever he wished. It was a silent threat. One motion, one snap of his fingers, and he could strip my half-brother of his flesh the same way Nerissa had just done to one of the fae. My stomach roiled.

"You were never going to let me live anyway," I protested. "I'm the only one who can send back the demons and seal off the underworld. The only one who could ruin your plans." A dagger of ice formed between my fingers, and I swung it toward his face, lodging it in his blood-red eye.

Preston sneered. "You're right," he said, loosening his grasp on Charles, who, weak from hunger or fear or both, collapsed to his knees. He slid the blade from his eye as if he felt nothing at all. Maybe he didn't—maybe pain was but a distant memory for him and Nerissa. Maybe their borrowed half-lives didn't offer nearly as much sensation or true life as they hoped. I cringed when he cast off the ice, his eye still attached. Nothing but a bloody, gaping hole remained in that socket as he stepped forward, lifting a hand toward me. He was like something from a nightmare, as awful as the demons surrounding us, clashing with the guards, slaughtering and consuming them. As terrifying as the animated skeletons using their bodies to fend off my friends. His remaining red eye glared at me with decades' worth of hatred and bloodlust. "Part of our revenge on Silverfrost is ensuring none of the royal family live, that all taste death. You are our vengeance incomplete. But not now. You've served our purpose, and now you can watch in despair as your kingdom falls. We'll leave your family for the beasts to feed on." He kicked Charles, who gave a dull grunt in response, his glassy eyes staring up at me in horror.

I sent a blast of snowy air at Preston's face, praying I could distract him even if I couldn't kill him. In the next moment, I had another blade of ice in my hand poised to throw at his other eye.

Preston laughed. "Yes, wear yourself out. Your strength is already flagging. You're not used to wielding this much magic for long."

He was right—my muscles were trembling, my mind growing foggy with the effort to concentrate on calling on my power.

Somewhere, dimly, I was aware of lightning crackling, of more magic roiling within the room. Roots were cracking through stone, pushing through dirt and stone to tangle the limbs of demons. Someone was calling my name.

I tossed my ice dagger, but Preston dodged it smoothly. Before I could try to stall him with something else, he made a cutting motion with his wrist. There was an awful crack as the bone in my forearm snapped, white-hot pain searing up the entire length of the limb. My cry of pain sounded animalistic in my ears, half-drowned by the shrieks of underworld creatures and the shouts from fae suffering and dying around us.

"Ren!" Charles cried. His arms were still bound behind him, and he struggled to get his feet beneath him so he could rise.

There was nothing he could do for me now. Tears sprang into my eyes. There wasn't anything I could do for him, either. Once I was dead, Preston and Nerissa would slay him in a blink, or leave him to be eaten alive by the terrifying monsters still pouring forth from the underworld. They'd used me, knowing my heart would never allow me to do anything else than protect someone more helpless than myself, and yet I'd failed Charles anyway.

Perhaps it would have been more merciful to let them snap their fingers and kill him earlier than force him to endure all of this.

My retaliating magic was half-hearted, a sheet of glistening ice that formed between Preston and me instead of encasing his arm as I'd intended. There was too much agony scattering my thoughts, and I was already weary.

He sneered, lifting his hand again, and I braced myself for the inevitable. Either he would consume me with more pain, taking his time tormenting me until I died, or he would end it all right there, breaking my every bone or sloughing off my flesh.

But instead of searing pain, there was nothing. Preston cried out, his concentration broken, and fell backward, skidding across the ice.

Charles was sprawled on the ground. In desperation, he must have given up trying to stand, and instead, he'd managed to throw enough strength into a kick with his bound legs to knock Preston off his feet.

I knew we only had seconds. With my magic feeling distant, as if for-get-me-nots clung to me instead of exhaustion, I pulled on it one last time, begging for enough power. The ice answered, flowing upward from the ground like a living thing and encasing Preston's limbs, locking him in place.

He roared in fury, his face contorting with his rage. I staggered backward, reaching for Charles to help him up, as storm clouds tumbled into view, permeating the room in shadows punctuated by flaring purple lightning. The hairs on my arms rose in response, but I wasn't afraid. I was elated.

Help had come. They must have broken past the skeletal army.

"Starlight." The familiar voice was close to my ear as Garrick grasped my arm, gently pressing the hilt of a hunting knife into my hand.

"Garrick," I murmured, "you have to—"

But he was already moving, brushing a swift kiss to my forehead and then darting away under cover of the thick clouds, vanishing back into the recesses of the catacombs before Preston or Nerissa could see and take control of him.

They can bind me to their orders, such as the one that will never allow me to let you escape, even when they're nowhere nearby, Garrick had explained to me, along with the Ashwoods, last night. *But they can't use my body as a weapon unless I'm within sight.*

Then you must stay out of their sight, Elle had proclaimed matter-of-fact-ly.

Despite knowing that Garrick would have to stay back, fending off demons as they slipped past our friends and me to ravage through the castle, it was still a comfort to know he was fighting on our side, never too far away. Gratifying to think that he was defying Preston and Nerissa after all the ways they'd used and abused him.

Now, as my eyes adjusted to the blanketing darkness, I turned to Charles, hurriedly slicing through the ropes binding his arms and legs. "What—is—happening?" he panted, breathless either from fear or his exertion after his imprisonment.

Don't open the door. It was the most selfless request he'd ever asked of me.

And yet I had, perhaps damning us all to grisly deaths.

"Don't worry," I said, seizing his arm and dragging him behind me, away from the hulking form of a demon that was approaching us. "The ones who wield this storm magic are our friends."

At that moment, Princess Elle dashed into view, clouds and lightning swirling around her in an intimidating, awe-inducing display. There was no fear on her face as she leapt between us and an oncoming demon, brandishing a blade sparking with electricity. But Prince Fitz was beside her in an instant, his usually cold expression etched into something bloodthirsty as he watched the creature charging for his wife.

I took this reprieve to whirl on Charles, seizing his shoulder with my good hand. My other hung limply at my side, the constant pain filling my mind with haze. "You have to run," I urged. "Find a horse and ride hard to Altidvale. Warn the citizens. Nowhere is safe, not until I can find a way to banish all these demons and stop Nerissa and Preston's plans, but the farther away you get, the more time you'll have until I can find a way to win."

Despite the exhaustion painted on his face, there was a fire in Charles's eyes. "I'm not abandoning you again, Ren."

"There's nothing you can do." Tears pricked my eyes. "You're sick and tired. I don't know what awful things they did to you—but I can imagine. And neither they nor the underworld creatures can be killed." My throat tightened, but I forced my words past the building sob. "I can't watch them harm you, little brother. I love you. Go and find safety. I pray the gods show mercy on us—on the world—and that I can protect us. That I'll see you again, someday."

"Ren..."

"Don't argue with me!" I shoved him, a little more firmly than I'd meant to.

He staggered back, his complexion pale, his eyes awash with remorse and horror and grief. "I can't…"

"You *can*," I insisted. "You didn't listen to me before, but you can in this one thing. This is all I want you to do. *Please*. For me."

My eyes darted toward the clearing clouds, lifting enough to give us a better view of our enemies—but unfortunately, it also gave them a better view of us. The entrance to the catacombs was clogged with piles of bones, the remains of the corpses Preston and Nerissa had animated, and already demons were pressing through it. I knew Garrick waited for them on the other side, that he would do everything in his power to hold them off. Even still, it wouldn't be easy for Charles to run past them.

"Before you lose your chance!" I begged.

Across the room, Nerissa prowled away from one of her former guards, dropping his mangled body. Blood smeared her mouth and chin, a clear sign she'd been consuming his flesh to feed off his life, and the urge to vomit pummeled into me. I stood my ground, fisting my one good hand as my mind screamed at me to gather enough energy to draw on the light flowing through my veins. The light that would be enough to not only repel the demons ravaging through the living, but to also stop *her*.

But Nerissa was faster, her magic quick to respond. With a flick of her fingers, her bloody gaze latched onto Charles. The snap of bone pierced the air and my half-brother crumpled to the stone floor. He gasped, too overcome with misery to even cry out as he clutched his contorted leg.

I shrieked as Nerissa strolled forward, passing demons and fae mid-fight as if they were nothing. A dagger sliced through the air and lodged in her neck, but she didn't pause as she wrenched it free, leaving a bloody hole behind, one that swiftly knit itself back together. She discarded the blade carelessly, her focus single-mindedly on Charles and me. I stepped between the two of them, pouring every ounce of my fury into my effort to call forth my magic.

An icy breeze tugged through my hair, tiny snowflakes grazing my nose.

Dismay clutched my chest. *This* was what was left of my power? I'd hoped after the avalanche I'd unleashed mere days after learning I had magic, that the time I'd practiced in the castle with forget-me-nots would have rendered me a little more adept and granted me more endurance. But my mind was fractured with agony, guilt, and fear.

Worse, I sensed the ice I'd encased Preston within was starting to dissolve, the way I could sense my own body's movements. My mind was releasing the magic I'd crafted, its strength shattering.

And perhaps that was why the demons surrounding us didn't even bother to approach—because they knew that Preston and Nerissa were both able to dispatch of the only person who was a true threat to any of them.

Out of the corner of my eye, I saw Preston converging on me, his strides as assured as his sister's. Neither made a move to use their death magic yet, and I knew why. They were drawing out these final moments, relishing the pain and terror that was doubtlessly etched across my face. They were enjoying their vengeance as they rained their bloodthirst and hatred on the one surviving member of the family they so despised.

Then they were mere feet from me, staring me down with their cold, death-like gazes. Nerissa flicked her wrist. The bones of my right hand fractured, each flare of red-hot fire making my stomach twist with nausea. I couldn't hold back my ragged cry, my throat raw from my animal scream.

Vague sounds informed me that Charles was attempting to rise, still trying to fight for me when all I wanted him to do was lie down and stay out of the siblings' notice. To survive. I caught sight of Aspen in her larger form grappling with a skeletal-looking creature, dodging adeptly to avoid its strikes. Prince Holden was calling upon vines to entrap demons as they charged. Princess Elle and Prince Fitz were back-to-back, holding their own against a group of guards who remained loyal to Nerissa and Preston, as well as a cluster of oncoming underworld creatures.

And rebels—rebels everywhere, fighting, bleeding, dying.

Somewhere outside, Garrick and other rebels were doing their best to hold back the tide of creatures flowing from the room. There was an unending stream of them emerging from the yawning entrance. Who knew how many thousands of furious, tormented souls and ravenous demons had been awaiting a moment like this for millennia?

I was alone against Preston and Nerissa, their fury, and their immunity to death itself.

With shaking fingers, I lifted my good hand, still clutching the knife Garrick had gifted me, and sliced open the palm of my mangled one. Scarlet bloomed across my pale skin as I ran the broad side of the blade through it, layering it in my blood. My strongest weapon.

Preston sneered, but Nerissa realized my intention a moment before I hurled the blade. She darted to the side. It was Preston who received the full brunt of it, the knife striking his forearm. He flinched away as if burned, and light flared. My light.

Hope blossomed, but only for an instant. The knife skittered across the floor, and with an angry hiss, Preston lifted the edge of his cloak to smear the blood off his skin, as if it continued to sting as long as it touched him.

But seeing both my light and my blood reminded me of what I could do. And somehow, I didn't think I'd have to touch them to hurt them...not if I commanded the full strength of the light glowing within me. I'd been born to command and chain these creatures. Born to protect this world. Born to hold these forces at bay and force them to yield to my will.

I just needed my weary mind to concentrate on that, and not on the throbbing sensation running through my wrist and fingers, or the nausea dancing along my tongue.

With a cry, I lifted my hand, palm out, willing my light to shine. To flare. To overpower every ounce of darkness in this room.

Preston laughed and snapped his fingers. I choked on a sob and collapsed, my ankle twisted unnaturally beneath me. "We could do this all night," he taunted. "Break every bone in your body. See how much pain you can endure before you succumb to death...or before you beg for it."

Another snap. Another flash of pain. More bones in my leg splintered. A keening sound mingled with the shouts of battle and groans of agony as others died around me, and it took me a moment to realize that the noise was coming from my own aching throat.

With every piece of strength left in me, I forced the agony away, shoving it to the back of my mind. Lifting my hands, I called on my winter magic, imagining countless daggers of ice raining upon the siblings, shredding them until even their undead bodies collapsed, too broken to be useful in this world. Too ruined to be a threat ever again.

Agony roared through my body as Nerissa gestured and broke another of my bones. I choked on a sob.

"*Starlight.*" There was a growl of pure, animalistic rage as Garrick—in his wolf form—launched forward, canines flashing as he charged for Nerissa.

My mind screamed at him to run, even if I couldn't blame him for rushing out to my aid. I wouldn't have been able to hold myself back either if I'd seen them tormenting him, heard him scream as I had.

Nerissa's eyes widened in surprise, flicking between Garrick and me.

The ice answered my call, hurtling toward the air with the force of a hundred archers shooting at once, heeding me in my most desperate need.

And then Garrick altered his course, his movements turning stiff and graceless at the same moment that Preston and Nerissa dropped to the floor. My daggers of ice slammed into him, piercing fur and flesh. Splattering blood across the stone as the wolf crashed into a heap, motionless.

CHAPTER THIRTY-ONE

White. Cold, white nothingness. That was all I saw as I screamed, my voice hoarse and broken. In my mind's eye, I clung to every moment I'd had with Garrick. A night under the stars, safe and warm. The rumble of his voice as he'd killed to defend me. His searing gold gaze. Each brush of his calloused hand. Our stolen kiss.

Every ounce of my helplessness, my rage, and my grief unfurled in my cry, until I ran out of breath, my voice cracked, and I curled in on myself.

But the white remained, bright and overpowering. I blinked, eyes burning, and found that I'd unleashed a *storm* of blinding white, the antithesis of Prince Fitz's and Princess Elle's billowing black clouds. It was a raging, swirling snowstorm right there underground—but it was more than that. Icy bits of snow clung to my lashes and coated my hair, and icy wind made the hairs on the back of my neck rise, but the blizzard was full of light. Pure. Strong. Furious and beautiful and cold and hopeful as starlight.

Bloodcurdling cries shredded the air as the light devoured demons and undead souls together, rushing through them as if they had no substance, until they disintegrated like mist. Some tried to flee, including Preston and Nerissa, who stumbled for the dark corners of the crypt. But the siblings weren't fast enough, not against my light. The glow pierced them, lighting them up in one awful instant in which they screamed, eyes wide and mouths gaping, and then—nothing. They dissipated like smoke on the wind.

Gone, never again to torment me. I'd banished them, sending them back to their eternal darkness.

As I gaped, the storm gradually died, snow descending into nothingness, evaporating as if it had never been. The white clouds melted. That bright glow vanished, dimming to the eerie glow from the flickering torchlight flooding the room. My light had swept wide—there was still a horde of demons crouching in the shadowy corners of the room, taking to the shelter they could find, but their numbers were heavily diminished.

The subsequent quiet was ominous, my ears ringing from the blizzard I'd created and my own screams. From the earlier din of fighting. Now, I found myself surrounded by bodies, some so desiccated I had to glance away in horror.

Of course, as long as the door to the underworld remained opened, its creatures could regroup and return.

But my mind couldn't linger on that or on this shred of hope, not for long. I was spent, my body was broken, pain pulsing through me with every breath, and Garrick...Garrick was motionless, shifted back into his fae form and lying in his own blood.

Voices echoed around me as I dragged myself forward, using my one good arm and my one whole leg to move. Each motion sent fresh agony sweeping through my body. "Garrick," I murmured hoarsely. Tears burned my eyes, but I couldn't let them fall. Couldn't let myself believe the worst.

"Ren..." I didn't know who was speaking. I didn't care. Unless it was Garrick, it didn't matter. I couldn't focus on anyone or anything else.

Claws and scuffling and a horrified cry rang out. The demons were fighting again. But I couldn't find it in myself to be afraid. Without Garrick, it was all for nothing.

Without Garrick...

"Help! He needs help." Where was Kinsey? "Kinsey! Someone!" My cries were feeble. Even if I hadn't broken my voice with my screams, I scarcely had the energy to call out. It was all I could do to crawl to Garrick's side, slumping beside him. Reaching for his ruined torso, pierced through once, twice, thrice... I stopped counting at half a dozen, unable or unwilling to fathom it. As I watched far too much blood stain the white fur of his vest, my horror grew.

"I did this to you," I whispered.

Hand shaking, I pressed my fingers to his neck, feeling for a pulse. I brushed my hand over his mouth, praying for the feel of his breath caressing my skin. Nothing.

Nothing. "No," I moaned. "You can't leave me. I'm supposed to save you."

I was supposed to tell Garrick how I felt, supposed to share a future with him. Supposed to find happiness. Supposed to finally share the freedom we'd fought for.

Without him, I was lost. Homeless. Purposeless.

"I love you," I choked out. "Please stay."

"Ren! Look out, *Ren!*" Charles was shouting, frantic.

I glanced up to see a wraith-like form breaking free of its bonds of vines and roots and sweeping toward me, its skeletal hand extended. Despair pommeled me, but I was no stranger to the feeling. I was already drowning in it. The tears I'd tried to fight slipped down my cheeks.

Hopeless.

Someone slammed into me, forcing me to a stand, where I teetered on my one good foot. Aspen. Her eyes were fierce as she tossed a glance at me, refusing to let me shy away from her order or break down any further. "Stop them."

"I can't," I blurted, but Aspen was already charging the wraith, her sword lifted high, fending it off so I had a clear path to the underworld entrance.

My heart throbbed in my head. I couldn't leave Garrick here. My breaths came out strangled. I'd sapped all my strength. Numbly, I lifted my still-bleeding hand, wondering if there was any light left in me. It seemed as if it had all drained from me when I'd watched Garrick fall, when I'd poured out my last bits of anger. Now I was a shell of myself.

Charles grasped my shoulder. Like me, he was crippled, staggering on one good foot. "Together," he said, and when I looked into his pale face, scrunched in pain and determination, I knew I couldn't refuse him.

For Charles. For Aspen. For the glamoured humans trapped here. For every last fae who had shown me a shred of kindness in this harsh land. For the humans in Altidvale.

I could summon one last bit of magic to save them, even if it was too late for me. Too late for Garrick. Our freedom—our dreams—were lost.

As my half-brother and I clung to each other, supporting one another in our uneven gait while we half-shuffled, half-hopped across the floor, the rebels cleared the way for us. Prince Holden entangled any looming demons with vines, or fended them off with a bow, each arrow a distraction. His brother and Princess Elle shocked creatures with their lightning, stunning them enough to drop them to the floor, twitching. Aspen flitted between her high fae and pixie forms, one moment tall enough to sword-fight the monsters, the next small enough to dart between their legs and seemingly vanish before their eyes.

Where's Kinsey? I thought desperately as Charles and I struggled over a crack in the floor, dodging roots that shuddered as if they were limbs attached to a living being, just waiting to seize their next victims. I saw no sign of the Ashwood healer among the dead or the living. If Garrick was still clinging to even a shred of life, surely the fae would be able to use his magic to save him.

Holden, Fitz, and Elle circled in front of Charles's and my slow progress as more demons poured forth from the entrance. A cluster of rebels joined them, unleashing battle cries as they poured all manner of nature magic—lashing rain and howling wind and tangling vines and roaring fire—toward their enemies, drawing them slowly away.

Until at last, there was nothing and no one besides Charles, that awful, yawning entrance, and me. Fighting raged all around us. The sounds of hissing and rattling bones echoed from the darkness within, but nothing else was emerging—not yet.

Sucking in a breath against my fear, my pain, and my grief, I forced everything away as I lifted my bleeding palm toward the entrance. I brushed my blood along the entryway, rough stone scraping against my stinging injury.

I have nothing left, I thought helplessly. My cheeks were sticky with drying tears. My body screamed at me to lie down, to lose consciousness and escape the agony of every broken bone I was trying so desperately to forget. I was empty, hollower than if forget-me-nots had forced my magic away. When I reached, there was nothing at all.

A voice sounded in my mind, as if my blood had awakened some ancient magic emanating from the stone door itself. Except it wasn't an unknown voice. It was mine, reminding me that *I* was connected to this door by magic and blood. *I don't need to fight to the entrance or send away the demons. The power to perform my duty as a Silverfrost is* in *my blood.* It was what Garrick had said—what he'd believed from the beginning, that my light lived on in me no matter what. The gods had given this calling to my ancestors, and I had inherited it. It was what I was made to do, with a light that burned in my veins as long as I lived. It didn't matter how scattered my mind felt or how depleted my magic and my body were—the power I'd been gifted was ancient and unstoppable.

I'd been trying too hard, attempting to force something that should have come naturally. Thinking I had to concentrate on my power and channel it, when it was as much a part of me as my silver hair or the breath in my lungs. I couldn't weaken the light that lived in me, not with my doubt or distraction, fear or regret. All I had to do was trust and lean into my power.

Leaning heavily against the frame to keep my weight off my ruined leg, I narrowed my gaze and reached into the darkness, groping to find where the open stone door rested. My fear evaporated, for nothing at the underworld's edge could withstand my light. My fingers brushed against stone, and despite the drying tears on my face, despite my shattered heart, I grinned.

It was time to send the demons back for good.

I slammed my hand against the door, feeling my light glow like a steady warmth through my body. Through my soul. Through the air itself. It pulsed outward, shimmering and silver and irresistible.

I could feel its power at work, like an extension of myself. Banishing darkness. Obliterating the oppressive sense of despair and terror that had permeated our surroundings. Dispelling demons and undead spirits like smoke chased away by a pure breeze.

Instinctively, I knew they were all being sent back, even those imprisoned within the fortress, awaiting the moment Preston and Nerissa had planned to unchain them upon the world. My connection to the land and to the power in my blood could feel it like the lifting of a burden, like a cleansing rain washing away dust and filth.

As I withdrew my hand, the stone door closed, clicking with a sense of finality that echoed in the suddenly-quiet room. I exhaled raggedly. Blinding pain turned my vision black, and I collapsed.

CHAPTER THIRTY-TWO

"We have a story of a woman cursed to sleep a hundred years." The teasing feminine voice drew me out of sleep, blinking blearily against the sunlight pouring through the nearby window. "Ah. It's good to see *you* suffer from no such affliction."

I jolted upright, finding myself in my bed in my own chambers within the Silverfrost castle, with Aspen perched nearby in her pixie form. She offered me a fierce grin as I met her gaze, her rich brown eyes alight with happiness. "How do you feel?" she asked.

"What happened?" My voice came out like a croak, throat aching. Snatches of the fight returned to me. A one-eyed Preston staggering after me. He and Nerissa breaking my bones. Demons consuming fae. A wolf pierced by my own ice daggers...

Garrick.

My heart twinged, and I bit my lip, trying and failing to stifle my sob.

Aspen leapt up instantly, compassion painted across her face. "Ren..." She set her tiny hand on mine. "Does anything hurt? Kinsey healed you, but with that many broken bones, and the amount of winter magic you wielded, you slept a full day afterward. He was a little worried that your body would be too exhausted to interact properly with his power, and the bones might not set correctly, or..."

"No," I choked out, tears burning my eyes. And it was true. I felt none of the agony that had consumed me before I'd lost consciousness. "I am unhurt. But Garrick...?"

Aspen squeezed my hand. "He's alive."

"What?" I breathed, relief spilling through me.

"He hasn't woken yet, last I heard," the pixie continued, her words cautious as she studied my hopeful expression, "but shifter magic protects him. And Kinsey was able to tend to him right after you banished the demons and sealed the underworld."

I squeezed my eyes shut, soaking in the news. "Will he make a full recovery?"

"We expect so."

Already, I was swinging my legs over the side of the bed, striding across the cold wood floor toward the door, heedless of the fact I only wore a nightgown. But I'd moved too quickly. My body was weak and my head spun, making me lurch awkwardly. I caught myself on the chair before my vanity as I crumpled.

"You make a terrible invalid," Aspen scolded, suddenly standing beside me in her high fae form. She seized my arm, gentle yet firm, and guided me back to the bed. "You can see Garrick soon, but first you need to eat and drink. I'll fill you in on what's happened since while you do. As our queen, you need to be aware of the state of your kingdom."

Queen. The sound echoed in my ears, filling me with equal measures of hope and worry.

"My kingdom," I managed as I sank back against the pillows, letting Aspen tuck me in. My head was spinning, but even more than the monumental news of my impending rule was what she'd shared about Garrick.

Garrick is alive. The knowledge eased my fears and filled me with unending warmth, like an expanding glow in my chest. Nothing could be wrong as long as he was all right. If he was alive, I could learn how to rule. I could do anything. Anything seemed possible as long as he existed in this world.

I needed to see him. Needed to be there when he awoke, ensure he was healed and well. Needed to tell him how I felt. Needed to be by his side, soaking in our newfound freedom and the future we could now embrace together. After the days we'd been robbed of being able to share our own feelings, I didn't want to lose a single moment, a single touch.

Aspen rang for a servant, and a fae woman slipped in a few minutes later bearing a tray of steaming stew and a pitcher of water. "Your Majesty," she said as soon as she saw me, her blue eyes widening. She dipped into a curtsey, carefully keeping the tray poised in her grasp. "It's good to see you well. Thank you for what you've done for Silverfrost."

Your Majesty. I was too overwhelmed to process it. "I...you're welcome." I blinked at her. Were the human servants gone? Had their glamour broken when Preston and Nerissa were banished?

As the servant left and Aspen poured me a glass of water—which I hastily drank down—and then handed me the bowl of stew, urging me to eat, she began talking. "We have fae, many of whom were former rebels, helping staff the palace. Others have been tasked with returning the humans to their homes. They're confused and afraid. Some served for years under Nerissa and Preston, and were quite disoriented the moment their glamour shattered and they found themselves here."

I shuddered, imagining what it must have been like for them. Had they been lost in other daydreams, believing themselves to still be in the human world? I couldn't fathom waking from such an illusion to find I'd been a slave to fae all that time, far from home and with years of my life effectively stolen.

"Charles?" I asked.

Aspen smiled. "Not a very good patient either, to tell you the truth. He's healed well, already gaining some color in those gaunt cheeks of his from a steady diet and rest. I could hardly get him to leave your rooms to rest though." She rolled her eyes, but her grin didn't lessen. "I think he truly is remorseful and wants to right the wrongs between you."

Grateful tears glistened in my eyes, and I nodded.

"The fighting has ceased. The Ashwoods have ordered their troops to stand down, and now they remain as guests in the castle. The crown prince and princess are committed to witnessing your coronation to display their support of your rule, and then remaining until the three of you can sign an official treaty between kingdoms."

She sighed. "For now, Silverfrost celebrates. We opened the fortress to the public, allowing all to flood the dungeons and see that the demons are, in fact, banished, and you have saved us all. But I know that in turn, dissenters will make their will known. Either out of loyalty to Preston and Nerissa or hatred of your human side, they will oppose you." Her expression hardened. "However, you have my surviving rebels at your disposal. They serve already as guards and servants in the castle, and they are prepared to take up places in your court as needed. They will defend you to their dying breaths—I'm sure of it." Standing suddenly, she knelt at my bedside, studying me earnestly. "And I will serve you, in whatever capacity you desire, Your Majesty."

Startled at her display of deference, I straightened, setting down my spoon. "Aspen, you're a friend. There's no need for formality. I...I don't even know how to be a queen."

She dipped her head. "But you deserve respect, and any who oppose you will need to see it. They need to view you as their queen." Glancing up, Aspen smiled proudly. "And you need to own it."

"I haven't the faintest idea how to lead a kingdom," I murmured. And even though Aspen and I had discussed this before, even though she'd assured me many times I wouldn't be alone and that I was the most fit person to rule, the full impact of what was about to happen settled on me. *Queen.* Surely it was madness. Surely another fae could take the throne instead.

But Aspen rose and shook her head, taking my hand and squeezing it reassuringly. "The power in your blood is proof that you're meant to rule. It's fate, Ren. If one can dare to believe the gods ever condescend to influence our lives anymore, then I'd even venture to say they chose you. Silverfrost tradition claims that the light in your blood not only commands the door to the underworld, but also that it brings light and strength and prosperity to our kingdom. There is power in who you are. And your connection to the land through your ancestry—it's greater than anything the rest of us possess. You are our best choice."

I clung to her words, trying to let her confidence seep into me, hoping she was right.

Before either of us could say more, a knock sounded at the door. Aspen bid the visitor to enter, and Charles rushed into my rooms, his face lighting up when he saw me awake. "Ren!" he cried, darting forward and seizing the nearest chair to perch at my bedside. "You look well. Do you feel well?"

Mouth full of my latest bite of stew and throat still aching, I nodded, warmed by the way he was fretting, by the reassurance that he truly did care.

Aspen's gaze flitted between us. "I know you're eager to see Garrick, Ren, but let me check with Kinsey and ensure he approves of visitors. For now, I'll leave the two of you to catch up."

While Aspen sauntered from the room, I patted the bedside next to me. Charles hesitated before settling in, wrapping an arm around my shoulders. His dark eyes glistened when I turned to him. "You really are all right?" he whispered.

"Yes, Charlie. And you?"

He shook his head. "Perfect. Fae magic is…" His voice drifted off. "*Your* magic is…"

"Terrifying?" I supplied, thinking of the night he'd cast me out in fear and disgust.

Charles hung his head in shame. "No, it's beautiful and awe-inspiring. I was a fool, Ren. I don't know how I could ever possibly atone for what I did. It's unforgivable."

"You're my family, Charlie. Of course I forgive you."

"I broke my promise to Father to provide for you and shelter you after he died," he choked out, a tear slipping down his cheek. "I let resentment grow in my heart. You'd always cared for me so well, were always the perfect elder sister. But as I started to get older, and my friends began to gossip about your hair and their ideas about what you could truly be… I let fear grow. I started to think I could become ostracized too. That I'd never have a happy future as long as I was associated with you, or at least as long as I was friendly and kind to you. So I tried to distance myself the only way I knew how." He clenched his hands in his lap, staring down at them. "I was so wrong. So selfish."

"And yet I still forgive you," I murmured, setting my tray on the bedside table and leaning my head on his shoulder.

"Still more proof that you are better than me. You've always been better than any of us. No wonder you carry such power. The goodness in your heart alone must be enough to repel a horde of those horrendous monsters." He chuckled softly.

"It's my fae blood, not any virtue on my part." I nudged him playfully. "If it was my goodness alone, they would have fled the kingdom as soon as I stepped foot here."

He laughed with me, and it felt good, like our sibling relationship had once been, in those years before Charles had started to distance himself from me.

As we quieted, my half-brother's voice turned sober again. "I've heard the talk. You're heir to the throne, the rightful queen of this land. I know you're half-fae, and you've found friends here, but is that what you want? To stay here? Because if not, say the word and we'll leave now. You'll always have a home with me, Ren. I promise."

Tears stung my eyes. I lifted my head to study Charles's expression, seeing the sincerity burning in his gaze.

"I want to stay. I haven't a clue how to rule" –I laughed mirthlessly– "but Aspen and Garrick will help. This is where I belong. And being here, where I can keep the door to the underworld sealed off, will protect our world as well as the fae one. This is where I'm needed."

Charles appeared thoughtful. "Garrick is the fae that can transform into a white wolf? The one who was wounded?" At my nod of assent, he continued. "Does he...treat you well? I can tell you care for him. And I by no means am in any position to give or rescind a blessing on your relationship—I'm well aware of this. But I only want to know, as your brother who wants to see you happy and secure, if you're happy?"

My smile felt radiant. "Charles, I'm the happiest with him that I have ever been."

Daylight streamed through the open curtains, illuminating the bed Garrick was asleep within. Despite the rich fur rugs on the floor before the hearth and beside the bed, the covers on the bed itself were scarce—likely because Garrick didn't need the layers to stay warm.

I stepped inside slowly, barely noting my surroundings even if I'd never been within Garrick's quarters. They were fairly sparse, with little to mark them as his but for his hunting knives laid out on the dresser and the swords, bows, and quivers hanging on the walls.

Heart in my throat, I settled on the edge of his bed, focusing on the steady rise and fall of his chest. Soaking in the sight when I'd been so sure I'd lost him. I found where his hand rested on the coverlet and set mine overtop of it, squeezing his fingers.

His eyelids flickered and he shifted his head. "Starlight?" His tone was gruff but soft as his gold eyes settled on me.

The sob of relief I'd been holding back burst out. "I thought you were gone. I thought I'd lost you." Tears streamed down my cheeks, and Garrick sat up abruptly, his movements smooth and assured as he wrapped his arms around me and drew me onto the bed, his embrace warm and comforting.

"You won't lose me so easily," he murmured into my hair, cradling my head against his chest. The beat of his heart was another reminder that he was alive. Whole. Mine.

I drew back, wiping my tears and studying him worriedly. "You're supposed to be healing. You were pierced by so many—"

Garrick shook his head. "Kinsey explained everything when I woke earlier, before he allowed you to come see me." His eyes swept over me. "I'm fine. Do you remember what I told you before? Shifters heal more readily when they sustain injuries in their other forms. I'm more resilient if I'm wounded in my wolf form and then transform back—that let me hold on long enough for Kinsey to work his magic. But you—they were *torturing* you."

"And now I'm whole. And they're gone."

"And we're free," Garrick whispered, lifting a hand to cradle my face. "Thanks to you."

"I don't want to run a kingdom alone," I blurted.

Garrick's lips twitched in a smile. "You won't. Aspen and I will be here."

I swallowed. "I mean..." My cheeks heated, a blush creeping from my neck all the way to my scalp. "Garrick, I don't know how the Silverfrosts do this. In my town, a gentleman would court a lady...he would be the one to ask to do so...and he would also be the one to propose. But I suppose now I'm the one asking you if...you would consider that with me? And ruling with me—as my husband?" I cringed at my own awkwardness. I was going about this all wrong, hadn't even said I loved him yet.

But Garrick smirked. "Starlight, after that kiss we shared, whatever made you think I'd not want to…" He raised his eyebrows. "Court you, or ask for your hand, or any other of your human traditions that would bind us?" Moving his palm from my cheek, he lifted one of my hands in his and pressed a kiss to the back of it. "I want it all with you."

I sobered. "But are you sure? You would be binding yourself to the crown again. You couldn't live freely in the mountains, hunting and adventuring. Your life will be consumed with politics and diplomacy and formalities and—"

Garrick's grasp tightened on my hand, his expression earnest. "None of that matters. Those dreams are hollow and lonely without *you*. Besides, I should be the one asking if you, a queen with far more magic and power than I will ever possess, could ever condescend to want me, a lowly wolf shifter. And *when* we marry" –his smirk widened– "for of course I will have you, I will gladly give up my life as a hunter. I will happily bind myself to the crown again, because it will mean binding myself to you. What matters to me is you, Starlight, and living out the rest of our days together."

Blinking back overwhelmed tears of joy, I threw my arms around him, leaning in close and basking in the light of his smile, of his brilliant eyes. "I love you," I confessed. At last. The words felt so good to say aloud. "I should have said it before, when you told me how you felt. You were worried I wouldn't feel the same, and I suppose I was shy trying to find the words. You're right—love doesn't seem like enough to describe it. But still, I should have—"

But Garrick cut me off once again, this time with a kiss, sweet and languid, a delicious reminder that we had an entire future ahead of us.

CHAPTER THIRTY-THREE

Somehow, even with the gathered crowd in the vast space of the throne room, the roaring fires and floor-to-ceiling windows behind the dais offering a view of falling snowflakes made the space feel cozy. Perhaps it was the absence of Preston's and Nerissa's disgusting presence and the lack of empty-eyed, glamoured humans haunting the castle. Maybe it was the sense of joy and celebration even during a traditionally solemn affair. Or maybe it was Garrick at my side, clasping my hand firmly in his, or Aspen perched on my shoulder, whispering commentary in my ear as I walked down the aisle created between the assembled guests, all silent as they watched me pass.

Beneath the light of sprites fluttering through the air, twirling with ribbons in Silverfrost colors, the Ashwoods sat together. Crown Prince Fitz's expression was solemn as usual, but he gave a subtle dip of his head as I approached, his silent approval. At his side, his wife grinned without restraint, and I offered a quick smile back. I hoped in the future we would be able to visit one another's kingdoms regularly. Having a fellow human in this world as an ally—and maybe even someday a close friend—would be invaluable.

Not far away was Charles, adorned in fae clothes that made him look strangely out of place. The fact that he'd stayed to witness this moment of mine, the fact that he watched me now with eyes glowing with pride...it made my chest warm. I bit my lip to keep my eyes from watering when he nodded to me, as if silently telling me that this truly was what I was meant to do, who I was meant to be.

And then I turned my gaze forward, toward the awaiting thrones. Both were wrought of white birchwood, engraved with delicate snowflakes and winter animals, and cushioned in rich blue velvet. The weight of those symbols was heavy on my shoulders, but not as heavy as it would have been without Garrick and Aspen with me. Without the Ashwoods as neighboring allies.

You were born for this, I reminded myself. What would Mother and my stepfather think of me now? What would my real father think, the fae man I'd never met who had died protecting both her and me? I hoped they would be proud.

"Keep your speech brief. And don't forget your show of magic once you accept your crown!" Aspen urged as I ascended the steps.

It was the sage hag, the one who kept memories, who awaited us at the top of the dais, clothed in simple silver and blue robes that matched the Silverfrost banners strung in the beams overhead. Though her stooped posture made her shorter than me, when I paused before her on the dais, I felt small. Garrick released my hand and held his up for Aspen to hop into his palm, and then the two of them retreated to the edge to watch.

Slowly, I half-turned so as to face the crowd and the hag at once, my skirts rustling. My gown was all silver, only a few shades lighter than my hair, and glistening with lace and white beads and pearls in shapes that mimicked frost and snow. It paired well with the silver crown resting in an open box in the hag's hands as she shuffled forward and lifted her voice.

"Dear court of Silverfrost—and guests from Ashwood and the human world—you are gathered here this morning to bear witness to a most momentous occasion. For decades we have longed for hope and peace and despaired that our land would fall to chaos. We thought the line of royal Silverfrosts had ended and that our destiny was darkness. But here we are, with a woman of mortal blood no less, who bears the powerful winter magic of her forebears, and most importantly, who carries the light of her ancestors. She's saved us all, and for that, we owe her our gratitude and our allegiance. As she accepts this crown that is hers by birth and battle, please kneel to show your respects."

My breath caught in my chest as everyone stood and dropped to their knees. Recognizing me. Even the sprites paused their dancing to perch in the beams overhead and dip into postures of deference. At the edge of the dais, Garrick knelt with Aspen in her pixie form at his side. She lifted her chin, just a little, to meet my gaze and wink at me.

"Florentia Silverfrost," the hag intoned, drawing my attention back to her, "please step forward."

I did so, and she lifted the crown from its cushioned place, setting the box on the floor so she could use two hands to raise the headpiece high. "Please, call me Ren," I whispered.

She paused to grin at me, silently acknowledging she'd heard my request.

"Kneel to show your willingness to humble yourself before your people, to serve them first." I did as she bid, tugging at the train of my dress to sweep it out of the way. "Now repeat after me."

I followed her lead, vowing to serve and protect Silverfrost: "I accept this crown and take my throne with a heart dedicated to serving my kingdom. May the land accept me and strengthen me, and through my strength, may my kingdom and my people grow in power and might too. I swear to protect the Silverfrost people above all else, and to seal the door to the underworld, as is my gods-given duty."

As the crown settled on my head, I stood and turned to my people, who rose and erupted into applause and cheers.

"Greet your new ruler," the hag announced over the tumult, "Queen Ren Silverfrost!"

I smiled softly, grateful she'd agreed to use my preferred nickname in this moment, when formalities fell away a little. Lifting my hands, I leaned into my power and my tie to the land. Snowflakes, fluffy and huge, fluttered from the rafters, and everyone paused to ooh and ahh. Then I banished them with a thought, making them melt away as I cupped my palms and let my light shine, bright and powerful and hopeful.

What I prayed would be a symbol of the days to come.

EPILOGUE

Under *aeveld's* pure light, the fresh snow gleamed like fallen stars, twinkling and enchanting. It crunched beneath my boots as I looped my arm through Charles's and lifted the hem of my skirt. Glistening like frosted snow itself, it shimmered beneath my layers of fur. I felt like a proper winter queen, clothed in the element I wielded and shining as brightly as the power that burned in my veins.

"With all due respect, I hope your vows won't take long," Aspen said from where she was huddled on my shoulder. Despite being bundled in the fur I wore along with her own coat, she shivered.

"I promise."

With a warm kiss to my cheek and wet eyes, Charles released me silently when we emerged at the top of the trail. Leading out from the castle grounds, it climbed to the mountain's peak and offered a stunning view of Northelm and its lake, as lovely as a sheet of glass under the stars. Near the edge of the overlook, Garrick waited with a crooked grin.

Dressed in matches shades of white and silver, he was breathtaking. His eyes shone with love and warmth that made my heart pound against my ribcage as I strode forward. This was all I wanted. A lifetime with this man. Whatever challenges came with bearing the crown, whatever dangers arose from living among the fae, I could bear it all as long as I had Garrick at my side.

If I was his starlight, he was my sunshine.

"Ethereal," he murmured as I drew near, and despite all we'd faced together, I couldn't help the blush that flooded my cheeks.

Aspen made an exaggerated gagging sound on my shoulder. I shot her a look that pretended to be annoyed. "Don't make me send you away," I threatened.

"Then who will bear witness to your union?" she scoffed, hopping down from her perch and transforming into her larger size in midair. "Now, face one another and let's make this official."

As Garrick took my hand, his touch tender and his gaze even softer, I couldn't hold back my words another moment. "Garrick Darkgrove," I began, "I vow before the gods and our trusted witness to love you for all my days. I give you my heart, my soul, and my kingdom. I take you as my equal, my husband, and my best friend." Tears burned my eyes. "You are the brightness to my days and the joy in my laughter. I love you and choose you, above all other souls on this earth, and I give myself to you alone. With our marriage, I unite our lives and I share with you a portion of my magic." I drew an elegant hunting knife Garrick had gifted me—one with a hilt marked by a collection of stars and snowflakes—I sliced a shallow cut along my palm. Following the instructions Aspen gave, I drew the traditional runes on Garrick's face.

When I'd finished, Garrick brushed a tear from my cheek. "Ren Silverfrost, I vow before the gods and our trusted witness to love you for all my days. I will serve you as my queen, my wife, and the deepest treasure of my heart until my last breath. You are my home, my purpose, and my strength. You are my light, the good I cling to in the darkness. I choose you alone and a life with you, forsaking my immortality."

I froze, eyes widening. Aspen gasped aloud. But Garrick went on calmly, slipping his hand from mine and unsheathing one of the hunting knives strapped to his belt. This time, it was his turn to slice his palm. With aching tenderness, he brushed his own blood on my face, his thumb tracing unfamiliar patterns unlike the ones I'd marked on his forehead and cheeks. "I don't want to live countless years without you, my Starlight. So, since the gods grant us fae the choice to give up our immortality and live out mortal years with a beloved human, I accept that gift."

This time, more tears slipped free from my eyes and Garrick grinned as he wiped them away. "I give myself wholly to you, and no one will ever come between us again," he whispered, leaning forward to press his lips to mine.

I flung my arms around his neck, pulling him against me.

"I..." Aspen giggled. "Let me say my part!" she groaned, but when Garrick and I ignored her, only deepening the kiss, she sighed. "As your witness, before the gods themselves, I recognize your marriage and the binding vows you have made today."

Garrick smiled against my mouth, pulling back just enough to nibble at my bottom lip playfully.

"That's enough! Let's return to warmth," Aspen proclaimed, hands on her hips.

Laughing, I offered my palm as the pixie returned to her true form, taking her place once more on my shoulder. Hand in hand, Garrick and I descended the path back toward the castle. Toward the future.

Toward home.

THE END

NOTE FROM THE AUTHOR

Thank you so much for reading *Fortress of Blood and Power*! If you have a moment, please consider helping me out and leaving an honest review on Amazon.

Chosen by truth. Marked for death. Halia must choose to save her kingdom, or let it fall.

Misroth's king has died, and the entire kingdom is in mourning—or so it seems. After her father is crowned regent in his brother's stead, Princess Halia discovers a terrible truth that could end her life. But when she flees to live in hiding, she discovers that the Royal Guard are not all she has to fear. Dark creatures stalk her, reports of oppression and war reach her ears, and her burden to protect her kingdom—at any cost—will not be silenced.

Acknowledgements

This book was especially challenging, which makes getting to this point feel extra rewarding. It also means everyone on my team deserves extra thanks, because I'm not sure I could power through without their support (and my amazing readers' enthusiasm!)

I'm always afraid I'll forget someone, so I like to add that my acknowledgements isn't really any exhaustive list. After all, even those who weren't early readers, etc., but just messaged me throughout the process or believed in me also played an important role. So to anyone who's ever taken the time to check in on me while I'm in the writing and editing trenches, or to tell me they believe in me even when I'm not sure I believe in myself...thank you!

Thank you to my alpha readers, Sheree, Beth, and Tricia. Your insight and enthusiasm for this book was invaluable. I couldn't have made this book (or Garrick!) what it is without you. Thanks to my beta readers, Rai, Kriszta, and Brittany, for helping me polish up this book and giving me early reader feedback.

Sheree Whitelock and Malcolm Carter—thanks for always cheering me on and sending cat memes as needed.

To my husband, for your support and excitement, always. :)

Thank you to my street team for your support in spreading the word about this book: Courtney, Crissy, Erin, Hannah, Heidi, Kim, Lauren, Manda, Meaghan, Rai, Taylor, and Tricia.

For all my friends on Instagram: the fellow authors who commiserate with me, the fellow readers who fangirl/fanboy with me. The ones who tag me in posts about my books, comment how excited they are about my books, share stories about my books, and send me messages about my books. Thanks for reminding me I have an audience who actually wants to read about my characters and the vivid worlds in my head. Thanks for reminding me, on the days when I get stuck in my own head, that these stories serve an even bigger purpose outside of myself, bringing you smiles and maybe a bit of hope and light. Hopefully some swoony "squee" moments too!

And thanks to the One who always keeps me going and has helped make my wildest dreams come true.

ABOUT THE AUTHOR

Rachel L. Schade was born on the first day of summer in a small town in Michigan. She attended The Ohio State University to learn how to write obnoxiously long papers, cite people who use big words, and discuss her passion: books. She has a great love for the color blue, sunshine, chocolate, and not folding her laundry. Currently she lives in Ohio with her husband, daughter, and fur babies, and surrounds herself with books and coffee on a regular basis.

You can email Rachel at rachelschade@gmail.com, or find her on Facebook and Goodreads: Rachel L. Schade, and on Instagram and TikTok: @rachelschadeauthor.

www.rachelschadeauthor.com